2 PROMISES

2 PROMISES

A novel by Phil Armstrong

9 780557 231263
ISBN 978-0-557-23126-3
90000

I dedicate this novel to my wife Roseanne.

She has provided love, guidance, compassion, and unwavering support for every crazy idea that I come up with.

She continues to be my source of pure energy!

Contents

Chapter 1

Where do thoughts go?

The rain came heavy and sudden. The gale was fierce and constant. Beth turned her face away from the wind and shivered. She was cold and hungry, and her clothes seemed to soak up the water. The cobbled streets glistened in the rain. The old fashioned streetlights bled a dim amber light onto the quaint street. The village of Haworth is a popular place for visitors. Haworth is located in West Yorkshire, England. The village has a picturesque main street lined with Dickens curiosity shops selling a variety of interesting things. Haworth remains a magnet for tourists seeking a glimpse of the past, and a connection to the literary world of the Bronte sisters. Beth lived in Haworth, but her immediate needs masked how picture perfect Main Street appeared. At the top of Haworth Main Street was an old fashioned telephone booth. It was painted bright red and looked like a prop from a movie set. The phone booth was located at the main entrance to the church adjacent to the Black Bull pub. Beth dashed into the phone booth to shelter from the rain. She composed herself before dragging a strand of wet hair from her face.

The stench of urine suddenly became overwhelming. She looked down at the floor, and kicked a couple of spent cigarette butts into a corner. Beth peered around frantically through the foggy glass. All of the shops were closed for the night. She could see the rain lashing the windows of the Apothecary. A sign was anchored to the pavement by two large rocks. It was swaying as the wind tried to loosen the heavy anchors. The sign read.

Free lecture at the Church Hall tonight - starts at 7pm

How the Universe Works by Dr. David Harrington

The Mountain of Thabor room

All guests welcome

Beth glanced at the black sports watch wrapped around her left wrist. The time was 6.50pm. She decided to run for the shelter of the church hall. She arrived at the door and waited to enter. She was still panting from the run. It was a wicked night on the Yorkshire Moors, and Haworth was getting the brunt of the storm. Beth could see a warm glow emanating from the hall inside. She looked up and caught the eye of a cheery looking middle-aged woman. Sheltering in the doorway she gave Beth a warm welcome.

"Come inside quickly love, and get out of the rain you're soaking."

Beth smiled and hurried past the greeter. Beth needed a place that was warm and dry. She cautiously entered a long corridor. Rooms were visible from each side. Each room had a unique name. Beth could see,

The City of Jerusalem, Canterbury Cathedral, Mecca, Konark, Constantine, and more. People were gathering around the room named, The Mountain of Thabor. It was a square shaped room with rows of worn wooden benches. A low wooden stage was positioned at the front. Along one side of the hall was a long table supporting coffee and cookies.

Beth made her way to the refreshments table. She poured herself a large cup of hot coffee. Gripping the ceramic cup she felt the warmth seeping through into her hands. She grabbed a couple of cookies and a paper napkin. She was hungry. Beth headed to the rear of the hall. The doors were now closed keeping the hall warm. She took a seat on the back row close to the coffee. Beth balanced her coffee cup on her thigh, and with her other hand moved a cookie to her mouth. She raised her head and realized that the hall was full. Beth sensed something was happening.

The activity level in the room had changed. Key people were making their way to the front of the hall. People gathered their refreshments and quickly settled into their seats. A thin man walked onto the stage. Beth didn't hear what the man said. She noticed he was one of those annoying people who seemed to have the talent of smiling when he spoke. Beth's mind wandered. She finished the cookies and sipped hot coffee. Beth could never seem to focus. She had an active mind that wandered easily when bored. Beth's favorite game at school was to count the ceiling tiles. Her school reports always mentioned her lack of focus.

"Beth has potential if she would only apply herself."

Beth smiled as she recalled the consistency of her report cards. Her grades at school were average, and she was a constant disappointment to her teachers. Beth's work record had been unimpressive. At 25 she had gained experience in a number of low paying jobs. When it came to her employment record she cheerfully described herself as, "Still searching for my passion." Beth knew her lack of focus had held her back. She recognized that she was intelligent; she had a quick mind and an equally quick mouth. Beth would often describe herself as, "An independently modern woman." She was proud of that moniker. Beth was a strong woman orphaned at the age of seven. Her parents died in a car accident. She was raised in foster homes and childcare facilities. She made it through keeping her self esteem intact. Beth would credit her survival to her cunning, intellect, and wits. One foster parent described her as being, "Sly." Beth initially resented the word, but later she learned to love it. Yes, she was sly, because being sly had served her well. Beth was a loner; she did not have any friends, and was not interested in men. She trusted no one and was fiercely independent.

When Beth was old enough she left the protective care system. She landed a job and rented a flat. At the first opportunity she visited a tattoo parlor. She selected a design for the inside of her right wrist. A fox is the embodiment of sly. Sipping from her coffee cup, her sleeve rode up to expose the small tattoo of a sitting fox. The bushy tail was folded between its legs, and the face pointed towards her. Beth stared at the image of the fox. The lights in the hall started to dim. The man on stage came back into focus.

"It's my great pleasure to introduce to you the leading expert in spirituality, Dr. David Harrington," said the smiling man. A brief but polite round of applause followed.

Dr. David Harrington was a tall man with great posture. He strode elegantly across the stage. He wore shiny black Ferragamo shoes and a striking blue three-piece Canali suit. David had a look that did not fit the surroundings or the audience. David's shock of grey hair reflected in the solitary spotlight fixed upon the podium.

"Thank you all for coming out tonight in such foul weather," said David. "There's a lot of energy in the heavens tonight, and clearly there's a lot of energy in this room. Let me start my lecture by asking the audience a question. Where do thoughts go? More important, where do thoughts come from?"

David's English accent was crisp and somewhat refined for this venue. Beth seemed transfixed. She had entered the hall as a place of refuge, and immediately David had stimulated her interest. David resumed after a pause for water.

"I want to explain concepts for you tonight that will challenge your traditional ways of thinking. The task before me is to explain a complicated set of ideas in a way that can be readily understood. I won't shirk from this challenge. Let's begin." You could hear a pin drop as David continued, "Let me start by laying some foundations. I would like to describe a core assumption based in scientific fact. Imagine you can break down our bodies to its smallest element. That element is held together by energy. You can talk to me about atoms, particles, whatever granularity you may want to reach. We are all held together by energy. Our bodies resonate at a certain frequency. As James Arthur Ray suggests, whatever is present in your life right now you're resonating with. Whatever is missing from your life right now you're clearly not in harmony with. When European travelers came to North America they started to communicate with Native Indians. They were told strange stories. The Indians spoke of being connected in one universal energy system," said David moving from behind the podium. "This means that you, the bear, the tree, and the rock are all connected by the

same strands of energy. We are part of one interconnected system. This was quickly dismissed as the folk-
lore from a primitive culture. Science has now proven
this to be fact. Perhaps the Native Indians were more
advanced in their thinking than we gave them credit
for," said David with a tinge of distain in his voice.

Beth listened intently as the speaker continued. "Our
universe is comprised of energy. The thoughts outlined
in the discipline of Indian Yoga describe a connected
universe. This is not new thinking, and many cultures
have described this connection in various ways. Modern science is catching up with ancient belief. You've
probably heard of monks meditating, and radically
changing their body temperature. They use their inter-
nal energy to do this. Have you heard of monks being
able to leave their physical bodies to experience out of
body travel? Why is it that certain people spend their
entire life in search of enlightenment and personal
growth? These are radical ideas that depart from your
established thinking. Please try to stay with me."

Beth did not need encouragement. This was her
first exposure to a new way of thinking. She was
totally engaged and focused. David paused, looked at
the room and started again. "Some people can meditate to quiet the mind. What does this mean? Can
you meditate to a point where you stop all of your
thoughts? Can you stop the noise inside your head?
Let me explain another point, and then I feel the need
to tie some of these ideas together for you. The scientists will describe our world as the physical domain.
What does this mean? It suggests that all things have
a place, a location. This microphone, chair, you and I,
all have a physical place. We're all composed of matter
that we can see and touch. In the physical domain we
understand the concept of time; you all arrived here
before 7pm for example. Time is linear in the physical

domain. Everything in the physical domain requires energy and is interconnected. Everything in the physical domain vibrates at a certain frequency," said David as he grabbed his water bottle. He started to pace.

David paused for effect; he knew his next statement would take a while to grasp. "What if I told you a non physical domain exists? It's called a spiritual domain. Now this is where it gets hard to explain. You can't see or touch the spiritual domain. Time, as we know it does not exist, and no energy is required in this world. Things can't be seen or felt. Nothing is made of physical matter. I'll give you an example that I will credit to Deepak Chopra. This should make the idea a little clearer. When you go to the movie theatre your eyes show you that the movie is a continuous stream of animation and action. We know the movie reel is composed of a series of frames strung together in a sequence. When the film is moved through the projector at high speed you don't see the edges of each frame. You also don't see the gaps between each frame. We know that they exist. Imagine an on and off switch. The picture represents the on. The space between the frames represents the off. Get it? It's important that you follow me on this. The universe that you currently inhabit is constantly switching between on, and off. The universe is pulsing like the switches."

David's dialogue started to speed up, but Beth listened intently. David continued, "The physical domain is the world that we can see. For example Haworth Main Street. The spiritual domain is more complex. It's the space between the pictures, and the space we don't see. What lives in this space? The answer is everything and nothing. When monks chant to clear their minds they can elevate to the highest level of awareness. They manage to still their thoughts and enter into the spiritual domain. This domain does not occupy any location. You're not an individual when you enter the spiritual domain. You give up the ego based self. You are so connected that you become part of the universe. People who get addicted to drugs sometimes report that they enter the spiritual domain. Their issue is they don't know how they got there. They spend their entire lives using drugs. They're trying to emulate that feeling of total euphoria."

Some of the audience members were starting to look a little lost. Beth had never felt so emotionally attached to a subject or speaker. She paused to reflect on how focused she was. David explained complex ideas in a way that Beth could relate to. David began to pace again. He took a deep breath and continued.

"The scientists have names for these domains but these are just labels. Perhaps you can relate more to these labels, physical world and spiritual world; awake and dreamland; earth and heaven. These are merely labels as long as you understand the difference. Let's move onto something even heavier. We all agree that we're made of flesh and bone. I have suggested that we are made of energy. We know we have a heart and other organs such as our kidneys. Let me now ask you the following question. Where is your soul located? How would you answer that? Is it in your head? Is it in your heart? Modern science can't answer this question. Your soul is everywhere in your body. That's because your soul is made of pure energy, and it lives within your entire body. We all know the mechanics of making a baby. When a new physical being is conceived where does the new soul come from? Where does the soul go when the body physically expires? These are eternal questions that great minds constantly debate."

Beth was piecing together the answers before David completed his thoughts. "There's now a ground swell of opinion that suggests the soul comes from the spiritual domain. It enters the body, and returns to the spiritual domain when the body expires. We are not physical beings with a spiritual side. We are spiritual beings existing briefly within a physical body. In the spiritual domain souls don't require energy. They don't need space or occupy a location. Souls are totally connected existing in a highly creative domain. All creativity comes from this domain. The linear construct of time does not exist within the spiritual domain. I started this lecture by asking two questions. Where do thoughts come from and where do they go? I can now give you this answer having confused most of you here tonight. I recognize this is mind-numbing information. Everything that you thought was real in your world is a movie still. The enlightened world exists in the gaps between the stills."

David walked toward the edge of the stage to ensure he had the audience's full attention. "If you think about it, a thought is something that you conjure up in your mind. A thought is made from your minds energy. Thoughts can transfer into the universe of connected energy. Your thoughts can affect the events of the universe and your physical health. There is substantial evidence around the subject of self-healing. This demonstrates how powerful your thoughts can be. Mankind has accomplished many great things starting with a simple thought. The creative side of mankind manifests through thoughts. These thoughts start in the spiritual domain and then move into the physical domain. Thoughts are transferred through energy. Thoughts are sent into the universe and eventually return to the spiritual domain. This describes the path where thoughts start, form, flourish, and eventually end."

David talked at length to illustrate the differences between the spiritual domain and the physical domain. He had lost most of the audience, but a few seemed to

understand. Beth enjoyed the lecture and was fasci-
nated by the material. She quickly forgot about her
wet clothes. She felt enlightened and liberated. This
was indeed sly stuff, and she wanted to hear more.
David was wrapping up. Beth could not believe she
had listened intently for ninety minutes. She noticed
the hall was half empty. When David concluded his
remarks the remaining crowd clapped politely. Beth
did not clap she just sat in awe. The information had
swept over her like a tidal wave. She could not believe
how interested she was in this topic. She had never
felt so engaged and so intrigued before. She decided
to visit the library tomorrow morning. She would try
to find reading material on this subject. Beth returned
her empty coffee cup to the table. She nodded politely
to a few people and made her way to the door. She
entered the hallway and stepped out of the church
hall. Thankfully it had stopped raining, but the cold
stinging wind hit her face as she stepped outside onto
the cobbled street. It was dark outside, and the cobbles glistened like mirrors in the rain. The rain made
the cobbles slick, and Beth tried to remain on her feet.
She descended Haworth Main Street being careful of
its steep drop. She passed the glowing lights of the
Black Bull pub. She could hear the distant sound of
voices and laughter emanating from inside. As she hurried home toward Sun Street she thought of David and
the messages he had just delivered. Beth's body felt a
sudden jolt of energy. A burning sensation started to
circle the crown of her head and then consume her
entire body. Beth's impatient stride was broken. Her
knees felt weak and she collapsed onto the hard cobbles. Beth could feel little rivulets of water stream over
a cobble and splash her face. She could see the dim
glow of an amber street lamp from the corner of her
eye. Everything went dark.

Chapter 2

The Spirit Warrior and the Gieging Teachings

In the spiritual domain there is no need for energy and no physical matter. This domain does not resemble our world. There are no buildings, no trees, and no physical structures. Subra is a Spirit Warrior, a unique soul, hand selected for a specific purpose. Subra had been studying under the expert tutelage of Master Xu. Master Xu was a presence unlike others; he was a spirit guide of the highest level. When a person's life expires their physical body is discarded and left behind in the physical domain. Their soul is released from the body and returns to the spiritual domain. The soul assimilates back into the universe. In the spiritual domain unique souls are selected carefully and taught to become individuals. These souls will assist other souls return from the physical domain. They help with the transition from self, back to the whole of the universe. Subra had been selected for a very important task; he was paired with Master Xu. Master Xu was the most trusted and influential teacher in the spiritual domain. Master Xu had trained Subra in the ancient art of Gieging (*guy-jing*).

Gieging is a mental discipline. Gieging will produce outstanding results if practiced with intensity. The universe can be manipulated using Gieging. A small amount of Universe can separate from the collective conscious. This small amount will then be transformed into an entity with self like qualities. It can be taught to behave in an individualistic way. With continued Gieging training this new entity can enter the physical domain. The entity can form individual thought patterns and develop its own energy signature.

A successful Gieging is achieved almost every one hundred linear earth years. The entity can separate from the collective spiritual domain. It can enter the physical domain of existence. The entity will possess the skills to retrieve precious cargo and quickly return to the spiritual domain. The entity and cargo will then be absorbed back into the collective universe. This is a very difficult and unique skill to perfect. Of the billions of souls in the universe only a few can ever reach this level of sophistication. Only one will be selected as a Spirit Warrior. Master Xu was a tough teacher. He pushed his students and quickly narrowed his selection to two candidates. Badra was a talented student, but Master Xu began to pay less attention to him.

Badra demanded to talk with Master Xu. Would he be selected as the Spirit Warrior? Master Xu was honest with Badra. Badra did not appreciate the blunt message delivered. Master Xu explained that Badra was obsessed with crossing over into the physical domain. He had asked countless questions about taking a physical form. Master Xu had suspicions about Badra's motives to return to the physical domain. Badra would not be selected.

Subra had shown great promise and a passion to learn. Master Xu had dedicated his recent efforts to develop Subra as a Spirit Warrior. Subra had started to show signs of individualism, and ability to harness, use, and release energy. In Master Xu's opinion Subra was the one. Subra was a Spirit Warrior. After an intense instructional lecture Master Xu signaled to the whole universe. Subra had completed his instruction. Master Xu was a brilliantly gifted teacher, but he did not have the natural talent of Subra. When Subra trained as an individual he felt scared and excited. Subra could feel energy flowing through him. He could sense doubt, fear, and emotions that self-based energy sources could feel. Sending a Spirit Warrior into the physical domain is a dangerous mission. He is trained to survive anything that may go wrong; sometimes that is not good enough.

Once the Spirit Warrior crosses into the physical domain he cannot transform into a physical being. He is sent to locate and retrieve a specific cargo of energy. The cargo is brought back and shared by all. Danger occurs when a Spirit Warrior is unable to find his way back from the physical domain. Historical teachings talk of an energy portal. The portal can transport souls from the physical domain to the spiritual domain. A trapped Spirit Warrior would need to find the energy portal quickly. When the portal is used it will close instantly. Another portal will open in a different physical location.

The location of the new portal is never known, but a fleeting vision is provided to the soul traveling through the portal. The last soul to use a portal was Damascus. He reported seeing the vision of a shell. This was the clue to the location of the new portal. The legend of Damascus, and the image of the shell, is important in the education of any new Spirit Warrior. The amount of linear time allowed in the physical domain is unknown. When a Spirit Warrior becomes trapped finding the location of the new portal is critically important. Master Xu had previously mentioned a Spirit Warrior whose label was Corom.

Corom was Master Xu's most talented student. When he was ready he accepted a dangerous mission willingly. Corom managed to summon a vast quantity of energy. He broke free from the collective universe and passed into the physical domain.

Corom has not returned to the spiritual domain. Master Xu fears the energy that Corom gathered is not enough to sustain him or help in his return. What happens when a Spirit Warrior stays too long in the physical world? Corom has not returned to deliver his cargo or tell his story. Master Xu has assumed that Corom's soul has died, similar to a physical body expiring.

In the physical realm there have always been individuals of great intellect. Throughout history humans have had great thoughts. Many of these thoughts were spoken aloud. The spoken thought travels as a sound wave. Some thoughts are preserved by the written word. These thoughts are transmitted as streams of energy into the connected physical domain. Where do they go? Eventually thoughts are trapped within a cosmic energy net. After approximately one hundred linear earth years the energy net becomes full. It is the Spirit Warrior's mission to cross the domain divide. He must quickly retrieve the cargo of thoughts. He will transport them back into the spiritual domain to be shared, accessed, and appreciated. Emptying the cosmic net is the most dangerous and skillful mission.

The moment had come where Subra knew he had to fulfill his mission. He had trained hard for this and was ready. Master Xu had declared him ready and he did not intend to fail. Subra started to concentrate; he could feel heat forming.

"That's the start of the process," thought Subra. Subra was starting to channel energy into the spiritual domain. He was becoming an individual. He could feel the process happening and was starting to formulate thoughts. "Keep going. It's working," he thought.

Energy was starting to gather, and it felt like warm water flowing through him. He could sense a separation from the universe. "I have to follow through and continue as trained," thought Subra. He concentrated and started to use the energy. He could feel a gradual separation occurring. He could sense fear and doubt. A strong feeling of being alone washed over him. The separation from the collective universe had started. Subra was starting to feel heavy. He had turned back at this point when practicing with Master Xu. He knew exactly what he needed to do to continue. He started to feel the anxiety.

"This is further than I have ever gone; can I go through with this?" Subra was overwhelmed with fear and self-doubt. Voices screamed for him to stop and return to the collective universe. He felt disconnected and alone. Subra was panic stricken; he had never felt so isolated. Could he continue? One of the voices was calm and sounded different from the rest.

"Apply the training, and remember Master Xu said this would happen. Move forward and focus on the projection technique. Gather more energy. Only listen to the affirmative thoughts and collect more energy."

Subra felt calm. He used the technique taught by Master Xu to harness the energy. It was flowing toward him easily now; he felt full. He knew it was time to move forward. He was now on his own. He was an individual.

"This is it. I'm ready. I need to project into the next domain," thought Subra. A rush of blue light filled his consciousness, and any trace of self-doubt was slowly being eradicated. Subra was now an energized entity in the wrong domain. He felt a surge of energy as a strong blue light pulled him forward. He started to resist, "I have to be one with the blue light. Stop fighting it and somehow focus on becoming the blue light," thought Subra.

The blue light continued to swirl around Subra. Subra used a powerful technique that Master Xu had described to him. He had repeated this technique back to Master Xu hundreds of times but was forbidden to practice it. The technique was an ancient secret and only taught to those advanced in the art of Gieging. Subra focused and applied the technique. He visualized the blue light gathering into a ball that enveloped him. He visualized the light streaming forward carrying him into the next domain. Subra immediately had a feeling of immense fear a paralyzing feeling that he clearly did not like. He felt weightless in this domain. He knew he had left the spiritual domain and entered the physical domain. Subra could see wondrous things. He was surrounded by black with small blinding points of bright light.

Subra could feel himself feeding on these energy sources. He was absorbing the light to fuel his thoughts. In front of him lay a magnificent spectacle. It was a large blue orb like mass. It shone and reflected light. It was a huge source of energy. It had swirls of white and colors of green and blue. You could see distant crackles of pure white energy in dark spots on the orb. Subra resonated with a specific frequency; a technique Master Xu had taught him. The space behind him drew his attention. The space contained a gaseous cloud like entity. It was not solid like the object in front of him. A cloud of blue and purple gas sent out a strong repeating frequency. It resonated perfectly with the vibration Subra had sent out.

"That's it," thought Subra. "I've found the cosmic net; my cargo!" The final part of the process was the most difficult and the most dangerous. Subra knew this would deplete him of most of his energy. He needed flawless execution. Master Xu had taught him how to resonate in harmony with the cosmic net. The net had a cargo too precious to lose. It contained insightful quotes from the greatest minds. The net contained knowledge that could be stored and shared with the collective universe.

"I need to resonate at the same frequency as the cosmic net to attract it to me," thought Subra. "If I can mimic its frequency then I can tow it back into the spiritual domain." Subra started to oscillate at various frequencies.

"I'm not making the right connection. I'm not resonating," thought Subra. "Master Xu warned me about the panic, the insecurities, and the doubt. Control it! Think about the outcome not the noise around it. Focus on the outcome and feel it."

The feeling was instant. A thread of blue and purple light shot out at Subra filling him with information. It flowed quickly into his very being. Subra had found the frequency match, and he was harvesting the content of the net. Subra felt utter euphoria. He was feeling the wisdom held within the net. Subra was overwhelmed; he could feel the passion, the love, the pain, the jealousy, and the emotions contained within the quotes. He felt an immense feeling of pride. This was a new experience for Subra, and he enjoyed these new feelings.

He knew the net had been emptied. Subra secured his cargo it was time to move into the final stage of his mission. Subra needed to tow his cargo back into the spiritual domain. He did not see the shaft of burning white energy shooting skywards from the orb. It was so vibrant that it blasted its way up through space. Anything in its path was robbed of energy instantly. Subra struggled to remain focused. He did not know what was happening but he knew instantly that something was not right. He was in trouble. Regaining his focus he realized quickly that he could not absorb energy. He had somehow been damaged.

"What now? What do I do?" questioned Subra in a heightened state of agitation. "I need to get to an energy source." Subra felt a sensation new to him. It struck fear into his whole being. "I'm falling, I'm falling, this is what falling feels like, oh no," thought Subra.

Master Xu had explained the idea of falling. It was hard to grasp and Subra had not understood the descriptions. He knew it was serious; if he fell he would be in grave danger. Subra knew what he had to do. He was falling towards the orb still towing his cargo. He needed to do something quickly. He needed to remember the lecture and follow Master Xu's instructions.

"Find a strong, purple colored, energy source, emanating from the orb. Make sure you head towards the purple energy source. The energy source will lead you to an Indigo Child. Resonate at the purple frequency. This will attract you to purple energy sources on the orb. Indigo Children are receptive to your energy. You have to find the nearest source and head for it. Find an Indigo Child." The orb was getting bigger. The shaft of hot white light pulsed back towards the orb and quickly faded from view. Subra continued to fall; he scanned the orb frantically looking for purple light.

"Resonate, resonate," he thought. Subra continued to send out purple energy waves. He could not see purple light through the white wispy strands that covered the orb. Subra was getting weak. The fear response was starting to cloud his judgment and his ability to focus on his task. From beyond the wispy mist he could finally see a bright purple dot. It was small but it was bright and strong. "That's it. That has to be the purple energy I need," thought Subra. Subra did not resist the fall. He felt calm as the purple light became stronger. He was heading for the energy, and he continued to focus on resonating at the same frequency. During his fall he kept his cargo with him. Subra passed through the wispy vapors surrounding the orb. He could see the energy of the purple light. It shone brightly like a beacon guiding a distressed ship. Subra did not let the fear overwhelm him; he felt calm as he guided his precious cargo toward the purple light.

Subra was soon entering a warm envelope of welcoming energy. It was a soft landing. He had entered an energy source with his cargo intact and managed to survive a fall through a hostile environment. Subra could feel another energy source. All the energies were resonating at the exact frequency. They were in harmony and coexisting. Subra had access to a range of feelings that came flooding into his consciousness. That is when he realized what had just transpired. Subra had entered a physical being inhabited by a soul. A single spirit was living inside this physical being. The clash of energies had rendered the physical body immobile and Subra felt remorse. The body and soul had been disconnected due to the shock the body had suffered. This disconnect was the body's defense response. Subra had to find a way to communicate with the resident spirit. He needed to reestablish the connection between the body and the soul. Subra had to heal this Indigo Child.

Chapter 3

The Sly Fox

Well, look what the cat dragged in," said Nurse Jones in a sarcastic yet friendly manner. "Didn't know you were working this shift tonight."

Nurse Edwards smoothed the covers on the bed and looked up sharply. "Hey, good to see you Annie, I'm just finishing up. Have to go and get our Kevin from my Mum's, and then off home to rustle up a spectacular frozen dinner for Kevin and hubby."

"What's the story with this one then?" asked Nurse Jones.

"Not sure," said Nurse Edwards as she moved to the door. "They thought at first she was a boozy slag. Found her on the street floor collapsed outside of a pub. I guess they thought she'd keeled over from having a skin full. Toxicology didn't find any alcohol in her and she looked almost singed. Now the theory is that this poor love might have been zapped by lightning."

"Really," said Nurse Jones waiting for the punch line of the joke.

"She's lucky to be alive. I guess some old codger staggering out of the pub found her and called for

21

help. They had her in an ambulance and over here sharp. They could tell it was serious and couldn't smell alcohol on her breath. Keep an eye on her. The drip instructions are on the sheet, and they don't look like the others, so read 'em carefully, okay, Annie?" Nurse Edwards waited for the response.

Nurse Jones looked deep in thought. "Yeah, yeah, I will thanks." Nurse Jones moved slowly to the bed in a concerned manner. She bent over and studied Beth's face.

Nurse Edwards had made it to the door and was about to leave. She turned and waved. "Ta ta Annie, see you tomorrow?"

The goodbye suddenly registered with Nurse Jones. She wheeled around quickly and faced the door. "Karen, do you know if she's got parents, or family, visiting tonight?"

Nurse Edwards paused before answering, "Don't know. Check with the Duty Nurse. Sandra's working tonight, she'll know the dirt. I have to boogie, see you love." Nurse Edwards left to complete her hectic evening routine.

Nurse Jones read the drip instructions, and she reread them to ensure she understood it. She watched Beth's motionless body, and she listened to the sound of her heart pulsing through the monitors. Beth was in a coma. Nurse Jones had seen healthy looking bodies waste away to nothing. She had also seen people who looked dead suddenly sit up and recover. There was no set formula for this state. Curious, Nurse Jones placed her hand on Beth's forehead. It was warm but not alarming. She did it to make a connection. It was not meant to be a temperature test or any established procedure. At that moment she caught a glimpse of something and looked down at Beth's right wrist. She noticed a tattoo of a small fox.

"Poor lass," she thought as she headed for the door and the short walk down the hall to the Duty desk. Nurse Rhodes was working the Duty desk tonight. Airedale hospital was a busy place, but the witching hour was usually close to pub closing time. Tonight had been unusually light. The storm and the foul weather had kept people indoors. The halls seemed quiet, and the hospital was settling down for a peaceful nights rest. Nurse Jones walked slowly down the hall. She rounded the corner and leaned against the Duty desk. Behind the desk illuminated by a soft-targeted reading light was Nurse Sandra Rhodes. Sandra was the senior Nurse. She was liked by all of the Nurses. She knew her job and she was fair. Nurse Rhodes looked up from the papers she was reading sensing a hovering presence.

"A nice quiet night so far Annie love."

Nurse Jones nodded, "Foxy lady, does she have any visitors scheduled tonight?"

"No. From what I can gather Dr. Ablett is the on call physician. He's told me that she's an orphan and has no registered next of kin." Nurse Rhodes lowered her voice to a whisper. "Saw the tattoo did you?"

Lowering her voice Nurse Jones asked, "What about girlfriends or roommates?"

"Nope, I think she's on her own poor love." Nurse Rhodes shuffled some papers and looked up. "I think her drip will run out in about a couple of hours. Check the sheet, it's a bit non standard."

"Yes done it, I know the deal. Okay, I'll go now and do what I get paid to do. See you later."

"Bye love, give me a shout if anything exciting happens." Nurse Rhodes returned to her reading.

Above the sound of the equipment you could hear the howling Yorkshire wind. The rain rattled the windowpane in Beth's room. Beth lay motionless; she was lying in the dark. A faint green glow from the equipment monitors provided poor illumination. Her eyes were closed, and the neatly pressed sheets were covering her lifeless body. Subra could sense a strand of Indigo in his dark world. He needed to attach himself to the Indigo light and follow the energy stream. Subra struggled to move. He finally connected with the energy within Beth's body. He could now tap into Beth's feelings. She was hanging on but she felt weak and polluted. There was a pollution happening within her body. External contaminants were flowing into her. Subra could sense a consciousness, but it was not connected with her body. He needed to get her to reconnect. Subra managed to catch a wave of Indigo colored energy. He tried to communicate with Beth.

"Can you hear me? I need you to focus all of your attention upon my voice. Can you hear me? Come on try. Try harder." Subra could sense a small swell of energy. "There it is. Speak to me."

"Am I dead? I'm afraid I'm dead and I'm not in heaven," thought Beth.

"No, you're not dead yet. Dying is a dull, dreary affair, and my advice to you is to have nothing to do with it."

"Great, I'm knocking on death's door and chatting with the grim reaper!" thought Beth.

"Never knock on death's door: ring the bell and run away! Death really hates that!" Subra could sense a smile even if it wasn't physical. "You're not dead, and you're not going to die if I can help it. I'm not the grim reaper, but I do need to explain who I am."

"Well, if I'm not dead it sure feels like it. I'm talking but I know I'm only thinking. I'm thinking and I know I'm not moving. I'm lying here motionless," thought Beth.

Subra responded, "On the plus side, death is one of the few things that can be done just as easily as lying down. There are worse things than death, have you ever spent an evening with an insurance sales man?"

"I'm dying and I get to chat with a comedian."

Nurse Jones stopped at Beth's door and peered in to examine her patient. All was calm and Beth lay motionless. The crisp hospital sheets were undisturbed. Beth looked sweet, innocent, with her hair falling around her face onto the pillows. Nurse Jones made a face. She scrunched her mouth to acknowledge what a shame such a beautiful girl was struck down in her prime. She had a feeling this was not going to end well. One final look at Beth, and Nurse Jones turned and walked away. She needed to check with her next patient. She was unaware of the conversation occurring in Beth's mind.

"I told you. You're not dying. You'll live to be one hundred and you've got it made. Very few people die past that age. Life is pleasant. Death is peaceful. It's the transition that's troublesome. Trust me I should know. Seriously, I'm just trying to lighten the mood but you must not die. I'll help you get back to normal, and then you must help me. Do we have a deal?"

"This is like some cheesy movie where I make a deal with the Devil, and will live to regret it for the rest of my life. I don't know who you are. For all I know I could be talking with myself. It's probably the drugs," thought Beth.

"Half of the modern drugs could well be thrown out of the window, except the birds would eat them. No, you're not feeling the effects of the drugs yet, but you need to get off them quickly. I'm in here with you but I'm not you," explained Subra.

"Who invited you here? I sure as hell didn't."

"Agreed, fish and visitors smell in three days. Let me first introduce myself. I'm known as Subra. I'm not your conscious or your intuition; I'm not your alter ego or another personality. I'm a soul. I'm a different person who needs to share your body for a while. I desperately need your help. You can trust me." Subra continued, "I need to help you. Right now the drugs that are being drawn into your body are killing you. They're not making you stronger. I'll take the time to offer you a full explanation of both our circumstances, but I can sense that the drugs are making you weak. You need energy to function, and the drugs are blocking your energy flow."

"I do trust you. What you say sounds right, but I need to know more about you? Why are you here? What type of help do you want? I also want to know how to get rid of you? In the meantime, how do I get these drugs out of me? How do I wake up?"

Subra had started to map out Beth's energy patterns. He could tell that Beth's body was starting to shut down. He needed to get Beth off the fluids being drawn into her. Subra knew that Beth did not have much time. He was killing his host and his chance of finding the portal.

"My name's Beth by the way."

"Nice to meet you Beth. I'm going to use your body to send a message to the doctors. You have to be removed from the drugs. You don't need these drugs or the kind of fluids they're feeding you. Please don't panic or fight me. I know what I'm doing; this will be the first time that you need to trust me. You'll feel your body starting to reject the drugs. I'll trigger this using your energy, but Beth you are still in full control of your own body."

"I'm game Subra. Just don't kill me, I'm not ready to go to heaven yet," thought Beth.

Subra tapped into Beth's energy and started to gradually raise her temperature.

The green glow in Beth's room changed rapidly to a bright red. Loud alarms indicated to Nurse Jones that Beth was in distress. Nurse Jones quickly entered Beth's room. She turned the light switch on and called for Nurse Rhodes. Nurse Rhodes was entering the room as Beth started to convulse and shake wildly. The drip instructions were followed to the last detail. The drip was removed instantly as Beth's body seemed to reject the drug treatment. The fluids for nourishment remained active and intact. Nurse Rhodes tried to hold Beth's shaking body still. The drugs had stopped but the fluids continued. Beth continued to shake violently and her temperature rose steadily. Beads of sweat formed on Beth's forehead; her hairline was damp and her face flushed with blood. With different pitches the alarms sang like a choir.

"Quick, call the doctor on staff and get him down here now," said Nurse Rhodes in a manner not to be questioned.

Nurse Jones scampered from the room to head for the nearest phone. After what seemed a long time Doctor Ablett and Nurse Jones entered the room. Nurse Rhodes was swabbing Beth's forehead with a damp towel. Beth continued to spasm on the bed. Dr. Ablett quickly assessed the situation and determined that another course of treatment was required. Beth's body had rejected the drug being used.

"Her temperature keeps rising steadily. I haven't seen anything like this before. She's getting hotter and hotter," said Nurse Rhodes in a shaky voice.

"Get the fluids out of her. I'm going to try something else," barked the doctor.

As the doctor prepared the next plan of attack Nurse Rhodes extracted the fluid feed. The doctor was busy working with Nurse Jones. They were organizing the next set of treatments. Once the fluids were stopped the temperature indicator started to fall immediately and Beth's body stopped shaking. The temperature indicator continued to fall; everyone present watched Beth stabilize. Her temperature soon returned to normal and she was calm.

"She won't live long without fluids. Please reapply the fluids. We'll give her a rest from the drugs," said the doctor in an efficient manner.

Nurse Rhodes reapplied the fluid feed. She was greeted with spasms and a rapidly rising temperature. She did not wait for the doctor to instruct her, and perhaps she should have, but she instantly removed the fluid feed. Beth responded with a calm body and a normal temperature.

"Let her settle and monitor her closely tonight. I want to see how she's doing in the morning once her body has had time to adjust to the drugs." The doctor shook his head and passed through the door. "Call me if she starts to do that again or if you see anything unusual."

"Yes, doctor," the Nurses, replied in stereo.

As the doctor left the room the Nurses quickly tidied up. Silence fell in the small room. The monitors were chirping, but Beth's breathing was now strong and regular. Both Nurses felt calm, and a sense of relief washed over them.

"Enough excitement for one night. I'm going back to the desk. Check in with her frequently and give me a shout the minute you see any change," said Nurse Rhodes as she headed down the hall. Nurse Jones looked at Beth; she was peaceful and seemed happier with no feeds. She seemed to be sound asleep. Nurse Jones smiled and watched Beth for about ten minutes before heading off to complete her other duties. Throughout the night Nurse Jones would check in on Beth. Occasionally Nurse Jones and Nurse Rhodes would speak. They would conclude the best course of action was to leave Beth as she was. They monitored

Beth through the night and did not call the doctor again that evening.

"Beth, you've gone quiet on me. Are you all right?" inquired Subra.

"I'm here, but that was scary and weird. Subra, thanks. I feel stronger and my energy is starting to build. It's like a battery charging. My thoughts are clearer. Subra, I can feel you inside of me. I can feel what you're feeling. My body feels dead, and I'm trapped in my own mind with you."

"Beth, it's time to tell you who I am and why I'm here. It's time to tell you the truth. I think you're starting to trust me now. Remember that the truth is more important than the facts," said Subra, opening up to Beth.

"You've helped me, but I have to admit, you still have to gain my trust and my friendship."

"That's fair; misfortune shows those who are not friends. The shifts of fortune test the reliability of friends," whispered Subra softly.

"Wait! That's Cicero. You're quoting Cicero! I remember that from school. I had to do a paper on Cicero. Subra, who are you?"

Subra paused and started to explain to Beth. Subra talked about his studies with Master Xu. He told of his selection process and his Gieging teachings. He described to Beth the domain he came from, and how hard it was to separate from the collective universe. He told of how difficult it was to leave his world. He talked at length about the mental process he used to project himself into the physical domain. Beth was silent; she was listening to the story with interest. She related the story to the messages delivered in the lecture. She could understand the difference between the physical and spiritual domains.

"Are you still there? It's all gone quiet," inquired Subra.

"I'm here. Carry on. I'm sure there's more?"

There was indeed more. Subra continued to communicate with Beth. He told her about the rush of feelings he had felt during separation. He told of his fear and anxiety. Subra described his wonderment at being an individual and having energy to use. He described his excitement at having his own thoughts. Subra continued detailing his journey from the spiritual domain to the physical domain. He described his sights and the sensations of harnessing energy. He described the experience of feeding on energy. He described the beautiful orb that houses the physical world and how it looked from afar. Subra then described the cosmic net. He told Beth of his mission and his cargo.

Beth interjected after what seemed an age of silence. "A cosmic net that stores all of our most important quotes. You have millions of quotes and right now they're all in my head. This is a little hard to believe. I think you're stretching the truth."

"Stretching the truth. Truth is generally the best vindication against slander: Abraham Lincoln. There are few nudity's so objectionable as the naked truth: Agnes Repplier. Believe those who are seeking the truth. Doubt those who find it: Andre Gide. Chase after truth like hell and you'll free yourself, even thou you never touch its coat tails: Clarence Darrow. As scarce as the truth is, the supply has always been in excess of the demand: Josh Billings. Do I need to go on or have I proven my point?"

"So you have a massive store of the world's quotes. What the hell were you going to do with them?" thought Beth.

Subra continued with his explanation. He described his mission in more detail. He detailed how he was to retrieve his cargo, and transport it back to the spiritual domain where this collective wisdom would be shared with the connected universe. Subra explained how he collected the quotes and began to tow them. He described the shaft of hot white light bursting from the orb towards him. He detailed his fall, and the procedures that Master Xu had taught him in case of emergency. Subra described the energy source that he was instructed to find. He detailed his frantic search for a purple light source and how he continued to fall. Subra could sense his descriptions speeding up as if he were falling at great speed. Beth remained silent and listened intently. Subra could feel Beth getting tense. Subra described the falling process as he passed through the wispy atmosphere. He explained his relief as he saw an energy source emitting the right signature; an Indigo colored light. It was the aura of an Indigo Child. It was a physical being receptive to his type of energy.

"Subra, what's an Indigo Child? I haven't heard that term before, and that's how you describe me. I don't know if I like that," thought Beth.

"I can only tell you what Master Xu has passed down to me through his teachings. An Indigo Child is a special physical being. The Indigo Child is connected to the spiritual world with a special type of Indigo energy. Some physical beings can see this purple glow and call it an aura. An Indigo Child is usually different and misunderstood. They have difficulty concentrating yet can do things that others can't," Subra paused.

Subra wondered how Beth would react to this information but he had to continue. "They tend to be able to hear voices with connections into the mind. They have ESP and other types of talents. They tend to be loners and they don't easily fit in. Beth, you have a strong Indigo aura and have open energy channels. That's why I was able to locate you and seek refuge. The cargo I carry is in you at the moment. Our collective energies have shocked your physical body, but I know I can work with you to restore you back to your original state. You just have to trust me. I can only communicate with you when you sleep. Your thoughts need to be still and quiet. Do you understand?"

"The lion and the calf shall lie down together but the calf won't get much sleep."

"That's right. Woody Allen, Without Feathers," said Subra.

Beth tried again. "A lie told often enough is a truth."

Subra corrected. "A lie told often enough becomes the truth; Lenin."

Beth didn't have many left. "I'm just a person trapped inside a woman's body."

"Now that's one I can relate to: Elayne Boosler. Great quote. Sounds like you're finally getting it. I need to tell you a couple of things. We'll work together to reconnect your mind and your body. When you wake up I'll not be able to talk with you. I'll still hear your thoughts. Are you ready for another interesting side effect you'll need to adjust to?"

"This is getting stranger by the minute. You're not going to tell me that when I wake up I'll be a man or anything stupid like that are you?" thought Beth.

"No. That would be fun though. When you wake up you'll have an abundance of energy. You'll use this pure energy to fuel your body. You'll not need any food or water while I live inside of you. Your body will reject them violently."

"All right. Where were you when I needed to lose a few pounds," joked Beth. "Come on, how will my body get the vitamins, minerals and energy that it needs to function? I'm not buying this."

Subra responded calmly. "You won't lose any weight but you won't gain any either. Your body will not be harmed. It'll be living off pure energy, the type your body likes."

"No food or water until I get rid of you. We can only communicate when I'm asleep. Anything else? If that isn't weird enough," asked Beth.

"Beth, one last thing. I think we should work on waking you up. This is the part where you'll need to help me."

Subra explained to Beth about Master Xu's Gieging teachings. He relayed the teachings and legends surrounding the portal that connects the physical world with the spiritual world. He explained the legend of the last soul through the portal. He described how that soul is afforded a glimpse of an image that would help locate the new portal. He talked of the famous Shell image, and how this was the clue to the physical location of the new portal. Subra explained the story of Corom and the dangers associated with his mission. He told of his fears; that he would meet the same fate and never return. Subra's voice became more serious and direct. He went on to explain that he needed Beth's help in locating the portal. Subra talked about the portal. It was his only hope of returning home with his cargo. This was the only way that Beth could remove him from her thoughts. Beth was starting to understand. She could not believe this was happening to her but what choice did she have? Either she was going crazy talking to an imaginary friend, or this was true. She had to wake up and find this portal. Perhaps if she woke she would see the world differently and this voice in her head would go away. It seemed an interesting story. Could she be sure that it wasn't the product of her fertile imagination; could it be the drugs? The quotes could be suppressed memories. She had watched enough TV in her young life.

"I know this is really hard to grasp Beth, but remember I can read your thoughts and feel what you feel. I'm real, and my plight is real. You will learn to trust me. We'll work together to realign your energy flows and get you to wake up. Before we start I need to give you some instructions. This is important. You must concentrate as I need you to remember this." Subra paused for effect before he resumed. "I'll work with your energy flows and we'll align them to help you wake up. When you wake I will not be able to communicate with you. I'll really need your help. Together we'll need to find the Shell and the portal. I don't know where the portal is or even how to find it. Master Xu gave me some instructions but could not elaborate more. I need to pass these through to you. Beth, my future lies with you." Subra sounded serious.

"Master Xu always said that journeys will always bring you home. This is similar to a quote from Herman Melville; Life's a voyage that's homeward bound. What Master Xu was trying to tell me was if I wanted to go home I need to start with a person who has been there. This means finding someone who has had a near death experience. As part of my training, I used to assist with the transition of souls from one domain to the other. Some souls had too much energy, and it was clear that it wasn't their time. They returned to the physical domain. Beth, I need you to think. Is there someone you know who has had a near death experience?" asked Subra.

"I do! What a coincidence. I know a guy who has talked to me about this," thought Beth.

"Good, but there are no coincidences. Coincidences are spiritual puns. When you wake Beth you must seek this person out and talk with them. They will tell you something that will be useful, and it will lead us to the location of the portal. This person is the start of our journey."

"What will he tell me? I don't know if I can do this on my own," thought Beth.

"I don't know what he'll tell you. You'll have me to guide you in your sleeping hours. You can do this," assured Subra.

Beth did not know why she said it, but she felt Subra needed to hear it. Before she could halt she had thought it. "Subra, I promise you, I will help you find this portal."

As Beth and Subra continued to communicate Subra was sensing a small but steady rise in her energy levels. Beth could feel it too. They continued to dialogue. Subra informed Beth that he was working in the background to open up energy blockages in her body. As Subra worked Beth could sense parts of her body that she could not feel previously. Whatever he was doing was working. Subra could start to feel the energy in Beth's body flow more rapidly. It was gathering intensity. Beth started to feel different parts of her body and knew she was close to waking.

* * * *

"How's the sleeping fox this morning?" Inquired Dr. Ablett. Nurse Jones arched her back as she turned to the sound. Dr. Ablett and Nurse Rhodes entered Beth's room looking for a response.

"She's had a good night. After we took her off the fluids she really calmed down. Her temperature remained normal. I just have to finish up a few things and then I'm on my way out. My shifts done so I'm waiting for the cavalry," said Nurse Jones in a tired voice.

"I'm concerned about hydration. I think we need to get her back on the fluids, but after last time, I wanted to give her a chance to wean off the meds. She looks pretty good. I think what we should do is take some blood; I'll run some tests and come up with a new plan. Can you take a couple of vials before you go? I'll have a look see and decide what we can do to get her through the day. Later, we can come back here and try again," explained Dr. Ablett.

"All right, I'll get the blood drawn and down to the lab. Then I'm heading out," said Nurse Jones.

Nurse Rhodes and Dr. Ablett nodded as they walked out into the hall. Nurse Jones could hear them talking softly. The sun was streaming through the window in stark contrast to the night before. As Nurse Jones read the charts she was startled. She moved backwards instinctively. Beth suddenly opened her eyes and adjusted to the light. She raised her hands to her face and surveyed her new surroundings.

"Doctor Ablett! Come quick," cried Nurse Jones. The doctor quickly appeared and was greeted by Beth looking directly at him.

"Hello young lady, you're in Airedale Hospital. You had an accident but you're quite safe. Do you know who you are?" inquired Dr. Ablett.

The hospital insisted that Beth remain available for tests and observation for another day. Beth was fully coherent and felt fine. The tests came back negative for any abnormalities. Beth had to be resourceful at meal times; she could not consume the food or the liquids. Subra had been explicit; no need for food or liquids while he was inside her. Beth noticed that she never felt hungry or fatigued. She did need to play a game with the hospital staff. Beth only ordered water with her meals, which nourished the hospital Fichus. The food was a little tricky. She lined her bedside drawers with absorbent paper towels. She scooped the food into the drawers and disposed of the remains after meal-time cleanup. Beth would grab the paper towels, leave her room and dump the remains into a garbage bin. The staff was happy and amazed that she was walking and getting exercise. Beth fell asleep quickly when lights out was announced on the ward. Subra entered into Beth's thoughts.

"Cute trick with the food. You're sly," said Subra.

"Sly, you say. You're not the first one to say that. Good to hear from you. It was a fairly lonely day with my head all to myself. I need to get out of here. I feel great but they won't let me go," thought Beth.

"I know. Tomorrow you can force them to let you go by signing the liability release waiver. I heard Nurse Rhodes talking with the doctor about it for another patient."

"I know you've been working on me; I'm feeling stronger and stronger. Do you know what would be really good? If you could help me lose a couple of pounds off my butt," joked Beth.

"The butt thing is not in my repertoire unfortunately," laughed Subra.

"I'm worried about getting out and letting you down. I hope I have the courage to see this thing through," thought Beth.

"You need not worry, you'll be fine. Courage is fear that has said its prayers. You'll not let anyone down," assured Subra.

As the night progressed Subra and Beth continued to discuss their release plan. Beth told Subra about the kind-hearted man that she knew down at the allotments. He spent his time there growing flowers and tending to his garden. Beth often passed the allotments, and as if by fate, he was always there. She didn't know his name but she had talked with him often. At first it was small talk about the weather or his flowers. He was a kind man. Beth had mentioned her interest in Indian cooking. The next time she saw him; he gave her a couple of old Indian recipe books. He was the type of guy that was just genuine and not creepy in any way. Some guys appear friendly. You just know what they want, and you feel like you need a shower after a short conversation. The allotment guy was different, calm, honest, and helpful. Beth's conversations with him grew longer and she enjoyed passing the time. They never arranged to meet; it was still left to chance. She would talk with him about three or four times a week. It was obvious to Beth that he was not in good health. He would cough often; a deep rasping cough that you would suggest gets looked at, if you were familiar enough.

When Beth described him to Subra she realized that neither of them had taken the time to introduce themselves. He would call her, "love" and "dear." She would call him, "old friend" or "Sir." Beth described the Indian man to Subra. She told him of his allotment full of roses. Beth dwelled on one particular conversation they had recently. The allotment man had a slight Indian accent, but it was tempered by a seasoned Yorkshire twang. The old man had talked about not feeling well. He had been rushed to hospital. He described in detail seeing a bright light and not being ready yet. He talked of unfinished business. Beth recalled how uncomfortable this made her feel. She didn't want to probe into what was wrong with him. This was probably the only person she knew who might have had a near death experience.

"Does this guy fit the bill Subra?" inquired Beth.

"I'm not sure, but it's the best lead that we have so far. I'm confident that he can tell us something that will help us. Let's try to get to this guy when we can. First, we have to get you out," said Subra.

Morning came quickly and Beth felt prepared. She had discussed plans in detail with Subra. She was eager to get going and help her new friend. She felt compelled to help. It was a burning sensation driving her forward. Beth felt great, strong, and alive. She liked the pure energy diet. It was like having a dozen "Red Bull" energy drinks. Beth needed to get the waiver signed, force the release, and get out.

Chapter 4

The White Rose

Beth looked at her watch; it was 1.15pm. She headed for the green exit sign in the hospital lobby. She strode confidently to the door where she had arranged a taxi. Medical staff had advised Beth of her foolish and risky decision. She thought she might lose her composure. They could not know she was completely healed and running on pure energy. She would not tell them. She could quickly be transferred to the psychiatric ward. As she left the hospital she felt the cold sting of fresh air rub her face. The sun was bright but the wind was still cold.

Beth jumped into the back seat of the taxi cab, "Going to Sun Street in Haworth please."

The taxi sped away. Beth was not in the mood to talk and pretended to study her release forms. The driver got the hint. She could see his brightly colored red turban. Strands of dark hair were peeking out from the bottom at the neck. He was a large man. He kept glancing into the mirror to look at Beth. She stared at the release form but did not read it. Beth looked at the roundabout near Cliff Castle and the thin road winding up the side of the Worth Valley. It was a busy time of day, and her mind wandered to the old Indian man at the allotment. The Taxi turned and Beth noticed the Bronte Pub. She knew she was close to home. They passed Haworth steam train station and the old Aire-dale Springs factory. When the taxi turned left onto Sun Street Beth let out a quiet sigh. It was good to be home. Beth could get out of her clothes and have a bath.

"Right there. Three doors down from the Fish 'n' Chip shop on the right," said Beth pointing.

She paid the taxi driver. He thanked Beth in broken English. He had a large grin that looked strangely soft. Beth jumped out of the taxi and headed towards the door of her small cottage. She reached into her purse for her keys. They were still there; that was a relief. Beth entered her cottage and got undressed. Time was slipping away. Beth quickly showered deciding a bath would take too long. She changed into a pair of jeans, a tee shirt, and a sweater. She slipped on a pair of black runners. Beth pulled her auburn hair back into a ponytail. She grabbed her bag and left the cottage. Beth walked quickly through the park before heading up the alley towards the allotments. It was a glorious sunny day but a little on the brisk side. Her cheeks were rosy red, but she hardly gasped as she climbed the steep cobbled alley. Walking past the allotments she noticed a few people tending to their little patches of fenced land. She quickly reached allotment number four and scanned the scene. Behind a sea of color was the Indian man.

"Good afternoon sir. How are you doing today?" chirped Beth in a cheery voice.

The Indian man turned and looked to see who was talking to him. He had to squint into the sun to rec-ognize her, but when he saw it was Beth his face lit up with a broad smile. Being Indian, and of darker skin, this seemed to exaggerate the whiteness of his teeth and make his smile more charming. Beth often thought his smile illuminated his entire allotment.

"I'm doing better for seeing you young lady. Haven't seen you in a few days, been keeping out of trouble?" said the old man. It was followed by a rasping cough. He caught it quickly by covering his mouth with a fist and bending over sharply.

"Yes, I was busy but in a good way. The allotment looks good. The roses are beautiful," said Beth noticing a lion. It was made from marble and faced the gate to the allotment. Beth leaned on the flimsy metal fence. The Indian man walked over to Beth and wiped his brow with the sleeve of his shirt.

"What's you name love? I talk to you like you're my own daughter and I don't know your name."

"My name's Beth sir, Beth."

"I'm Anwar. It's my pleasure to talk with you Beth, my angel," he said.

Beth thought it was sweet being called an angel. "It's a coincidence; I was just thinking recently that we talk often and didn't know each other's names."

"There are no coincidences my dear. I have another reason to introduce myself to you today because I really need to impose upon you. Come in, sit, I would like to talk with you about something really important, if you have a minute?" He motioned to the wooden bench surrounded by sweet smelling roses. Beth felt safe and entered the allotment passing through the gate and over to the bench. It was a long bench and she positioned herself at the far end. She was immediately hit by the strong fragrance of the surrounding roses.

"What's on your mind?" inquired Beth.

"I don't really know where to start with this one," confessed Anwar looking nervous.

"Start at the beginning or where you feel comfortable," said Beth, proud of her response.

Anwar positioned himself at the other end of the bench and rubbed his dirt-covered hands on a cloth. He was clearly nervous and Beth could sense this as she waited for him to start. "I had a dream you see. A spirit came to me in a dream and spoke to me while I slept." Anwar coughed repeatedly as he struggled to get his message out.

"Damn cough. I know this sounds weird but you have to believe me. For the last couple of nights a voice has talked to me while I've slept."

Beth smiled and moved closer to Anwar, "It's not weird, I understand."

Anwar continued, "The spirit told me that you, my angel, would be coming to the allotment today seeking me out. I was instructed to tell you of my dream and that you would understand. Beth, I'm dying and I don't have a long time left."

"Oh I'm sorry, I ..." started Beth.

"Let me finish," interrupted Anwar. "I have to get this out. Beth, I don't have much time and I need to ask a favor from you. It's so imposing that I would expect you to decline. Beth, you have to do this for me. Really, you just have to. I know it's such an imposition and I may have left it way too late," pleaded Anwar.

"You're talking in riddles. Just slow down and simply tell me what you want."

Sitting on the bench in the sun surrounded by roses Anwar began his tale. Anwar told of a time long ago when he was a young man growing up in Mysore, in the Indian State of Karnataka. Anwar was 21 years old when he first delivered food to the house of a wealthy family. The most beautiful girl he had ever seen in his life greeted him. She was so beautiful that she made the famous Ambavilas Palace pale in comparison. He knew instantly that she had captured his heart and there would never be another.

Over time Anwar managed to talk with the girl and slowly melt her heart. Week after week Anwar would snatch precious time with her. He wooed his love with notes, poetry, and sentiments of affection. Anwar fell in love with Aklina Akhter. She was the daughter of a wealthy Mysore businessman. Aklina had shiny long black hair. She wore beautiful pale blue saris. She had deep hazel eyes that always laughed and sparkled like the sun reflecting off Karanji Lake. Aklina had one unusual feature. Her left forearm was beautiful and strong, but she had a skin pigment blemish. This blemish was white colored contrasting with her deeply tanned arm. The white birthmark was clearly in the shape of a rose. Anwar called her his "White Rose."

At first Aklina jokingly referred to Anwar as "Mahishasura." This was the name of a famous demon from the Mysore Hindu mythology. After a while she referred to him as her "Tiger," after the large bronze tigers that lay in the Mysore palace grounds. Slowly, Aklina fell in love with Anwar and would sneak away from the house to spend time with him. Like the star crossed lovers Romeo and Juliet, Anwar and Aklina were deeply in love, but they were never meant to be. They had realized their families would never agree to this union. One evening Aklina was asked to speak with her Father. Aklina was nervous; she thought that their love had been exposed. Her Father was in a good mood and looked very excited. She was asked to sit and she felt more nervous. Her Father seemed happy, and her Mother looked pale and tense. It was that evening that her parents informed her. Aklina was to be married to a wonderful boy from a prominent family. He was the son of a trusted business associate from Bangalore. Aklina was stunned but remained composed. It was arranged that Aklina would meet with him soon. She was instructed to be a "perfect lady," and not squander this chance or embarrass the family. Aklina knew this signaled the end of her relationship with Anwar. How could she tell him? What should they do? One afternoon Aklina slipped out of the house unnoticed and headed for the store that Anwar worked in. They met and went to Anwar's modest place to talk.

Aklina described her predicament and cried. Anwar consoled Aklina. Without thinking they shared their love for each other. As coincidence would have it the young suitor fell ill. He could not make the journey from Bangalore to meet Aklina. She would have to wait before she could meet her future husband. Many months went by, and Aklina hoped that the marriage would fall through. To her dismay she discovered that she was with child. She concealed this fact as long as she could until one night she shared the news with Anwar. He was excited and frightened. What should they do? They would have to leave the "City of Palaces," bringing disgrace to both sets of families. They needed to plan, as neither had enough money to execute an escape.

Anwar delivered food to the home for weeks but something seemed wrong. Each time a different person would take the order. Where was Aklina? After a while Anwar decided to discretely inquire. What he heard hit him so hard that he was physically sick. The daughter had fallen ill, and the Akhter family had moved from Mysore to get her some treatment. Anwar was desperate and asked everyone he could; no one knew where the family had relocated. On chance, Anwar searched nearby Bangalore and established that the wedding had fallen through. He could not locate Aklina and it seemed he had lost his love, and his child, forever.

Anwar would often visit the Ambavilas Palace. He would rub the nose of the bronze tiger for good luck.

Aklina had done this in the past. He hoped that they would see each other again one day. After a few years Anwar had heard the family had moved to Cochin. He then heard they had relocated to somewhere in Europe. Aklina and his baby had been lost forever. Anwar was given the opportunity to move to England, and this was a move he could not turn down. He talked of the hard time adjusting to life in England and understanding the West Yorkshire dialect. He worked hard and opened a bakery. It was such a success, and he managed to open seven bakeries before eventually retiring and selling his business. Anwar explained that he never did marry or even court another woman after Aklina. Anwar pointed to fate for bringing him to Yorkshire. Yorkshire is famous for the "War of the Roses." Its county symbol is the "White Rose."

Anwar continued, "I have a green thumb Beth. Everyone is complaining about insects this year yet my roses grow strong and beautiful. The white ones are the most beautiful. I often take flowers down to the senior center to spruce the place up a little. I'm known for that. They call me the "Rose Man," down there."

"What happened to Aklina? Do you know?" asked Beth gently.

Anwar coughed violently before continuing. "I was taken ill recently Beth. I was rushed over to Airedale. The doctors were pleasant enough but the message was concerning. They told me that I needed to do a series of tests. I knew it was serious. I nearly died. I think I shared that with you, didn't I?" Anwar avoided eye contact and looked at the dirt. "The doctors say I don't have much longer. It's my lungs Beth and it's spreading. Here's where it gets strangely interesting. I was sitting having a tea in the small canteen they have at the hospital. I was waiting for my results. A person came and sat at my table. Indians tend to sit together Beth.

When we started to chat we realized that we knew each other. More than that, we grew up together in Mysore. Kirit was a servant at the Akhter family house! Now if that isn't a coincidence, I don't know what is!" Anwar was shaking his head and rubbing his temple with his left hand. "I remembered this person as a skinny little boy. Here we were a million miles away, both old men, having tea in a hospital in West Yorkshire. I asked him Beth," said Anwar staring deep into Beth's eyes. "I asked him if he knew what happened to Aklina."

"Did he?" inquired Beth leaning in across the bench.

"He did," said Anwar, his tone of voice deep and shaky. "He did."

Anwar, slowly and deliberately, outlined the rest of the story to Beth. Puffy white clouds sailed by high above. Shadows danced across the allotment. It could have been raining cell phones, and Beth would not have noticed for she was totally absorbed. Anwar continued with his story. Kirit had talked like two old friends catching up on gossip. The Akhter family was furious at Aklina and held several closed-door meetings. Shouting and the sobbing could be heard. All the servants and staff were sent home for the evening. It took a while for word to filter down to the staff but slowly the story came out. It was apparent that beautiful Aklina had disgraced the family by becoming pregnant out of wedlock. Key members of the staff were let go. The remaining staff was told that the family and their employment were relocating to Kolkata in the Indian State of West Bengal. Kirit decided to leave with the family. The Akhter family relocated to a large house in Kolkata. The Father had a cousin who helped him reestablish his business.

Aklina was under great pressure to reveal the Father of her child, but she had stubbornly refused.

This infuriated her Father who disowned Aklina and the child. Aklina's Mother tried to help, and ensured that Aklina was taken to a medical facility to have her baby. Her Father was not supportive.

"I was close to tears as Kirit told me the story Beth. I had to stay composed as he would have guessed it was me," said Anwar coughing badly.

Kirit continued with what he remembered. "Aklina and her Mother went to the medical facility the day of the birth. It was very basic and not well equipped. The Akhter family could have afforded top quality medical care but the Father was a proud man. Aklina seemed to be doing fine until she started to bleed internally. Aklina gave birth to a beautiful, healthy, baby girl. Aklina insisted that they name her Rose. It was an unusual name for an Indian girl, but she insisted the girl was to be named Rose Akhter," said Kirit shaking his head.

"What happened to Aklina?" asked Anwar in an even but quiet voice.

Kirit just shook his head and looked down at his steaming cup of tea. It was as if the answer was too painful to state. He looked up at Anwar and said, "Anwar, she was a beautiful girl. It was a real shame. She refused to name the Father. I considered stating it was I to give her some release from her torture. I was too young, and no one would have believed me. I wasn't very good at lying. Anwar, she had a real grace about her and she wouldn't give in. They say her body was cremated but I don't know for sure. I loved her eyes, her kindness, she was beautiful."

Anwar asked, "What happened to Rose?" trying not to sound too desperate.

"That's where it gets sad. The family abandoned little Rose in an orphanage in Kolkata. I have no idea if she made it; the family was disgraced and moved to rejoin another branch of the Akhter family in France. They met a cousin. Srini, I think was his name. I didn't go with them. I moved back to Mysore and then over here twelve years ago."

Anwar and Kirit talked for a while, exchanged phone numbers, and vowed to meet for tea. Kirit lived close to Anwar in Oakworth, a small village near Haworth.

"That's so sad," said Beth moving closer to Anwar. Beth could feel tears welling up but convinced herself it was the wind stinging her eyes. "So long as little children are allowed to suffer, there is no true love in this world," said Beth. Beth surprised herself with a quote that she was not remotely familiar with. This was Subra pushing quotes into her consciousness reminding her that he was still there.

"You're a sweet intelligent child quoting Isodore Duncan to me. For that I thank you," stated Anwar returning to his coughing.

"Doubt is not a pleasant condition, but certainty is absurd," responded Beth unwillingly.

"Beth, I was a Baker, but in my retirement I have read many books. Voltaire is not a person that I would expect you to know. You're an interesting individual. I do get your point. No more uncertainty. You need to know what I'm about to ask," responded Anwar.

Anwar stood awkwardly, and he almost stumbled as his weary legs took on the strain of his weight. He walked carefully over to his dark duffle bag and withdrew two similar sized envelopes. Anwar held one in each hand. Waving the two envelopes in the air, Anwar let his weight hit the bench hard, as his legs gave way from under him.

"This is important, really important, to me. I need you to believe in Rose. I need you to have faith that you can win in this request. If you think you can win, you can win. Faith is necessary for victory. Faithless is she that says farewell when the road darkens," Anwar said reaching out to hold one of Beth's hands.

"I'm still not sure what you want me to do, but you know that you can trust me. Quoting William Hazlitt and a modified J.R.R.Tolkien gets me curious, but I'd rather hear what it is that makes you procrastinate so," said Beth with a touch of impatience.

Anwar smiled, "You're bright. I have two envelopes and a massive ask. In this envelope is a private letter. It belongs to a woman named Rose Akhter, daughter of Aklina and Anwar. I can feel it; she's alive. She deserves to know who she is. She needs to know; this letter explains everything. I don't have long left on this Earth, and my little "White Rose" deserves to know who she is, and how beautiful her Mother was."

"Her Dad's a neat bloke too. She's a lucky girl," said Beth.

"Thank you. You don't know your parents do you Beth?"

"No," responded Beth sharply.

"Then you know how it feels to live in ignorance," suggested Anwar.

"Stupid is forever, Ignorance can be fixed," said Beth without thinking. Subra was starting to get good at pushing timely thoughts through.

"Exactly!" said Anwar knowing that Beth was getting this. "This is why I need you to set out on an adventure. I need you to find Rose and give her this letter. I'm too sick and may not have enough time. You're my only hope," pleaded Anwar.

"Charm is a way of getting the answer "Yes," without asking a clear question," responded Beth.

"Then I take it you find me charming?"

"Yes," responded Beth. Their eyes locked as smiles broke on each face. Beth moved her hand forward and held Anwar's hand. "I will help you," stated Beth confidently.

"In this envelope is the means to find Rose. I have the address of the orphanage she was taken to in India. I have her full name. I have an Indian access visa for a six-month period starting in one day from now. Don't ask me how I got this. I pulled in a large favor at the Indian consulate. This needs to be glued into your passport. You have a passport don't you?" asked Anwar.

Beth nodded; she had a valid passport but had never used it.

Anwar continued, "I trust you Beth. You're like my own daughter in so many ways. If she turns out to be half as smart as you, I'll be pleased. The envelope contains money, a considerable amount. You may need this to go to India, find Rose, bribe officials, and of course, return. I'm sure you have plenty in here, but the rest is for your faith in me and your troubles."

"I can't..." started Beth.

"Yes. You can," interrupted Anwar. "You must go home and plan immediately. I need you to find Rose and deliver this letter to her. I've left you some instructions in your letter, and I hope you have the courage to let your heart guide you into this great adventure. Many people say that when they go to India it touches them and changes them forever. Beth, you need to do this, not for me, but for yourself. I know you think that you're doing me a huge favor, and you are. You have to trust me. Later, you will think that I have done you a large favor." Anwar was holding out the two envelopes. One had "Rose" written on it; it was sealed. The other had "Beth" written on it; the flap neatly tucked into the lip.

Anwar smiled, and his eyes started to sparkle as he offered the envelopes to Beth. Beth scrunched her forehead as she struggled to understand Anwar's comments. She felt her body extend her hands outwards in slow motion to take the envelopes. She had noticed Anwar had not coughed in the last five minutes; he was calm. When Beth took the envelopes Anwar lunged forward and hugged her. Beth was not alarmed; she imagined it would feel like this, to be hugged by your Father. It felt good, safe, loving.

"Thank you Beth. Thank you so much. You've made this dying man happy," said Anwar excitedly.

"I've agreed to look, but you know it will be difficult finding Rose," tempered Beth.

"You'll find her Beth; I just pray that she's in good condition and in safe surroundings when you do. I've left instructions for you in your envelope." His coughing returned, this time it was a bad fit. Beth noticed a small amount of blood quickly folded into the handkerchief used to conceal his coughing. Anwar recovered and continued. "Beth, I can't go with you. I will support you, as best I can, from here. Just assure me that the two of us will form a tight, small group, on this mission. We need to be totally committed."

"Never doubt that a small group of thoughtful, committed citizens can change the world. Indeed, it is the only thing that ever has," responded Beth. Beth smiled, as she knew this was Subra's way of telling her to accept the mission, and the small group now had three members, not two. This group was growing in size. Anwar snapped Beth back to attention.

"I don't know that one but it's beautiful."

"Margaret Mead," said Beth instinctively.

"Beth we've chatted enough. I want you to go home and read the instructions. I need you to prepare and pack, before you change your mind. I can't begin to tell you how happy you've made me. This is an adventure that you're destined to be part of. My voice at night told me that you needed to do this. This is not just for me but it's for you also. Please go now and stay safe my child. I love you like the daughter I never had," gushed Anwar. Anwar leaned forward slowly; he kissed Beth on the forehead and placed something in her left hand. Beth looked down. Anwar had placed a beautiful white rose in her palm. She raised her eyes to meet his.

"Anwar, I promise you, I will find your daughter, but I have a strange question to ask you," said Beth. "Your spirit talked with you in your dreams, and I have a similar spirit guide. My spirit guide indicated that you'd tell me something important. It will help me with my life's mission. I have to ask you one thing."

"Go ahead. I will help where ever I can."

"I would like you to think hard about a Shell, yes a Shell. Where in your life does a Shell become prominent? Where have you seen a Shell? If I said Shell, what would that mean to you?" asked Beth hopefully.

Anwar thought hard. "Beth, I'm sorry, I'm drawing a blank. I've never lived by the sea, I've never owned a Shell, or had a Shell prominent in anything that I can recall. This is one that I can't help you with. I don't know how I can tell you anything meaningful about a Shell." Anwar looked disappointed; he wanted to help so badly. He looked deep into Beth's eyes. "Please find my little Rose, and make sure you return home safe."

He picked up his duffle bag, coughed loudly, and trundled along the allotment path leaving Beth to wonder what she had just signed up for. As they had talked the clouds had moved in. The afternoon sun, once so strong and bright, had taken its leave.

The light was fading fast and the feelings of darkness were starting to settle. Beth could not believe how quickly the time had gone. Anwar was a kind old man, but listening to his cough Beth agreed he did not have long to live. It was natural that he wanted to send one last letter to his daughter. Beth was still sitting on the bench surrounded by swaying roses. She held a white rose in her hand and two envelopes. The night continued to draw in quickly and the weight of her promise now started to play on her mind. Had she done the right thing? Did she even know what she had signed up for? Could she pull this off or would she disappoint?

Beth suddenly became aware that she was alone in the allotments; everyone else had gone home including Anwar. The wind was picking up again and the temperature had dropped. Beth shuddered and wrapped her arms around herself. She quickly placed the rose on the bench and gently placed the two envelopes in her purse. She left them sticking out as her purse was not deep enough. Pulling the strap over her shoulder she stood, shivered, and hurried out of the metal gate, closing it behind her. Beth thought the alley looked different at night, too many shadows, and too many mind games. She rarely used the alley after dark. She hurried down over the cobbles and headed home briskly, not looking back. At the end of the alley she suddenly remembered, she had left the white rose on the bench. She stopped momentarily but continued on quickly, leaving the rose behind.

"I lost one rose but I'll find another," she thought.

Beth passed a couple of teenage boys hanging out at the corner. She immediately thought of what Anwar had said. One of the envelopes contains money. She glanced quickly at the boys; they were not paying any attention to Beth. Beth hurried past the boys. She clutched her purse tightly, as she started down the cobbled hill. She entered Sun Street with a feeling of relief. She noticed the street lamps illuminating. She will just make it home before it gets too dark. Beth approached her cottage, and at the front door, she fumbled for her keys. She entered and reached for the light switch, closing the darkening outside world, behind her. Feeling safe and calm, she bolted the door, and sank into her favorite chair. It was quiet, except the faint drone of a passing car, and the sound of some distant voices.

"What have I done?" said Beth aloud to herself.

As she looked around at her modest little rented home she recognized her neatly organized belongings. This was her place. It was not much, but it was hers, and she felt safe. What would she feel like in India? She did not have travel gear; she had no immunization jabs, and knew nothing about what lay ahead. This was more than a day trip to Scarborough seaside. Beth remembered the quotes popping into her head when she spoke with Anwar. Clearly Subra was at work finding a way to communicate with her during her waking hours. The quotes were positive and Beth took this as Subra's way of endorsing her direction and decisions.

Beth looked down at her purse. It was lying on the floor, at the side of her chair, with two white envelopes protruding. She reached down slowly and retrieved them. The first was sealed, with "Rose" written neatly on the front. Beth placed this back in her purse. She looked at the second envelope labeled "Beth." She flicked open the folded flap with her fingernail. Numerous items were inside, but Beth selected the letter from Anwar.

Chapter 5

Focus on the outcome that you want

Dear Beth,

What I have asked you to do is a favor so large I was ashamed to ask. The fact that you are reading this note means that you have graciously accepted my request. If truth were told, I should have visited India years ago, when I was a younger man, in better health.

The news of my love and of our daughter has shaken me to my very soul. I was filled with joy that my daughter had lived, and shame that I had not sought these answers earlier. I was happy to toil away in the allotment of life, comforted in the fact that I did not know. Now that I do, I feel helpless.

Beth, you are my only hope of salvation. I believe that every little girl needs a Daddy, and that absence is something that now bonds both you and Rose. I know in my heart that Rose is alive, but I have a fear for a young girl in an orphanage, in that area. Many bad things can happen to her, especially if she has her Mother's looks.

I know this is a daunting task for you Beth. You are sharp, quick minded, healthy, and full of life. You are strong willed and resourceful. You are the perfect person for the job. There is one other quality that you have Beth, I trust you with all of my heart.

I will try to make sure that you are safe. India can be charming but it has its dangers. I have taken the liberty of booking you into business class to India. I have arranged a driver for you, when you land in India. Your hotel is booked; your journey is well planned. I would not want my daughter traveling to a strange land without these basics being arranged.

I have included money for you in English pounds and Indian Rupees. I'm sure you will have enough, but my home number and mobile number are attached at the bottom of this letter, should you need more. Your flight is prepaid on Emirates leaving from Manchester tomorrow at 2.05pm. You will fly through Dubai to Kolkata and land in Kolkata in the early hours of the morning, around 8am. I will have the driver hold a sign with your name on it. You should have no issues. I have also attached the name, address, and number of the hotel that you are staying in, should there be a mix up. The small wooden elephant faced figure is "Lord Ganesha." He removes obstacles; please keep him with you. He will bring you good fortune.

I can never thank you enough Beth. I know that you will not be working, so please use some of the money to pay for your rent. I have tried to put myself in your shoes, but quite simply, I would have said "No." The fact that you said, "Yes," is a miracle. For that, I cannot do enough for you. Please accept my eternal gratitude. I have attached more details, but for now make sure you are on the plane from Manchester airport at 2.05pm tomorrow. Good luck and stay safe.

Regards,
Anwar Patel

Beth looked into the envelope and examined its contents. She glued the Indian Visa into her passport as instructed. She went to her wardrobe and started to fill a backpack. She knew she wanted to travel light; some tee shirts, a sweater, a rain jacket, underwear, and more. Beth put the little wooden Lord Ganesha inside her backpack and smiled.

"Remove obstacles," she thought. She kept her packing to a minimum. Guided by a sense of urgency, Beth phoned her landlord. She informed him of the future rent payments, contained in an envelope, on her dining table. She told him that she needed to go away for a while; she did not know when she would be back. She had prepaid two months in advance. With the details planned, and her bag packed, Beth was now starting to feel excited. She hung up the telephone after speaking with the Taxi Company. She had arranged to be picked up at 11am. Beth had taken care of everything that she could think of. She was now ready to find Rose. Beth had a sudden urge to talk with Anwar; should she call him? She picked up the phone and dialed the number.

"Hello?" answered Anwar softly.

"It's me, Beth."

"Is there something wrong?" asked Anwar.

"No, not at all. That's why I'm calling. I just wanted to call and tell you that I'm packed, ready to go, and excited about this opportunity. I'm feeling confident that I'll find your daughter Rose. Anwar, I will find her, I just thought that it was important that I tell you that," said Beth.

"I know you will Beth, I know you will."

"Have a good night Anwar."

"Good night my dear, you're on the right path," said Anwar as he paused and then hung up the phone.

"On the right path," repeated Beth. "I wonder what he means by that?"

Beth felt warm inside. She had never been more certain she was doing the right thing. She knew it felt good to help Anwar, but she couldn't help feeling a sense of urgency. She didn't know why, but she wished she could be on the plane now. Tomorrow morning will drag until she could start her adventure. Why was she so wired? Was she excited about helping Anwar? Was she excited about giving Aklina some family roots? Was she excited about the prospect of an adventure, pushing herself out of her comfort zone?

Beth realized that she was caught up in a host of frenzied possibilities. She stared at the wall in horror. Beth realized that she had neglected her most pressing mission. She needed to help Subra! Beth would hear from Subra tonight, and she would not be surprised if he was disappointed. Beth had spent the day taking on another task. She had let Subra down, and she could feel this impending darkness growing within her.

"Oh, no!" Beth said to herself. "I got caught up with the Aklina mission, and I didn't find anything to help Subra." Beth sat quietly and replayed her conversation with Anwar in her head. She felt uneasy, as she could not recognize the message that she was supposed to hear. What was it? Beth was getting tired, and she knew she had a big day coming. She felt a little apprehensive about falling asleep. Beth knew when she fell asleep she would have to converse with Subra. What would she tell him? Would he scold her for accepting the Indian mission ahead of finding the portal? It seemed that Subra wanted Beth to accept the mission but did she misread his quotes? Beth was apprehensive about Subra's reaction. He had stressed that time was running out and finding the portal was critical. Going to India, on a side mission, was probably not what Subra had in mind. She did not look forward to the upcoming conversation with Subra, but she could not stay awake any longer. Beth headed upstairs. As she climbed each step, she felt heavy and sluggish. This was the first time she had ever felt this way running on pure energy. The stairwell in Beth's cottage was narrow and dimly lit. Beth could feel her body rising with anxiety. Why did she feel this way? She had completed her nightly rituals of turning the lights off and checking the locks. Beth entered her bedroom. She opened the set of drawers at the side of her bed.

She pulled out her warmest, heavy wool pajamas, and quickly changed into them. It was good to sleep in her bed tonight, back in familiar surroundings. She hoped Subra would not be too mad with her. Beth watched the shadows dancing on her bedroom ceiling, as the traffic outside created its nightly light show. Beth slipped into sleep quickly.

"Good job today Beth, you're on your way, and you handled it great," said Subra in a cheerful voice.

"What? I accepted a mission in India that I can't back out of now," explained Beth.

"Beth, I asked you to help find the portal for me. We'll set out on this journey together and it'll lead us to the portal. I said that Anwar will tell us something that will help us locate the portal and he did," said Subra.

"Oh, great, you figured it out then. I'm so glad. I tried and I think I missed it. What was it?" thought Beth.

"I don't know yet, but we will. We've been offered a road to travel together and I'm proud that you said yes. I'm proud that you agreed to help Anwar. That act will be rewarded. Beth, you did this for all the right reasons, your insights will come. Your wisdom will be provided through uncertainty."

Beth was relieved at Subra's reaction. She had been worried, but she felt she had done the right thing. Subra confirmed this as they continued to talk. That night Subra and Beth discussed the day and the interaction with Anwar. Subra shared with Beth that Anwar's aura was weak. His statements of "Not having long," were probably accurate. This would explain his immediacy at finding his daughter.

"I felt sorry for Anwar, he waited too long. Now he has a glimmer of hope, his body is too frail to go and seek it out. He so wants to give his daughter the truth," thought Beth.

"Matthew Arnold; Sohrab and Rustum," suggested Subra.

"Yes, I've located it; Truth sits upon the lips of dying men," answered Beth. "Neat trick by the way; injecting quotes into my conscious waking hours."

"That's the best I can do. I still can't talk with you, other than when you're asleep. I can position the odd quote for you."

"I wasn't hungry today, that pure energy really works. I was weak climbing the stairs on route to my bed. Why is that?" inquired Beth.

Subra responded quickly, "Any negative thoughts that you have will weaken you. You were creating an anxiety around my reaction to your fantastic deeds today. This was self-imposed, you responded perfectly. You did exactly as you should have done."

"I told Anwar that I felt confident that I could find Rose, and...."

Subra quickly interrupted, "Turns out if you never lie, there's always someone mad at you."

"Thanks Subra, you're a true friend," thought Beth.

"I have a quote from Jay Leno for you. Go through your phone book, call people and ask them to take you to the airport. The ones who will drive you are your true friends. The rest aren't bad people; they're just acquaintances. Beth, I can't drive you to the airport, but I will stay with you for your entire journey. Adversity does teach who your real friends are."

"I would be lying if I didn't say that I felt nervous. I know I'm going to meet Rose. I really hope she likes me," thought Beth.

"If you make it plain that you like people, it's hard for them to resist liking you," assured Subra.

"If I'm honest, I'm still worried about this India thing. You can sense that, right?"

"What worries you masters you, we are passengers together," responded Subra. "Do not anticipate trouble, or worry about what may never happen. Keep in the sunlight," said Subra. "Keep your sunny disposition."

"Okay Benjamin Franklin, but that's another thing I'm not used to. How will I deal with the sunlight, the heat?" thought Beth.

Subra had an answer yet again, "Don't knock the weather Beth. If it didn't change once in a while, nine out of ten people couldn't start a conversation."

Beth reflected on Subra's words. "I suppose you're right. I just can't predict my future and it's making me a bit nervous."

"Prediction is very difficult, especially about the future. When you relinquish the desire to control your future, you can have happiness."

"I know, but I still worry about the future. Can I find Rose? Can I find the Portal? What am I going to do with my life? These are all things in the future and it's pressure I've not had before," thought Beth. She felt the weight of responsibility building.

"It's rather simple. The best way to predict the future is to create it," answered Subra.

"Subra, I have tended to always trust my gut, my instincts, it felt right saying yes today, but what if I was wrong? What if India is the wrong direction for the portal?"

"There can be as much value in the blink of an eye as in months of rational analysis. Creativity comes from trust. Trust your instincts. You will creatively solve this portal problem," reassured Subra.

"I will need to have this motivational chat with you often. I know I'll need some luck to pull this off," thought Beth.

"You'll make your own luck. You're doing the right things. I'll not have this conversation again with you. You must focus on what you want and align your positive feelings to it. If you don't believe, then stay in bed and don't go to India. I know that's not you. You're a fighter Beth, an optimist," said Subra in his best motivational tone. "I want you to start to talk to yourself differently. I will teach you to send out energy patterns of what you want. Are you game?" Subra questioned Beth's openness to learn.

"Yes. I need all the help and positive energy I can get. I'll keep an open mind, even though you're in it already," thought Beth.

"Let's start. This is a fundamental principle of Gieging. Beth, you seem to focus on what you don't want. What I want you to do is focus on the outcome that you do want. When you say, "What if I can't find the portal," you're sending out energy. The energy says, "I can't find the portal." Focus on the outcome that you want, "I will find the portal." This sends out a different type of energy. The energy now says, "You will find the portal." This will open the positive energy flows within your body. Energy flows where attention goes. Do you understand?" asked Subra.

"Yes, I get it; I need to reprogram my language to get different results."

"You're a fast learner; it takes some people a lifetime to understand this important lesson. It's more than just having a smiley face and a positive attitude. You're trying to force the answer to the portal location. I'm as motivated as anyone to solve that problem, but you can't force it Beth. I have confidence that you'll solve the problem. If you can solve your problem, then what is the need of worrying? If you cannot solve it, then what is the use of worrying? Don't worry; focus on your desired outcome. You'll solve it and you will find Rose," reinforced Subra.

"You're right. We won't have this conversation again. I'm confident in my abilities to find both Rose and the portal. The days of self sabotage are over."

"Our upcoming journey is an exciting one of discovery. There's never a traffic jam on the extra mile."

Subra and Beth continued to discuss topics throughout the night. Beth told of her experiences growing up. She talked about the rejection and self doubt that lived with her constantly. Subra worked with Beth to reprogram her thoughts, language, and energy flows. The noise of the traffic outside started to increase indicating the arrival of morning. The sun began to rise and illuminated Beth's bedroom window. Birds started to sing announcing the dawn chorus. It was going to be a great day. Beth started to wake as she rubbed her eyes and tried to remove her hair from her face. She looked toward the light and squinted quickly at the sun's rays. Beth thought about her night and the advice that Subra had given her. She had a busy day ahead. She knew the morning would appear to drag, until she was traveling. She spent the morning trying to keep busy. She caught an early bus to a nearby town. Keighley town center was a busy, bustling place in the morning. Beth spent the time shopping for some last minute items. She had bought tee shirts, sunscreen and sturdy runners. The morning seemed to linger until the taxi arrived outside her door as planned. Beth grabbed her backpack. She quickly checked for her passport and headed for the door. She could see the brightly colored yellow paint of the taxi through her cottage window.

Glancing at the rent envelope on the dining table, she took a quick look around, as if to say goodbye for a while. Beth opened her front door and stepped out onto the street. The door locked behind her, and she tested the handle to make sure it was locked. She made her way to the taxi and slipped into the back seat.

"Manchester airport isn't it?" said the driver turning to face Beth. "You! Didn't I pick you up at the hospital a couple of days ago?"

"Right," said Beth recognizing the red turban.

"Where are you going and which airline?" inquired the driver in broken English.

"Kolkata, India and I'm flying Emirates," said Beth with butterflies in her stomach.

"You're going to India so soon after coming out of hospital, is that wise?"

The taxi was speeding away over the Yorkshire moors. Beth thought how she would miss the lush green valleys, clean air, newborn lambs, and dry stonewalls. This was home and she was heading for a very different land. "I'm fine thank you," said Beth.

"I see you're traveling light, how long are you going for?" asked the driver.

"Not sure yet," answered Beth.

The driver was clearly in a talkative mood. "I'm from Delhi myself, further North, West of where you're going. It'll be hot. Are you traveling alone?"

"No. There's a group of us," said Beth hoping to avoid a lecture on the dangers of India.

The taxi had taken the back route over the moors. It had been a while since Beth had been out this way.

She looked at the small villages and beautiful old Inns she passed on route.

"It's not my business, but I think you could find yourself in difficult situations going to India for the first time," offered the driver. Beth was stunned and could not think of anything witty to say. She felt her cheeks flush. The driver held her gaze in the rear view mirror.

It came out without thinking, "At the age of eleven, or thereabouts, women acquire a poise and an ability to handle difficult situations which a man, if he is lucky, manages to achieve somewhere in his later seventies." "Thank you, Subra," thought Beth.

The driver sat and mulled over Beth's response. To his credit he attempted to match wits with Beth. "I happen to feel that visiting India will raise conflicting attitudes for you, as your type have led a very privileged life over here."

Again Beth was left with no response. "I happen to feel that the degree of a person's intelligence is directly reflected by the number of conflicting attitudes she can bring to bear on the same topic."

Subra was in fine form. That seemed to work. The driver went quiet and paid attention to his route. Beth was left to admire the countryside. It was beautiful, wild, and stunning. The Yorkshire moors quickly gave way to the Lancashire countryside. Beth was snapped out of her day dreaming by the driver who decided to start again. Beth braced herself for more negativity but the tone was different this time. She thought the driver tried to break the silence because he felt uncomfortable.

"You have a strong spirit, do you believe in energy and the mind?" asked the driver.

"That's a broad subject, but generally, yes I do."

"I'm sure you're aware of the Indian traditions, Yoga and such," pitched the driver.

"I know Yoga means "Union," and that it's a heck of a lot more than standing on your head and doing poses!" said Beth.

The driver laughed. "Good," he said. "When I was a little boy growing up in India my father and I were very close. Unfortunately he's passed now. He taught me a game that we often played together. I tell you this because India is the land of traveling. This is maybe something you'd enjoy when you do your traveling. We used to lie on our backs on a hillside. You don't have to be lying down to play, "Cloud Busting." Have you heard of it?"

"No," said Beth intrigued.

"It's a game where you pick a big, white, fluffy cloud. The wind in India is still and hot, not like here where the clouds race across the sky. The clouds hover and stay still in India. The game is to pick a cloud in the sky, a solid one. You imagine your energy concentrating and flowing out of your forehead, or your third eye. Do you know where that is?"

"Yes," said Beth rolling her eyes.

"You direct it at the center of a cloud and you just keep focus. We did this all the time, my father and I."

"What happens?" inquired Beth.

"Magic and wonderment,' answered the driver. "You can punch a hole right through the cloud. It starts to drift apart in the middle forming a hole. Cloud Busting, do it when you get bored," offered the driver smiling.

"Does it work?"

"Only if you believe it works," answered the driver.

Beth had heard this point before. "I will try it."

"Trying is a graceful way of failing, do it," said the driver.

"Thanks, I will."

The driver smiled and they continued with their journey. The Lancashire landscape slowly started to change from a rural setting to the city of Manchester. Traffic increased, and the driver became tense as he concentrated on his immediate surroundings. "Emirates is located at terminal two. I will let you out at terminal two. This fare is prepaid and the tip is already included."

"Thanks," said Beth looking into the car's rear mirror. "How much longer?"

"About fifteen minutes, not long. I'll take you to the curb at terminal two. It's a busy place. I would appreciate it if you can hop out quickly when we get there," the driver asked.

"Sure," said Beth.

The taxi pulled up to the curb. Beth was on her way when the driver looked back and shouted. "Thanks. Have a good trip and keep your wits about you." Beth grabbed her backpack and smiled at the driver as he took off.

Beth entered Manchester Airport terminal two. She was met by crowds of people, all heading in different directions, all moving with a purpose. She saw families and couples saying goodbye and hugging. It suddenly hit Beth that she had not flown before. She quickly convinced herself that this was exciting, the extra mile; no traffic jams on the extra mile. Beth saw the red illuminated Emirates sign and joined the long orderly queue of people. A rather small-framed woman stepped out of nowhere and smiled at Beth. Beth's first thought was "Wow, she's pretty." Beth quickly realized the refined looking woman in the beige pantsuit was an Emirates employee. She was assisting passengers. Beth's mouth hung open and she didn't know what to say.

"Hello, can I see your passport please Miss?" asked the attendant.

"Sure," said Beth searching for her passport and duly handing it over. The attendant scanned it into a mobile device and smiled.

"Miss Martindale? You're flying business class to Kolkata?" inquired the attendant.

"Yes," blurted Beth.

"Please follow me, you have your own queue for business class. It's much shorter," informed the attendant.

Beth followed the efficient attendant. She couldn't help noticing how neat her hair was; pinned up in a bun design. Beth had thrown her hair into a ponytail as usual. The attendant stopped and waved Beth into the shorter line. She used a swift extension of her arm accompanied by a smile. It was a motion Beth had seen countless times on TV game shows, but it looked smooth and effective today. Beth smiled at the attendant as she moved into the queue. The attendant returned Beth's passport and wheeled away in an efficient manner. Beth was soon at the check in counter. A well-groomed attendant advanced her through the check in process. Beth now had her boarding pass and continued through the security screening process. After her bag was scanned she had to remove her belt, shoes, watch, and coat. She needed to get dressed again before she could move into the lounge area. She looked at the large illuminated board and could see her flight details. The next thirty minutes was a blur for Beth. She suddenly found herself walking to the end of a boarding ramp and stepping onto the front of an airplane. Her stomach churned constantly. More professionally groomed young women greeted her.

"6D," said one attendant smiling cheerfully, "This way please." Beth was shown to her seat.

It was not a seat, more of an enclosed pod. She had never seen anything like it before. Beth enjoyed her first flight experience; the flat bed, the movie screen, the drinks and food that she had to politely decline. She enjoyed the constant attention of the cabin crew.

This was the way to travel. The flight to Dubai departed at around 2pm. Beth managed to sleep during the seven-hour flight. It was just enough time to have some friendly banter with Subra. Beth enjoyed herself, but she suspected she would not enjoy the next part of her journey. She was about to experience her first international connection. When Beth landed in Dubai it was just after midnight, local time. She now had to find her connecting gate. The walk to the next gate was painless, but she was facing a ninety-minute wait before her connecting flight to India.

The airport was quiet and calm. There were a few people milling around but the pace and excitement had dropped. Everyone seemed tired, lifeless, and bored. Beth sat quietly in her chair waiting to be called. She watched other people. Beth sat opposite a man reading a mathematics book on prime numbers. He had a computer bag with him and short-cropped hair. Beth saw him jump to attention hearing his Blackberry phone ring. He quickly reached down and flipped the cover of his holster open. Grabbing his Blackberry, and moving it to his ear, he stood abruptly and started to walk away.

"This is John," Beth could hear him say in an American accent as he walked off deep in conversation.

Beth did not see herself as an attractive girl. She often used her directness as a shield. She was an insecure person and did not have a strong positive self-image. Beth always wore jeans, tee shirts, and baggy sweaters. Today was no exception. She was a "no fuss" type who wore her hair in a ponytail; held in place with elastic. No one could doubt that Beth was intelligent, but she was constantly told that she needed to focus. She needed to channel those smarts. Beth never wore makeup and was never really interested in boys. She knew she was not gay; she definitely liked the male torso, and had stared longingly at a fashion poster. It was hanging on a billboard, in front of a store she had worked at. Beth once had a teacher she was fond of. He taught her for a whole term in one of her many schools. He was from Calgary, Canada. He was average height, slim, articulate, kind, mature, and had a Canadian accent that was easy on the ears. She secretly liked him, liked him a lot. So did most of the girls at the school.

"He's so fit," they would say in that Yorkshire slang.

Beth's image of herself was always inconsistent. She had often joked that she could lose a few pounds off her backside. She meant it as self-deprecating humor. Beth walked a lot. She did not have a car and was clearly fit and toned. Beth ate sensible foods and could not afford to eat excessively. She had long, auburn, healthy, hair that glistened in the sun. Beth had a natural beauty about her. She was about five feet five inches tall, 25 years old, and her face glowed. She inherited high cheekbones and large green twinkling eyes. Beth had a strong smile that could melt a man.

Most men would look at Beth and see a beautiful young, fit, natural, woman. Most women would see Beth as a fresh, youthful, woman; someone they would want to be. What Beth lacked was confidence. She always felt she was not good enough. Waiting for her connecting flight Beth couldn't sleep and it was getting late. She thought about the day and her mind wandered to Anwar and Aklina. Beth saw a neon Coffee sign. She picked up her backpack and quickly headed off down the hall for a walk and a distraction. Beth spotted a washroom sign and paid a quick visit. She approached the hand basins and began to wash her hands. She splashed cold water on her face and dried herself with a paper towel. As Beth disposed of the towel she caught a glimpse of herself in the mirror. She lingered to study her reflection. She looked good, considering it was midnight. She had been trapped on a plane for the last seven hours, and she thought she looked good. Perhaps it was the pure energy but she looked fresh. It was the first time, in a long while, that she felt this way.

Staring into the mirror she mouthed the words, "You can't even drink a coffee. You're on the pure energy diet."

Beth returned to her seat in the lounge and waited for the gate staff to get organized. John was seated reading his Math book. He glanced up and smiled at Beth as she sat. Beth could hear Anwar coughing badly in her mind, and she started to think about the Shell.

"Where will I find this Shell?" thought Beth.

Beth glanced around her. The lounge area had filled in with people waiting for the flight to India. A few people were westerners but most looked Indian. She saw Mothers with sleepy children and Fathers pacing impatiently. Beth saw men dressed in tunics that looked like a smock with trousers underneath. Most women wore traditional Indian dress, and Beth tried to study them from the corner of her eye. They looked so comfortable. She was in a pair of tight fitting jeans, a snug blue tee shirt, and a wool sweater. She noticed that some saris were plain, while others had delicate beading, and looked more expensive. She tried to imagine herself in a sari and sandals. She would wear a pale blue sari of course; just like Aklina.

One of the women had painted hands in intricate designs; Beth had never seen this before. There were a few Indian looking women in the lounge that dressed in a western style. One woman sitting opposite Beth intrigued her. She looked Indian from her appearance, but she was dressed in white sneakers, comfy sweat pants, and a sweatshirt. She had no trace of an Indian accent and carried a black computer bag. She was holding a Canadian passport. She was traveling with two men; both had English accents. They also had matching black computer bags and Canadian passports.

"Not many western faces on this flight," thought Beth.

Eventually the gate staff announced the boarding order. Beth moved forward with the computer bag business crowd. She boarded the plane with ease. She was greeted with a smile and shown to her seat. The flight to Kolkata was just under five hours. Beth would land at 8.15am local time, according to her itinerary. After a frustrating connection in Dubai, Beth was finally seated and ready for takeoff. She wanted to get going. She was eager to get to India and start her mission. This was the final leg of her long journey to Kolkata. She could feel the butterflies deep in her tummy and she smiled at the thought.

"This is it," thought Beth. "No more messing around now. When I step off the plane, I'll be in India! I'm going to find Rose, and I'm going to make Anwar a happy man."

Beth settled into her pod. She had to refuse Champagne, orange juice, food, coffee, meals, nuts, and popcorn. It was difficult not to appear rude, but she felt she had done her best to be polite. Beth watched a couple of movies. She finally covered herself with a blanket, positioned her bed in the flat position, and nodded off. This gave her a chance to have a quick chat with Subra.

"So, what do you do when you're not chatting up your favorite girl?" thought Beth.

"I've been working on you," said Subra sounding stern.

"What's blowing your skirt up? You sound like you're in a snit," thought Beth. Beth could sense that Subra was not right.

"I have some bad news. It's Anwar; I don't feel his life force anymore. Even though I'm not connected to the spiritual domain, I can sense he's joined them," Subra said in a quiet, sad, voice.

"Oh no," thought Beth. "Are you telling me he died?"

"I'm sure that's what I'm feeling," replied Subra.

"I don't understand, why do you sound so sad?" asked Beth. "I thought you'd be telling me that he's gone to a better, happier place, with no wretched cough."

"He is," snapped Subra quickly. "I guess this is the first time that I can truly understand grieving. I'm sad that he couldn't hold on long enough to talk with his daughter. He was so close. Now, she'll never know him, in this life."

"It's good that you can feel this but she'll know him. I'm going to find her and give her the letter. I'll tell her what a wonderful man he was," thought Beth. "It's all right to feel bad Subra. That's what we do over here in this domain. Waste not fresh tears over old grief's."

"Euripides, 484 BC to 406 BC. You're right Beth, the only cure for grief is action."

"Thank you George Henry Lewes. Remember, I can access the quotes freely when I'm asleep. I'll miss him sorely, but this has made me more determined to complete his wishes. I now have total confidence and belief."

"Some things have to be believed to be seen."

"Agreed, like Cloud Busting," replied Beth.

"I would rather have a mind opened by wonder than one closed by belief."

Beth responded in a flash. "Oh, what a tangled web we weave when first we practice to believe. Enough with the quotes now, I want to communicate with you."

76

"My dear Beth, the point of quotations is that one can use another's words to be insulting," said Subra in a lighter mood. "Be careful with quotations, you can damn anything."

"Subra, I'm being serious," pleaded Beth. "Listen to me. I miss my dreams, I know it's fun talking with you, but do you understand? I miss my dreams."

"To accomplish great things we must dream as well as act, it's time for you to wake and act Beth. Talk with you soon."

Subra faded and a compelling feeling washed over Beth to wake up. Beth opened her eyes and found herself strapped into her seat on the plane. The cabin was busy now. The attendants were moving quickly and with purpose. Beth caught the sight of a beige uniform approaching.

"Please move your seat back to its upright position. We're preparing for landing; fifteen minutes. Please fill out your customs card," said the attendant in a helpful and efficient manner.

Beth complied and was soon feeling the slight bump as the landing gear deployed. A smooth landing, and a quick announcement by the cabin crew, signaled her arrival in India. Beth stood as soon as the seat belt sign went off. She grabbed her backpack from the overhead and opened the zipper. The announcement said the temperature was 32 degrees Celsius. She tucked her sweater into the backpack. Beth glanced at her watch. It was 8.17am; she was really excited. She headed for the exit and thanked the cabin staff for an excellent flight. They looked very smart in their beige uniforms.

Chapter 6

Adventures in another world – Kolkata

Beth stepped from the plane; a wave of hot air welcomed her to India. She carefully walked down the steep metal stairs and onto the tarmac slip.

"I'm standing in India," thought Beth.

She joined fellow passengers as they waited for transportation. Within a minute, a large white bus stopped and opened its doors. Beth followed the group and sat in the bus. It had large windows that curved into the roof. The available space filled quickly. The doors closed leaving behind passengers for the next ride. The bus moved slowly. It made its way to a white, flat roofed building, where everyone entered. Beth moved into the building, she walked through the customs area and joined a long line. After shuffling her way forward she eventually made it to the front of the line. A young man in a uniform waved her forward. Beth strode towards the desk and presented him with her passport and customs form. He searched for the page with the visa.

"I hope this works," thought Beth.

The young man seemed disinterested as he picked up his stamp. He stamped a clean page in her passport book. He did not ask any questions. He tossed back her passport and waved at the next person in line. It was as if Beth were not there. Beth walked out of the customs area and into baggage claim. She passed rows of metal baggage trolleys with blue plastic handles. The terminal looked dated. It was white with an interesting ceiling made of illuminated triangles. Beth looked at the large columns supporting the structure. Each column had a floor to ceiling advertisement pasted to it. Cellular phone companies had the space brightly decorated in bold red colors. A very large poster had an exotic looking Indian woman fawning over a man. Why? He was wearing the new, black and gold, light powered, Citizen Eco-Drive watch. Beth headed for the exit.

She stepped out of large glass doors. She was not expecting the reception. A large metal fence ran about thirty feet from the door. She noticed people straining at the fence. They were four or five people deep. A large number of people held signs bearing names. They all shouted at Beth as she emerged from the terminal. It was hot and Beth was dressed in a tight fitting tee shirt. She walked the line looking for her name. She noticed a couple of the men were looking at her, in that way. As she glanced around she noted most of the women wore saris. Beth felt a bit self-conscious; a loose fitting tee shirt would have been better. More people shouted at her and waved small placards bearing names. "Beth Martindale;" it read on a large sign at the back. Beth's eyes were drawn to the familiar arrangement of letters in a sea of names and faces. She caught the man's eye and nodded. That was all that was needed. Dressed in a white tunic uniform, he sprinted to the end of the fence to greet Beth.

"Miss Beth, it is so nice to see you. My name is Sanjeev please follow me. Stay close, come please," said Sanjeev.

Sanjeev grabbed Beth's backpack and headed across a narrow road to a parking lot. In a flash, something brushed up against Beth's leg, and she whirled around out of instinct. A blur of brown; it was running past her being chased by two others. Beth finally recognized them as thin, mangy, looking dogs.

"Stray dogs. Big problem around here, just ignore and don't feed," instructed Sanjeev.

Beth continued to follow as she passed rows of yellow taxis with black stripes down their sides. The cars looked dated, an old style that was unfamiliar to Beth. She felt a hand on her elbow as she walked. Beth turned and saw a young man.

"You need to give me money, yes please," he said. "Please, you give money?" he asked.

"Go away!" shouted Sanjeev. "Don't stop walking. Just follow."

Beth made it to the parking lot. They stopped at a white Toyota. The bright sunshine hurt her eyes and she knew it was starting to get hot. Sanjeev had loaded her backpack into the back of the car and closed the boot.

"Please," he said motioning to the open passenger door.

Beth climbed in and attached her seat belt. The interior of the taxi smelled minty, due to the air freshener hanging from the mirror.

"It's a crazy place the airport. It's full of beggars and tricksters. Please, only talk to people you know," said Sanjeev.

The car was in motion and he pulled out onto a main road. The tall, lush, green, trees that lined the exit struck Beth. For some reason she had a mental image of a dusty brown barren land. As the car pulled away the air conditioning kicked in, and she could feel the cool, calming, air flow.

"Good temperature, yes?" inquired Sanjeev.

"Yes, good," replied Beth mimicking his broken English.

"First time to India?" asked Sanjeev. He turned his body taking his entire focus from the road as the car sped forward.

"Yes, first time."

"Eat vegetarian," said Sanjeev trying to be helpful. "That way you won't get sick."

"I will, thank you," said Beth.

Beth noticed that Sanjeev wobbled his head, from side to side, in a curious way when he talked. His words said yes, but his head motion said no. She smiled as she noticed this peculiar trait. A screaming horn broke the silence. Another horn and then a chorus of horns followed it.

"This is our turn signal; we sound it to let cars know we approach, that we are passing, stopping, and turning, used for everything. You'll soon get used to it and not hear them," laughed Sanjeev.

He was right; horns blaring everywhere, for everything, with no one seeming to mind or getting upset. In Yorkshire, sounding the horn would be seen as an act of aggression. She noticed painted on the back of trucks, and rickshaws, the words "sound your horn." Beth had heard a saying that it was a small world. She did not feel that way. She felt she was a long way from home. Every sight, smell, and sound, was new. Little rickshaws had barefooted drivers and passengers crammed into the back seat. Some had whole families squeezed into the back seat. She was learning rapidly; expanding her experiences, growing as a person, and pushing the boundaries of her comfort zone. She had experienced more in the last twenty minutes than the previous month. She liked it.

Beth felt alive and energized. She had discovered a thirst for new experiences. She had made the right decision. She was going to help Anwar and Subra, but she was going to have some fun doing it. There was an awkward silence forming in the taxi, and Beth decided to initiate some conversation.

"Sanjeev, I saw a woman getting on the plane with unusual hands. They were painted with intricate designs, what does this mean?" asked Beth.

"Yes, this type of work is called, Mahndi. It's very famous in India. It's an old Indian custom. The bride will get her hands painted on the eve of her wedding, but she will keep the paint on for about two weeks after her wedding. Everyone who sees her hands will give her well wishes." Sanjeev explained with his eyes firmly placed in the rear view mirror, and his head wobbling from side to side.

"What kind of paint is it?"

"It's a Henna paste. An artist normally does it by hand. These days, you can get..." Sanjeev paused as he searched for the English word, "templates?"

"Yes," affirmed Beth.

"Templates, that takes the skill out of it. Progress they say," complained Sanjeev.

"Maybe it is a small world, everyone seems to dislike progress," thought Beth.

The taxi swerved wildly to the left throwing Beth around in the back seat. Sanjeev sounded the horn, and he sped past a slow moving vehicle missing it by inches. Beth looked at Sanjeev; he was calm, very calm. The sudden change in direction caused Beth to divert her eyes. Her gaze moved from the side windows to the front of the taxi. She stared through the windshield. She noticed Sanjeev's hands on the steering wheel and the watch strapped to his right wrist. It was an old watch and the glass had discolored. The glass had a large crack reflecting the light. The strap looked worn. It was fake leather and had started to flake due to wear. On the dashboard was a small wooden figurine; the elephant headed Lord Ganesha. To start a conversation Beth asked Sanjeev a question.

"What's the significance of the elephant statue?"

"This is Ganesh, or Lord Ganesha. He's the lord of success, the destroyer of evils, and the remover of obstacles. Lord Ganesha is very popular in India. He is one of the five prime Hindu deities. There is a big festival for Lord Ganesha, but you need to go to Pune to experience this. You will see Lord Ganesha everywhere that you go in India," explained Sanjeev.

Beth glanced outside and the scenery had changed. She saw large fields of garbage, at the side of the road people were milling around, searching for anything of value. She noticed groups of men finding shade where they could. Some wore trousers, sandals and shirts. Some were dressed only in cloth, wrapped around their hips. Bright colors seemed to be reserved for the women. They wore saris, hair clips, bangles, and earrings.

"They look beautiful," said Beth quietly.

Beth's attention was snapped by a sharp knock at the window. She was jolted to look at the face peering in. The car had stopped at a light, and an old woman pushed her face close to the window. She had a pained expression, begging eyes, and a weathered, wrinkled face. A faded green scarf wrapped around her head hid her hair. With one small withered hand, she wrapped her knuckles on the window, keeping eye contact with Beth. Beth could feel an anxiety rising deep within her. Was it pity, shame, or sorrow that she felt? Perhaps she felt uncomfortable because she simply did not know what to do in these circumstances. She looked at Sanjeev for some type of signal. Sanjeev was stoic; he stared forward at the light and totally ignored the old woman. She did not exist.

Beth looked at the old woman, she was clearly begging. She was shouting something in desperation, but it was illegible, it was not in English. The old woman sensed the light was about to change. She shuffled quickly to one side and pushed her other arm close to the window. She had a very thin appendage, bone thin. The bone was bent backwards and stuck out 90 degrees from her shoulder. Her arm was horribly deformed and had no muscle or flesh on it.

It had been an unfortunate liability for this woman throughout her long life. The old woman shouted something in desperation, as she quickly moved back to let the taxi speed off. Beth was in shocked silence; that experience was not very pleasant. Sanjeev sensed this and offered words of advice.

"There are many beggars in India Miss. You must not give anything. If your heart becomes weak and you give money, food, water, you will attract a crowd of beggars very quickly. This is very dangerous they are very desperate people. They will try to take advantage; they will do anything to survive. If you keep yourself to yourself, then no harm will come to you."

"Got it. Thank you Sanjeev," said Beth still shaken.

"My pleasure Miss," replied Sanjeev. "We're close to the hotel now Miss, a few more minutes only," said Sanjeev wobbling his head. "The airport that you arrived at was closed for a while last week you know. A pig strayed onto the runway and stopped a British Airways flight," laughed Sanjeev. "Perhaps the pig knew more than we did," he said laughing loudly.

"Pigs and dogs," said Beth.

"Like a farm at the airport," laughed Sanjeev. "It used to be called the Dum Dum airport, because it's located in Dum Dum. Then some official thought that a better name was in order. Now it's called the Netaji Subhash Chandra Bose International Airport. International, that's a laugh. Seventy five percent of the flights are domestic. Not such a great name choice. Not easy for international foreigners to remember. People still call it Dum Dum, much better."

Beth had to agree. The taxi sped southwards into the city.

"You're staying at The Astor Hotel, very beautiful hotel, we are close," informed Sanjeev.

He pulled into a driveway flanked with a black metal railing. Beth was struck by the tall, thin building, that was, The Astor. As the car stopped, a couple of men in uniform approached Sanjeev. They seemed friendly enough. One had a pole with a mirror attached to it and was inspecting underneath the taxi. The other walked around the taxi looking in.

He looked at Beth and smiled, "Good morning Miss, welcome to The Astor," has said.

Sanjeev leaned back, "More security than normal due to the elections," he explained.

Beth looked at the hotel as the car was being inspected. This would be home base. The morning sun was shining brightly on the hotel, which was spectacular. The hotel was a hundred years old. The building was an example of stunning Victorian architecture. You could not miss it, due to the bright red brick and white trim. The hotel glowed vibrant red in the strong sun.

Beth looked at the wall with a large white arch and a red brick interior. In the center was white lettering set against the red brick; "The Astor Hotel."

"This was going to be good," thought Beth.

It was a short walk to the front entrance, a door surrounded by white trim. Sanjeev approached Beth.

"Do you know about the news with Mr. Anwar?"

"Yes."

"I'm very sorry. I will give you my card; it has my cell number on it. Mr. Anwar hired me to look after you. You need not worry; Mr. Anwar has taken care of my expenses and your hotel expenses. You need not pay anything. Please call at any time, when you need transportation. I'm at your service Miss. I will be taking my leave for now and wait for your call," explained Sanjeev handing Beth a small business card.

Beth tucked the card into her back jeans pocket. A uniformed hotel attendant was carrying Beth's backpack and motioned her in the direction of the hotel entrance. Beth noticed a tall tree growing inside the small courtyard. Beth thanked Sanjeev and walked towards the front door. She was in the heart of the city and could hear traffic and horns. Beth took a deep breath and entered the hotel lobby. The sun was scorching her back. She walked into The Hotel Astor and realized how comfortable the air conditioned reception felt. The rich colored wood that framed each door well and the reception desk impressed her. Behind the reception desk was a young woman standing to attention in her bright red tunic. She beamed a welcoming smile Beth's way and waited for Beth to approach. The reception desk was made of wood and was waist high. The walls were a cream color contrasting with the wood wainscoting and shiny cream floor tiles. The walls behind the reception were also wood panels. Beth could see a waiting room off to the right. It had a large red leather couch and a couple of green potted ferns. She was impressed. The hotel looked older from the outside. Inside, the hotel looked very modern and clean. As Beth approached the desk the young woman greeted her.

"Welcome to The Astor Hotel, can I see your passport please?"

Beth fumbled for her passport and handed it over.

"Miss Martindale, we have you down for a double room. Our instructions say it is prepaid for three weeks with a rolling three week renewal, is that correct?" asked the receptionist.

"That's correct," said Beth trying not to sound surprised.

The receptionist placed a form and a pen in front of Beth. She asked Beth to fill out section A. It contained basic information, name, address, country, and email address. She completed the information and turned the form around.

"Is one room key sufficient?" inquired the receptionist.

"Yes, that's fine, thank you."

The receptionist gave Beth her plastic card room key. She peered into her computer screen and said, "Oh, please wait. I have an envelope for you when you check in. This came from England," she said giving Beth the package. She motioned to the attendant to escort Beth to her room. The attendant jumped to attention. He was carrying Beth's backpack and quickly walked over to Beth.

"Room 323 please," said the receptionist.

The attendant walked Beth to the elevators and delivered her bag to the room. He entered the room with Beth, and began a long story about the hotel, how to work the air conditioning, where the fridge was, and how to establish an Internet connection. Finally, Beth understood the motive for his delay. She reached into her pocket and pulled out some Indian Rupees. She did not recognize the bills and pulled the first one out. She gave it to the attendant who stopped talking and thanked Beth. He glanced down at the note in his hand and began to thank Beth repeatedly.

"If there is anything you want, you call the desk and ask for Ved," he said.

Beth did not know how much she had given Ved but he seemed very pleased. Ved wheeled away and closed the door behind him. Finally she had made it to India and was now safe in her room. The room was really clean and spacious. It had light colored wooden floors, beige walls, and earth tones, with peach and brown furniture. It was modern, with a double bed, LCD thin TV, and Indian wall prints, with accent lights. Beth approached the desk in her room. It was neatly arranged with a writing pad and stationary. The stationary was beige colored, like the room, with gold, embossed writing. The notepad read; The Astor Hotel, 15 Shakespeare Sarani, Kolkata, 700071, telephone - 91 33 2282 9957/58/59.

Beth tore a page from the notepad and tucked it into her backpack.

"At least I will remember where I live," she thought. "Well Beth, I think Anwar's looking after you," she said looking upwards to the heavens. "I will make you proud Anwar, I promise," said Beth gently.

Beth explored the room, the bathroom, the closet, the safe, and the mini bar. Everything was exceptionally clean, modern, and she was pleased. She did not know what to expect, but this exceeded her expectations. Anwar may not have selected the largest hotel in Kolkata but he picked a good one. Beth looked at the alarm clock and it informed her that the time was 10.30am. Beth had a long shower to clean her body and refresh her mind. She felt better as she dressed in the hotel robe and slippers. They were comfortable and smelt of flowers. Beth lay on the bed and reached for the envelope she had been given. Marked on the front, in neat handwriting, were the words, "Beth Martindale." Beth opened the large brown envelope and emptied the contents onto the bed. Inside, was a letter with a yellow post-it note attached? A sealed envelope lay unopened. Beth picked up the letter and read the post-it note. It was handwritten in the same neat style as the front of the original envelope.

The post-it note read, "This letter was emailed to the hotel. Specific instructions were left to print and deliver this to Miss Martindale when she checks in." There was a signature, but unlike the writing, it was difficult to read. Beth removed the yellow sticky and attached it to the original envelope. She unfolded the letter and started to read. The letter contained a company name which read, "Ruby, Clary and Fitch; Barristers and Solicitors."

My Dear Beth,

I've left strict instructions with my lawyers to get this note to you should I pass away. The fact that you are reading this means that I have left this world and started my journey to that better place. I'm devastated that I did not get a chance to meet my Rose. I wanted to tell her how much I loved her. I'm very happy to have met you Beth. I'm proud of your wonderful generosity to help me convey this message of affection to Rose. I think I know you Beth. I know you will find Rose and deliver my letter to her. I hope you find what you are looking for in life and I'm sure you will.

We had a simple relationship, and for you to put your life on hold, to do this for me is an unexplainable miracle. I knew I didn't have much time left and that my health was failing. I trust the Hotel is adequate and that Sanjeev is looking after you. I have known Sanjeev since he was a little boy. He's a good soul and will continue to help you.

Good luck and may Lord Ganesha remove all obstacles for you on your search. I will be cheering for you in whatever place I find myself, but I'll be supporting you. Beth, I cannot thank you enough. I have enclosed another letter for you. Indulge me. This letter is for you to open privately, once you've found Rose and delivered the letter.

Your Eternal Friend,

Anwar

Beth put the letter on the bed and felt her eyes starting to tear. "Eternal friend," thought Beth.

Beth placed her head onto the soft pillow. She had only managed to sleep briefly on the plane ride. Beth's body clock was confused, and she could feel herself drifting into sleep. She tried to fight it but it was useless. She was asleep in minutes.

"You made it to India," Subra said in a voice tinged with excitement.

"My body clock is a bit out of whack."

"True, that will last about a day. You're only allowed a quick nap. I will make sure that I wake you after we've talked. You should try to stay awake during the day and sleep at night. It will help you adjust to local time faster. I can sense your energies are not resonating with the local energies yet. We need to fix that quickly," said Subra.

"That's good. I'm sad from the news of Anwar and his letter," thought Beth.

"Anwar was a good and honorable man. He's now in the spirit world and cured of that wretched cough. Happiness is nothing more than good health and a bad memory. Health is not valued till sickness comes."

"I need to get started and find the trail to Rose. I won't find her here in the hotel room," thought Beth with a feeling of impeding urgency.

"The address where Rose was taken to the orphanage is close to the hotel. You should be able to pay a visit today. That would be a good start. Listen to your body we need you healthy and fit to do this. I have a feeling Beth. I'm feeling that the search for Rose will help us on our journey to the portal. It just feels right," affirmed Subra.

"Really. It's good you feel that way. I was feeling guilty for doing this and not finding the portal," thought Beth. "You knew that didn't you?"

"The two are connected. We'll find Rose together and she'll help us find the portal. She may not know that she's helping us but I suspect she will," said Subra in a hopeful voice. "You need to start your journey again. You go, just remember that a foreign country is not designed to make you comfortable. It's designed to make its own people comfortable. You will travel the world in search of what you need and return home to find it." Subra's voice tailed off.

Beth could recognize the feeling. Subra had decided it was time for her to wake. He would well up energy and shoot it into her brain. This made her senses acute. Any sound or thought would wake her. She woke to the sun streaming through the hotel window. It beckoned her to come outside and begin her adventure. She felt better, full of energy and raring to start her quest. Beth jumped up off the bed, flipped off her hotel slippers, and dropped her robe to the floor.

"This is going to be a great day. I'm going to make you proud Anwar," said Beth.

Beth dressed quickly in a loose fitting white tee shirt and jeans. She picked out a pair of clean socks and laced up her running shoes. Beth grabbed a small leather wallet. She loaded it with money, ID, and a credit card. She slipped it into the front pocket of her jeans. Beth retrieved Sanjeev's card from her rear pocket. Beth started to panic there was no contact information? Beth turned the card over and in black ink was scribbled a cell phone number.

"Off to a fine start," thought Beth. "No. Don't beat yourself up just go with the flow. Don't fight fate," thought Beth.

Beth moved towards the hotel safe and placed the envelopes, letters, cash, and passport inside. She closed the safe and entered a pass code that she would remember. "4545" was the code she selected. "45" was the number of Beth's cottage on Sun Street in Haworth. Haworth felt a million miles away as she entered the code. Beth had removed one document from the pile. It was a letter signed by Anwar that contained the name and address of the orphanage. It identified Rose's last known location many years ago. Anwar had provided a contact name, a person he thought worked at the orphanage. She folded the paper and tucked it into her back pocket. Beth went into the bathroom, brushed her hair, and tied it back with an elastic band. She looked at the business card and headed for the phone. A small plastic card was placed next to the phone. In several languages it gave instructions to secure an out-side line. Beth followed the instructions and phoned Sanjeev.

"Hello?"

"It's Beth; can you pick me up at The Astor? I need to go somewhere."

"Sure, sure, ten minutes," said Sanjeev.

"Thanks, I'll be waiting in the lobby."

The phone clicked as Sanjeev hung up. Beth replaced the receiver and tucked the business card into her back pocket. She headed for the door and grabbed the plastic room key from the light slot in the wall. Beth unlatched the door and headed out into the hall. She closed the door behind her. She headed for the elevators to take her to the lobby.

Beth waited in the lobby; she did not want to sit in the large red couch. The desk attendant looked at Beth and smiled.

"Do you need transportation Miss?"

"No, thank you, I have a driver. Thank you for asking."

"My pleasure," was the response.

Beth looked at her watch. It had seemed a long time and she was getting impatient.

"Where was Lord Ganesha? Why wasn't he removing the obstacles? Damn it," thought Beth. "I didn't bring my Lord Ganesha. He's late, I'm going back for it." Beth raced back to her room and quickly retrieved the small wooden Lord Ganesha. She tucked him into her jeans front pocket. You could see a small lump in the front of her jeans but you would hardly notice. When Beth arrived in the lobby Sanjeev met her with a large smile.

"Miss Beth, are you ready to begin the day?" he said.

"I am, let's go."

Beth climbed into the back of the white taxi as Sanjeev held the door open. Sanjeev closed the door and walked around to the driver's seat. As Sanjeev got into his seat he leaned over to the front passenger's side. He straightened up and leaned back to offer Beth a bottle of water.

"Keep drinking, it's very hot, and you're not used to it," he said.

Beth accepted the water and thanked Sanjeev. She tucked the unopened bottle into the pouch of the back seat. She reached for the paper containing the address from her jeans. Sanjeev was talking with the guards. After some conversation they pulled out of the hotel.

Chapter 7

Remove the obstacles

Where to Miss?"

"We need to go to the Calcutta Muslim Orphanage, it's located at 2 Shariff Lane, Park Street," said Beth reading the page.

"I know it, no problem," said Sanjeev.

"I need to speak with Amba Chawla."

"Amba Chawla," repeated Sanjeev, "let's go and find her."

"Her," thought Beth, "It's a her."

Beth looked at Lord Ganesha still sitting on the dash. She ran her fingers over the lump in her pocket. "Remove the obstacles," she thought.

Sanjeev was speeding along. He darted in and out of traffic while sounding the horn. They were passing an area green and lush, before turning onto Outram Road. "Not far now Miss."

A few turns and they were traveling down a narrow run down street. Sanjeev pulled in front of a brightly painted blue building with white accents. The building was only a couple of floors high and looked like a motel. It had an entranced flanked by blue railings and a blue colored security gate. The gate was at the end of a tunnel made of blue steel bars. It was unclear if this was meant to keep people out or in? Above the tunnel was a bright yellow sign in a semi circular shape.

A.K. Fazul Haque Girls Higher Secondary School.

English Medium.

A Project of The Calcutta Muslim Orphanage.

Sanjeev rolled the window down to speak with the guard hovering at the gate. He looked annoyed leaving his comfortable shaded chair.

He walked slowly towards the taxi, "Yes sir?"

"We're looking for Amba Chawla, very important, Miss Martindale needs to see her immediately," explained Sanjeev.

The following set of exchanges was not in English but Beth heard Sanjeev say, Amba Chawla and wondered if he was getting through. Finally the guard walked away to open the gates. Sanjeev turned to Beth and started to explain.

"Mrs. Chawla is in today. She's teaching a class and you can see if she will talk with you." As Sanjeev pulled inside there was nowhere for him to go. He entered the gates and stopped almost immediately. Sanjeev got out of the Taxi to open Beth's door. "I will come with you in case you need any help."

"Thanks, that's good," said Beth climbing out of the car into the heat.

Beth and Sanjeev headed into the blue and white building. It was cool inside but not air-conditioned. The guard had clearly alerted the front door. A smart look-ing woman in a purple sari arrived to greet them. She started to talk with Sanjeev before turning to Beth.

"Hello, I understand you're looking for Amba? Is she expecting you?"

"No, she doesn't know me," explained Beth. Beth asked the woman to mention to Amba the following information. She had been sent by Anwar Patel and needed to talk urgently.

"Let me see if Amba is available," she said in a voice tinged with a faint English accent. Before she left she motioned to a small area filled with seats.

Beth took a seat. Sanjeev looked at Beth, "Miss, I'll be in the car. Call for me if you need anything."

Sanjeev took his leave and left Beth in the recep-tion area. It was a quiet building like the inside of a library. The walls were white and cool. Occasionally she could hear distant conversations but they didn't seem to be in English. Beth was rehearsing how she might approach Amba when a small Indian woman appeared wearing a green sari.

Beth stood and stretched out her hand in greeting. "Amba, my name is Beth Martindale."

The young woman looked at Beth coldly and ignored her hand. "You're the friend of Anwar Patel yes?"

"Yes," said Beth dropping her hand.

"Amba will see you now. Please follow me," she said turning and walking away.

Beth followed the woman and noticed the length of her hair. The hair flowed down her back held only by a cloth ring. They continued down a long hall-way, up a stairwell, and down another hallway. They stopped at a wooden door painted white. The woman knocked meekly and opened the door slightly. She said something and stood aside allowing Beth to move forward.

"Come on in please," said a warmer voice from inside. "Good afternoon, Amba Chawla. I heard you were looking for me, how might I be of assistance?" said a heavyset woman sitting behind a desk.

The room was ridiculously small. It had a large desk facing the door with only one chair in front of the desk. Behind Amba was a window allowing sunlight to stream in. The desk supported neatly stacked paper piles of all shapes, sizes and colors. Around the desk were wooden shelves brimming with binders and books. The wall housed a row of battered metal filing cabinets. The room looked like an overloaded library about to explode. Beth accepted her invitation to sit signaled by a hand gesture. She sat and looked at a mature woman with silver hair pulled back from her face. She wore a rich brown sari with gold flecks that caught the light.

"My name's Beth Martindale, I'd like to ask you how you knew Anwar Patel?" inquired Beth.

"I knew Anwar from my time in London, England many years ago. I'll never forget him. I was taking a Masters in Education and could not afford to continue. I was in jeopardy of not completing my term. Anwar was a complete stranger; he didn't know me at all. He had heard through the Indian community that I was taking a Masters. When completed, I wanted to return to India and teach orphaned girls." Amba partially covered her mouth with her hand. She could not hide the smile as she recalled Anwar. She looked down at her desk and the papers that lay spread in front of her.

Beth looked over her shoulder and saw a framed sign hanging on the wall, it read, "He who gives to Orphans lends to God."

Beth took the opportunity to speak. "Please continue it's important for me to know. Then, I'll be happy to tell you why I'm here."

Amba collected her thoughts and regained eye contact with Beth. Dropping her hand she continued. "Anwar heard about my situation and sent me a letter. At first I thought it was a hoax but attached to the letter was a check. I cashed the check. It paid for three years worth of rent and tuition in one payment. I never got a chance to thank Anwar in person. I tried. I tried to meet with him and ask him how I could repay his generosity. He wrote me a couple of times and told me that to repay him I must make good on my promise of teaching orphans. I have dedicated my life to that and it's always been my passion," said Amba. "I never got a chance to meet Anwar. I tried to imagine if he was old or young. All I know is that it was a significant amount of money to give to a complete stranger. There were no strings attached. Now, tell me how you know him and what is your business with me?"

Beth explained what a wonderful man Anwar was and how he grew Roses. She told of his failing health and the story of Aklina and Rose. She detailed her assignment and finally revealed that Anwar had sent a letter. Amba sat and listened intently. She never moved. She just breathed steadily and concentrated on every word.

"I've received his letter and I feel sad. The only assumption I can make is that Anwar knew he was days away from death. Unfortunately he will never get to meet his beloved Rose. I have this letter signed by Anwar giving me this address and your name. This is the location of the orphanage that Rose Akhter attended when her Mother, Aklina, passed away," explained Beth.

Amba looked at the letter and Anwar's signature. "Of course I will help you," said Amba. "What you have to realize is that the situation has changed over the years. The girls that come here now had a rough start to life but they can consider themselves fortunate. Thanks to this facility and generous donations they have a fighting chance. Beth, back then, being an orphan left you vulnerable. Being a female orphan could mean a couple of things both options were bad. We have records that I can look at to see if Rose Akhter attended. I might have records of where she went."

"I would really appreciate it if you could locate her records."

"You know it's a real coincidence that Anwar helped me. He didn't know that he would indirectly help the orphanage that his daughter came to. The same place, what a coincidence, no?"

"There are no coincidences," responded Beth without thinking.

Amba smiled, "Please wait here. I'll be right back." Amba left the room and headed down the hallway. Beth looked around the small office full of papers and books. It smelt musty; Amba was obviously not a neat freak. Beth sat still; she could hear the faint sound of birds chirping in the tree outside of the window. The sun was bright and the air was getting hot. On a cluttered wooden shelf was a brightly colored statue. The figurine had many arms. It played a flute and had peacock feathers behind its head. It looked both female and male. It was hard to tell. Amba came back into the room and caught Beth's gaze.

"It's Krishna," explained Amba as she sat. "I have the file right here. She was left here as a newborn with a small donation. She was raised by one of the orphanage helpers. Rose was transferred to the Kalam family at the age of seven. Beth, I don't know who the Kalam family is? I don't even know if this is legitimate?" Beth looked at Amba and fixed her with a stare.

"Amba, you're talking to a girl raised in the green hills and valleys of the Yorkshire Moors. If a fight broke out in a pub then stick with me but when it comes to Indian subtlety I'm lost. You'll need to be blunt and explain this to me."

"I will Beth, as best I can," said Amba. "In India when you have a child, Indian culture values sons over daughters. We are talking thirty years ago Beth but times haven't changed that much. Many orphanages are full of girls. Mothers often abandon their daughters in railway stations or high traffic areas knowing that they will be found and hopefully cared for. Social workers often bring them to orphanages, if they're lucky."

Amba looked down at her desk and continued. "Some Mothers went the direct route and brought their daughters directly to the orphanage. Under a dowry system the bride's family would pay the grooms family a specified amount of money or property to ensure the union takes place. You've probably heard of the dowry system? After the marriage the wife is the responsibility of the husband and goes to live with the husband's family. The dowry system was made illegal in 1961, yet it's still commonly practiced today. This would explain why baby girls continue to be abandoned. Beth, being an orphan in India has a far greater stigma than elsewhere. It's due to the importance society places on family, lineage, caste and religion. As an orphan you're truly an outsider. Many decide to spend their entire life in the orphanage," said Amba. "Beth my dear, these are the unfortunate ones. What I'm not telling you about are the truly wretched. Years ago when money was scarce some desperate orphanages would select, then sell, young girls at about 11 or 12 years of age. They were desperate for the money. Local women would come and 'adopt' girls for a fee," Amba looked down ashamed.

"Like the Kalam family with Rose," said Beth?

"Most of these women were Madame's. They would take the girls and they wouldn't be seen again. The girls would be housed in brothels and live that life until they died," explained Amba.

"Are you saying that's what happened to Rose?"

"I don't know what happened to Rose. Every adoption needs a home address. No address was ever checked. Things are different now. I have an address on file and it's probably legitimate. What may not be legitimate is that a family actually lived there with Rose? The only thing I can do to help is giving you the address and let you continue your investigation from there. I shouldn't do this but Anwar has helped me in my life and I want to help you."

Amba wrote down the address and gave it to Beth, "Good luck! You should know your odds are slim. I'm sorry Beth, I have to get back to class." Amba stood and walked to the door. Beth moved out of the little office to give Amba a chance to exit. "I will walk you to the door," said Amba.

No words were spoken during the walk down the hallway and the stairs. When Beth got to the door she turned and shook Amba's hand. The look on Amba's face told Beth that she suspected this would not turn out good. Beth did not say anything but she smiled and walked out of the door clutching the piece of paper that Amba had given her. Beth emerged into the sunlight. She saw Sanjeev opening his door and moving quickly to open the rear passenger door. She fought back tears as she entered into the back seat and fastened her seat belt.

As she sat she could feel Lord Ganesha in her jeans, "Remover of obstacles," thought Beth looking at the dashboard figurine.

"Where now Miss?" said Sanjeev, unaware of the gravity of the situation and its possible outcome. At that moment Beth hated men. Sanjeev was helpful but he was a man. "Back to the hotel?" he inquired.

"Yes, back to the hotel," snapped Beth, going with the suggestion.

Beth was silent through the ride back. Sanjeev sensed his place was to remain quiet and drive. He did this admirably. As the taxi approached The Astor Hotel the gate staff performed the familiar security check. Sanjeev reminded Beth that he was at her disposal. Beth strode into the lobby feeling deflated and a failure. This was not the way it was supposed to be. Beth had thought that Rose would still be working at the orphanage and they would later meet for tea at The Astor Hotel. This would be where Beth delivered the envelope to Rose. This was turning out to be harder. It did not sound good for Rose. Amba felt Rose's chances were slim. Beth was starting to feel down. She felt like a failure. She had let everyone down before she even got started. In all the excitement she had forgotten to ask about the Shell or the portal. Nothing that Amba told her related to the portal.

"Great job, failed on two counts," said Beth quietly to herself.

"Welcome back," chirped the desk attendant, "its happy hour at Plush our lounge bar, two drinks for the price of one."

"I could murder a drink," thought Beth as she respectfully declined and walked towards the elevator bank.

Beth was in her room quickly enough and placed the plastic card in the slot in the wall. Beth placed the address page on the desk before taking her heavy clothes off and slipping into bed. She could not sleep but she did cry. Eventually Beth did fall asleep and she knew who would be there to greet her. Beth wanted to fall asleep, she wanted to hear a familiar voice and get some reassurance.

"You don't need to cry or feel bad Beth. You're doing what you can. Let's talk this through. So far you've made it to India, started your search and got a new lead. That's a decent start. You've confirmed Rose was alive up to 11 or 12 years of age. All you have to do is keep going and follow the trail until you find her," Subra reassured.

"I thought it would be easy, all obstacles cleared, because this is so right," argued Beth. "It's really shaken my confidence."

"I was always looking outside myself for strength and confidence, but it comes from within. It's there all the time," Subra responded. "You have to have confidence in your ability, and then be tough enough to follow through."

"I've lost an opportunity today, don't you see Subra?"

"Opportunity is missed by most people because it's dressed in overalls and looks like work."

"I didn't find Rose and I'm sorry but it seems I can only do one thing at a time. I didn't discover anything about the portal or the Shell. I'm useless," thought Beth dejected.

"I thought you said that you refuse to beat yourself up anymore. It's the first day and you've made significant progress. Small opportunities are often the beginning of great enterprise. A handful of patience is worth more than a bushel of brains," replied Subra.

"I'm thinking that I should just stop now," thought Beth in a serious moment.

"Others can stop you temporarily; only you can do it permanently." He paused and waited for the response.

"Of course you're right. I've made a decent start. I didn't find Rose on the first day but I guess I was the only one that thought I would? Anwar knew I wasn't a quitter or a slacker. I'll work harder, like Lord Ganesha and remove the obstacles," thought Beth with more optimism.

"The wisest mind has something left to learn. You will learn quickly Beth. This is a new country, new people, and a different game than what you're used to. You'll need to adapt to your new surroundings and become sly, like that fox on your wrist," Subra suggested.

"Yes, it's time to get foxy. We might be in India but I'm a Yorkshire lass, a hardy, stubborn breed us folk. I'm not giving up on Rose. I will simply try harder," thought Beth with an air of defiance.

"That's the spirit. Force without wisdom fails of its own weight. To acquire knowledge, one must study, to acquire wisdom one must observe," said Subra. He was directing energy to wake Beth and signal to her their discussion was over.

Beth woke with study and observe, ringing in her mind. "I'm missing things," said Beth to herself. "I need to be more observant." Beth called the ever-ready Sanjeev and instructed him to be primed for another trip tonight.

"Where to this time?" said Sanjeev sitting in the driver's seat of the taxi. Beth handed him the note given to her by Amba.

188 Raja S.C. Mallik Road

Kolkata 700 032

Sanjeev studied the address and nodded to Beth. "We go, take a while," he said with a smile.

The taxi pulled away from The Astor Hotel and made its way into the city. The streets were bustling with people and energy as the light faded into darkness.

When Sanjeev arrived at the destination he peered out of his window. He confirmed that they were at the right address.

Sanjeev pointed to a sign, "Miss, this is the place," he said looking down at the written note. Beth saw the sign attached to a wooden frame by rusting nails. Three, large, circular, lamps illuminated the sign.

Jadavpur University

Faculty of Engineering and Technology

188 Raja S.C. Mallik Road

Kolkata 700 032

This was the place but the building had been converted into a technology campus. Beth did not know what to think. Was this the house? Had it been sold? Perhaps demolished? Was this always a false address given to secure Rose? Beth could feel her heart sink again. She was starting to feel each door closing on her; she stared at Lord Ganesha as if to ask why. Sanjeev was waiting for instructions as he peered into the rear view mirror.

"I need to find Rose Akhter, she was a little girl given to the Kalam family twenty years ago. She supposedly lived here at this address," blurted out Beth in frustration.

The street was getting dark and a group of young students were making their way home. They talked and laughed loudly. They stared at Beth as they walked by. Sanjeev started the taxi and headed down the street. He found a small lane opening and parked the taxi at the side of the road.

"Stay here."

Sanjeev left the taxi to talk to three old men sitting on the storefront steps. Beth watched from within with the taxi windows rolled down. Sanjeev struck up a conversation with the men. They were all smiling and laughing. This was followed by Sanjeev mentioning, "Rose Akhter," and the family name "Kalam." Beth could barely hear the old men. They mentioned "Rose," it was the only English word she recognized. She could see them pointing fingers in the direction of the University. The old men continued to talk with Sanjeev in a cordial manner. One of the old men struggled to get up and support his weight. After some effort and a slight stagger, he managed to turn into the open doorway. He shouted something while waving his arms. An old woman appeared dressed in yellow; she talked with the old man and pointed down the street. She quickly disappeared and the old man continued to talk with Sanjeev.

"Sanjeev, you smooth talker," whispered Beth in the taxi.

Sanjeev offered a card to one of the old men. He bowed slightly and bounded off to the car with excitement flowing through his steps. "I think I have a lead Miss," he said. "The old men have lived on this street since they were kids. They're true historians."

"What did they say?" asked Beth impatiently.

"They remember the Kalam family and they recalled them having a little girl," said Sanjeev proudly. "They thought they remembered a name like Rose. One of the men's cousins had a daughter. He thinks she and the Kalam girl played together. His cousin's at a wedding and won't be back until tomorrow. He said he would call me and we can talk with his cousin directly," explained Sanjeev proudly.

"Thank you Sanjeev, you did a great job, but do you really think he'll call you?"

Sanjeev looked deep into Beth's eyes, "No. I think we'll need to come back here tomorrow where these three old men will still be sitting. Back to the hotel?"

Beth nodded, "Yes, enough excitement for one day." Beth thought, "Sanjeev has kept this mission alive. It's one thing to look at old orphanage records; it's another to rely on the memory of old men. This assumes his cousin will remember his daughter's little friend."

This was the only lead that Beth could follow so what choice did she have? The search for Rose felt like it was beginning to be a long shot. The portal search had stalled before it had started. Beth watched the people, the dirt, the rickshaws, and the trucks. They all weaved a dance across white lane lines and any resemblance of order. The taxi moved through the darkening night, headlights, and horns all part of the melee. Sanjeev looked calm as he sounded the horn to let a slower truck know he was approaching. Beth looked at the truck they were about to pass. The words "Sound Horn," was painted on the rear, in white letters. A few cows were wandering around at the side of the road in an uncaring manner. Little kids played in piles of garbage and families huddled in make shift accommodations. People dressed in white shirts leapt out of the shadows while others blended into the darkness. The taxi pulled in to The Astor Hotel and the guards completed their routine.

"Good evening Miss, hope you had a pleasant day?" said one of the guards as he circled the white taxi.

Sanjeev was motioned forward into the small courtyard. The tall, thin, tree was swaying in the wind. Beth thought they might get some rain tonight. She thanked Sanjeev and he offered his assistance for the coming day.

"I'll wait for your call as usual; I've left my number at the front desk. They can call me anytime. Have a good night Miss," said Sanjeev smiling with a little bow and a head wobble.

Beth thanked Sanjeev again before entering the hotel and heading up to her room. Beth entered the plastic card key into the wall slot and the lights came on in her room. Someone had been in her room. Items had been moved and the room looked tidy. The bed was turned down. A small chocolate was placed on a silver tray with the room service breakfast menu. Beth looked at the chocolate longingly. Beth did not feel hungry or thirsty at all. She missed eating. Meals provide nourishment but they are also a form of socialization. Even when you eat alone you are greeted and interact with your server. You can sit with others and watch others, as you eat. You can imagine scenes being played out, like a movie at each table. You are alone and yet connected to the energies within the room. Beth missed that. Each meal has a different energy about it. The vibrant or subdued breakfast; the lunch with friends or colleagues; the dinner with family or a special loved one. Beth had a chocolate she couldn't eat and an empty room. She loved chocolate.

It was early evening and Beth turned on the television in hopes that it would provide some entertainment. She wanted to stay enlightened; perhaps some important messages would be delivered. She wanted to be aware, open. As the TV flickered into life she pointed the remote and searched the channels. Most of the channels were not in English some had high energy, Bollywood dance scenes. Beth settled on BBC World News. The prim looking anchor was talking about global financial equity prices and mid cap stocks. Beth did not really listen. She thought the woman's accent was a bit plumy, that type of forced posh voice. It was however English and it felt like home. She left the news anchor babbling as she undressed and slipped into her hotel slippers and robe. Beth stretched out on the bed and propped herself up with the pillows. She placed the tray gently on the nightstand and focused on the TV. The news had moved to sports report. Beth was not a big sports fan. From what she could gather it looked as though Liverpool Football Club had defeated Manchester United at Old Trafford by a score of 3 to 1. The interviewer flashed to a good-looking man who Beth instantly recognized. "Steven Gerrard" was the caption under his picture. He was the Liverpool captain. Beth did not listen to the words but she studied his face and his smile. It was the first man of her type she had seen for a while. It was also a bit of home. Beth was starting to drift as she turned off the TV. She turned the room lights off and laid back to rest. It was not long before Beth was asleep.

"Where are you my friend? Do you follow Liverpool or Manchester United?" Beth joked. No response. "Perhaps my joke was in poor taste?" thought Beth. There was still no response.

"I'm here," said Subra. "I've been working on your energy flows."

Beth could immediately sense that something was wrong, perhaps Subra was annoyed, "Are you angry with me? Subra?" asked Beth.

"Not at all, you did a great job today. You've accomplished a great deal."

Beth felt better, but there was something that she had felt, even though she could not explain it. Beth talked with Subra throughout the night. She discussed her interactions with Amba, Sanjeev, and the comments from the old men. Beth spoke of her frustration at not eating and her lack of progress on the portal and the Shell. Subra reassured Beth that her journey would provide insights into the location of the portal. Beth did not agree. All of her interactions had been functional, providing no insights into the location of a portal.

"Yes. Food is important, tell me what you eat and I will tell you what you are. That could be difficult with you Beth you're an enigma!" teased Subra. "Einstein said nothing would benefit human health and increase the chances for survival of life on Earth as much as the evolution to a vegetarian diet. Beth, most people in India are vegetarian."

"It's fine with me, chocolate is vegetarian. Well, it's meatless at least," thought Beth. "I felt fear today Subra. I feared that doors were closing, and my chance of finding Rose and the portal were slipping away."

"No one but a coward dares to boast that he has never known fear," reassured Subra.

"It's not like that," shared Beth. "I felt like I didn't fit in here. I was ignorant."

"At least you recognized that. It is worse still to be ignorant of your ignorance. You have to remember Beth it's innocence when it charms us, ignorance when it doesn't. All you need in this life is ignorance and confidence; then success is sure," responded Subra trying to bolster Beth's feelings. "Ignorance gives one a large range of probabilities."

"I understand that, and don't get me wrong, I can't know everything but I really started to doubt myself again. That's what scared me."

"Doubt whom you will but never doubt yourself. A mind troubled by doubt cannot focus on the course to victory," Subra responded.

"I should know this and I've made a commitment to myself to be positive. I can't seem to stop criticizing myself."

"Remember what I told you about your choice of words, they're intentions that come true. By saying that you can't, you are asking for this to happen. Focus on what you can. As for others, if you're not criticized, you may not be doing much. Any fool can criticize, condemn, and complain. Most fools do," assured Subra.

Subra and Beth talked at length about her feelings that night. They shared ideas on how they might unearth some clues to the location of the portal. Subra asked Beth to be more direct in her interactions. She needed to ask about the Shell. She needed to find any hidden meaning. Beth was feeling better about the progress made to find Rose. She hoped that Amba's feelings were unfounded. She felt better about finding Rose in good health. Beth still had this nagging uncertainty about the portal. She was concerned about how she would get the right clues. This lack of control was eating away at her insides. She did not like the helpless feeling it created. Beth was sure about one thing. She would find Rose. She had told Subra that Rose was the key. She would still ask everyone about the Shell in hopes that she would gain some insight. She believed it was Rose who would give her the next clue to help her find the location of the portal. She just had this feeling deep inside her chest. Subra and Beth talked at length and Beth was feeling stronger for it. She did not feel so alone, Subra really helped. He had a familiar calming voice without all the sexual politics of talking with a man. Beth liked that. Morning came quickly and Beth woke to the sound of traffic, birds, and a stream of sunlight bursting through her window. Beth showered and dressed quickly. She felt energetic and ready to tackle the day's challenges.

"Today is going to be a good day," she told herself as she looked at her reflection in the mirror. "Today I'm going to take the letter for Rose with me. I will need it," she said setting the intention. Beth prompted the front desk to call for Sanjeev. Within minutes he had arrived outside The Astor Hotel.

"Where are we going today?" asked Sanjeev as Beth strapped herself into the back seat.

"I'm assuming you didn't get a call yet so let's go visit the old men again. Let's see if his cousin enjoyed the wedding?" said Beth smiling.

"No I didn't get a call. So, back to the old men."

They drove to the previous day's location the small street was busier. She could see students arriving at the University and more people going about their business. The night before the fading light had made the street look quaint. In the hot, harsh, light of day, the street looked dirty and worn. The taxi sped past the University entrance sign and stopped outside of the store. It was no surprise to see the three old men sitting in the door well, in the same position as the previous night. Beth wondered if they had gone home or stayed there all night. Sanjeev did not ask Beth to follow him but she did anyway. Sanjeev noticed that Beth was standing behind him as he started to talk to the men. They talked with Sanjeev but they were not looking at him. All three stared at Beth with silly smiles painted on their faces.

"His cousin's back and working in the grocery store across the street." Sanjeev turned and pointed at the store. "Let's go Miss."

Sanjeev headed into traffic and boldly walked across the street, Beth followed. Sanjeev entered the grocery store and started to talk with one of the clerks. He pointed Sanjeev to a portly looking man quietly working at the rear of the store. He wore sandals, brown trousers, a blue shirt, and a dirty white overall tied at the waist. Sanjeev motioned for Beth to stay back as he approached the man. Beth could see Sanjeev smiling and the conversation seemed cordial. After a while the man reached into his overalls and wrote something on a label he was using to price goods. Sanjeev seemed to thank the man and headed towards Beth.

Beth couldn't contain herself, "How did it go?"

"Well, get in the car first, and I'll tell you what I know," said Sanjeev with a sense of urgency. Beth followed Sanjeev into the taxi. "I need to find a place to park that's less crowded, then we can talk," he said. Sanjeev drove to a nearby street and parked on a quiet lane. Sanjeev turned the engine off and turned to face Beth. "That man has lived on this street for 35 years, he knew the Kalam family. The wife was barren and they wanted to have a child. The Kalam family was moderately wealthy and could afford to adopt a daughter. A daughter is not always desirable but the wife wanted a daughter to talk with. The grocer recalls them adopting a girl from the orphanage. His daughter "Mituraj," used to play with the little Kalam girl." Beth looked at Sanjeev with inquisitive green eyes. Sanjeev continued "Miss, he told me she had an unusual name for an Indian girl; Rose!"

"What happened to her?" asked Beth directly.

"He doesn't know but he said his daughter may know what happened to Rose."

"How do we find his daughter?"

Sanjeev smiled at Beth. He noticed she was beautiful with emerald green eyes that sparkled in the strong sun. Sanjeev turned and pointed at a door across the narrow lane. "There, Mituraj lives there, this time you come."

Sanjeev and Beth left the Taxi in a hurry and crossed the narrow lane. A small thin, two-story house lay ahead of them. The house was modest but it looked well maintained. A wooden door lay at the top of three small stone steps. Either side of the door was narrow windows covered in black iron security bars. Beth approached the door first and knocked firmly using her knuckles. Both looked at each other while waiting for a reply.

Chapter 8

Mituraj, a good friend

Restrained by a brass colored security chain the door was allowed to open a small distance.

"Who is it? What do you want?" said a nervous voice from within.

"My name is Beth Martindale I'm here with my driver Sanjeev, we were hoping to speak with Mituraj," explained Beth.

"I'm Mituraj, what do you want?" she inquired again.

"Just five minutes of your time. I'd like to talk with you about a little girl that you grew up with called Rose. I'm desperately trying to find her. I have a message that I've sworn to deliver to her. I need your help, please," said Beth trying to see Mituraj through the narrow gap.

"Perhaps you can come in but leave your driver outside," suggested Mituraj.

Sanjeev instantly smiled at Beth, crumpled the label with the address in his hand and retreated back to the Taxi to wait. With perfect timing the door unlatched and Beth was invited in. When Beth entered the narrow hallway she could see a tall slender woman in her early thirties. She looked healthy and had short hair with large gold colored earrings that dangled. Mituraj wore numerous gold bangles on one wrist and a simple thin red colored twine around her other wrist. Beth angled her arm inwards to hide her fox tattoo. She pressed her wrist into her hip. Mituraj did not smile at Beth she looked nervous and untrusting. It was then that Beth noticed a figure, a small boy hiding behind his Mother. He peered out from around her legs. He was about 10 years old and very shy. He had large brown eyes and neatly parted black hair. He wore a white shirt partially tucked in to his black trousers.

"School uniform," thought Beth.

Beth closed the door behind her and smiled. "I just need to talk with you if that's all right?" she explained.

"Is Rose in some kind of trouble?" asked Mituraj.

"No, I have news from her family. I know the Kalam family adopted her, but I bring news from her Father. Her real Father," explained Beth waving the envelope. Mituraj looked at Beth with a stern face. "Rose was adopted and the Kalam family were very good to her. She considers them her parents. Rose's Mother died at birth and her Father abandoned her. I'm not sure news from him would be welcomed."

Beth tried again to melt the frosty reception. "I understand how Rose would feel, but I need to put the record straight. Rose's Father was an honorable man; he was a kind and generous man. He didn't abandon Rose, he was only informed of Rose's existence a week ago. He asked me to deliver this letter to her, to let her know. He lived in England and unfortunately has passed away. I promised him I would get this to Rose. Do you know where she is?" Beth could sense that she was starting to get through. Mituraj's body language suggested she was relaxing and starting to trust Beth. Beth was pleased with herself; she was starting to observe these things.

"I do know where I can find Rose, perhaps if you give me the letter I can deliver it to her. I'll be seeing Rose in the next day or so," explained Mituraj.

"You are indeed a good friend but I promised I would deliver this letter to Rose, and I can't rest until I've done so in person, you understand?" said Beth.

"You too seem like a good friend. I'll call Rose and ask her first before I give you her contact information. I'm sorry but I don't know you and this could be a tale. A good friend watches over her friends, you're a woman, you understand?" said Mituraj. "Please wait here and I'll call her."

Mituraj disappeared into the house leaving the little boy to watch over Beth. He kept his distance knowing he was safe with distance between them. Within seconds he was safely tucked in behind his Mother's legs. Mituraj fumbled with the silver colored cell phone. It reflected the light in the hall. Beth thought it looked odd, a woman dressed in a traditional yellow Indian sari using a modern cell phone. Mituraj finally completed her dialing and held the phone to her ear. Beth was still at a distance but she could hear the ringing noise. This woman was calling Rose. She was about to speak with Rose. At least Rose was alive and presumably close. Beth felt very excited, her mouth felt dry as she licked her lips.

"Rose, hello Mituraj," the conversation continued but not in English.

Beth listened intensely, she could hear a woman's voice through the cell phone speaker but she could not hear actual words. The voice belonged to Rose; the woman she had flown half the way around the world to meet. Mituraj stood between delivering her promise to Anwar and failure. Beth stared at Mituraj who responded by looking down quickly at the floor, unable to meet Beth's piercing eyes. The conversation continued and Beth could pick out a couple of familiar words. After a short conversation Beth heard Mituraj say, "Bye." Beth stepped forward a short distance.

"Can I talk to her?" said Beth. Too late, the phone call had ended and Mituraj had disconnected.

"I talked with Rose; she wants me to give you her work address. You can go over there it'll take about 40 minutes from here. I'll give you her address," said Mituraj bending down and whispering something to the little boy. Mituraj was still cautious but she seemed to be pointing Beth to the path leading to Rose.

"Don't blow it Beth," she thought, "you're so close."

The little boy ran back to the hallway and presented his Mother with a piece of paper and a pencil. Mituraj wrote on the paper and offered it to Beth.

"Rose will meet you at her office, it won't be open for another 2 hours, meet her at 11.30am. My advice is to stay close to your driver, now go please; my husband would not want me talking with you."

Beth felt a little offended by Mituraj's choice of words. As she reached for the paper her fox tattoo was exposed. Mituraj looked down at the fox as Beth took the paper. Thinking quickly she decided to take her chance.

"I know this is a strange thing to ask but does a Shell mean anything to you? You know a sea Shell or the shape of a Shell? Does it have meaning for you?"

Mituraj moved past Beth and opened the door, "No, you must go, please, go."

Beth could see concern in her eyes, she was not concerned about Beth there was something more, something deeper. Beth felt ignorant. Mituraj had helped Beth; she felt that she should not outstay her welcome. She looked deep into Mituraj's brown eyes and said, "Thank you." Beth held her gaze to make her point. She thought she saw a slight smile as she moved through the door and down the stone steps. Beth walked confidently towards the taxi Sanjeev was holding the door open. In that short walk it struck Beth just how hot it had become outside. The sun's heat was blazing down. The taxi was hot inside with the windows down and the air conditioning off. Beth felt the warmth in the seats as she fastened her seat belt. She felt good.

"What did she tell you?" asked Sanjeev.

"Good news, good news," repeated Beth. She leaned forward and gave Sanjeev the paper, "She told me Rose was alive and she spoke with her on the phone. She called Rose to let her know we're coming to visit her. She's expecting us at 11.30am." Sanjeev studied the address.

"That's good news Miss; I will get us there in about 40 minutes. We'll have some time to kill." Sanjeev started the engine, closed the windows, and turned on the air conditioning. The cool air felt great. Beth leaned back in her seat and pulled at the elastic band, releasing her hair. She combed her loose hair with her fingers and pointed her face to the cool air vent. Sanjeev looked at Beth through the mirror and smiled. "Close now Miss, you are close to finding her."

"Yes, and I wouldn't have been able to get this far without your help Sanjeev. I want to thank you for that," said Beth catching his gaze in the mirror.

Sanjeev said what he always said, "My pleasure, Miss."

Beth had told herself that she would find Rose. It was not until she received the address and heard her voice, that she really felt certain. It was now starting to sink in.

It will happen if you truly believe. It sounded like a cliché or a snappy Subra quote but Beth finally understood. She did not gaze out of the window during the drive. She was preoccupied thinking through a number of things. She found herself looking at Lord Ganesha and thinking about the obstacles she had overcome. She was about to find Rose in record time. Beth could tell she was traveling in one consistent direction as if she were heading due north. The buildings and streets looked smarter more refined. She saw mature trees, gardens, and larger houses. A very large house caught Beth's eye.

"Sanjeev what's that?" inquired Beth.

Sanjeev pulled over and parked the taxi. He told Beth to follow him. "It's closed to the public today but we have some time to kill. We'll go up to the gates and look in, you need to see this," explained Sanjeev.

It was scorching hot. Beth followed Sanjeev to an entrance where two square marble pillars adorned with decorative urns announced a long driveway. Beth's hair blew in the warm wind as they both peered inside. Beth started to see the building again. She marveled at the palace with its six large marble pillars holding up a decorated roof. The building was marble colored with stone steps leading up to what looked like neoclassical architecture. Beth thought this building would have been better suited for a Greek Island rather than Kolkata, India. It was surrounded by a high black wrought iron fence, which enclosed a beautiful garden. In the center of the garden was a tall fountain made from stone. The fountain was dry. Three large flagpoles were placed on the roof but no flags flew today. The lush green lawn surprised Beth. The garden was an oasis in a poor, busy city.

"Someone here had money," thought Beth.

Next to the majestic house pillars stood two tall palm trees. The palace had walk out balconies complete with railings and an ornate brown colored roof. A corner of the garden housed a collection of flower urns made from marble. Beth could see the garden filled with large green plants with pink flowers. Facing outwards from the fountain were chiseled marble lions.

"Anwar and his marble allotment lion," thought Beth. "There are no such things as coincidences."

Sanjeev explained to Beth that the house was very famous in Kolkata. It was appropriately named, " The Marble Palace." It looked a little out of place a nineteenth-century mansion in North Kolkata. Sanjeev leaned in and told Beth that she was on Muktaram Babu Street. Sanjeev informed Beth that the Mansions floors and walls were made of solid Marble. A wealthy landlord called Raja Rajendra Mullick had the house built. Sanjeev mentioned the house was completed in "Eighteen thirty something and his descendants lived in the house today. The house is open to the public on certain days of the week but clearly not today. The house has over 100 different types of Marble and had its own Zoo at one time. Inside was a room decorated with mirrors and famous paintings from artists like Ruben. The house has an impressive collection of clocks, over 80 types, I think," said Sanjeev. "The garden has a lake and statues of Hindu Gods, Jesus, the Virgin Mary, Lord Buddha and other things."

Sanjeev was clearly not an art specialist but he was doing a fine job as impromptu tour guide. Beth appreciated the effort. He sounded as though he was proud to show Beth something beautiful about Kolkata. Beth smiled at Sanjeev and she gazed across the lawns through the fence. At that moment a loud screech could be heard. Loud enough to drown out the constant noise of horns and traffic. Beth wheeled around quickly to look at Sanjeev.

"Peacock Miss, they live in the palace aviary," explained Sanjeev.

Beth felt her forearms starting to burn in the blistering hot sun. She had no idea how long she had spent looking at the palace. She imagined the tigers guarding the palace in Mysore. She wondered if this palace was anything like the one Anwar had described. Beth needed to get back to the taxi and the air conditioning. Her jeans felt heavy and she could feel Lord Ganesha still lodged in her pocket.

"Time to go," suggested Beth. "Thank you for stopping and showing me this."

Beth knew what Sanjeev's response would be and he did not let her down, "My pleasure, Miss."

Sanjeev smiled, nodded his head as his brown eyes glinted in the sun. He turned and walked in the direction of the taxi. Returning to the taxi the inside was hot. The windows had been closed and the air was uncomfortably hot. Sanjeev placed the air conditioning on high to cool the interior quickly. He looked out into the busy road and nudged the taxi back into traffic. Rickshaws buzzed in and out of small gaps, and the taxi continued north. Sanjeev drove for a while before looking in the mirror. Beth combed her limp, loose hair with her fingers. Strands of hair were wet and sticking to her neck. She had cooled down considerably since she returned to the taxi. Beth caught Sanjeev's glance in the mirror.

"Miss, I have to tell you something."

"What is it?" asked Beth recognizing a new concerned tone from Sanjeev.

"Located North of the Marble Palace, where this address lies, is not a very pleasant place. I should say it's not the sort of place where a woman like you should go alone. I will need to escort you Miss. We are heading close to the Sonagachi area. It's very famous and not very safe. You understand Miss?" asked Sanjeev.

"No, I don't understand Sanjeev but I'm smart enough to trust you. You've looked after me so far, and I can't see any reason to doubt you. If you say that I need to stick close, that's good enough for me," said Beth feeling butterflies in her stomach.

As they continued North Beth she could see the surroundings change. As she gazed out of the taxi window she saw poverty, squalor, and desperate people trying to survive. The opulence of the Marble Palace seemed a million miles away. Beth's face tightened as she saw people living in shantytowns, the streets covered in garbage. Occasionally Beth would lock eyes with women from behind the safety of the taxi window. They would either stare at her with hollow eyes or immediately look down and hang their heads. No one smiled and the energy surrounding this place felt bad.

"Where are we Sanjeev?" asked Beth.

"Sonagachi, Miss. In English Sonagachi means, "The Golden Tree." You won't find any gold or any trees, just really unhappy, miserable, people. This is Kolkata's largest red light district. It contains several hundred brothels and over ten thousand prostitutes. This place started as a home for a rich persons mistress. Now it's not a safe place for women. Many of these women are dying from disease and are addicted to drugs," Sanjeev explained.

Beth stared at the narrow lanes and the multi-story stone buildings hiding desperate women. She did not know but most of the women were controlled through cruelty. Beth shivered as the scorching sun blazed through the window. Sanjeev pulled the taxi onto Beadon Street and looked for this intended address. He slowed the taxi allowing people to stare inside. Once they saw Beth they would realize it was not an opportunity for business. Sanjeev found a place to park without disrupting the flow of traffic. Down the side of the road ran a narrow gutter where dirty water trickled. The road was strewn with garbage, small pieces of paper and trash. The place had an odor, a strong pungent smell that turned the nose. The taxi was stationary and Sanjeev stopped the engine. He leaned back over the driver's seat and looked at Beth.

"I think we need to go over there," he said looking to the left. "I need you to come with me and stay close."

"I will," said Beth feeling a little anxious.

They got out of the taxi and moved towards a dark stone building that blended in with the rest. It was a dirty building with no real characteristics. On the left side of the door was a small hand painted plaque. It had been blistered with the sun and the paint was starting to peel. The plaque was painted black with white letters. It read, 'The Reika Foundation.'

Beth looked at Sanjeev, "This is the place?"

"Yes," replied Sanjeev simply.

"Then what are we waiting for? Let's go talk with Rose," said Beth sliding her hand to her rear jeans pocket. She made sure she had Rose's letter with her.

They entered through a black colored door streaked in grime and dirt. Beth noticed fingerprints on the door, near the handle, imprinted in the dirt. She grabbed the metal door handle, turned it and pushed the door open. The handle was still warm from the sun. The door swung open onto a surprisingly large square room. Chairs were backed against the walls. At the far end of the room a window cut into the wall with a small counter. Behind the counter Beth could see the outline of a woman. To the right of the window was a closed door. Beth walked confidently to the counter and waited. The woman glanced up quickly. Upon seeing Beth she held her gaze. The woman spoke to Beth but it was not in English. Sanjeev jumped to attention and took over the conversation. He explained that Beth was here to see Rose and that she was expected.

Sanjeev looked at Beth, "She's not here, she's expected any minute and we need to wait."

Sanjeev took a seat. He looked at the two women sitting in the room and immediately turned his eyes to the floor. Beth remained on her feet and looked at the posters adorning the walls. They had vivid pictures of abused women living in wretched conditions. She was attracted to two posters with bright pastel colors. One was in English, it read.

The Reika Foundation

Reika – "Lovely Flower" in Japanese

The poster contained more messages in smaller print.

> The Reika Foundation is a privately funded foundation, established to assist women in need. The foundation provides assis- tance, advice, intervention and practical help. This center is conveniently located for the inhabitants of Sonagachi whom need advice or help.

Beth looked around the room before reading the rest of the text.

> Many of the women who come here are abused and have addictions. With no edu- cation, skills or hope, this foundation pro- vides a safe haven in a troubled world. We work closely with the Durbar Samanwaya

Committee (DMSC) and recognize their efforts. Thank you for supporting The Reika Foundation.

The poster had designs of flowers and trees. Beth thought the design of the poster was a cheerful change to the stark reality of the other posters. The door opened and a striking Indian woman stepped into the room. She looked around and locked her stare upon Beth. She wore gold colored sandals and a purple colored sari with gold accents. Her wrist supported many gold bangles. She wore a single gold ring on her right hand and a small gold colored watch. She had long shoulder length black hair and a small diamond nose stud. She walked over to Beth.

"Miss Martindale?"

"Yes, Rose?" said Beth extending her hand.

"Miss Akhter," said Rose curtly ignoring Beth's hand.

"Rose Akhter?" inquired Beth.

"Yes, come with me I understand you have some sort of news that you want to share with me, is that correct?" said Rose.

"Yes, I've traveled a long way trying to find you," responded Beth feeling nervous.

"Trying to find me? I've worked here for the last 10 years. Come," said Rose motioning Beth to follow her.

Beth smiled at Sanjeev as she passed him sitting and waiting. Beth thought Rose looked familiar. "She looks like Amba, a much younger and slimmer Amba. Rose had Amba's beautiful cheek bones and deep brown eyes," thought Beth.

Beth followed Rose through the door and into a small office area. They turned right and passed a closed door before entering into a meeting room. It was a simple room with a small round table, no windows and four chairs. The wooden furniture was old and worn. The room smelled of body odor.

"What are you doing here? You're clearly not Indian."

Beth closed the door and mustered up some courage. "I'm doing a favor for a wonderful man. I've traveled half the way around the world and put my life on hold to find you, so I don't need your attitude, get it?" said Beth leaning forward and drilling Rose with her glaring green eyes.

"I'm sorry," said Rose in a startled tone. "I'm not sure I want to hear what you have to tell me."

"Rose, I'm an orphan too. I will never know my parents. I know how it feels. You live your life feeling incomplete. You feel like a tree in the wind clinging to the earth with no roots. We have no roots," said Beth. "Even the word "Orphan" grates; I know what it's like to feel incomplete. People stare and laugh at you. I grew up in childcare; I hated family celebrations and holidays. I was given a chance to give you some answers, answers to questions that every little girl asks."

Rose listened; she was not so confident now that Beth had pushed her back. Rose was a striking woman in her early thirties and clearly had her Mother's beauty.

"Your Father was a generous honorable man. I knew him briefly, and I must inform you that he's passed away recently." Rose did not register a reaction. "I'm sorry Rose your Father didn't abandon you. He didn't even know you existed until a few days ago. He was seriously ill and asked me to find you as quickly as I could. He grew roses in an allotment in Yorkshire, England. He lived in my little village called Haworth. Rose, he grew roses and delivered them to the hospital and old age pensioner's homes. He told me of your Mother Aklina and the reason you were called Rose. I'm spoiling the letter."

"What letter?"

Beth slid the envelope over the desk towards Rose. She felt a rush of satisfaction as she pictured Anwar smiling. Rose looked at the envelope refusing to touch it.

"Tell me what he looked like? A letter won't tell me that," asked Rose.

"He was a gentleman, about five nine and in bad health. He coughed hard and deep. He had a smile that would light up a room, a broad smile with brilliant white teeth. He had a cheery disposition and always had a friendly hello. He was a quiet man but an educated man. I think he started as a simple Baker but I suspect he became wealthy. He seemed to help people and enjoyed doing that. He was a popular man. Anwar had deep brown eyes and a full head of black hair with some grey coming in at the sides," explained Beth.

"Anwar," repeated Rose. Her body was sinking into the chair and her aggressive nature had started to subside.

"Are you going to read the letter?" asked Beth.

"No, not until I get home in private, I'm a proud woman," explained Rose.

"Promise me that you will read it. I haven't done this just for you to throw it away when I leave," said Beth forcefully.

"I promise, I will. I want to know about my parents, I'm curious. In some strange way the fact that they're both dead makes it a bit easier. I won't have to offend my other parents," explained Rose with tears in her eyes.

"What do you do here?" asked Beth trying to lighten the mood.

"I'm a counselor; I help the poor women across the street. That's Sonagachi, The Golden Tree. We have over ten thousand women making a living in the red light district. We educate them on the risks of HIV and Aids. We talk to them about using condoms and the dangers of unprotected sex. Women are controlled and drugged. Many girls come from rural centers where they were sold. Some money in a family of girls helps to feed the other mouths. Ten of your pounds will buy a young girl that traffickers can route to The Golden Tree. Some are simply drugged or kidnapped. We hear stories of girls being beaten with hot iron bars and confined to a small shared living space," Rose looked down to her right. "We see the marks left after these beatings. It's a horrible existence these girls have no education and no chance of escape. Most are at the mercy of their captors. Their day starts at 6am and they'll need to look after at least a dozen customers before their day ends at 3am. Some customers insist on not using a condom and the girl accepts this if she has not met her quota. We don't know how many girls are infected but we suspect it's about 60 to 70 percent," Rose clasped her hands.

"Can you get them out of there?" asked Beth.

"Some we do, but we have to do it carefully we don't want to raise the anger of the pimps. We do it quietly and reintroduce the girls to their families. Some women spend their entire life in The Golden Tree. Kids are born and raised there. The Golden Tree, it sounds so beautiful but Beth, there is nothing beautiful about this place," explained Rose.

"Why do you do this?" asked Beth.

"I've seen some of these girls; some are very young, scared and covered in bruises. I have to help them," said Rose.

"You can't win can you?" Beth asked quietly.

"We won't win if we don't try. If I help one girl a week it's worth it. There are thousands that pass through that door, and thousands more who don't," explained

Rose. "We work with the Center for Communication and Development. It's an organization aligned with ours to get them home."

"Rose, you're a lucky woman; you had two Mothers and two Fathers. After you read this note you will see they were deeply in love and didn't get the chance to meet you. You weren't abandoned. Now you have roots, firm ones. This letter is a chance to hear from one of your parents about their story and their love. Many don't get this opportunity," Beth said leaning over the table and pushing the envelope closer to Rose.

"Thank you, I appreciate you doing this for me and for my family," said Rose in an emotional shaky voice.

"My pleasure," answered Beth smiling and thinking of Sanjeev waiting. "Rose, I need to ask you something that is vitally important to me. I'm afraid I can't explain why and I'm sure the question will seem a little odd. I promised another friend that I would ask."

"Ask away, I'll answer if I can," said Rose puzzled.

"I feel silly doing this but here goes. Rose I want you to think of a Shell. Try to think if that means anything to you. A Shell, what comes to mind instantly when you think of a Shell?" asked Beth expecting the worse.

Rose smiled. "Ms. Kaigara Tanaka," offered Rose immediately.

Beth looked at Rose with a puzzled frown. Rose gave an instant answer. Was that the clue? "Who is Ms. Tanaka? Why her?" asked Beth.

Rose answered in a slow and deliberate voice. "The Reika foundation is the brainchild of Mrs. Sakura Tanaka. She's the principal donor to the foundation. Her daughter, Kaigara, is our chair of the board."

"What does she have to do with a Shell?" asked Beth perplexed.

"Kaigara is an unusual but beautiful Japanese name. It means Shell," Rose said smiling for the first time.

"Shell in Japanese. Where would I find Kaigara? Is she in Kolkata?" inquired Beth excited at the prospect of following her first portal lead.

"No," laughed Rose. "Toronto, Canada. Ms. Tanaka is a successful businesswoman living in Toronto. I've met her a couple of times and she's a no nonsense woman. I'm not sure if I should give you her contact information. I could find myself in a lot of trouble."

"I need to speak with Ms. Tanaka before I decide on the amount of my donation to the Reika Foundation. I've been impressed with you Rose and the work you're doing here, but I wanted to speak with the chair of the board, before I donate," said Beth with a glint in her eye.

"Very well. I'll contact Kaigara directly and inform her that we've spoken and that you would like to request a short meeting. I'm assuming that you would like to meet with her in person?" asked Rose.

"Yes," said Beth quickly without thinking.

"I'll let her know that you'll be coming to Toronto. Why don't you contact her when you get there?" offered Rose. "I'll get you her address and details. I'll send her an email today and inform her of our conversation. I'm not going to mention this envelope or our conversations about my parents and the Shell," said Rose in a matter of fact tone. "Please wait here and thank you again for this," said Rose, waving the envelope and leaving the room.

Beth stared at her watch five minutes had passed. Rose returned with a sheet of paper. Beth had a smile on her face as she rubbed the bump in her jeans pocket, "Lord Ganesha was working his magic," thought Beth. She could not take that silly grin off her face. Against the odds she had found Rose and completed her assignment.

"Here, please remember our agreement. Giving out our benefactors information under the wrong circumstances could get me fired," explained Rose.

"I'll not let you down. I'll make a donation and I do appreciate the help. Trust me, there's an important reason that I need to speak with Kaigara. I just need to find out what it is," said Beth grinning.

Beth took the typed page and glanced at it briefly. It contained Kiagara's full name, business address, and phone number in Toronto. It also contained an email address and a company name, "Swan Property Investments." Beth carefully folded the paper and pushed it into her front jeans pocket opposite. As the two women stood, both smiled and Rose extended her hand in a gesture of friendship. Beth shook her hand firmly.

"I can't thank you enough," said Rose. Rose noticed a mark on Beth's right wrist and turned her hand to examine the tattoo. "A sly fox," said Rose.

Beth smiled, "Hmm, sly; no such thing as coincidences," thought Beth.

"I want you to have this," said Rose handing Beth her business card. "It has my email address and I'd like to know how you make out. Beth, can you email me please? I'd like to ask you about my Father, if I think of questions after you leave."

"Rose, I don't have a computer right now. I may get one soon. I can always access email through my local library, when I get home. I'll send you my contact information," said Beth.

"You promise," said Rose.

"I promise," responded Beth.

The two women smiled and moved towards the door. As they were leaving Beth tucked the card safely into her jeans pocket. She felt she had just made a permanent connection. Under different circumstances she would not have given Rose another look. Two women from very different worlds yet now they had a bond. Beth respected the work that Rose was doing. She was an exceptionally smart and beautiful woman and she had decided to help these poor unfortunate girls. Beth felt a warm glow inside and wondered what Subra was working on. Perhaps it was contentment; she had helped Anwar and delivered on her promise. Despite all the self-doubts she had done it. She had also developed a lead on the portal, and she could now focus on finding a way home for Subra. It had been a good day. Rose was the only person who had answered the "Shell" question instantly with a concrete connection. Beth had a strong feeling she would. This must be the right lead.

"All this time I've been looking for a Shell, when I needed to be looking for a name," thought Beth. "This wasn't a coincidence. There are no coincidences," thought Beth.

Beth arrived at the door; she smiled warmly and shook hands with Rose. Beth entered the waiting room; it had filled with seven women all looking at Sanjeev. Sanjeev looked desperate to leave, "Bless him for staying," thought Beth. Beth walked past the women and glanced at the colorful poster. "There are no coincidences," said Beth softly.

"What?"

"Nothing, let's go I'll fill you in," said Beth.

Sanjeev and Beth left the foundation and made their way back to the parked taxi. Sanjeev opened the door and Beth entered the back seat. She clipped the seat belt around her lap and let out an audible sigh. Sanjeev started the taxi and cranked the air conditioning to maximum. Sanjeev looked in the mirror but did not pull away. He let the engine idle. He looked into the rear mirror at Beth waiting for an update.

"Mission accomplished Sanjeev; I delivered the letter to Rose as promised. I've fulfilled my promise to Anwar. I feel good about that, and I want to thank you personally. I couldn't have done this without you Sanjeev, thank you for your help," said Beth. She could see his laughing brown eyes in the mirror.

Sanjeev broke into a broad smile. "My pleasure Miss, back to The Astor Hotel?" asked Sanjeev as the taxi pulled away.

Beth gazed out at the wretched Golden Tree area. "Back to The Astor Hotel" she confirmed nodding her head. After a while driving, the only noise was the rumbling of the road and the constant sound of horns. Beth turned her thoughts to Anwar. She tried to picture a young Aklina and Rose's face came to mind. Aklina must have been as beautiful as Anwar had described. "Poor Aklina, the women over here have it tough," thought Beth.

She looked at Sanjeev concentrating on the upcoming traffic. "Sanjeev, how did you meet Anwar? He told me that he knew you as a child?" inquired Beth.

"Yes, Miss," replied Sanjeev. "I knew Mr. Anwar when I was five years old. My Father had an accident at work and unfortunately passed away. My Father knew Mr. Anwar from his Mysore days. News of his demise traveled to Mr. Anwar. He was in England at the time. Mr. Anwar knew that my Mother was sick and I had three sisters. He is a very generous man. For years he sent money to help with the family. My Mother passed away when I was twenty. Mr. Anwar made sure that we all went to school, spoke English, and had a place to live."

"How did he manage to help so many people?" asked Beth.

"Mr. Anwar had a big heart. He personally helped each of my sisters marry. He found very good husbands, all are happy. He bought me this taxi and helped me establish my business. He has provided me with business contacts and corporate accounts. I would have done anything for Mr. Anwar and his friends," said Sanjeev in a sincere tone.

"Wow, I didn't understand how helpful he was. I feel good to have helped him but it sounds like he has touched so many people," said Beth.

Sanjeev continued, "When I heard about the news I was devastated. My sister told me to be happy, as Mr. Anwar was not well. He's in a better place and the karma will flow back to him in abundance. Mr. Anwar will be happy knowing the good deed that you've done. I feel privileged to have played a small part. He'll be reunited with Aklina, his one true love. I'm a man Miss and don't understand these things, but even I know it's romantic. My sisters tell me so, yes?"

Beth laughed as she pulled her fingers through her tangled hair, "Eternal love, yes very romantic."

Both smiled as the taxi sped towards The Astor Hotel. It was a long drive, the traffic was heavy but the red and white hotel came into view. Beth recognized the location of a couple of advertising boards as she approached the hotel. A few streets away, up high on a billboard an exotic Indian woman was still fawning over the man with the cool watch. The taxi pulled up to The Astor Hotel and the guards went through the regular entry ritual.

"Good afternoon Miss," said one of the guards with a sunny disposition.

Beth smiled in response. She felt alive and serenely calm. She could now concentrate on finding the portal and helping Subra. It was a weight off her mind. She also had a great lead, Toronto.

The taxi pulled through the gates. Sanjeev jumped out of his seat and opened the door for Beth. "Call me when you need me again Miss."

"I will and thank you again Sanjeev." Beth touched Sanjeev's forearm and gave it a light squeeze.

Sanjeev bowed slightly, smiled and said what he always said. "My pleasure, Miss."

Beth entered the hotel and walked to the elevators. She smiled at the attendant on the front desk and stopped in her tracks. "Excuse me, is Ved the porter around please? I would like to talk with him."

"Certainly Miss he's in the back but let me call him right away. I'll have him come to reception," answered the smartly attired attendant.

"You wanted to see me Miss?" asked Ved in a nervous way.

"Yes, I have an errand that I'd like you to do for me, if its not too much trouble?" asked Beth smiling sweetly at Ved.

"Oh, no trouble at all Miss," replied Ved.

"Good could you come with me and I'll tell you what I need?" asked Beth.

"Certainly, Miss," responded Ved politely.

Beth led the way to the elevator bank and Ved followed dutifully. Once they reached Beth's room she invited Ved inside. Beth noticed Ved getting visibly nervous, unsure of the favor that Beth wanted. He shuffled and fidgeted while looking for direction. Beth walked over to the closet and opened the door to block his view to the safe. Screened by the open door, Beth punched in her access code and opened the safe. She removed money and the second envelope from Anwar. Beth closed the safe door and the wardrobe door. She placed the envelope on the desk. She looked at Ved searching for a reason to be in Beth's room.

"I need you to do an important favor for me. It's really important. Have you seen the new black and gold Eco-Drive Citizen watch, the one on the billboards?"

asked Beth.Ved nodded unable to speak. "Do you know where to get one of those around here?" Beth asked.

Again, Ved nodded.

"Take this money, it should be enough. I'd like you to get me one of those watches and bring me the receipt. Can you manage that?" asked Beth as she placed the money on the table.

"It's a man's watch Miss?" responded Ved looking at Beth's fox tattoo.

"I know. I want the exact model in the poster not a knock off. Get me an original man's watch," instructed Beth.

"Miss, I can get you one tonight when my shift ends at the hotel. I will bring the watch back to you later tonight," explained Ved.

"Very good," said Beth walking over to Ved and standing deliberately close to him.

"Don't let me down now," she said pushing her cute face close to his.

Ved was very nervous, as he looked deep into Beth's beautiful green eyes. He had never seen green eyes before and managed to stutter a response through his personal fog. "I won't Miss."

"Good, thank you Ved," said Beth smiling and moving to the door. Ved followed quickly. "Ved, I think you'll need the money," said Beth.

"Oh, yes," said Ved nervously rushing back to retrieve the money from the desk.

As Ved left the room he did so with a smile, a bow, and a slight wobble of his head. Beth laughed and thought he was a sweet boy. She just knew she would see the exact watch, receipt and precise change that night. Ved was a good kid, honorable. Now Beth had to find a way to get to Toronto quickly. "How am I going to do that?" she thought.

Chapter 9

Trees standing in water – Toronto

Beth rang the front desk at The Astor Hotel. The attendant answered politely, "Hello Miss Martindale how may I assist you?"

"I need to make flight arrangements to get to Toronto, do you have someone who can help me with this?" asked Beth, trying to be polite.

"Of course Miss, just come down to the front desk and our travel concierge will be happy to assist you," said the attendant.

"Thanks, I will." Beth grabbed her passport and wallet from the safe. She made her way down to the front desk. The attendant was already talking to a tall, slim man in a hotel uniform. He looked up and caught Beth's eyes.

"Miss Martindale, this is Raj, he will assist you with your travel plans. I hope your stay with us has been satisfactory and we do hope to see you again," said the attendant in a cheery voice.

"If I find myself in Kolkata again, and I just may, I would not consider staying anywhere else but The Astor Hotel," said Beth honestly.

"Thank you," said the attendant looking over to her colleague. "Raj, please assist Miss Martindale."

Beth followed Raj into the sitting area next to the check in desk. The sitting room contained a small desk with a computer screen, two chairs, and a large red sofa. Raj sat in the chair behind the desk and motioned for Beth to take the other chair directly in front of him. He swiveled the computer screen so Beth could see what he was doing. He logged onto a web site that prompted for information.

"Toronto, Canada was it Miss?" inquired Raj.

"That's right, I need to get to Toronto," said Beth hardly recognizing the words coming out of her mouth. "I'm going to Toronto," thought Beth. "I don't even know where Toronto is," thought Beth in a panic. Beth thought of Anwar and replayed his words from the allotment.

"Many people say that when they go to India it touches them and changes them forever. Beth, you need to do this not for me but for yourself. I know you think that you are doing me a huge favor, and you are. You have to trust me; you will perhaps later think that I've done you a large favor." Anwar's words echoed in her mind as Raj punched the keys on the keyboard.

"I get it now," thought Beth. "You really did me a great favor. Anwar could have chosen Sanjeev, Amba or any of his Kolkata contacts to find Rose, yet he chose me. Probably the least equipped person to do this mission. He chose me and I've not let him down. I've grown more this week as an individual than I've grown in the past ten years. If I can do this, I can do anything. That's the lesson that Anwar is teaching me. Yes, India has changed my life and I'm sure Toronto will broaden my horizon even more," thought Beth proud of herself.

Raj peered into the monitor and then looked at Beth staring at the screen with a blank expression.

"It's not looking good Miss. It's hard to get to Toronto from here. As you can see there's no direct flight. You will need to connect," said Raj.

"I'm fine with a connection," explained Beth.

"Twice," said Raj in a higher pitch. "I'm afraid this is not a pleasant route. Do you want to fly business class Miss?"

"Yes," said Beth hardly thinking.

"I have to let you know, not all domestic flights in India offer business class, so you have to fly coach. I'll try to keep you in business class where I can. I'll also try to keep you on the same airline that way no mess up with the luggage or boarding pass," explained Raj.

"Thank you," said Beth, "I only have carry on luggage."

"That's easier, but they still mess up boarding passes when you cross airlines. It's better to stay with one airline the whole way," explained Raj. "I have your route locked in, is leaving tomorrow good for you?"

"Yes, if possible," reassured Beth.

"It is, let me read this to you so that you understand," said Raj. "This is with Jet Airways. You will leave Kolkata at 6.05am, an early start Miss. This flight will be domestic to Mumbai it arrives at 8.40am, that's two hours and thirty-five minutes. Good so far?" asked Raj.

"Sounds easy except for the early morning start," said Beth smiling. She was rubbing Lord Ganesha through her jeans.

"Here's where it starts to get ugly Miss. Your flight from Mumbai leaves at 12.55pm. This means over four hours of waiting. I'm sorry it's the best I can do. The next flight is Jet Airways to London, Heathrow landing at 5.55pm local time. This will be an enjoyable nine and a half hours of flying," said Raj.

Beth pulled a face. "London is nearly home for me," thought Beth. She nodded at Raj to continue the horror story.

"You'll be happy to know that Jet Airways does fly direct from London to Toronto. It's a quick hour layover in London leaving at 7pm. After a little over eight hours you should make it to Toronto at 10pm local time. I'm sorry Miss this is an ugly 25 hours and 30 minutes with layovers. Not a great schedule. It's the best I can do if you want to get there quickly. It avoids overnight layovers," said Raj in perfect English. "There is good news. All of the flights are business class except the first short flight to Mumbai."

Beth thought about the prospect of traveling for more than 24 hours straight through. "I can do this," she thought, "I can. I'll sleep and talk with Subra."

Beth nodded and Raj started to confirm the booking. "Can I borrow your passport?" he asked.

"Do I need a visa to go to Canada?" asked Beth.

"Canada is still part of the commonwealth, you don't need a visa to visit," explained Raj moving his fingers rapidly over the keyboard. "Sanjeev will get you to the airport. I will call him and make plans for him to collect you at 4.30am."

"4.30am," repeated Beth in mock horror.

"You'll need to leave an hour earlier to give you time to check in," explained Raj.

"Yikes that's early. I better hit the hay early tonight," said Beth watching Raj pretend he understood what she just said.

"I'm ready to confirm your tickets now. I can use the billing information on your hotel account." Raj turned the screen fully towards Beth so she could see the prices. They looked large until she noticed they were displayed in Rupees. Beth could not figure out the cost and rather than look silly she just nodded and smiled. Raj hit the confirm button and said, "You're booked Miss. I'll just print your e-ticket at the front desk if you'd like to follow me." Raj rose from his seat and Beth followed. They entered the reception area and Beth realized she had not read Anwar's letter.

"He told me to read it after I located Rose. Damn, I might have jumped too soon organizing this trip to Toronto. Damn, Beth. Damn," thought Beth getting angry with her self. Beth waited as Raj went behind the check in desk. The attendant smiled and graciously moved to one side allowing Raj access to the printer. He took the papers and folded them into a sleeve with "The Astor Hotel" emblazoned on the front.

"Here you are Miss, your e-ticket. You'll need this at the check in counter tomorrow," said Raj.

"Thank you for your help."

"My pleasure," said Raj smiling almost as brightly as the attendant.

Beth felt a presence over her right shoulder. She turned and found Ved looking a little stressed. "Miss, I'm so glad I caught you. I've been worried sick but I'm pleased to report that I've completed my assignment." Ved handed over a gift wrapped box and a handful of bills with some coins. "Here's the receipt," he said looking relieved.

"Are you all right?" asked Beth.

"I'm not used to walking around with so much money; they looked at me strangely when I bought the watch with cash. Then I had to walk back to the hotel with all this money in my pocket. It wasn't mine and I was worried," blurted Ved.

"No need to worry now," said Beth trying to calm Ved down. Beth glanced at the receipt; it read "Citizen Eco-Drive Model."

"Good job Ved," thought Beth. "Ved, thank you for doing this. I know this will deliver positive karma to you," said Beth smiling.

Ved returned the smile as Beth reflected on her statement. Curiosity got the better of her.

"I must go and get ready for tomorrow," said Beth making an excuse to retreat. She walked briskly to the elevator carrying the package. Once inside she selected the 3rd floor. In her room she slotted the plastic room key into the wall and the lights activated. She could clearly see the envelope sitting on the desk. Beth latched the door and got undressed. She pulled on her hotel bathrobe and slippers. Looking at the crumpled pile of clothes on the floor she bent over and picked up her jeans. Beth paired the hems together and held her jeans upside down. Lord Ganesha fell to the carpet softly. She tucked the leg hems under her chin and let them fall over her forearm. Beth took the folded jeans and gently placed them on a chair. She picked up her Tee shirt, underwear and socks and placed them on the table next to the letter. Her life was going to be orderly; she was going to get her act together from now on. It was a new Beth. Beth took the envelope and reclined on the soft bed. Staring at the envelope she wondered if Rose was having the same feelings before opening her envelope. She had received a message from Anwar, a message from the spiritual domain, as Subra would call it. Beth took a deep breath before gently tearing a corner of the envelope. She placed the torn paper into the trash bin next to the bed.

She slid her finger into the hole created and pushed it along the seam of the envelope. She glanced down at her fox tattoo. The fox was staring directly at Beth with his body positioned side on and his tail tucked between his haunches. Beth loved the design of the tattoo. She told the tattoo artist that she wanted a small fox and he came back with this design. It was uncertain if this was a product of his fertile imagination, or if he lifted it from some piece of artwork. She knew instantly that she liked it. Some people get bored of their tattoos and then wish they had never gone through with it. Beth liked her fox more with each passing day. She reached into the envelope and extracted the folded letter. Beth unfolded the paper and she could feel her heart rate starting to race.

"Inhale," she told herself. Beth opened the letter and began to read it aloud.

My Dear Beth,

I never doubted you for an instance! Congratulations and a big, thank you. You've made me feel complete. To know that Rose was living with the impression that her Father simply didn't care was simply unbearable.

I know in my heart you've stretched your comfort zone on this journey. I hope you take something positive away from India and that it's provided you with some personal growth. It's a complex place full of pain, suffering, decency, honor, and pride. The wonderful people in India are open hearted and kind. I know Sanjeev will do anything to assist you.

I could go on about how grateful I am that you delivered my note but words cannot adequately express my gratitude. I feel heavy in my heart for one reason. I haven't been entirely honest with you. I have always told people that I was a simple Baker. I managed to string a few stores together and make some money to retire on. This is a fanciful tale that has allowed me to live a normal life.

Beth, I have always enjoyed helping people. It was ironic that when my time came near I was the one in desperate need of help. I was most grateful that you willingly offered that help! I have tried to live my life as a simple man and I knew that I would never marry or date another woman. Aklina was my one true love and there could be no other.

My bakeries provided a decent income and I invested wisely. I started by buying land in India. When I was advised to sell it provided me with a handsome return. I took the profits, and on the advice of a dear friend, invested in high tech startup companies such as Infosys, Wipro and Tata. When the year 2000 came, and the technology boom reached its heady heights, these companies returned large. I cashed in at the right time and invested in real estate in London, New York, Paris, Toronto and Tokyo. I bought properties that generate income streams. Renters pay their rent and I get to see my building investments rise in value.

I'm sorry, this is a long, boring, investment story. I'm avoiding the truth. Beth, I'm a little wealthier than my allotment appearance might suggest. The note you've graciously delivered to Rose outlines just how wealthy she has now become. I'm sure the shock is setting in and she will be checking the references I provided. Given a note like this, I would assume it's a hoax too!

I know that you've benefitted from your journey to India but you had to have guts to do this. I've contacted the Bradford and Bingley building society. Your rented cottage on Sun Street is now bought and registered in your name. You may want to visit the building society branch on North Street, in Keighley. Talk with Mr. Davis; he's the manager and has the paperwork ready for you to sign upon your return. A Mr. Wilks from the Blue Phoenix Group will advise you more when you return. Mr. Davis has been instructed to contact Mr. Wilks so that the three of you can talk. Beth, Mr. Wilks is on your side. He is paid to give you good advice and has never steered me wrong.

Beth, remember how good it felt to help someone in dire need? This is a life lesson that hopefully you will not forget. You have a fire inside and it burns bright. You have a special glow that I can't quite place. I know you'll help others and I know you like to help others. Trust me that will come back to you many times over.
I will leave this world a happy man. I challenge you to make your life fabulous. You should do all the things you can to help others. I know that people will seek your help Beth, choose wisely and provide it freely.

When you talk with Mr. Wilks he will explain to you the operational aspects of the "Generosity Account," specifically the source of the deposits into this account. I have professionals manage my real estate assets and investment portfolio. I just decide what to do with the returns. I would like you to run this part for me now Beth.

Mr. Wilks will make sure that you are fully briefed on how it works. It's simple really. We have great people managing the investments and all you have to do is decide which worthy cause should get the rewards. There's a little more to it than that but I'm sure a "sly fox" like you will pick up the reins quickly.

First, I ask you to help and then I burden you with a great responsibility. I know you can do this. Rose will get wealth beyond her imagination, I will see to that. I didn't want to burden her with running an organization primarily based in England. I couldn't think of a better person to leave this responsibility with.

India was a prerequisite for this, when you see the opulence of the palaces and the contrast of the slums you know that this world caters to all. Some people just need a helping hand at the right time in their lives and they will go on to do incredible things. You now have the power to help people Beth, use it wisely. The "Generosity Account" will pay for your expenses and flights. I hope you feel excited by this opportunity. It's natural to feel skeptical and a little overwhelmed. Once you get comfortable and realize how this works you'll be excited.

A quick chat with Mr. Wilks and you'll be set to change the world. Beth, you're my little fox. I know you'll make me proud and I'm confident that you'll learn quickly and grow this business.

Thank you for giving me the chance to be a better Father to Rose.

I will always remember your act of kindness and hope you enjoy a lifetime of giving.

Fondest regards,

Anwar Patel

As Beth's eyes welled up with tears a thought suddenly popped into her mind, "One must be poor to know the luxury of giving: George Eliot." "Thank you Subra," said Beth softly. "Subra, I have one for you," said Beth, "The price of greatness is responsibility: Sir Winston Churchill."

Beth could feel the weight of the letter sinking in. She was delighted that she now owned her little cottage but at what price? She was now going to head a charitable organization. She had no idea how big it was or what was entailed. She knew very little but there seemed to be an expectation to grow it. Beth wondered how she would choose worthy causes? How would she know if the investment professionals were doing a good job? She felt way out of her league.

"I just started to feel that my promise had been met and you load me up with this!" said Beth looking at Anwar's signature on the letter. "Right," Beth said, "I have to ask myself what am I grateful for?"

This tip was given to her by a counselor at one of the many childcare facilities that Beth cycled through. She rattled off a dozen things quickly and immediately felt better.

"I can do this, focus on what I want," thought Beth. Beth reorganized her backpack and got her fresh clothes ready for the long journey in the morning. As she packed she looked down at her fox tattoo. "Well, it's you and me fox. Looks like we both have to be sly to deal with these investment types. I hope we can live up to this challenge. For now we have to stay focused and solve this portal problem first. We need to help Subra get home." The fox did not respond but Beth needed to talk with someone. She had always thought of her fox as a he. Beth retrieved Lord Ganesha from the carpet and placed him with her clothes. She was startled by the shrill tone of the ringing phone.

"Hello," answered Beth.

"Sorry to disturb you Miss, it's the front desk. Due to your early morning checkout time we've taken the liberty to put you through advanced check out. You don't need to stop by the front desk unless you use the mini bar, Internet, or the phone tonight. Have a safe flight, and we'll slip a copy of the final bill under your door tonight. Have a safe trip Miss Martindale and thank you for staying at The Astor Hotel."

"Great, thank you," said Beth hanging up the phone. It was evening and Beth felt the need to sleep before her early start. She repacked her backpack and carefully placed Anwar's letter inside. Beth set the alarm clock and settled in for a chat with Subra. She was looking forward to having this exchange. It was not long before Beth fell asleep.

"I told you I would find Rose and how about that Kaigara? Japanese for Shell!" thought Beth. No answer. "Come on Subra stop tinkering," thought Beth. No answer. "Subra this isn't funny, I need to chat with you."

Subra might not be able to comprehend linear time but Beth could. After a while the unconscious mind has to wander when you sleep. Beth was floating in a stream of clear blue water. She was surrounded by beautiful white roses and could smell incense. Little foxes were playing on the banks of the river darting between marble lions. Beth felt something, just strong enough to register in her mind. She focused on the force it was Subra. Beth dialed him in like finding the right frequency on a radio. She had not needed to do this before. Perhaps he had been roaming around fixing her energy flows?

"Well, good of you to show up mate," said Beth sarcastically.

"I've been busy," said Subra faintly.

"I told you I would find Rose," thought Beth in a proud way, "now I want to find the portal. Kaigara is Japanese for Shell, who would have thought that?"

"It's a great lead. Congratulations on finding Rose I'm happy for you. A discovery is said to be an accident meeting a prepared mind," said Subra sounding a little stronger.

"I feel good but again I'm stepping into the unknown with the new task, the Generosity Account."

"What's money? A person is a success if you get up in the morning and go to bed at night and in between you do what you want to do."

"Hmmm, you modified that a little," thought Beth.

"True but Bob Dylan won't mind," responded Subra.

"Looks like we're going to Toronto, I don't know much about Canada. I know they have Maple Syrup and snow, but hopefully not this time of year?" Beth blurted trying to fill some dead time.

"A lot of people like snow, I find it an unnecessary freezing of water," replied Subra.

"It's very hot in Toronto this time of year you'll be fine."

"I have a brutal travel day planned tomorrow, I'm just going to grin and bear it," thought Beth making small talk.

"Although the world is full of suffering, it's also full of the overcoming of it," replied Subra. "The watch was a bold gesture Beth, Sanjeev has helped considerably. No act of kindness, no matter how small, is ever wasted."

"Aesop: from The Lion and the Mouse," offered Beth.

"Forget injuries, never forget kindnesses," Subra tested again.

"Confucius, (551BC to 479BC)," answered Beth.

"You're getting good at this; it won't be long before you have waking access to this knowledge."

Just as he finished his thought, Beth felt a sharp pang. It was not pain. It was the same uneasy feeling she had experienced last time she had chatted with Subra. What was it? Subra could not be mad at Beth for she had found Rose and secured a great lead on the portal. What was it? It was so frustrating because Beth had never experienced anything like this before. She could not identify this strange feeling. As the night wore on it was soon time to wake and begin a long day of traveling. Subra asked Beth to do something he normally did as a matter of course. Beth was asked to focus her energies on waking up so she could start her day. She was used to a Subra induced surge of energy pulsing her brain and waking her instantly. She followed Subra's instructions without questioning and managed to wake herself. She turned on the lights and made her way to the bathroom. It was still dark outside and the birds were quiet. As she moved towards the bathroom she spotted an envelope poking out from beneath the room door.

"My hotel bill," she thought, "better grab that."

Beth picked up the envelope and pushed it into her backpack. She turned and entered the bathroom. Beth showered and stood naked in front of the mirror. She was about to brush her hair when her thoughts strayed to the trip ahead. She grabbed an elastic band and produced a ponytail in short order. She dressed quickly and did a final check of the room. Beth took Lord Ganesha and tucked him securely into her backpack. She checked each drawer, the safe, and the desk for her belongings. A final check of her money, her contact details, the hotel bill, her letters and she was on her way. Beth threw the strap of her backpack over her shoulder. She grabbed the shiny gift-wrapped box and headed for the door.

"Come on fox we better run." Beth closed the door and glanced back at room number 323.

"Good morning Miss," said Sanjeev as Beth stepped off the elevator. Beth offered Sanjeev an exceptionally warm smile this morning. It was the same smile she had used with Timmy Haggerty when she was 14 years old. Beth was very impressed with this fit boy. She had just discovered that girls had power over boys. She was about to experiment with how good it felt to tease. Timmy looked at Beth for a fleeting moment. He must have thought she was a gorgon, hair of snakes and fish scale skin. He took one look at his potential seducer, turned and walked away with Karen Whitehead. That concluded Beth's experimentation in wielding her feminine powers over the opposite sex. Beth's smile this morning came from a warm place, a place of gratitude. It was met with an equally respectful smile from Sanjeev. He grabbed Beth's backpack as usual and walked to the taxi. Beth kept the package close to her and nodded respectfully at the young man behind the reception. Beth entered the taxi and as usual Sanjeev held the door open.

"Thank you Sanjeev," said Beth.

"My pleasure," responded Sanjeev.

"Before we go to the airport I have a little something for you. It's a token of my appreciation for all that you've done for me during this visit." Beth pushed the package onto the armrest between the two front seats. Sanjeev looked at the package and then looked at Beth.

"Miss, I can't."

"It would offend me if you didn't." Beth held Sanjeev's look within her piercing green eyes.

"You know I would've done anything I could for you and Mr. Anwar," said Sanjeev honestly.

"I know that. Now please open it before we start our drive," instructed Beth. Sanjeev cautiously lifted the small package and again looked at Beth for reassurance. "Go ahead," said Beth in an impatient tone.

Sanjeev opened the wrapping. He looked like a little girl delicately unfolding a flower. After a couple of attempts he managed to take the paper off. He looked at the design on the box, "Citizen" it said. He removed the cardboard cover and held the hard plastic case. Shaped like an oyster he popped the top open revealing a beautiful shiny new watch. Ved had done well. It was the exact watch featured in the poster; gold and silver metal strap; black and gold face; silver bevel and a crystal case. The watch glistened in the exterior lights of the hotel. The second hand was moving on reserve power. On the dashboard it looked as if Lord Ganesha was smiling. Beth felt warm inside. Sanjeev just stared at the watch in amazement.

"Do you like it?" asked Beth.

"It's spectacular Miss," said Sanjeev. "That's the first time I've ever used that word," he said grinning wildly.

"Well, it's of no use in your hand, try it on," said Beth.

Sanjeev placed the watch on the armrest and fumbled with his plastic watchstrap. He placed his old watch in his shirt pocket and reached for his new Eco-Drive watch. He slipped his left hand through his watch and snapped the metal clasp closed. It fit great.

"You never need a battery with this watch it's powered by sunlight and you get plenty of that around here. I want you to remember Anwar when you look at your watch. You have to promise me that you'll keep your eyes on the road though," laughed Beth.

"Miss it's beautiful, thank you so much," laughed Sanjeev.

Beth got to say what she had always wanted, "My pleasure."

Sanjeev merged into the familiar road to the airport, "You are flying domestic first, right Miss?"

"Yes 6.05am, Jet Airways to Mumbai," said Beth confidently.

"Plenty of time," said Sanjeev glancing at his new watch. Occasionally Beth would catch Sanjeev looking down at his wrist in disbelief. Half way through his route to the airport Sanjeev entered a familiar stretch of road. "Miss, Miss, all I need now is the girl!" Sanjeev laughed as he pointed to the Citizen Eco-Drive bill-board. Beth laughed with him. The traffic started to thicken around the airport.

"If I can avoid the stray dogs and pigs on the run-way I should be off soon," said Beth retrieving her backpack from Sanjeev as they stood at the airport check in gate.

Sanjeev had gone as far as he could without a pass-port and a flight itinerary. "Miss, I wish you a safe flight, it was my pleasure to serve you," he said bowing his head slightly.

"Sanjeev, I've had to follow your customs since I've arrived here. I hope you understand, in my country when you leave someone that has helped you as much as you have, we do this." Beth moved in and gave San-jeev a big hug.

Sanjeev went stiff not knowing what to do or how to respond. He smiled and looked a little flushed. With her backpack thrown over her shoulder Beth turned toward the check in counter. She left Sanjeev and looked backwards once to see him walk away. Beth was impressed by the Jet Airways check in staff. They could all have been participants on a reality show, India's top supermodel. The young women were immaculate in their striking yellow blazers contrast-ing with their dark hair and tanned faces. Beth had a smooth check in process and received an apology for not having a business class seat available on her flight. The young woman assured Beth that she would be sat at the front of the plane affording ample legroom near a bulkhead. Beth did not know what a bulkhead was but she thanked the woman who was clearly trying to please. It was an early flight yet it looked as if it was going to be full. Beth received her boarding pass. She had requested "no meals" and the attendant confirmed this. Beth thought this was easier than trying to politely decline the food offered. She could see the attendants face skew as she realized Beth had no meals booked for her entire journey.

The attendant looked up and asked again, "Sorry Miss, just to confirm again, no meals on any flight?"

"That's correct," said Beth confidently.

"Have a safe journey Miss and thank you for flying Jet Airways."

Beth finally made it to the plane. The aisle was full as she tried to locate her bulkhead seat. She was seated in a row of three facing a wall at the front of the plane. Beth felt self-conscious being the only western female in a plane full of locals. The plane contained a few Indian women but was mostly comprised of men. Delaying the boarding process was an elderly man who struggled to get his bag into the overhead. A very attractive flight attendant dressed in a long yellow jacket and black skirt arrived promptly. She assisted the man and he thanked her. It was clear from his accent and his Dallas Cowboys tee shirt that he was American. He sat promptly in an aisle seat. As Beth walked by he caught her eye and gave her a reassuring nod of the head. Beth smiled in response and advanced to her seat. Her row of three seats had an overweight Indian man slumped into the window seat. He glanced up at Beth and seemed to dismiss her instantly before she could acknowledge his look. She looked at her ticket again and heard a loud "Yes" echo inside her head. She realized she was positioned in the aisle seat. Beth pushed her backpack into the luggage overhead. She sat in the aisle seat and stared at the wall. The flight was cramped and the seats were small. The middle seat remained empty and Beth managed to lean back and eventually fall asleep.

Chapter 10

Kaigara, Japanese for Shell

A re you there, Subra? I don't have much time on this flight," thought Beth. Subra did not respond and it was starting to annoy Beth. She concentrated and could feel a small energy signature that she recognized. She focused intensely and could finally feel Subra. It felt like she was pulling him into her immediate consciousness.

"On your way to Toronto?" inquired Subra.

"Don't you want to talk with me?" thought Beth. "You seem to be hiding these days."

"Sorry, that's not the case. I have something important that you need to learn. It will help you as you concentrate on finding the portal," offered Subra.

"All right, I'm all ears."

"I don't know that quote?"

"It's an expression, it means I'm listening. Go ahead we don't have much time," thought Beth.

"Listen to me carefully," Subra was talking but it sounded to Beth like she was listening to a radio with weak batteries. Subra would start strong then he would fade and the volume would fluctuate like a weak signal. She focused on his voice, as she knew this was going to be important from his tone.

"I found you Beth because of your aura. Everyone has an aura. It's an energy source than emanates from your body. Head dresses worn by Native Indian Chiefs and Mayan priests are thought to represent flames coming from their heads. These are thought to represent auras. Old paintings in Italy, Greece, India, Egypt and more, show halos around the head, often golden in color. People have tried to photograph auras starting with Kirlian, a Russian." Subra was rushing to get the information into Beth's unconscious mind. "Many people today accept the fact that auras exist and many claim to be able to see them. You have a strong Indigo aura. This is rare; it means caring, nurturing and humanitarian qualities. You're a perfect choice for this current assignment from Anwar. This man sitting next to you in the window seat; has a mostly Red aura. That stands for sensuality, vitality and aggression," explained Subra.

"What does Gold mean?" asked Beth.

"Unlimited potential, you won't see too many of those. There are many ways to see or feel auras. You will need to develop this technique quickly. I firmly believe it will help you in your future quest. When you can see auras you will see many colors within the aura. A single color will always be dominant. This is called the ground color. You have a ground color of Indigo but occasionally you also have a small amount of Blue and Yellow," explained Subra.

"You have me curious, Blue and Yellow?"

"Blue is teacher, traveler and seeker of wisdom. Yellow is creativity, intellect and slyness," explained Subra.

"Slyness, no way. You made that up," thought Beth.

"Just seeing if you're paying attention, this is important. I need you to start to develop an ability to see auras. You're an Indigo ground so this should come naturally and easily for you. You just have to be taught how to hone your ability. I want you to grab a white piece of paper. In a soft light, place your forefinger tips together and stare at them for about 10 seconds. Slowly start to move your fingers apart and try to see the thread of energy between them. Most people stop seeing the thread when they get to about half an inch apart. Keep honing this until you can see energy between your fingers on the same hand. You are predisposed to seeing this you just haven't looked before. Practice this for me and I will talk with you again when you sleep. This will give you something to do when you get bored. Just to mess you up a little bit. Most people say they see the auras using their third eye, the mind's eye. Beth you should wake yourself and try to practice this," Subra's voice faded.

Beth was curious why Subra felt strongly she would need this skill. She sensed that same old familiar feeling. It was at its strongest when Subra faded away and it annoyed her that she could not identify the feeling. Beth jolted herself awake and shuddered as she regained consciousness. The man with the Red aura looked at Beth with disdain.

"Wonder what I did wrong?" thought Beth.

A shrill pinging noise sounded above her head and the announcer could be heard through the intercom. Beth could not understand it was clearly not English. After the announcement completed an English sounding voice with an Indian accent followed. She informed the cabin that the captain had illuminated the fasten seat belt sign. She instructed passengers to prepare for landing in Mumbai.

"I've been sleeping for almost two hours," thought Beth. "I must have been really tired. Pure energy isn't what it used to be," thought Beth.

The Jet Airways plane landed in Mumbai within minutes of its stated time. The attendants donned in their elegant long yellow jackets wished passengers a pleasant journey as they left the plane. Beth saw the man with the Red aura. She did not expect him to push her in the back as he rushed past scampering up the boarding ramp.

"Red means aggressive," thought Beth. "Maybe I should practice this aura thing."Beth took her time walking off the plane; she had four hours to kill. She walked past the "Welcome to Chatrapati Shivaji International Airport" sign and smiled. She recalled the Dum Dum story and thought, "Yeah, I bet this is known as Mumbai Airport!" Beth saw a familiar stylish yellow coat worn by another potential super model. "Where do they get these girls?" thought Beth.

"Hello Miss, are you connecting to a flight out of India?" she asked.

"Yes, to London Heathrow."

"Are you flying Jet Airways?"

"Yes," said Beth as people barged by her.

"You should have your boarding pass already with your travel documents. You're in terminal one domestic you need to follow the signs to terminal two international where you'll find your gate. You'll need to go through security," said the attendant. Beth followed the signs and paused to look at her paperwork. The woman in Kolkata had slipped three boarding passes into her card folder. She found the Mumbai to London boarding pass but the gate information was empty. Going through security was the part Beth least liked. She recognized the American man from the plane near the front of the line. She imagined him traveling through London to get to Dallas. At security Beth was pulled out of the line and motioned to go into another line. They seemed to have one line for men and another for women. Once through the scanning machine she was invited into a canvas screened off area and told to step up onto a wooden box.

"What are they doing?" thought Beth.

A woman in a uniform patted Beth down. Beth laughed to herself as she wondered where she would smuggle anything in her tight jeans and tee shirt. Even Lord Ganesha made a bump when he was tucked into her pocket! She was then ordered to regain her place and pick up her scanned backpack. She glanced over at the men's line and saw the American in a state of semi undress standing high on his wooden box. No canvas screen was afforded to hide the men's blushes as they were patted down. Beth retrieved her backpack and headed into the waiting area for terminal two international. She walked towards an illuminated board to see if she could recognize her flight number and find her gate. As she looked up into a list of destinations she spotted London, Flight 118, on time, gate 323. Beth headed for the 323 sign in the distance. When Beth arrived at the gate she was surprised to see that it was full of people of all ages. She glanced up at the board behind the yellow jacket at the check in desk. "Brussels" it read.

"These people are going to Brussels, I have hours to kill," thought Beth.

Beth walked around the terminal building; she browsed the stores, fingered through some magazines and bought a paperback book. It was a slow moving spy novel set in Berlin. Beth practiced her finger aura reading technique but garnered strange looks and stopped quickly before yielding any results. She glanced down at her watch; she smiled as she thought of the Citizen Eco-Drive that Sanjeev was proudly wearing.

Her mind wandered and she imagined Sanjeev leaving the airport and dodging the stray dogs to return to the taxi. There, in the distance was an Indian super model wearing a beautiful yellow jacket and dripping in gold jewelry. Her sultry eyes locked onto Sanjeev and his head wobbled provocatively. He flashed a smile as he glanced at his watch. It was very important to know what time it was at that moment. The super model gazed at the watch and was instantly mesmerized by its beauty and power. She could not resist and pledged her undying love to Sanjeev. Beth chuckled out loud and a small Indian man dressed in a smart tunic gave her a solemn look.

Beth continued to stare at her watch, it was 10am local time and she still had hours to kill. This was going to be a long day but Beth was trying to keep a positive attitude about it.

* * * *

12.30pm
The United Way Charity Black Tie Gala
The Royal York Hotel, Toronto, Canada

Ms. Kaigara Tanaka laughed and leaned closer to the Premier, "Please excuse me I really must be going Mr. Premier. Thank you for a wonderful evening." Kaigara bid farewell to the premier, his wife and the remaining couple at her table. She looked around the charity gala main ballroom decorated in a gold and black theme. The ballroom guests were now starting to thin out as the late hour and dancing started to take its toll. She picked up her black satin purse and began to make her way over to the exit. Kaigara was an elegant woman, slim and shapely. She worked out at a local upscale women's health club, had a private dietician and used a personal trainer. Most people would describe her as driven.

Kaigara was wearing a black evening gown that flowed as she walked. It was tied at the neck and had elegant crystals sewn into the dress. Her long gown covered the tops of her stunning black high heels. At this point in the evening they were starting to pinch her feet. She wore a simple thin rope of gold around her neck. A large diamond was suspended from the elegant rope accompanied by matching diamond earrings. A gold Cartier watch hung loose from her left wrist. Kaigara had a Swarovski crystal brooch in the shape of a Swan pinned to her gown; it shimmered as it reflected the light. Kaigara would normally be seen with her long black hair pinned up in a severe business look. Tonight she had it styled where it fell naturally and flowed onto her shoulders. She looked desirable. A successful businesswomen in her mid thirties she commanded attention. Kaigara was educated at the London School of Economics; spoke English, French, Japanese, Mandarin and Cantonese. She was the only daughter of a prominent Japanese socialite and a respected Canadian/Japanese business entrepreneur. Kaigara was raised in Yokohama and Toronto, educated in London and lived in Toronto.

Kaigara had deep piercing brown eyes and a smooth complexion that made men stare at her exotic features. She had a combination of a strong western face with traditional Japanese bone structure. She was beautiful and she knew it. She walked from the ballroom smiling and nodding her farewell to various guests. She walked into the coat check area and found a quiet place to lean against a wall. Kaigara opened her purse and retrieved her Blackberry device. Twelve new email messages it proudly announced. She examined her inbox but her eyes stopped at a note from Rose Akhter. The email heading read "Urgent: Potential new investor." Kaigara read the email quickly. Rose had received an unannounced visit from a Miss Beth Martindale. Beth had asked many questions about the work being done and the foundation. She headed a large charitable organization and wanted to meet with the Chairperson of the Reika Foundation. Miss Martindale would be traveling to Toronto immediately and would call the office to arrange an appointment. She seemed serious.

Kaigara was immediately suspicious; some times reporters will pose as investors and dig around to try to expose misappropriation of funds or to find an angle on a story. Wasting money on helpless causes is the favorite angle these days. Kaigara was slightly annoyed as she started down a wide carpeted hallway. Guests were milling around and retrieving their coats. She spotted David Attman and his wife Gloria. David was a prominent investment banker and Gloria was a journalist.

"Perfect," thought Kaigara. "Gloria, David, how wonderful to see you both," faked Kaigara. Her greeting was met with equally fake smiles and handshakes. They asked how she was doing as they struggled to dress in light raincoats.

"I'm doing some work with Beth Martindale, have either of you worked with Beth?"

Beth was a mystery and this couple knew most of the money people. This irked Kaigara and she became more suspicious. She bid goodnight to the Attman's and turned her attention back to her Blackberry. It was late but that did not matter. She clicked on her address book and pulled up J.P. Webster. J.P. was perhaps the most connected guy in the city. His reach extended into New York, London, Hong Kong and Beijing. J.P. owed Kaigara a few favors after she had pulled his clients out of a tricky spot. If you were a somebody then J.P. would know you or knew someone who knew you. She clicked the green call button and the ringing tone started.

After a couple of rings a slow voice answered "Hello?"

"J.P. It's me Kaigara," she said curtly.

"What time is it?" said J.P. sounding half asleep.

"It's late but I need some information," demanded Kaigara in a tone not to be argued with.

"Can't it wait until morning?" pleaded J.P.

"No, Beth Martindale, who is she and what organization does she represent?" fired Kaigara.

"I've never heard of her but I'd guess Astral out of Edinburgh," said J.P. hoping that Kaigara would go away. It worked as Kaigara thanked J.P. and disconnected. She looked at her Blackberry battery indicator; it was getting low but had enough for one more phone call. She located Jenny McGovern at Astral. She looked at her Blackberry world clock; Edinburgh would now be 5.45am. Jenny would be up and getting ready to go to the gym. Kaigara called and could hear the ringing on Jenny's cell phone.

"This is Jenny," she said in a rolling Scottish accent.

"Jenny its Kaigara, I need some info dear."

"Jesus Kaigara are you burning the midnight oil or what? Make it quick I need to leave the flat and get on the road in 5 minutes."

"Yeah, I'm busting my hump over this one and drawing a blank. I need some info on Beth Martindale. J.P. thought she was one of your lot but I suspect she's a reporter, do you know her?"

"Definitely not one of ours, name doesn't ring a bell, tell you what, after the gym I'll ask around and look at our contact lists. I'll send you an email this morning and by the time you get to work tomorrow morning it should be sitting in your inbox. I'll dig up some dirt for you love," said Jenny trying to be helpful.

"Thanks Jenny I don't have a good feeling about this one," responded Kaigara.

"OK love, bye for now," said Jenny clicking the disconnect button.

"Damn it," thought Kaigara, "I bet she's a reporter." Kaigara was a clever businesswoman and she knew to stay in business you had to have high ethical standards. Her upbringing and education supported this. She would not do anything that would sully her family name. Her business dealings were impeccable and audited meticulously by PriceWaterhouseCoopers. She was not worried about the facts. What concerned her was that often facts get in the way of a good story. She remembered poor old Berty. Berty was a very wealthy man from Wales who moved to Canada when he was 35 years old. He started a company, worked hard and became wealthy. He founded an organization dedicated to helping war veterans; his father was killed fighting in the line of duty. His organization did some fantastic work. A junior reporter at a local paper started to question the financial dealings of Berty's organization. It was all over the news about the skimming, the irregularities, the wastage and the abuse of funds. The press had a field day in Canada, the United States and the UK. Most of his connections were established through the building trades and his sponsors and contributors dried up overnight. No one seemed to care about the fact that Berty was devastated by these malicious accusations. He decided to sue the reporter and the newspaper.

A year later when he emerged from his trial it was discovered that the reporter had made gross errors and had misinterpreted certain complex legal and financial obligations. Berty's accountants had followed the law for charitable institutions, which was radically different in Canada, the US and the UK. In order for Berty to be compliant his organization had to do things differently for each jurisdiction, hence this was seen as irregularities. The case was won easily, a settlement was reached but the damage was already done and poor Berty's reputation was shot. The paper ended up winning by selling more newspapers. The real losers were the veterans, who cared? Kaigara did not want this to happen to her, her family's reputation and the good work that was underway at the Reika Foundation. Kaigara looked at her watch; it was 1am she had not intended to stay this late. She tucked the Blackberry into her satin purse and pulled out a valet ticket. As she walked toward the hotel valet station a young man in a red uniform with gold trim jumped to attention. Kaigara gave him a smile and the ticket wrapped in a $10 dollar note.

"Right away Miss, we parked it up front so it'll only be a few seconds."

Kaigara waited in the lobby under the chandeliers. Through the glass revolving doors she could see people getting into their cars and speeding away into the night. A small group huddled together as they waited then wished each other a good night. Kaigara could not see her car but she could recognize the distinctive sound of the engine as it fired up. She loved that sound, it was powerful and yet classy. The car started to roll into view and stopped outside the front doors. People stared at the car and smiled. The young man hopped out of the driver's seat and looked for Kaigara. Kaigara pushed through the revolving doors as the crisp night air hit her naked shoulders with a sting.

She glanced at the sleek lines of the car and listened to the engine ticking over. Kaigara loved her car it was an extension of her, what she stood for and how she approached life. She drove a black Maserati Granturismo, V8, with Birdcage 20 inch wheels, bright red

Brembo brake calipers, walnut trim with black leather interior and red stitching. This car looked awesome and it drove like a dream with the Maserati skyhook suspension system; its license plate read, "SWAN." Kaigara elegantly entered the driver's seat and swung her legs into the car. The seat was positioned too far back; she could not reach the pedals. She leaned forward and took her shoes off placing them in the passenger seat with her purse. She used her left hand to press the preset number "1" button on her seat. Everything in the car adjusted to her personal setting. The seat, steering wheel and side mirrors all moved in concert. Now she was ready to go. She checked for traffic in her mirrors. The lights had activated automatically and she pushed the walnut encased gearshift into drive. A large green "D" appeared between the Maserati's blue colored gauges. Kaigara gently tapped the accelerator and with a growl in the exhaust pipes the car lunged forward. The sound echoed in the enclosed valet area and it sounded powerful. Kaigara passed two golden lion statues and merged into the traffic on Front Street. She quickly turned south towards Lake Ontario.

She drove a few short minutes stopping and starting through numerous traffic lights. She was soon on the harbor front and Queens Quay. She weaved between the slower moving cars before veering to the right. She proceeded down a ramped entrance to the private parking area of a luxury condominium building. Kaigara reached upwards to press a button on her sun visor. It was programmed to open the security door leading to the parking area in her building. The security camera mounted high above the ramp tracked the Maserati into the building and identified the license plate. With a distinctive car like this the security guard knew it was Ms. Tanaka. Kaigara drove into the building, turned a sharp left and counted three concrete pillars. A sign announced parking space number 32 was reserved for Ms. Tanaka. This space was a particularly good one as two concrete support pillars flanked it and no one could share the space or accidently dent the door.

Kaigara drove past the space, shifted into reverse and backed into the parking spot. To her rear was a brick wall, the parking system showed a graphic on the computer screen between the gauges. The car sounded a beep and the parking sensor icon was green colored. As Kaigara slowly backed up the icon went from green to yellow to red. The beep intensified and sounded like a patient had flat lined in hospital. Kaigara did not look backwards; she looked at the parking sensor readings. At the flat line sound she shifted into park and the Maserati automatically applied the electric brake. She glanced downwards and pulled her key fob out from the steering column. Kaigara grabbed her purse, slipped on her shoes and locked the car listening to the beep echo in the underground parking lot. She approached the exit door and saw the night guard holding the door open for her.

"How's Tony tonight?"

"Fine, thank you Miss. You're out late tonight so I thought I would walk you to the elevators," offered Tony.

Tony was 28 years old and he could not decide what he liked the look of most, the Maserati or Kaigara. He knew he did not have to make a choice because he would not get either. Tony opened the door to the parking garage leading to a long narrow passage. At the end of the passage was another door. Kaigara walked through the first door and Tony followed. Tony decided to check her out now. Once they entered through the second door they would be in the main lobby area of the condominium. It was completely mirrored and she would catch him sneaking a peek. As Kaigara walked towards the second door Tony's eyes dropped immediately to the small of her back partially naked in the low cut dress. He stared at the fabric of her dress and how it moved over her rear end as she walked in those heels. He lifted his eyes just in time as she spun around and stared at him.

"I'll get that," said Tony smiling innocently and opening the second door. Kaigara walked through and waited at the elevators. Tony pressed the elevator call button. A high-pitched sound announced the arrival of one of the elevators. Kaigara had retrieved her key from her purse. She stepped into the wood paneled elevator and inserted her key into the security slot before turning it clockwise. She tapped the number 7 and looked at Tony waiting in the lobby.

"Good night, Tony," she said with a smile.

"Good night, Miss," said Tony desperately trying to keep eye contact.

The elevator doors closed and Kaigara started to laugh. She knew what affect she had on Tony. Her taste leaned towards a more refined man when she decided it was time for such a luxury. The elevator announced its arrival at the seventh floor and the doors opened on cue. Kaigara knew Tony was now watching her over the security system until she stepped into her apartment. She walked to the end of the hall and approached the door with gold numbers showing 732. Kaigara's apartment was a corner unit overlooking Lake Ontario and providing city views of the Toronto skyline. It was professionally decorated with original oil paintings, tapestries, sculptures and antiques. Kaigara stepped inside and immediately disabled the alarm system. The apartment lights were motion activated and she glanced at the clock on the wall, it was 1.30am. She knew if she went to bed now she would never sleep.

"I'm calling David Wilks, it'll be about 6.30am in London, he's an early bird," thought Kaigara. "Damn," said Kaigara softly punching her fist into her thigh. "I don't have his number in my Blackberry. Yes," she said excitedly, "I have it in my day timer." Kaigara walked into her study and picked up her leather briefcase leaning against her desk. She clicked open the briefcase flap and pulled out her day timer. She opened the book to today and laid it flat on the desk. "When did I speak with him last?"Kaigara thumbed through a couple of pages until she saw the handwritten note. "David Wilks, Blue Phoenix Group." The phone number was printed next to it. Kaigara dialed the number using her apartment phone and perched on the edge of her desk. The phone rang a couple of times.

"Hello, David Wilks," was the greeting.

"I knew you were a morning person, it's Kaigara Tanaka calling. How are you?" she said sounding tired.

"I'm fine Kaigara but if you're calling about the Kingston project my client has decided against it, I thought we discussed this?" asked David in an irritated tone.

"No, sorry, that's not the nature of my call," said Kaigara sounding apologetic. "I've a question to ask you, more of a favor really?"

"Shoot, I have a meeting in 15 minutes, how can I help you?" said David.

"I know that you're well connected and I wondered if you had come across a certain name who claims to be the head of an investment group. She says that she might be interested in making a donation to my foundation but I'm suspicious of her motives and credentials," said Kaigara as quickly as she could.

"What's the name?" asked David curtly.

"Miss Beth Martindale," offered Kaigara. There was silence on the other end of the phone as David ran possible responses through his head and assessed the consequences of each.

"I can vouch for Miss Martindale being the head of an Investment company and should she decide to donate she has the means to do so. I cannot comment on her decisions but I can say that she is a wealthy client of mine," said David.

"Which organization does she represent David?" asked Kaigara bluntly.

Again after some silence David responded, "It's now public record so I think that I'm within my rights to disclose that information. Miss Martindale has assumed control of the Generosity Account and its global operations."

"What happened to Anwar?" inquired Kaigara.

"Didn't you hear? Anwar's passed away, Beth Martindale is Anwar now," said David.

"Thanks David, I really appreciate this, I'm sorry to bother you," said Kaigara disconnecting. Kaigara was stunned. Anwar had died; he was a true friend in a world of fakes. Now she knew she was going to meet Miss Beth Martindale.

* * * *

12.15pm
Jet Airways Gate 323
Mumbai Airport
Mumbai, India

Beth handed over her boarding pass and passport to another yellow jacket wearing supermodel and smiled. The Jet Airways attendant scanned her boarding pass efficiently. She returned Beth's passport and the boarding pass stub. Beth walked confidently forward to start the next leg of her journey, the flight to London. As she reached the front door of the plane, another yellow jacket welcomed Beth onboard escorting her to her seat.

Beth looked at the cabin layout and thought, "Great! Pods again." The pods were arranged in a herringbone style giving her ultimate privacy. Beth stored her backpack in the overhead and settled in for a long flight. She browsed her itinerary, nine and a half hours flying time landing at 5.55pm local time. A woman arrived and crouched in front of Beth.

"Hello, Miss Martindale, my name is Bindi. I'll be looking after you on this flight. I just wanted to confirm that our records show that you have elected not to have any meals on this flight is that correct?"

"Yes, thank you," said Beth feeling guilty.

"Very well, but if you change your mind just give me a call," said Bindi with a wide smile.

"Thank you," responded Beth. She really liked their service approach it was refreshing. It reminded her of the service at The Astor Hotel. Beth had to refuse Champagne; nuts; juice and water it was starting to become embarrassing. She soon settled down into her pod to watch a movie. Bindi arrived with a small bag of popcorn. How wonderful was that? This airline was great. Unfortunately Beth had to refuse that also. Beth could smell the popcorn and it smelt fantastic. Bindi was again polite and gracious in accepting Beth's refusal. The movie was a romantic comedy. It centered on an American boy who falls in love with an Indian call center girl. Romance and cultural differences were the key themes. The movie was entertaining and funny. Beth appreciated the change of pace, bubblegum for the mind. After the movie finished she took her headphones off and looked around. The cabin was quiet; it was the perfect time to practice her aura readings. She found the menu card, which had a plain white back. She held her fingers together and slowly drew them apart about a quarter of an inch while concentrating. Subra started to open her energy paths and chakras. Beth was skeptical but became instantly engaged as she saw a thin luminous strand of violet energy pulsing between her two fingers. She stared at the light and moved her fingers gently apart breaking the luminous strand. She held her hand up to her face and concentrated. Between her fingers, for an eighth of an inch, surrounding her hand she could see a light border. She could see a fuzzy looking Indigo colored energy layer. She stared at her hand concentrating hard when a man walked by and gave her a questioning look. Beth pulled her hand down quickly but her eyes tracked the back of the man as he made his way to the bathroom. Beth's mouth hung open as she could see three colors surrounding the man. His ground color was definitely Green with layers of Yellow and Silver.

"Wow," said Beth under her breath. "I can see these things."

Subra had figured out the energy flows and had managed to unblock the aura energy from her eyes and focus it through her third eye. Subra was having fun; he was limited to Beth's physical body as his current universe. Not having a physical body he could navigate along Beth's meridian lines. He always thought of a body as a discarded shell after the soul moved on. He was amazed at how intricate this organism was. When the man disappeared into the washroom Beth felt herself relax and sink into her reclined chair.

"There," she said aloud.

Beth could sense that familiar strange feeling again and she honed in on its source. Subra had strayed into an energy channel and was having difficulty navigating his way out. The man in the washroom emerged and walked slowly past Beth looking at her outstretched body. He flicked his eyes in her direction. She paid no attention as she was singularly focused on the source of this strange feeling. Another strong feeling started to wash over Beth like a wave. She finally recognized what was happening. She connected with the strange feeling and she immediately felt panic. Her mouth opened slightly and her eyes darted from side to side. Beth was shocked; she was trapped on a plane and could feel the cold sweat clamming up at the base of her hairline at the neck. She wanted to get up and run, but she knew running would not solve anything. If she ran, this problem would run with her. The problem was inside her.

Beth said to herself, "Breathe, breathe Beth."

Beth tried to relax and started to breathe deeply, she needed to talk with Subra immediately but how could she? She would not be able to sleep in this agitated state. She was annoyed and stressed, neither was a good companion for deep sleep. Beth unclipped her seat belt, stood and reached for the overhead storage clasp. She fished around in her backpack and found her paperback novel. She closed the overhead and returned to her seat. Beth buckled her seat belt and started to read. Stanton was dashing and handsome, women swooned over this man in his Army uniform.

"Well, if he's that interesting and handsome no wonder women threw themselves at him. I've yet to witness a scene where women throw themselves in a swooning manner at any man," thought Beth. "Read Beth, it will make you drowsy," she thought.

Stanton scaled the castle walls and singularly overpowered the guards using his silent combat techniques learned deep in the Burmese jungles. He made his way to the inner chambers of the Nazis fortress. The romantic interest was Francine, a French underground captive being forcibly held. The hero never seems to get a chance to rescue Chuck or Fred. It always seems to be Francine, the incredibly beautiful, long strawberry blonde haired waif. She sounded intriguing and she managed to keep her makeup in pristine condition throughout her days of torture and abuse. That's essential for a girl. The book described Francine's form fitting gossamer like dress and how it clung to various parts of her female body. Beth chuckled at how corny this book was. Tortured for secrets yet she looked stunning wearing her form fitting summer dress, those Nazis had no appreciation for female fashion. The book was obviously written by a man because it left the reader wondering what shoes Francine was wearing. That's important. Beth worried about Francine's shoe choice; flats, pumps, sandals what? She smiled.

In Beth's mind she started to rewrite the novel. Stanton was now Sanjeev, bursting through the front gates of the castle in his heavily armored taxi. Sanjeev was dressed in commando white from head to toe with his Citizen Eco-Drive glinting in the moonlight. He could sense the pain and anguish of the heroine waiting for rescue. She had been shouted at. She had refused to cough up information about flight plans or menu choices. All the while she had kept perfect posture and managed to keep her long yellow jacket in pristine condition. Her lipstick and make up remained unblemished. Beth laughed to herself but it was working. This novel was so bad, her mind was drifting and she started to fall asleep. She lost track of time. Beth did not know how long it took her to reach deep sleep but she had now regained control of her thoughts.

"Subra where are you? Subra we need to talk, do you hear me? Show me your energy and I will pull you through," thought Beth. Slowly, a faint energy signature started to resonate. Beth spotted it quickly and honed in on the energy pattern.

"Can you hear me?"

"I'm here, you're doing great with the auras, I've been trying to develop your cognitive recognition with your third eye," said Subra.

"Many big words, is there something else you want to tell me?"

"About the auras?" responded Subra.

"No about you personally," thought Beth.

"I'm not sure what you're getting at?"

Beth started with her explanation, "I've been feeling a little odd recently. It's happened when we talk. I've had a certain type of feeling and I couldn't quite place it. I've struggled with this. I've never experienced this before but I now know what it is. When I started to have conversations with you Subra you were strong, powerful and vibrant. Pure energy is what I think you called it. It's different now. You fade in and out. I have to pull you into my consciousness instead of you instantly being there. I have to wake myself from our conversations. You used to do that. I felt tired for the first time and now I know why. When were you going to tell me?"

"I'm not sure what you're asking me Beth?" responded Subra faintly.

"You know exactly what I'm talking about. Your energy source is running out. You're fueling both of us and you're dying. It requires energy to do these things. What happens to you when you run out of energy?" asked Beth.

There was a silence followed by a long pause, "I don't know," admitted Subra.

"How much time do I have to find the portal?" asked Beth.

Another pause, "I don't know?" said Subra.

"You had a moral obligation to tell me this instead of making excuses."

"Compassion Beth is the basis of all morality. There is no moral precept that does not have something inconvenient about it," responded Subra.

"Inconvenient! I'm talking about losing my friend and having to live with the guilt. You didn't see any risk in not telling me that I was on a time limit to find the portal?" stormed Beth.

"If you don't risk anything you risk even more. Take calculated risks. That is quite different from being rash," said Subra.

"George S. Patton, but he was talking about battles and war. We're talking about your existence and a time limit. You should've shared that with me," demanded Beth. "Again, how much time do I have?"

"Calendars are for careful people, not passionate ones. Time is a cruel thief to rob us of our former selves. We lose so much to life as we do to death," replied Subra evading an answer.

"How much time?"

"A single day is enough to make us a little larger but I really do not know. I know I'm growing weaker, that's all I know," said Subra honestly. "Can you forgive me?"

"Forgiveness is a gift you give yourself; it is a virtue of the brave."

"Two interesting and very different women, Suzanne Somers and Indira Gandhi, I believe," said Subra impressed at Beth's ability to access the quotes.

"Subra, I need to find the portal quickly don't I?" asked Beth.

There was a long silence and Beth decided to wait him out.

"Yes," was the response from Subra. "There's no grander sight in the world than that of a person fired with a great purpose."

"I get that, trust me I'm motivated, but when will I know that I've found the portal?" asked Beth.

"Some things arrive in their own mysterious hour, on their own terms and not yours, to be seized or relinquished forever," said Subra trying to explain. "You may occasionally give out, but never give up."

"You can't build a reputation on things you are going to do," said Beth.

"Beth, I didn't want to burden you with a ticking time limit. You're doing fine and you'll find the portal. I have the utmost faith in you. If you don't I know you've done everything in your power to help me," said Subra reassuringly.

"I'll try harder Subra, some of the best things in life aren't things. I promise you I will find the portal," thought Beth.

"I need you to keep finding leads and follow your heart; it'll lead us to the portal." Subra faded away.

Beth surged a stream of energy to wake her and slowly opened her eyes allowing them to adjust to the cabin light. Her novel was perched on her thighs. She closed the book and tucked it into one of the pod storage pouches. Beth felt sad and determined. She had already lost Anwar; she was not going to lose Subra by letting him down. Beth glanced at her watch, 5pm. It was still on local Mumbai time, which meant she had been flying for four hours. That left another five and a half to go before London.

* * * *

7.30am
Apartment 732
Habourfront Toronto, Ontario
Canada

Kaigara sipped her ginger tea and stared out of her apartment window. She could see the sun reflecting on the gentle waves as the wind buffered Lake Ontario. Her eyes moved to a blinking red landing light attached to a small plane as it started its landing approach at the Island airport. As if in slow motion the small plane elegantly landed on the runway and then steered to one of the holding areas. Kaigara was staring off into space allowing different moving objects to catch her eyes, like a cat. Kaigara placed her cereal bowl on the edge of the coffee table. She was sitting in her robe allowing the morning sunrays to stream through her window. She picked up her teacup and took a small sip. Kaigara had experienced a restless night. Her mind was thinking through the possibilities with Beth Martindale.

She had only managed a couple of hours of sleep. Kaigara walked over to the exterior glass wall of her condominium. From where she stood she had an excellent view of Toronto. She could see over the lake to her left, it looked calm and serene. As she panned around, the Island airport looked calm with little traffic. She liked the Island airport it was useful to get to Montreal, Ottawa, New York and Chicago in a hurry. Better than the busy Pearson airport with its lineups and International traffic. As she continued to inspect the view she sipped some tea feeling its warmth penetrate her hands through the bone china cup. She could see the long winding Gardiner Expressway full of commuters approaching and leaving the city. The Gardiner Expressway was filling in as commuter traffic tried to catch an early start to the day. She could see the railway tracks and the green and white commuter trains bringing in the daily crowd. To her right was the city skyline of Toronto. She looked at the curving shape of the Rogers Center. When they first build this stadium it was called "The Skydome." The roof retracted and allowed for open-air lakeside baseball games. The dome was the home of the two-time World Series champion Toronto Blue Jays. People still called it the dome. Kaigara thought back to when the dome was being built. She could still vaguely remember her father pointing out the native Indians working in the steel rafters. They had no fear of heights and would walk around steel girders high in the sky with no safety tethers. Positioned next to the dome stood the CN Tower. Kaigara's eyes followed the corkscrew like structure to the very top. This building for many years held the title of the world's tallest freestanding structure. Its shaft corkscrewed slightly to counter act the earth's gravity and rotation. The skyscrapers and the high-rise condominiums reflected the sun in a dazzling mirror effect. It was going to be another hot day in the city of Toronto. Standing in her condominium penthouse Kaigara was soaking in the view and sipping tea peacefully when the shrill sound of the phone pierced the silence. She gently placed her teacup on a coaster and walked to the phone.

"Hello?"

"Hi, it's me," Kaigara instantly recognized the voice as her Mother's. "Did I wake you?"

"No, I was up, just finishing breakfast before I make my way into work."

"Just calling to say that your Dad's plans have changed and he's going to Yokohama this afternoon. I'm teaching tonight and have a busy week but I wanted to go to lunch with you on Thursday. We can go to Far

Niente restaurant at 12.15pm, will that work for you?" asked Sakura Tanaka.

"Sounds good Mum," said Kaigara half asleep.

"OK, see you then, and don't be late, you're always late. I may come and pick you up at your office," said Sakura in a Motherly tone.

"Bye Mum," said Kaigara hanging up. Kaigara walked slowly in the direction of the shower to start her busy day.

* * * *

6.05pm
Terminal 3
Heathrow Airport
London, England

Beth knew she had an hour and was initially worried that she would not make the connection in time. The Mumbai flight landed a few minutes early and the transfer between gates was efficient. Beth soon realized she had plenty of time before she needed to board her next flight she was relieved. She looked around and was dazzled. Why could she not have a longer layover here! Burberry; Chanel; Cartier; Emporio Armani; Dior; and Bulgari, so many shops and not enough time to look around. As Beth moved to her gate she stopped dead in her tracks. She felt grungy, sweaty and unclean. She had another eight hours remaining in the same clothes. She looked at The Body Shop and smelled the clean fresh aromas emanating. Did she have time to stop in and get something? Beth decided to go in and get something that would make her feel clean again after this long journey was over. She had little time to browse and headed straight for the bath products. Beth instantly zoomed in on the Coconut

Foaming Bath product. She could see herself kicking back in a foam-filled Toronto bathtub smelling the scent of Coconut. She snatched a bottle and headed for the check out.

A small thin man rang the sale up, "Nine pounds and fifty pence please," he said cheerily. Beth handed over the money and left the store heading towards her gate. She started to see a crowd of people and the familiar sight of yellow jackets. She approached the gate just as the announcement to board business class was being made. After the normal courteous boarding process Beth settled into her 'pod' and started to relax. She had some anxiety associated with the Heathrow connection. It was one of the busiest airports in the world and she only had one hour. She reflected on how smooth it had been. The flight took off on time at 7pm and she smiled thinking about Toronto.

"Kaigara," said Beth quietly, "Japanese for Shell." Beth glanced over to her right and could see the face of the pod occupant. It was a man, approximately 28 years old and dressed in a light blue tee shirt and jeans. He was sitting high in his chair as he was untying his sneakers and kicking them off onto the floor. Beth caught a glimpse of his face and liked what she saw.

"Easy on the eyes, hard on the heart," thought Beth. She stared at the man as she was sitting slightly behind him and across the aisle. He emanated a Blue aura with strands of Silver. Beth was feeling a strong attraction to his energy and to him. She had not felt like this towards a man for a long time and it surprised her, she could feel her cheeks flushing.

"I don't know what you're doing with my energy flows Subra," thought Beth. Beth could see a flight attendant pushing a trolley but she could not see what was on offer. She would most likely have to refuse.

When the attendant got closer Beth could see newspapers and magazines. As the trolley stopped at her pod she quickly looked at the magazines. The travel magazine looked interesting with Yokohama on the cover. The cover contained a beautiful colored skyline shot complete with skyscrapers, Ferris wheel and schooner. Intrigued by the pictures, Beth turned to the page on Yokohama and started to read.

The city looked modern, fresh and exciting. Yokohama is the capital city of Kanagawa Prefecture. It is found South of Tokyo on Tokyo Bay. Yokohama's population of 3.6 million makes it Japan's largest incorporated city. It has a large foreign population of nearly 75,000. Beth started to read about its origins as a small fishing village and how it established itself as a base for foreign trade. She read of the great earthquake on September 1, 1923. It destroyed most of Yokohama killing over 30,000 people and injuring more. Vigilante mobs killed innocent Koreans. They were falsely blamed for using black magic to cause the earthquake. Today Yokohama is an exciting place with the Landmark Tower standing 70 floors tall being the tallest in Japan.

You could see monsters in Yokohama, the magazine suggested. Two Godzilla films were based upon and made in the city. The Kishamichi Promenade offers wonderful city views. Beth looked at the full-page photographs and admired the color, lights and architecture.

All were very modern and different from the little village of Haworth in the Yorkshire Dales. She wondered if Toronto looked similar. In the photographs she could see a large Ferris wheel it was illuminated at night with neon lights that undulated and made fascinating patterns. In front of the Landmark Tower was the centerpiece of this beautiful scene. Beth could see an old-fashioned sail ship. Its tall masts and brilliant white hull were stunning. The ship was floating in water but looked tethered to the dock. Brilliant lights bounced off the white hull giving the appearance of a mirror image reflection in the dark water beneath. The ship was called the "Nippon-Maru" and was open for the public to tour during the day.

There were buildings of all shapes and sizes making an interesting skyline. Beth thought this would be an eye opening experience. Very different from the landscapes she had witnessed in India. She wondered about Toronto, what would it be like? The rest of the magazine had an article and pictures showing the Winding Street in San Francisco, the Chateau Frontenac in Quebec City, the Guild Houses in Brussels and the Topkapi Palace in Istanbul. The pictures were beautiful but Beth had done enough reading. She just flipped the pages and looked at the images. It was dark outside and the cabin lights had been dimmed so that passengers could sleep. Beth looked around; the cabin was quite full for a business class section.

Occasionally she would see a flight attendant but the activity level was low as people slept. Dinner had been served and cleared away. The man seated in front of Beth unclipped his seat belt and rose from his seat to retrieve some papers from the overhead compartment. Beth raised her eyes at the motion and lingered her gaze upon him. As he reached up to retrieve his papers his tee shirt rode up exposing his abdomen above his black leather jeans belt. Beth's eyes immediately settled on the bare skin. Just as she looked he turned his head her way and caught Beth looking. She saw him smiling at her and immediately realized she had been made.

"Shoot, what do I do now?" thought Beth.

Beth did not smile back; she immediately looked at her magazine because, sheep farming in the Orkney

Islands, was far more interesting than this guys fit body. As she glanced up again he was still looking her way and grinning. She politely smiled and returned to her magazine. He returned to his seat turned his back on Beth and resumed his journey.

"Smooth Beth, real smooth," she thought.

Beth opened the entertainment screen and lightly tapped her movie selection. She chose a movie set in California, a romantic drama of love unfulfilled. Beth realized she was subconsciously looking for a mate. She adjusted her headphones and settled back into her chair to watch the movie. Beth had been running on adrenaline and decided she was far too tired to sleep. After the movie had finished and the credits had rolled she made another selection. She selected a short segment film entitled 'Your Destination.' Inspirational music played as the distinctive Canadian flag with a red maple leaf flapped furiously in the wind. The scene changed to a helicopter ride over tall skyscrapers. The narrator mentioned that "Toronto" came from a native Indian expression it meant "Trees standing in water." One of the buildings seemed to be made out of gold colored glass reflecting brightly in the strong sunlight. An odd shaped building which looked like an upturned cereal bowl came into view. A grand looking building rose majestically. You could tell it was from a bygone age. It was not made from modern glass but instead a copper roofed stone building. The signage read, "The Fairmont Royal York Hotel." Images of a modern subway train service with TTC logos were shown. Streetcars like San Francisco rumbled through the streets on wires. A modern town hall building in the shape of an eye from above was profiled. Parks with ponds, beautiful golf courses and gardens were shown. The Rogers Center came into view and the film was viewed at high speed as the domed roof opened. The camera switched to a night view showing the bright lights, large crowds and thrills of the Blue Jays Baseball team rounding the bases. The same location now hosted the Toronto Argonauts of the Canadian Football League. The stadium was filled with large men in uniforms, cheerleaders and crowds. Continuing on with the sports theme the camera zoomed in on an oversized woodpecker; a piece of art located outside of the Air Canada Center. This is the home of the Toronto Maple Leafs NHL ice hockey team. Toronto is known as an ice hockey city. The film showed the flashing blades, white ice, slashing sticks and pucks flying into heavily armored goaltenders. More images were shown of white uniforms and blue maple leafs adorned by players of the Toronto Maple Leafs ice hockey team. The ice disappears and makes way for the hard court. Now showing was the Toronto Raptors Basketball NBA team exciting the crowd in their purple and silver uniforms. The film cuts away to the Hockey Hall of Fame with large silver trophies and old hockey jerseys. Finally the movie moves to a night scene showing the city with its traffic, bars and active club scene. It was now back to daylight and the helicopter had moved west to Ontario Place and BMO field, home of the Toronto Football Club from the MLS. Further West and the wineries of Niagara are profiled. The camera lingers on bottles of wine and Ice wine. The promotional film then moves on to the spectacular Niagara Falls. Various views of the falls are shown, the Maid of the Mist boat ride and the casino with its nightly shows. The short film wets Beth's appetite. Toronto looks modern, clean and exciting.

"Wow, what a place," thought Beth.

The Canadian national anthem completed the film with the obligatory shot of a Mountie in uniform and waving red Maple Leaf flag.

"This could be fun," thought Beth.

She had left the hotel booking to the travel concierge at The Astor Hotel. She hoped he had found her a place right in the heart of the city. She could sense her excitement growing as she traveled to Toronto. When she started her journey to India she felt a combination of excitement and fear. She realized that she had matured and the fear had gone. What remained was just pure excitement. Beth quickly became grounded as she reminded herself that Subra was on a time limit. She was in Toronto to find the portal not to be a tourist. Flight 5059 Jet Airways to Toronto landed at Lester B. Pearson airport on time at 10.05pm at terminal 1. After leaving the plane Beth walked up the boarding ramp and into the terminal. She had a long walk down a glass-enclosed corridor. At the end of the corridor she followed the other passengers and walked through many twisting corridors.

"How far away is this place?" thought Beth.

Beth continued walking through corridors and moving escalators. Finally she passed through a set of glass doors and entered into the customs hall. It was a large rectangular hall with a bank of customs officers facing inwards towards the oncoming crowd. Beth walked towards a booth and stopped at a red line painted on the floor. The customs officer could see Beth but ignored her for a while. He looked up and motioned for her to join him. Beth walked forward; he had a dark uniform with silver buttons, badges and epaulettes. He was wearing a scowl as Beth presented her customs form and passport for inspection.

"Where are you coming from?" he demanded looking at her passport?

"Kolkata, India."

"What were you doing there?" he asked.

"None of your god damn business," thought Beth. "Vacation," she said.

"What are you doing here?" he asked.

"Vacation."

"You like to vacation. How long are you staying?" he said with a glance upwards.

"A couple of weeks," said Beth.

"Got any alcohol or cigarettes?"

"No," said Beth.

She was handed back her passport with a fresh ink stamp applied to one of the pages. He wrote some letters in red ink on her customs form. Both were returned to her and she was dismissed.

"Have a good visit."

Beth moved through the customs booths and reached a man in uniform sitting on a chair and looking thoroughly bored. He seemed to be looking at the customs forms. Beth handed him her form and started to walk away.

"You keep this for now," he barked.

Considering Canadians are known for their politeness she hoped this was just airport protocol. She smiled as she envisaged customs training and how miserable that place must be. Beth walked down another escalator and into a large room with luggage claim carousels. She walked past them and saw an exit sign. Two uniformed guards flanked the exit while collecting customs forms. Beth gave her customs form to a young man who checked the hand written code. She walked through two sets of sliding doors and into the greeting area. Toronto's greeting area was nothing like the chaos experienced in India. She walked out onto an elevated platform with exit ramps either side. There were about 30 people waiting to greet passengers as they came through the door. Beth moved down the ramp to her left and walked towards another exit door. As she approached the door she saw an illuminated sign for Limo she headed left along another corridor towards the sign.

"This place is a maze of corridors," thought Beth.

She saw a foreign exchange money counter and stopped. After changing her Indian money into Canadian dollars she continued towards the Limo sign. She reached a sliding door and exited from the terminal. It was dark but the artificial lights cast long shadows. She walked through the exit door and turned left where a long line of shiny black Limousines were parked. Drivers in uniforms were milling about. Beth approached the lineup and the trunk of the front car popped open as if to greet her. A driver moved out of the front seat and greeted Beth with a smile.

Chapter 11

The Prettiest Skyline in North America

L imousine Miss" he inquired? Beth nodded and he took her backpack and placed it into the trunk. The trunk closed with a thud and he held the rear door open. Beth noticed his black uniform and the smart brimmed hat that he wore. He was older than Beth, in his early 40's. Beth slipped into the back seat and immediately noticed how wide they were after riding around in Sanjeev's taxi. The seats were made from luxurious black leather and the inside of the Lincoln town car was classy.

The driver got in and turned to look at Beth. "Where to Miss?" he asked.

Beth had looked at her booking details just before landing. She had read the itinerary given to her at The Astor Hotel. "The InterContinental Hotel, Front Street, Toronto."

"Thank you Miss, I know it," said the driver in a courteous tone. "May I ask where you're flying in from?"

"India," said Beth in a dog-tired voice.

"That's a long flight, settle back and just enjoy the view, I should have you at your hotel in about thirty minutes," said the driver sensing that Beth was tired and not very chatty.

The drive into Toronto was swift, the seats were comfortable, and the car powerful and smooth. It was dark and the highways seemed busy to Beth she had not seen roads like these in real life. Near the airport the roads seemed to have about six or seven lanes each way. The driver expertly maneuvered the Limo in what seemed a due South direction. Beth confirmed this by looking at the compass indicator illuminated within the rear view mirror. Beth looked at the magazines tucked into the back of the front passenger seat. She did not feel like reading. She looked at the dashboard and except for a pair of folded reading glasses it was bare. No Lord Ganesha proudly removing obstacles. There was something odd about the drive into town.

"Yes, it was deftly quiet," thought Beth. Beth could not hear the powerful engine; the roads were smooth and no blaring horns. She had become accustomed to the horns she missed them now. Beth stared out of the window as they left a large highway called the 427 and joined another called the Gardiner Expressway.

"This is the main artery into the city. On your right is Lake Ontario; we'll drive along its shoreline until we enter the city. At this time of night you'll get a beautiful view of the skyline and the CN Tower. Some say Toronto has one of the prettiest skylines in North America because of the lake and the shape of the buildings huddled around the Tower," said the driver in a proud tone. Beth strained to see the city but all she could see was the black water of the lake and many lakeside condominium towers.

"When we get past this tower complex, you'll get a beautiful view of the city. I take it this is your first time to Toronto Miss?" he asked.

"Yes," answered Beth as the highway rounded the building affording a stunning view of the downtown city at night.

The city appeared to jut out into the lake with skyscrapers that looked about 5 inches tall. The skyscrapers seemed to be grouped around the tower and a large green and white object. At the side of the road were steep angled grass banks but they were unusual. Corporations had paid to advertise on these roadside garden beds. The advertisements were made from natural hedges and shrubs forming a garden like appearance. Corporate logos were made from beautifully manicured plants. Bright white spotlights illuminated them. The centerpiece dominating the skyline was the majestic CN Tower. It seemed huge, at least a third taller than the tallest skyscraper. The driver was right, the city looked beautiful. It cast an image that reflected its many lights and colors into the lake, which looked like a mirror.

"Why is it called the CN Tower?" Beth asked starting to come to life.

"It was built by the Canadian National railway company. I don't think they own it now but for many years it was the tallest building in the world. You have to go up there if you have time," he said.

"What's up there?" asked Beth.

"An observation deck, a restaurant, a night club, even a glass floor to stand on and an outside elevator ride, it's really cool," he said.

"Sounds fun, I will," said Beth.

She noticed that the road had three lanes full of traffic snaking their way into the city. The city looked larger now, the skyscrapers were looking huge and the

CN Tower was starting to disappear into the night sky. Beth saw a large modern windmill with three blades motionless. The Limo sped into the city passing billboards advertising cars, cell phones, new condominiums and banks. Some of the billboards had moving pictures illuminated through large flat screens. She suddenly noticed that the road was elevated. She was high in the sky passing condominiums at the third and fourth floor level. Below the road was another road streaming two layers of traffic into the city. It looked modern and Beth was starting to feel a twinge of excitement.

"This was more like it, not at all like Haworth," she thought.

The Limo took an exit to the right and glided down an off ramp back to street level. People were walking around as she noticed a sight that she recognized; it was the Rogers Centre home of the Blue Jays. It was much larger than she had imagined and the white roof was illuminated with green lights. Next to the dome was the mighty CN Tower; she was practically underneath it looking straight up. It was indescribable, her heart raced. The Limo stopped at a traffic light and people crossed the street in an orderly manner. No one banged on the window and she could not see any beggars. This was not India. The Limo headed North for a couple of blocks and she passed the Air Canada center. The taxi turned left onto Front Street and the majestic Royal York hotel came into view. It looked a little odd proudly positioned within a modern city of steel and glass. The grey stone hotel rose high above the street as the Limo whisked by. It was once the tallest building in Toronto. The Limo pulled a U-turn.

"This is your hotel Miss, we're here." The Limo pulled up alongside the curb and the driver turned to look at Beth. "Forty-five dollars please Miss."

Beth pulled out a fifty and a five passing it to the outstretched hand of the driver. "Keep the change," she said.

"Thank you Miss," said the driver rushing to collect her backpack from the trunk.

Beth stepped out onto the sidewalk, it was still warm but the wind was cool coming in off the lake. She thanked the driver and slung her backpack over her shoulder. The Limo started to pull away into traffic and onto the next fare.

"Can I help you with your bag Miss?" said a friendly voice.

Beth turned to see a doorman dressed in black shoes, black trousers, a black tunic with silver buttons and a pillbox hat. He stood dutifully under one of two glass awnings. They were shaped like a large glass umbrella or perhaps the petals of a flower. Spotlights were sunk into the ground and lit the canopies.

"No thanks I'm fine," said Beth.

"Checking in Miss?" inquired the doorman.

"Yes," said Beth looking around.

"Welcome to the InterContinental please follow me," he said holding onto a large silver handle attached to a glass door.

Beth walked through into the hotel. To her left were a couple of steps leading to an area with stainless steel railings and a sloping glass roof. To the right lay the reception area. It looked large compared to The Astor Hotel. There appeared to be a lower level connected by two large moving escalators cut through the floor leading down to conference rooms. The floor was made of shiny beige marble and tall dark chocolate colored pillars. She followed the doorman to the check in counter. The check in counter was high technology with brightly lit panels of white lights illuminating the area. An oval shaped piece of richly colored wood seemed to float above the desk peppered with bright pot lights. The counter was a combination of brushed steel and shiny burgundy marble, all very modern. Behind the counter on the wall was an illuminated splash of yellow, white, orange and indigo. It looked thoroughly artsy. Three attendants were positioned behind the counter. A young man was talking to a lady checking in. Two women were standing at separate workstations looking into black flat screen computer monitors. The doorman led Beth to the first woman attendant. Beth was greeted with a large welcoming smile.

"Checking in Miss?"

"Yes," said Beth.

She noticed the woman was wearing a dark grey jacket, white blouse and a gold nametag. Maria had dark long curly hair swept back away from her face and held in place with silver clips.

"If I can see some photo ID and credit card please?" asked Maria.

Beth handed over her passport, "I'll pay by cash," she said.

Maria typed into the computer she was suspicious of any guest saying that they would pay with cash. She pulled up Beth's reservation from the name on the passport. A pop up window alerted Maria to some special instructions. Maria looked up and smiled at Beth, "I'm sorry I won't be a minute, my systems a little slow tonight please excuse me," she said buying time. The attached special instructions informed Maria that Beth was an "A" type guest. This status was reserved for the wealthy, celebrities and high-ranking VIP's. The instructions also informed Maria that the room and all incidentals had been prepaid using an authorized corporate account. A letter was waiting in the back pigeonhole. When Miss Martindale checks in she should be given the letter marked to her attention. She should be informed that it is from a Mr. Wilks. Maria turned and looked down, only two envelopes pushed out of the pigeonholes. She grabbed the nearest and it was marked "Miss Martindale." Maria turned to look at Beth who looked tired and irritable.

"I'm sorry this is taking so long Miss Martindale but the file had specific instructions upon your arrival," explained Maria. "This is for you, it's from a Mr. Wilks," she said handing over the envelope. "Is one room key sufficient?" inquired Maria.

"Yes, one's fine," said Beth half asleep.

Maria completed the online registration and looked up at Beth. "Here's your room key, you're in room 732, a city view. Your room and incidentals is all prepaid Miss Martindale on corporate account. Just let us know when you need to check out. Sorry for the delay, would you like assistance with your bag Miss Martindale?" asked Maria.

"No thank you, I'm tired, I'd just like to go to my room," stammered Beth feeling dirty and tired.

"Of course Miss, the elevators are to your right just before you reach the Azure bar and lounge, have a good night's rest," said Maria.

"Thank you," said Beth.

She headed for the elevators stopping to look at the impressive sloping glass and steel roof. As she looked into the Azure lounge she could hear gentle music accompanied by laughter and eating. She saw a narrow corridor with a thin area rug. There was a dark wood frame surrounding metal elevator doors. Above each door were modern oblong shaped lights. Beth pressed the elevator button and a soft pinging noise announced the arrival of an elevator. She rode to the seventh floor observing in a mirror how tired and disheveled she looked after more than 24 hours of traveling. It did not take her long to find room 732.

Beth swiped the card key and entered placing the card into the slot in the wall. It was a tasteful room quite modern in its decor. The carpet was chocolate brown with cream colored waving stripes. The bed was King sized and had crisp white sheets and a beige duvet. Multiple pillows were stacked against a high headboard made of dark richly colored lacquered wood. Either side stood a square table and drawers. They each sported a tall metal lamp whose bright white shades contrasted starkly against the dark wood. Two brown comfy armchairs surrounded a small glass table with flowers and magazines placed upon it. A dark colored desk supported a thin screen LCD television. The window had a window seat and Beth could see the bright lights of city skyscrapers through the blinds.

She approached the window and closed the heavy set of drapes blocking out the city and the lights. Beth locked the door, dropped her backpack and got undressed. She threw her clothes in a pile on one of the armchairs. Naked, she walked into the bathroom. It consisted of marble, glass and mirrors. She grabbed the white terry cloth robe and slipped into it. Beth was getting used to hotel living but it was starting to lose its appeal. She grabbed the envelope from the chair and fell back onto the bed.

"Wow, this is a soft bed," thought Beth.

She opened the envelope discarding the outer layer onto the bedside table. She opened the folded letter. The letter was a printed version of an email sent to the hotel. On the top of the letter was a corporate logo. The logo displayed the head of a snarling tiger with the words "The Generosity Account" underneath. Beth looked at the tigers face. She recalled Aklina calling Anwar her tiger. She recalled the tigers guarding the palace at Mysore. She looked down at the letter.

Dear Ms. Martindale.

I received a phone call from Ms. Kaigara Tanaka from Swan Property Investments inquiring about your whereabouts, credentials and intention to meet with her in Toronto. We have not had a chance to formally introduce ourselves but I do know that Anwar has informed you that I am a trusted servant to the Generosity Account and to your new responsibilities. At the bottom of this letter I have included my contact details with phone number, mobile, fax and email address. Please, do not hesitate to contact me at any time, day or night. I took the liberty of contacting The Astor Hotel and they have informed me of your travel arrangements. I assumed that you were heading to Toronto to meet with Ms. Tanaka. I hope you don't mind. I've arranged a meeting for you with Ms. Tanaka tomorrow (Thursday) for 11am.

Ms. Kaigara Tanaka,
CEO, Swan Property Investments,
Royal Bank Plaza,
Suite 323 (about a 10 minute walk from your hotel).

Her calendar is quite full and I feared without the right context you may have been screened and kept waiting unnecessarily. The Generosity Account is Swan's largest customer by far, making you her most important client by a country mile. Ask her for the latest recommendations on the portfolio these are due. She provides a very good return and although she's a demanding person we've been pleased with her services.

Beth, I urge you to consult with me before making any immediate investment decisions but as always your word is final. I would like the opportunity to brief you on the strategy before you instigate any changes.
Kaigara can be a little direct. Don't let her push you around. We have not met but Anwar has told me that you are a strong willed individual. I like that and look forward to working with you. I have arranged for the Generosity Account to pick up your expenses while in Toronto. Call me for assistance with onward flights or other hotels and expenses.

I look forward to serving you and meeting with you upon your return to England.

Mr. David Wilks
CEO Blue Phoenix Group

Beth placed the letter on the side table and walked over to her backpack. She searched its contents until she found Lord Ganesha. She walked back to the bed and placed him on the nightstand close to her pillow. With relative ease Beth fell into a deep sleep. The bed was large and comfortable.

"Where are you?" she thought.

Beth had been looking forward to talking with Subra she had missed their discussions. Beth scanned the energy patterns as best she could. She searched for that familiar signature. It took a while but she concentrated and found a weak signal that she recognized. She honed in on it and amplified the energy trace.

"Hello, I kind of missed you," thought Beth hoping to hear Subra's familiar voice.

"When your heart is in your dream, no request is too extreme," said Subra.

"Ah Jiminy Cricket, a good opening line," thought Beth.

"Is your heart in finding the portal?" asked Subra.

"It is, it is. I'll find it for you I promised you that. I know I don't have much time, is this your subtle way of telling me that?"

"This is a team effort. If you can't put people up, please don't put them down. We're in this together Beth I need you to know that," said Subra.

"I do my friend, I do. Don't worry I'll find your portal, just as I found Rose. I'm going to find out why Kaigara and the Shell are connected. It's going to lead us in the right direction," thought Beth.

"The person who makes no mistakes does not usually make anything," said Subra.

"I've made mistakes already but I don't doubt I'll come through this with you intact."

"Success is an inside job," said Subra fading.

"This is starting to wear you out isn't it?" asked Beth.

"The more I communicate the more energy it takes from me Beth," said Subra in a stronger tone.

"You can't tell me how long I have but even Anwar knew he didn't have long. Can you give me any idea?" asked Beth in a concerned tone.

"Beth, I'm sorry I don't know, just find the portal as quickly as you can and I'll hang on as long as I can, deal?" asked Subra.

"Deal," responded Beth. "You know I'm stubborn and you know I'm not going to let you down. I don't know the answer yet but I will."

Subra paused and responded, "People don't really care how much you know until they know how much you care. I'm certain you care and I'm certain you'll find the portal. Beth, trust your instincts."

"Every time I chat with you Subra, you give me something to think about. I replay your words during the day and they give me inspiration. Some people march to the beat of a different drummer and some polka!" thought Beth.

"Beth tomorrow is a big day for you. I firmly believe there are messages for us. We'll need to be open to hear them. You'll need to ask questions and listen carefully. You'll meet people more worldly wise than yourself but remember I'm with you. I know you can make a breakthrough tomorrow, I can feel it. Eighty percent of success is showing up," said Subra.

"I'll get us moving again tomorrow," thought Beth. "I need to leave you now and dream, I can sense that I'm wearing you out, conserve your energy."

"Never compromise yourself. You are all you've got," said Subra fading away.

Beth entered into a dream state almost immediately. She enjoyed talking with Subra and felt sad that

her deep conversations were now reduced to snippets of time. Beth found herself in the middle of her
dream. She was restrained and locked in a tower. She
was wearing a beautiful fitted sundress and was being
kissed by the fit man on the plane. He grinned as she
woke and opened her eyes.

"Subra's going to think I'm a sex maniac," she
thought as she struggled to recognize objects in her
room. "Toronto," she muttered as she lay back and
scanned the dimly lit room. Beth glanced at the heavy
dark curtains blocking the natural sunlight. She
turned her neck to stare at the alarm clock with its
large red luminous numbers. 10.05am was displayed
on the clock. Beth stretched and smiled, "I must have
been tired," she thought.

Her smile dropped quickly when she realized that
she had less than an hour before she was due to meet
Kaigara. Beth sprung out of bed and ran for the shower
throwing her robe to the floor. She turned on the shower
and brushed her teeth while the water warmed up. The
shower kicked into life with great force, the water pressure was fierce. Beth opened the glass door, stepped
inside and showered. She dressed quickly in her trusty
jeans, yellow tee shirt and runners. Once her ponytail
was in place she was ready to go. She locked the safe
and looked at the letter from Mr. Wilks.

*I hope you don't mind. I've arranged a
meeting for you with Ms. Tanaka tomorrow
(Thursday) for 11am.*

Ms. Kaigara Tanaka,
CEO, Swan Property Investments,
Royal Bank Plaza,
*Suite 323 (about a 10 minute walk from
your hotel).*

She tucked the note into her jeans pocket. Her last superstitious act was to take Lord Ganesha from the nightstand and gently place him into her backpack. Beth locked her room door and quickly entered the elevator. A Chinese looking girl about 22 years old held onto her boyfriend. She had a fresh cute face her loose long black hair flowed freely framing intense brown sparkling eyes. She wore small black flats, Lululemon yoga pants and a cute blue Point Zero scoop neck top. He looked Caucasian with curly brown hair, an unshaven look, strong jaw and an athletic figure. He wore Puma sneakers, worn jeans and a black Lacoste golf shirt. They were clearly in love, as they could barely keep apart. Beth felt that twinge inside again. She needed someone to share her life with, not just a voice in her head. The elevator ride made her feel uncomfortable and she was relieved when she walked quickly to the main entrance. Beth walked into a beautiful Toronto morning, the sun was shining and the traffic was buzzing along Front Street.

It was about 10.45am and she turned to ask the door man, "I've been told that the Royal Bank Plaza isn't too far from here, is that right?"

"That's right, all you need to do is just continue East down Front Street," he said pointing in the direction, "for about three blocks or so. The Royal Bank Plaza is the gold shiny building on the North side of the street," he said motioning to the other side of the street. "You can't miss it, look for the mirrored gold tinted glass."

Beth remembered the short video of Toronto on the Jet Airways flight. She recalled seeing a gold colored skyscraper glistening in the bright sunshine. So that was where she was going, to the Royal Bank Plaza. Beth thanked the doorman and started to walk East along Front Street. She passed restaurants getting ready for the lunchtime crowd and came to a busy intersection. She waited for the light to change and squinted into the strong sunlight. On the North side stood a building that did not fit into its surroundings. Beth saw a tall stone building with a grand entrance complete with red carpet and a bellhop dressed in a red coat and tall black top hat. The Royal York Hotel stood proud, a symbol of a bygone age. The green copper roof pointed to a time when builders used different materials. The building looked impressive and Beth was caught staring at the stone gargoyles as the light changed. A swell of people moved across the intersection given permission by a small green light. Beth was swept along with the movement. It was all very civil, in the midst of cars and crowds of people the traffic signals were totally obeyed. Cars waited patiently for pedestrians to cross and move out of the way.

"There's that Canadian politeness," thought Beth.

She crossed the intersection and passed a hot dog stand. She walked along and stared at the full might of the Royal York hotel. The sidewalk opened up and she could see a statue of a man inside an iron sphere with metal birds flying around him. This was Union Station she could read the signage. For being in the heart of downtown Toronto she could not see one piece of litter and marveled at how clean it was. As Beth continued to walk the first hint of gold rushed into her eyes. The strong sun caught the reflection of the gold particles embedded within the reflective glass. The Royal Bank Plaza came into view. Beth saw people walking across the road where a wide median was placed containing trees and flowerbeds. She saw a gap in the traffic; she - was looking to her right, the wrong way! She walked to the median and crossed the street looking both ways. Looking right this time she spotted another gap, she quickly crossed the two lanes and stepped onto the

opposite sidewalk of Front Street. Beth saw a revolving door that led into the front lobby of the Plaza. She
entered and could feel the cool air conditioning on her
cheeks. She had been unaware of how hot it really
was outside. It was not India but it was warm. Beth
reached into her backpack and retrieved her meeting
instructions. She glanced at her watch, 10.53am.

"Right on time," said Beth to herself.

She glanced at the instruction sheet, 11am meeting, Ms. Kaigara Tanaka, Swan Property Investments,
Royal Bank Plaza, Suite 323.

"323, that was my room number at The Astor Hotel,"
thought Beth, as she walked towards the elevator
bank. She heard herself mumble, "There are no coincidences." She thought of her promise to Subra and
how she needed to find the portal quickly before she
lost him. She hoped the Kaigara-Shell connection was
a real lead and not a silly coincidence. "There are no
coincidences," she told herself again. Stepping into the
elevator she joined two men dressed smartly in suits,
ties and shiny shoes. Beth felt a little underdressed
in her runners, tight fitting jeans, yellow tee shirt and
black backpack.

One of the men asked Beth, "What floor would you
like?"

"Three please," answered Beth not raising her
eyes.

She saw the number 3 illuminate on a panel located
to her side. The doors opened and she could see a sign
indicating the third floor. Beth stepped out into a narrow hallway with elevator doors both sides. The floor
was black marble with white streaks running through
it. She thought of the Marble Palace. A sign on the wall
with gold lettering reflected the light. "Swan Property
Investments" was displayed with an arrow pointing to
the right. Beth turned right towards a double wooden

door with glass panels. She could see a reception desk and the outline of a woman through the glass panels. She opened the door and stepped into the reception area. It was carpeted in a luxurious deep cream carpet. Inside she could see a cream colored leather couch with antique wooden side tables. Beautiful fern plants were thriving in Chinese pots. Displayed in special cases were Inuit stone sculptures. Hanging on the walls were original oil paintings encased in large gold intricate frames. Beth walked confidently towards the reception desk where a middle aged woman stared into a computer monitor. She glanced upwards over her half cut glasses to meet Beth's stare.

"Good morning and welcome to Swan Property Investments how may I help you?" she asked in a professional tone with a crisp English accent.

"My name's Beth Martindale, I'm here to see Kaigara," said Beth making it sound like she had known her for years.

"We've been expecting you Miss Martindale, would you like to take a seat she'll be with you shortly," answered the receptionist. "Would you like a coffee, tea or water while you wait?" she inquired.

"No thank you I'm fine," said Beth.

Beth placed her backpack on the ground next to the sofa and watched it sink into the deep pile carpet. She had noticed the Swan logo on the reception desk. It was gold set against a black background. Behind the receptionist was a sign in gold lettering "Swan Property Investments" illuminated by a high intensity spotlight. She glanced around and saw a table displaying trophies and awards. Some were in the shape of a Swan. She did not sit as instructed she remained standing. She looked at the painting hanging above the couch. Beautiful art emit their own type of energy, it reflects the talent and time that went into its creation. Copies and reprints do not harbor such positive energy. Beth was drawn to the painting; it was original oil on canvas. The scene was an old tree standing on hard barren rocks, to the left was blue water and through the trunk and branches you could see the sky. The sky was cloudy with snippets of blue. Shafts of light could be seen streaming down through the clouds onto the water. The blue water had white crested waves as they lapped against the rocky shoreline.

Beth did not fall in love with the painting but its energy was strong and clear, magnetic. To the right of the painting was a small brass colored plaque mounted on the wall, the size of a matchbox. It read, "Old Pine, McGregor Bay, Arthur Lismer, Group of Seven."

"I was lucky to get that one, I paid more than I wanted to," said a polished voice from behind her.

Beth spun around to see a stunning looking woman. This had to be Kaigara, she looked exotic, and her dark long hair was slicked back tight in a hair clip. She had clear skin and high cheekbones her face was striking. A small nose slightly upturned with a narrow bridge that separated deep brown eyes. Kaigara wore a dark blue satin blouse that matched small blue earrings. She wore a black belt around her slender waist accenting a black pencil skirt that showed off her curves. Shiny black heels completed the outfit. Before Beth could take it all in Kaigara had approached her and extended a heavily jeweled hand.

"Welcome to Toronto Miss Martindale, how was your flight?"

"Fine thank you and please call me Beth," said Beth in a bit of a haze.

"Kaigara," she said shaking Beth's hand firmly. Beth noticed Kaigara's eyes immediately fall to the little fox tattoo. She watched her expression change instantly as she registered disapproval, "Please follow me."

Beth followed Kaigara through a large wooden door with gold handles; it led to a hallway with offices either side. The interior was made of wood, expensive looking wood. More oil paintings adorned the walls. The hallway opened to a wider area and a lady sitting at a desk.

"Can I get you anything?" she said rising out of her seat with a smile.

"No thanks I'm fine," said Beth.

"Get me a ginger tea, Karen please," said Kaigara sharply.

"Right away," said Karen heading off in a different direction.

They moved into Kaigara's office. She had an impressive office, bookshelves made of deep rich colored dark wood. Books, statues, awards and photographs adorned the shelves. Her desk faced the door; Beth could see a computer screen, a pile of papers and a high backed leather chair. Behind the desk the floor to ceiling windows offered a view of Union Station and beyond Lake Ontario. Kaigara motioned Beth to sit at the shiny meeting table made from one piece of solid wood. The chairs were heavy as Beth moved one back from the table and sat. Kaigara sat and leaned in with her elbows on the table and her hands clasped supporting her chin.

"Tell me about Anwar, what happened?" she asked.

Beth leaned back in her chair and thought, "Be sly Beth, be sly, you're completely out of your element." "Unfortunately Anwar passed away, he'd not been feeling well for a while now and knew he didn't have long. His cough had got worse and he'd been to hospital. He was a private man and didn't really talk about his illness much," said Beth.

Kaigara was just about to ask another question when Karen entered the room, she walked over to the table balancing a teacup and saucer. Kaigara leaned back and positioned a small coaster in front of her. Karen placed the cup on the coaster, smiled at Beth and started to leave the room. Beth studied Kaigara; she had a Pink aura (materialism, goal-setting, hard work) with bands of Red (sensuality, vitality, aggression) and a trace of Yellow (creativity, intellect). Beth noticed how smart Karen looked and felt a little shoddy. Kaigara was waiting for Karen to leave when Beth took the initiative.

"Please excuse my appearance, I'd packed thinking I was traveling in India not Toronto."

"Oh, I totally understand Miss Martindale; you've traveled a long distance. I'm just glad that you could come and speak with me in person," said Kaigara convincingly.

Beth was not buying it. "Call me Beth, please," she said forcefully.

"Beth it is," responded Kaigara.

"Kaigara is an interesting name," said Beth feeling a little more confident and trying to get a clue for the portal.

"Yes, it's Japanese, I have my Mother to thank for that," she said. "So Beth we have an hour today what would you like to cover?" asked Kaigara getting down to business and sliding her business card across the table.

"I'm afraid I don't have one yet," explained Beth looking at the business card. "I'm now heading the Generosity Account and would like to know more about the work you do."

"I've spoken to David Wilks to check your credentials Beth, I know who you represent. I also know that you spoke with Rose Akhter of the Reika Foundation in Kolkata. So you've seen some of our work, that was my Mother's foundation," said Kaigara. "Anwar never donated to the foundation because he said that he wanted to keep our relationship clean. We manage property investments for Anwar, or we did. We used to recommend to him what, where and when to buy. We managed the property and the tenants. He was very hands off," said Kaigara looking a little defensive.

"So I'm heading that now, I've not had a chance to speak with Mr. Wilks yet but Anwar has informed me that he's a professional," responded Beth.

"Mr. Wilks audits everything. Anwar was a special client to us Beth, you need to know that our families go back a long way. I have clients who demand a return, that's all. Anwar was family, yes he wanted a return but he also wanted to be fair and honorable to the people who lived in his properties. You may think it would be easy to scam a trusting soul like Anwar but Mr. Wilks had an eagle eye. I want you to feel that you can trust me also," explained Kaigara.

"How do your families know each other?" asked Beth.

"Once you have a certain net worth these individuals deal with the same people. I would advise Anwar to sell certain properties and buy others in different parts of the world from the proceeds. He started small and amassed a considerable fortune. All his assets drive a continuous revenue stream on a monthly basis. He would bank this into the Generosity Account and then simply give it away to needy causes. This is why I'm surprised with your visit. I thought that you would want to look at the portfolio that Swan manages for you? In the past Anwar was aware of the Reika Foundation but would not want to mix his business dealings," said Kaigara.

"Well, I'm not Anwar," said Beth feeling stronger as she fixed her green eyes on Kaigara.

"Clearly not," responded Kaigara.

"What do you have for me to take away on the current portfolio and your recommendations?" asked Beth.

Kaigara rose and walked over to her desk. Beth noticed how slim she was. How Anwar was connected to a woman like this was inconceivable. She pictured Anwar sitting on his dirty bench in the Yorkshire sun rubbing his soiled stained hands and growing his Roses.

As she turned to deliver the folder Beth asked, "Did you ever meet Anwar?"

Kaigara was taken by surprise, "No, I spoke with him a few times, most of my dealings were with David."

Beth asked, "David?"

"Sorry, David Wilks, Mr. Wilks," explained Kaigara. Kaigara slid a glossy folder containing papers over the desk to Beth. "Anwar never asked for these but if you wish to see them we will simply ship another copy. Mr. Wilks usually vets them and I presume talked them over with Anwar. Mr. Wilks was the one sending the instructions."

Beth glanced at the black shiny folder; it had a large gold swan logo in the center. She opened the front cover and slipped Kaigara's business card into the folder. "I will need to talk with Mr. Wilks when I return to England. We may or may not change the routine, I haven't decided yet," stated Beth feeling more in control.

She wore jeans and a yellow tee shirt but it mattered little, she had a huge fund and clever people backing her. She did not know Mr. Wilks but she liked him already. "Tell me more about the work that Rose Akhter and the Reika Foundation is doing to help the women in the Sonagachi," asked Beth.

"The Golden Tree, it sounds so beautiful but clearly it's a desperate place. My Mother founded Reika. When she visited Kolkata she was moved by the stories and what she saw. My Mother was born in Yokohama just south of Tokyo. She was raised in both Yokohama and Toronto, like me," said Kaigara.

"Yokohama, the magazine article, there are no coincidences," thought Beth.

"In Yokohama there's a majestic ship, it's located in the harbor. My Mother loves this ship it represents everything that is magical in this world to her and represents hope. She admires that ship. It's called the "Swan of the Pacific." This is why I chose the name and the Swan logo for my company. Beth, they really do great work," Kaigara explained. "Maybe one day, if you're lucky enough, you'll get to see the ship in Yokohama at night, it's a wondrous sight."

Beth felt a flushing of her cheeks and the faint swell of energy flooding her memory, "I've never been to Yokohama or the Kanagawa Prefecture. I've never had the chance to walk the Kishamichi Promenade or crane my neck upwards to look at the Landmark Tower. I've not marveled at the neon coated Ferris wheel overlooking Tokyo Bay. If I should ever get that chance I'll make it a priority to gaze upon the floodlit white hull of the Nippon-Maru, the Swan of the Pacific," said Beth holding her eye contact steady. "Thank you Subra," thought Beth.

"I'm sorry if I sounded, er, sounded," Kaigara struggled to find the right words.

"Just don't under estimate me, that could be bad for both of us." said Beth feeling like she just gained the upper hand.

"Agreed," said Kaigara looking downward at the table. A polite knock at the door broke an uncomfortable silence. The door opened and it was Karen looking like she wished she were somewhere else.

"I'm sorry to disturb you but your Mother's here for her lunch appointment," she said sheepishly before leaving.

"I know we have to end here but I'd like to ask one thing. Why did your Mother call you Kaigara? What's the significance?" asked Beth.

"That's the second time you've asked me, why don't you ask her in person on the way out?" offered Kaigara.

Kaigara thought lunch with Mother was not going to be great but it was better than continuing this conversation. She had talked to Beth like a young uneducated girl only to be surprised at her intelligence and preparation. Now she looked like the amateur and she felt embarrassed. Anwar would not give his operation to an idiot, and by the sound of it he didn't.

"Thanks I will," said Beth rising and walking to the door with Kaigara.

They traveled down the hall and into the reception area. Sat on the couch was an elderly woman dressed in smart clothes, pearls and pastel colors. Her hair was short, black with wisps of grey. "Very cultured and refined," thought Beth, obviously Kaigara's Mother from her beautiful looks. As they entered the reception area she stood and stared at Beth.

"Mom I need five more minutes then we can leave," said Kaigara quickly, "this is Beth Martindale she's the new Anwar." Kaigara turned and went back to her office.

"Sakura Tanaka, pleased to meet you Beth," said the smiling woman extending her hand. She was taller than Kaigara and just as slim. "The new Anwar? What happened to Anwar did he retire?" inquired Sakura.

"I'm sorry," said Beth, "Anwar was sick for some time and finally passed away last week." There was genuine sadness in her face as she sat quickly.

"Oh my dear Anwar," she said.

"I'm sorry," said Beth realizing she was a bit blunt, "I didn't realize you two were close."

"I've known Anwar for a very long time and consider him to be one of my dearest friends. My husband will be devastated at this news. Are you a relative of his?" asked Sakura.

"A dear friend selected to carry on his good work," explained Beth. Beth looked at Sakura bent over double with her head in her hands she was genuinely upset. She could see Sakura had an Orange aura (emotion, health) but she had strong spokes of Green (healing, love of nature).

"What are you doing for dinner tonight, if you're free I'd like you to join me?" asked Sakura.

"I'm probably going to skip dinner, my body clock is still messed up, thank you anyway," replied Beth.

Sakura was wearing an expression that pierced Beth; it was obvious she really needed to talk.

"You seem disappointed, is there something you need to say to me?" asked Beth.

"It's important, but not here, I'd like to talk with you in private. I think it'll be worth your while, but I do understand that you're tired. I'd like to meet with you tonight. Tomorrow I'm leaving to join my husband in Yokohama," explained Sakura. She looked desperate and upset.

"Perhaps we can talk later over drinks, my hotel has a decent lobby bar?" offered Beth.

"That would be great, I'd really like to talk with you about Anwar and get to know you a little better. You must be an extraordinary woman for Anwar to give you the reins of his business," said Sakura brightening up her expression.

"Sure, and I'd like you to tell me why you chose the name Kaigara, it's an unusual name," prompted Beth.

"Shall we say 7.00pm in the lobby bar?" asked Sakura.

"Sounds good, I'm staying at the InterContinental on Front Street."

"I know it, see you at 7.00pm. I look forward to our chat."

Beth shook her hand firmly. Sakura did not let go and twisted her hand to expose Beth's wrist. The sly fox tattoo was in plain view and Sakura smiled a genuine smile before releasing Beth's hand. Beth left the reception area and walked out into the hallway. She noticed the difference between the thick carpet and the hard marble under her feet. She pressed the elevator button and waited for the elevator to arrive. Beth entered the empty elevator and rode to the ground floor. Glancing at her watch it was 12.05pm. Beth felt good about her meeting with Kaigara; she felt she held her own.

"Not bad for a scrappy lass from Yorkshire," she thought.

She felt even better about the interaction that she had with Sakura. It was a gorgeous day and the lunchtime crowd flooded out from every skyscraper. Beth headed south on Bay Street exploring, she wanted to see the lake. She walked through a noisy traffic tunnel and across a couple of intersections before she reached Queens Quay. This was the entertainment district on the shoreline of Lake Ontario. Beth could see a beautiful building with an inviting entrance. Inside were stores of all varieties selling, food, clocks, puppets, souvenirs, clothes, jewelry, watches and coffee. Beth browsed the stores of the old terminal building and exited from the back near the water. A wide promenade was bustling with people talking, whizzing by on rollerblades, walking the dog and showing off there taught bodies. The lake was calm and a green blue color. The sun was relentless and uniformed people were shouting in excited voices as they tried to sell harbor cruises. A tall ship was moored at the dock. It was not the Swan of the Pacific but the blue hull and three large masts belonged to the schooner "Kajama." A sign said it was launched in Spain 1930. Beth was enjoying the day and the light cool breeze blowing in from the lake. She continued along the boardwalk until she came across a crowd of people. On a cement floor clearing she saw about 20 people dressed in the same green colored tee shirts. At the front she recognized the distinct accent of an Irishman organizing the group, his grey hair blowing in the wind. Lines formed quickly and Beth perched on a low wall to watch. An announcer was piped in over the loudspeaker system.

"Ladies and gentlemen, boys and girls we have a special treat today. We are honored to welcome the Burlington, Ontario, chapter of the Taoist Tai Chi Society."

His voice made way for gentle oriental music and the group moved in harmony transitioning gracefully through the Tai Chi moves. Beth noticed a small-framed woman on the end of a row. She was a little over five feet tall with shoulder length blonde hair. She emitted tremendous positive energy. She was a beautiful graceful woman as she moved in time with the music and smiled to the crowd. Beth was attracted to the strong aura surrounding her; she stood out from the rest. Her energy was different from the group with strong spokes of Gold and Blue. Her inner strength and beauty shone through her vibrant aura. Beth felt a connection and caught her gaze as she smiled enthusiastically. Her green eyes flashed at Beth as she gracefully pushed an imaginary force away from her. The group moved and swayed to the music, it was calming and beautiful. Beth felt strong. The demonstration was over too soon. The crowd applauded before surrounding the performers. Beth hopped off the wall and headed back to the hotel. She saw a store that sold spirits and wine. She knew she could not drink but she felt compelled to go in and look around. The store had products from all over the world. Inside it was spacious and painted in a calming hunter green. A small label caught Beth's eye. She stooped to read it more closely, "Ice Wine." Beth recalled seeing this in the promotional film she watched on the plane. It showed people picking the grapes in the cold of winter. Leaving the grapes to be harvested in winter meant they would contain more natural sugar and would be sweeter. The result was the world's best dessert wine. In front of her was a row of miniature-sized bottles with enough for a single glass.

"Perfect," thought Beth. "I'm going to buy this, it's a good size for packing and when I find the portal I'll celebrate with some Ontario Ice Wine."

After buying the wine it was not long before the doorman was welcoming her back to the hotel. Beth paused at the gift shop and bought a small teddy bear dressed in a Mounties uniform. She moved towards the elevators noticing the lobby bar Azure on her left. It was about half full as the lunchtime crowd drifted back to work. Beth entered the hallway from the elevator on the 7th floor and headed for her room. Her mind wandered to the woman in the Tai Chi demonstration and how happy and energetic she looked with Gold spikes in her aura. She entered her room. The hotel cleaning staff had been, it was neat and smelt fresh. Beth reached into her backpack, moved the newly acquired items to one side and found Lord Ganesha. She placed him on the desk.

"I need you to make this conversation with Sakura go well my friend," said Beth looking at his elephant trunk. "I need you to help me find a clue that'll help me locate the portal. Not just for me but for Subra," she said placing her faith in the little wooden figure.

Beth was not tired perhaps it was the lake air, the strong sunlight or the determination she felt in finding the portal. She was ready to have her meeting with Sakura now. The afternoon was spent drawing a bath and soaking in her body shop Coconut Foaming Bath. She relaxed and concentrated on her breathing to calm her mind and reenergize. She replayed conversations with Sanjeev, Anwar, Amba, Mituraj, Rose and Kaigara over in her mind analyzing where she felt she could have done better.

She recalled the sights she had witnessed over the last few days. She remembered Anwar telling her that she would grow from this experience. She still felt dirty after the long flight from India the bath rejuvenated her. She was pleased that she found the time to buy the Foaming Bath product at Heathrow. Beth felt cleaner outside and more energized inside having spent some time reflecting. She watched some local television, the news and a couple of sitcoms. It was getting darker outside. The clouds had moved in and the city lights seemed brighter. A local news anchor informed Beth that the time was 6.45pm. Beth removed her robe and headed for the bathroom. She combed her hair and left it loose. She looked into the mirror at her face; she had changed. She knew she was wiser but all she could see visibly was a darker tan.

A month ago she would not have been able to hold her own with Kaigara. Having Subra as a safety net made her feel confident. She was going to miss him. Beth dressed in the usual fair runners, jeans and a white tee shirt. She stuffed her old tee shirts into a laundry bag in her room and marked the instruction form appropriately. She included some socks and underwear. She hung the laundry bag on the back of the door as instructed by the form. Beth had one foot out of the door when she purposefully turned and marched towards the desk.

"You're coming with me mister," she said softly. She took the little wooden Lord Ganesha figure and pushed him into her front right jeans pocket. "For luck" she said as he disappeared into the denim.

Beth locked her door, slipped the plastic key into her back pocket and located the elevators. She was alone and pressed the ground floor. Looking at herself in the mirror she was surprised. She looked good, almost sexy. Her long flowing hair reflected the light from above her head. Her face was tanned and highlighted her eyes, clear white with emerald green centers. The white tee shirt made her tanned arms look darker.

"I could quite easily attract a man looking like this," she thought.

Her self appreciation was interrupted by the elevator stopping and the doors opening to reveal a couple in their sixties waiting patiently to get into the elevator. Beth exited in a hurry with a tinge of embarrassment. She walked the thin strip of Oriental rug and then onto the harsh polished marble floor.

Chapter 12

Sakura's Family Secret

Beth confidently approached the desk at the entrance to the Azure lounge. "Good evening, do you have reservations?" inquired a well-dressed man.

"No reservations, I'm meeting a friend for drinks," said Beth without thinking.

"Are you a guest of the Hotel Miss?" inquired the man.

"Yes," answered Beth flirting with her eyes.

"Certainly, please follow me I think I have a wonderful window table," said the man smiling at Beth.

Her thoughts went back to the last time she tried to use her sexuality and flirt a little. That wiped the smile off her face for a few seconds. Before she had realized she was standing next to their table at the back of the restaurant. The window table offered a great view of the busy street outside. The backdrop was the city with its lights and buildings. Beth sat and thanked the man with a polite nod of the head.

"I'll let your server know that you're here for drinks and if I can have your name I'll use it to direct your guest to this table," said the man waiting.

It took a while for his message to register and Beth responded, "Martindale, Beth Martindale." The man nodded his head and retreated.

"Bond, James Bond," thought Beth trying to recall ever using that format to address herself. She laughed inwardly as a young lady working the tables approached her.

"Good evening, would you like a drink now or perhaps wait for your guest?" she inquired.

"I'll wait, thank you," responded Beth with an earnest smile.

The smile was returned and the young lady moved on to wait another table. Beth glanced at her watch, 6.58pm. Sakura was not late yet. She felt a little nervous she knew she had one chance to make this conversation a positive one for Subra. She had recognized the desperation in Sakura's expression and the need for a private conversation; this intrigued her. Beth glanced forwards to a table in front of hers. Two men in their early thirties were talking in low voices. Both wore classy suits, crisp shirts and brightly colored ties.

"The business crowd," thought Beth.

The man facing her caught her gaze and smiled. He had a clean-shaven face, warm inviting smile and seemed interested. Beth immediately looked down at her place setting. Her peripheral vision saw the man with his back to Beth turn and glance at her over his shoulder.

"Why does this always happen to me when I don't want it?" thought Beth smiling to herself.

She flicked her hair back over her shoulders and immediately recognized that she was flirting with the men. Another man approached her table pointing to the empty seat. Sakura followed the man to the table. She had changed her clothes; she looked more casual yet still refined and elegant. Beth admired that. Sakura wore a sleek fitting black sweater, matching black trousers, small black purse and black heels with a hint of silver. She wore silver earrings and a silver necklace with black pearls forming a wispy design.

Sakura smiled and outstretched a hand, "Beth, so kind of you to see me, I know you must be tired."

Beth rose to shake Sakura's strong hand. "My pleasure," was the response reminding her of Sanjeev.

Sakura sat and looked at a young woman whom appeared out of nowhere. "Have you ordered Beth?" inquired Sakura.

"No, I'd like a Perrier," said Beth sheepishly. The young woman scribbled into her note pad and looked at Sakura.

"Gin and Tonic, Bombay Sapphire with ice please," said Sakura assuredly. "So, we are here and have a chance to chat, that's good."

Beth thought Sakura looked a little nervous perhaps uneasy. She felt her best course of action was to be open and blunt. "You really wanted to talk with me, what was so important?" asked Beth.

"Straight to the point I like that. I don't know where to start really but I did need to talk with you about a few things. I just hope you don't think I'm crazy," said Sakura with an apologetic tone.

"I'm sure I won't but you've intrigued me," responded Beth leaning in. She could see the man in front of her smiling and thought, "Pay no attention."

Sakura leaned back and waited. She could see the young woman approaching with the drinks. She raised her finger to Beth as if to indicate she needed a moment. The drinks arrived and Sakura reached for her Gin and Tonic. She positioned the lime wedge into her drink, stirred it and took a long drink through a straw as if to gain some courage. "I have a tale to tell you that's incredible. I wouldn't blame you if you just dismissed it as the ramblings of an old woman. When you listen I hope it resonates with you. I just wanted to give you the information. I felt compelled to, but I don't know what you'll do with it?" was Sakura's opening line.

"Go on," said Beth curious.

"First let me start with Anwar. I loved him as a friend and was shocked to hear of his untimely death. He was a great man. I don't know if you realize just how generous he was?" said Sakura with a tear in her eye.

"I'm just starting to find out."

"I first met Anwar in London. He didn't live in London but he was visiting and doing some business in the city. We met at a lecture and went for coffee and talked for hours. We had a lot in common but we were not attracted to each other sexually, just really good friends. I lent him some money once when his bakery business nearly went under. He repaid me by lending me a vast amount of money when I needed to setup the Reika Foundation. Nobody knows that. He also smoothed the path for my Foundation's registration through the intricacies of Indian politics. He was well connected." Sakura flattened out a wrinkle in the white linen tablecloth. She continued, "Anwar was in London one night when I came into our local watering hole with a friend I met at the university; Amba Chawla.

"Amba Chawla the lady I met at the orphanage," thought Beth.

"Amba was younger than I and was struggling to complete her studies. She was drop dead gorgeous and every man in the pub was staring at her. She was so bright, sorry I mean intelligent. She was on the brink of packing it in and I was trying to reassure her. I couldn't help her financially; I was just making ends meet myself. Anwar took one look at Amba and it sent him crazy," she said staring out onto the street.

"What happened?" asked Beth kicking herself for interrupting.

"We talked as a group of friends do and Amba talked of her frustration of not realizing her dreams of helping orphans. London was so expensive. Anwar sat and listened with the rest of the group. Much later he told me one night that he'd fallen in love with a girl in India and that she'd been his soul mate. He'd lost her and didn't know where she was. Amba looked strikingly similar to his girl and she reminded him of her so much," said Sakura staring at Beth and taking a sip of her drink.

Beth recalled how much Amba looked like Rose; she could see the resemblance a generation apart.

Sakura continued, "What I didn't know until much later was that Anwar contacted Amba a couple of times and helped her with her studies. Amba felt she needed to repay this act of kindness by fulfilling her promise to help teach orphans. That's what she's still doing today. Last I heard she was at the Calcutta Muslim Orphanage. It's a labor of love. I think Amba tried to start a relationship with Anwar but he kept his distance knowing that her looks weakened his promise to stay true to his one true love. I can't remember her name," said Sakura.

"Aklina Akhter," thought Beth.

"The Generosity Account made Anwar a fabulously wealthy man. He went out of his way to help Amba before he was rich. He gave me a lift when I needed it. He stimulated the funding and helped revive the work that the Calcutta Muslim Orphanage was doing. Let's not forget the help he brought to the Reika Foundation. I named it the Reika Foundation after Anwar. He always had a thing about roses, I never knew why? Reika is Japanese for "lovely flower," Anwar was my lovely flower," said Sakura tearing up again. She composed herself and continued, "Over the years we've remained close and Kaigara through Swan manage most of his investments. My husband and Anwar grew very close. Kaigara knows that Anwar is a special client; he is afforded the best choices and is given preferential treatment. I know this irks Kaigara but she wouldn't be as comfy today if it wasn't for the steady hand of Anwar." Sakura gazed out of the window again. Sakura spoke as if a thought pushed its way forward, "Nothing is as far away as one minute ago."

"That quote is from Jim Bishop," said Beth without thinking.

"You are a smart little fox aren't you?" said Sakura. "I can see why Anwar selected you," she said smiling in a reassuring way.

"Anwar didn't know that his generosity was actually helping Rose, his daughter. It's a coincidence that Rose worked at a center that he helped create. There are no coincidences," thought Beth.

Sakura continued, "I just thought you should know a little about the shoes you are trying to fill. I don't mean that in a condescending way, he was a smart man to select you Beth. You do have massive shoes to fill. I will always love him and will miss him dearly. There are probably thousands of things this man has done throughout his life that we'll never know about. He was one of a kind. Beth if you need advice or help you can always contact me and talk. I'll be only too willing to help where I can," Sakura held an Ivory colored business card between her two thumbs and gently positioned it for Beth to take.

"Thank you," said Beth graciously taking the card and slipping it into her jeans pocket.

"Now, I would like to switch topics on you, if I may?" said Sakura looking more serious.

"I'm listening," said Beth.

"When I was a girl I had a wonderful childhood. My family was moderately wealthy and I wanted for very little. I grew up in Yokohama and Toronto. My family had houses in both cities and we commuted, it was very exciting. In the Japanese culture Beth the women in the family are very close. They share a family bond and they talk about their history. I was very close to my Mother her name was Matsu Sato. Matsu means "Strong Pine" in Japanese and she lived a long life. She was a wise person, an old Pine," Sakura spoke softly and fondly.

"Kaigara's painting; Old Pine, Arthur Lismer, group of seven, there are no coincidences," thought Beth.

Sakura continued after a sip of Gin and Tonic. "Matsu was a very clever woman. She taught me how to listen to my body, still my mind through meditation and focus on what I want. She also taught me that this world, including people, is all made from energy. She spent a long time teaching me how to read people's energies. Is this sounding weird to you Beth?"

"No, I'm starting to become aware of this myself," said Beth feeling a little awkward.

"I'm going to continue but stop me if you've heard enough. When I first saw you Beth you had an energy field that I have only ever seen once in my long life. Take a drink of your water and I will continue," Sakura suggested as Beth looked at the untouched glass of Perrier.

"No thanks," said Beth, "please continue."

"I insist, just a little sip of water won't hurt," said Sakura.

Beth was starting to get suspicious, "Please go on you have me curious, energy you say."

"When I saw you for the first time Beth you were emitting a strong energy pattern. You are now. My

Mother Matsu taught me this skill over many years; Kaigara is not interested in the slightest. I can tell a great deal about a person from their aura," explained Sakura keeping eye contact.

"Interesting," said Beth, "What colors do I have?"

"Just one strong clean base color," said Sakura. "You have a rare profile, a very rare profile. Beth, yours is Indigo, you are a solid vibrant Indigo. Do you know what that means?"

"No idea," offered Beth looking down to the left unable to meet Sakura's stare.

"It means you're special," Sakura said quietly. "You're destined for great things. I'm not sure if Anwar could read auras but he knew you were special, different."

"Special means stupid where I come from," said Beth.

"Special means special where I come from. When I was a little girl I flew to Toronto with my parents one time. They were on edge and arguing. They never argued and I knew something was not right. When we got to Toronto a few days later an old lady visited our house. She made a fuss of me and stroked my hair. I was only young and I remember how old she looked. It was odd her skin was old, yellow and decaying. She emitted the strongest Indigo aura I've ever seen. I was trying to learn to read aura's at that age but I didn't need to concentrate on her she was that strong. She had a weird smell about her. I asked my Mother who she was and I was told she was my Aunt," said Sakura rolling her eyes.

Beth was enjoying the story but it was not getting her closer to the portal. "Why do you tell me this?" asked Beth.

"Patience dear, it's coming, I promise," Sakura continued. "My Grand Mother was called Sata Yamamoto; she was a traditional Japanese woman, a proud woman. She worried about our family name and reputation and she married well. She traveled extensively between Tokyo, Yokohama and Toronto. Her Mother was called Otome Osanami she would be my Great Grandmother. She was born in Tokyo in 1863 a very different time than what we're used to. Otome was a twin; she had a sister born immediately after her called Toshie. Toshie and Otome were inseparable; they played together, looked alike, grew up together and finished each other's sentences. Another Gin and Tonic please," said Sakura to the young woman as she walked by nodding. "These girls were like any other growing up in Tokyo at that time. They hoped to find a loving husband and raise a family. When they were 21 years of age Tokyo slept as a fierce lightning storm moved across the night sky. It's rumored that Toshie suffered from sleepwalking and was often restrained by Otome. That night Toshie rose from her bed and walked out into the courtyard of her home. Otome slept and was not aware that Toshie had left her bed."Sakura stopped to receive her next drink. She placed it by the empty glass. "Toshie stood in the rain and as the story goes she was struck by lightning."

Beth stared at Sakura; did she know what happened on Haworth Main Street? She did not register a change in expression.

Sakura continued, "Toshie was found the next day cold and wet lying in the courtyard. She was in a coma for four days. She finally woke and the family was grateful. Otome was very relieved as she carried around with her a feeling of blame and guilt. Otome was pleased that her twin sister showed no signs of damage. After a week Otome noticed something strange about her sister. She watched her intensely and spent every second of the day with her to prove out her suspicions."

"Suspicions?" repeated Beth hooked on the story.

"Otome realized that her sister was starving herself. She confronted Toshie and demanded that she ate or drank in front of her. Toshie at first denied that anything was different offering to take a small sip of water. The smallest of sips sent Toshie into convulsions and another week of bed-ridden coma. When Toshie recovered she went for a long walk with Otome and they both sat by a pond to talk."

Beth could feel her intensity rising but she told herself, "Remain calm, don't give anything away."

Taking another large drink Sakura continued. "The twins found a secluded spot and Toshie confided in Otome. Otome was the only person that she could trust. Toshie told Otome that she'd been struck by something but it had not been lightening. It was a raw natural spirit power, bathed in the color Indigo. She felt that her body had been invaded, that was the word she used, invaded. She didn't need to drink or eat; she was nourished by energy. Toshie told of a voice that visited her dreams at night. She described him as a warrior from another world, made from pure energy. He'd fallen in battle and sought refuge in Toshie. Toshie gave her captive warrior a name. She called him "Corom." Time went by and Toshie seemed to grow apart from Otome, she seemed to form a bond with Corom.

She didn't eat or drink. She managed to conceal this fact with the help of Otome who was sworn to secrecy. Otome watched over Toshie carefully month after month. She didn't eat or drink, yet she looked vibrant and full of energy."

"Didn't she start to feel sick or tired?" asked Beth immediately regretting the question.

"It's coming. Toshie felt great for a while then she would struggle to wake up in the mornings. The walk up the old familiar hill started to take more out of her. Signs were starting to show that she needed some kind of nourishment. What happened next is unclear. Toshie wouldn't tell anyone how she managed to harness energy but she seemed to be able to do things that others couldn't," said Sakura picking at her fingernail nervously.

"Say more," said Beth impatiently.

"Beth, do you know what Apport means?" asked Sakura spelling the word.

"No, I don't," said Beth honestly.

"The dictionary describes it as a paranormal transference of an article from one place to another, or an appearance of an article from an unknown source," explained Sakura.

"Wow," said Beth quietly mouthing the word and leaning in.

"Toshie only described it once to Otome. She said it was like entering the space between space. That's all she ever said on the matter. She could reach through time and space and make things appear. This took most of her energy and she only did this when she needed to. One hot day a close relative of the family was taken gravely ill. The infants Mother visited the courtyard distressed. Toshie asked if she could see the infant and was allowed to hold him. It was said that she managed to materialize water, with curing powers, sealed in a glass bottle from out of thin air. The infant drank the water and was cured instantly," said Sakura.

"Trouble," said Beth.

Sakura continued, "Trouble indeed, news spread around Tokyo and Toshie was now asked to perform similar feats for sick people with powerful families. It became known that Toshie could materialize Goshinsui or water of the gods, which had healing properties. She could make this water appear out of thin air sealed in glass bottles. Stories had emerged that Toshie was unable to eat or drink. People said that spirits possessed her. The spirits talked to her during her sleep. The authorities suspected a fraud and arrested Toshie in a blaze of publicity."

Beth was hooked waiting to hear the rest of the story. She glanced through the window as evening had given way to the darkness of night. People scurried around on the street outside. Beth glanced at the empty table in front of her; she had not noticed but the two men had left.

"Demand for Goshinsui was overwhelming and the family didn't welcome the attention Toshie was attracting. Upon her arrest the family disowned her but Otome stood by her side. In those days this was an act of great courage to defy her parents and family. Otome visited Toshie in the jail and pleaded with her to demonstrate her talents and tell the truth. Toshie knew that no one would believe her incredible story. Most likely she would be convicted of being mentally unstable and locked away." Sakura adjusted her wedding ring, she looked nervous.

"Go on, I believe you," said Beth impatiently tapping her fingers.

"It's not a question of belief, my story now starts to get strange. Otome and Toshie sat before a group of esteemed judges. There were five judges on the panel. Three of the judges had family members already cured by Toshie. Otome was asked to sit to one side. She was not on trial and would not participate. Toshie asked quietly, "What am I on trial for?" The answer given by the head judge was, "Fraud." Toshie asked the judges if she would be deemed fraudulent if she made Goshinsui appear in a sealed glass bottle. She offered to make the bottle appear in the center of the long table. The judges sat along one edge of the long table twelve feet away from Toshie." Sakura rubbed her hands nervously. "The judges agreed if she could do this they would have no option than to deem her genuine and not a fraud. When the judge completed his statement instantly a sealed glass bottle of water materialized. An Indigo colored haze surrounded the bottle. It was sitting on the table in front of the head judge. Toshie just smiled," said Sakura finishing her second Gin and Tonic in one large gulp.

"What happened to Toshie?" asked Beth.

"She was released but eventually committed to a mental institution where she sat alone haunted by the spirit that talked to her at night. She went from being a celebrity to a forgotten disowned woman. She didn't eat or drink for years. She fell quite ill and decided to drink some Goshinsui, holy water. She often said that this kept her Spirit Warrior strong. I know that sounds a little weird but it's supposedly true," urged Sakura.

"Let me get this straight, the thing inside her was dying and she kept it alive by feeding it holy water?" asked Beth.

"Why so interested in the holy water?" asked Sakura knowingly.

"Just trying to keep the facts of the story straight," said Beth in a sly tone.

"Shall I continue or am I boring you?" teased Sakura.

"No, this is fascinating."

"You sure you're not tired?" asked Sakura as if she were a cat playing with a mouse.

"I'm good keep going," said Beth getting irritated.

"All right but here's the part that I need you to stay open minded about. Toshie only had a one faithful visitor Otome. Otome had married a powerful businessman and she felt responsible for Toshie's fate. If she'd stopped her sister sleep walking like she had countless times before this would never have happened.

Otome and Toshie were now 44 years of age. Otome had a daughter and a son. Otome looked her age but Toshie who had not eaten in twenty years looked in her late twenties. She was aging much slower," whispered Sakura.

"So the daughter would be Sata," said Beth beginning to struggle.

"Yes, Sata Yamamoto," said Sakura. "That's good, you're piecing this together. Although Toshie looked younger and healthier she died suddenly at the age of 44, that's 1907 and was buried in Tokyo. The newspapers made a big thing of it dragging the family name through the mud again. Family reputation is an immensely important thing in Japan."

"She died 20 years after she was afflicted and she used holy water to keep Corom alive," summarized Beth.

Sakura let that message sink in before delivering the final shock. "Now, listen carefully. This is where it gets good if you can believe it. Toshie and Otome had been plotting an escape for years. They knew that if Toshie moved she'd be a freak and hounded by interested people for years to come. The family didn't want any more speculation and interest. Otome had married a very successful businessman. He had interests in construction and saw an opportunity to build in Canada. He set up an office in Toronto. He refined his English skills learned in the ports of Tokyo," Sakura made a slurping noise as she pulled melted ice through a straw. "Otome devised the plan, they faked Toshie's death. One of the dead mental patients is now lying in a grave in Tokyo marked Toshie Osanami, 1863 - 1907. Toshie was smuggled out of Japan and arrived in Vancouver in 1907. The family moved to Toronto in 1910."

"So she died here?" questioned Beth?

"Let me continue," said Sakura taking a look around to see who was listening. Azure was emptying and Sakura waved away the attention of the young drinks lady. "Otome died when she was 87 years old, she was buried in Tokyo. Sata Yamamoto looked after Toshie for many years. She was a wonderful woman, my Grandmother. I remember her being kind and wise. She lived in a little house in Scarborough, a suburb of Toronto. She had two boys and a girl. She lived to the ripe old age of 82. Hardy breed are the women of our family. My Mother was the only daughter, Matsu Sato the strong pine. Sata did not inform my Mother about the legend of Toshie until she'd just delivered her daughter, me."

"Wait!" interrupted Beth, "You forgot to tell me when Toshie died," asked Beth?

"I'm getting to that," said Sakura clearly unpleased with the interruption. "Toshie was very old and set in her ways. Since being struck by lightning she constantly talked about a gate. First it was ramblings in her sleep in Tokyo with Otome then throughout her life she became obsessed with finding this gate. My Mother told me that one day she asked her outright while sitting on a park bench in High Park in Toronto. Why do you obsess about this gate? The answer she got stunned her. She was told that the gate would provide Toshie with additional powers and access to unseen realms. It was the true fountain of youth."

Beth could not contain herself anymore, "Did she find this gate?"

"No, my story isn't done yet. My Mother Matsu introduced me to Toshie when I was about six or seven I think. We had just completed a journey from Yokohama to Toronto and we were all tired. My parents were fighting and I pretended not to listen. They never fought but my Father didn't want me to meet her. My

Mother was as strong as a Pine and she introduced me to my Aunt a few days later. She was old, musty, and had a bad smell about her. She had this extraordinary bright Indigo aura, blinding really. There was something fascinating about her and yet repulsive," Sakura looked up to see if she had caused offense.

"Say more," said Beth eagerly.

"I've met my Aunt many more times since then. In 1975 just before Kaigara was born I talked with my Mother. She informed me that she had numerous heated arguments with Toshie, as she was adamant that she wanted to move to Belgium. She said she'd spent years researching god knows what in the library and was adamant her salvation laid in Belgium. My Mother tried to talk her out of it and explained it would be difficult to get her through immigration. Times have changed since she landed in Canada. Fight after fight continued until Toshie threatened to take her story to the Globe and Mail newspaper. A compromise was struck. My father had connections into diplomatic circles and managed to get Toshie safe passage and citizenship in Belgium," said Sakura.

"Belgium," said Beth aloud?

Sakura ignored Beth and continued, "There's one small hitch we had to disguise her identity. Her name Toshie Osanami was too infamous so we changed her first name to a name that sounded similar. We registered her as Hoshi instead of Toshie. Hoshi means Star in Japanese. Before she left she was referring to herself as Hoshi or Star. She settled in a small village outside our Brussels and lives in it still."

"Still? That'll make her over 140 years old?" whispered Beth in a strained voice.

"I know," said Sakura, "My husband and I send her money monthly, I promised my Mother that I would look after her. She doesn't eat or drink. Her apartment is paid off Kaigara manages the property. The only thing she needs is a little money for expenses and clothes. I'm convinced that she's gone mad, but her obsession about the gate is harmless. She doesn't get into trouble and she causes no harm as far as I can see."

"What does she look like?" asked Beth.

"Like a woman in her 90's," answered Sakura, "she smells a bit odd but old people do so she blends in. She doesn't speak Flemish or French so living in rural Belgium is a challenge for her. She's a loner so she's content."

"Why Belgium she has no link to Belgium?" asked Beth.

"She's chasing this gate. It's a workable relationship, she lives in a little village and we send a check once a month to her apartment in Schelle," said Sakura watching a distinct change in Beth's expression.

"Where is she? The name of the place again?" asked Beth impatiently.

"Schelle, S-C-H-E-L-L-E, Schelle, Belgium it's a quaint little place. Eight or nine thousand people I think," explained Sakura.

Beth's heart sank to her stomach, Schelle, not Shell. Over a hundred years of research has led Toshie to Schelle and Beth was wasting time looking for seashells! Beth sat back in her seat and reflected.

"At the turn of the century Toshie was looking for a gate. With science fiction movies today we'd call that a portal. We're looking for the same thing," thought Beth.

Sakura sat patiently as Beth digested the information. Her expression was stone faced but her eyes pierced Beth's thoughts. "What are you looking for Beth?"

Beth felt her face flush; she looked down at her untouched drink. She slowly raised her strong green eyes and flashed them at Sakura. "You know, don't you?"

"A young woman can't live on fresh air; someone with your athletic body type would need to eat and drink regularly. Sure, I get it, you're health conscious. Perhaps you eat small meals but the truth is you can't actually eat anything can you? By the look of that glass you can't drink either," said Sakura nodding in the direction of the full glass of Perrier. "I've told you something that only my husband knows. I'll need to tell Kaigara about Toshie when she's ready. My fear is that Kaigara is different from our long line of caring women. You've met her she's,"

"Independent," offered Beth.

"Yes, Independent. She would not look after Toshie after I go. We made a promise that we would look after her, Mother to Daughter through the generations. When Toshie looked strong and vibrant all she could talk about was finding the gate. We all knew that she wanted this gate to grant her eternal life and unlimited powers. I suspect she hasn't found the gate for one of two reasons. Either she's crazy and there is no gate, or she's not destined to find it. I think she's looking for the gate for all the wrong reasons. Do you understand?" asked Sakura.

"I do," said Beth hoping she would continue. There was an uncomfortable silence as the two women avoided eye contact. Beth was determined to listen.

To her relief Sakura continued, "I've told you our most intimate family secret and you sit there accepting it without scrutiny, questioning or ridicule," she stopped abruptly.

"We're closing ladies, so I'll leave the bill with you but you're welcome to stay and chat as long as you wish," said the young woman sliding the bill and a pen onto the table.

Beth was eager to hear Sakura out so she grabbed the bill, filled out the total with the pen, added her room number and hurriedly signed the bottom of the bill stub. The young woman breezed by and collected both the pen and the bill in one smooth motion. "Thank you and have a great evening, stay as long as you like."

Beth stared at Sakura in silence; both women knew what that meant. "Most people would laugh this off as ridiculous, my husband did at first. You seemed to accept it readily and even asked for more details. Your Indigo aura is the same, you haven't touched your drink or eaten in front of me and you seem like you're on a mission of some sort. You're interested in Kaigara the English translation is Shell. Your face fell once I told you that Schelle is a village in Belgium. I'm not a stupid woman Beth, but it's time you were as honest with me as I've been with you, don't you think?"

Beth sat frozen contemplating the question; she felt a surge of energy flood her brain and the word 'Yes' reverberated. Subra had sent Beth a signal to open up and talk honestly with Sakura. "Thanks," she thought. "I know what you're talking about. I was struck by lightning just like Toshie," said Beth.

"I have to apologize Beth; I want you to trust me. I'm a well-connected person and I made a few phone calls after today's lunch to contacts in the UK. Let's just say that I knew that already," said Sakura sheepishly.

"I have the same aura, and I have a Spirit Warrior that communicates with me at night. I have to find the" Beth paused, "Gate. I think my warrior is dying and I need to get him through the gate." Beth looked at Sakura and wondered what she had done. Sakura could use this as evidence to claim that Beth was mentally unstable and unfit to manage the Generosity Account. "Can I trust you?" she asked leaning forward and making strong eye contact.

"Dear, I trusted you," responded Sakura. "I have some more information and a request, and then I must leave. At first Toshie, or Hoshi, as she's now known, was trying to find this stupid gate. I'm confident that her motivations have changed. She's a wily old bird Beth so I've got to be careful when I do correspond with her," Sakura looked down and sighed. "When she was living in Toronto and was researching in the library she confessed to something interesting. She told of her near death experience when she first drank water in Japan with Otome. She was given another image to help her find the gate. She was convinced that this was a clue. She was provided with the phrase "IN DEN VOS" she had no idea what it meant. She didn't know if it was French, Flemish or German? Toshie found a restaurant in Schelle called the "IN DEN VOS" she pestered the place until the owners banned her. I know she feels strongly that's where the gate is located," said Sakura glancing around to see who might be listening. "You can't tell her that I told you that. I now think that immortality is not her driving force. After living through two world wars, and two turns of the century, let's just say she's feeling dated. Can you imagine living in the eighteen hundreds and surviving in today's world? Internet, television, microwave ovens, computers, cell phones, automobiles, and credit cards that's rapid change," explained Sakura.

"People have changed, kids don't respect their elders and people aren't as trusting," offered Beth. "Why is she still looking for the gate?"

"I have to think its Corom. At her age you grow tired of life and seeing your friends and family die. Not having the pleasure of food and drink looking and smelling like she does. I hate to say this but I've often thought why wouldn't you throw yourself off a cliff or under a train? The answer is Corom. He's been her friend for over a century, I think she couldn't live with the guilt of killing him. She wants her life to end Beth, but she doesn't want Corom to die," explained Sakura.

Beth smiled knowing that there was a shred of decency left in this woman. "I think I can understand that. Perhaps she made a promise to him. I'm sure she would like to reunite with Otome and her family again."

"Beth, you're the only person I've ever met like Hoshi. I had to find out if you had been struck by lightning. I needed to know when you were struck to figure out how old you really are. I know you're a young woman. You need to go to Schelle and meet with Hoshi. The two of you need to combine forces and find this damn gate. She needs to be released from her living hell and Corom needs to go home. I want to give you her address. Will you go and talk with her?" asked Sakura losing her composure slightly.

Beth leaned forward and held Sakura's hand in a reassuring gesture. "I'm looking for the same gate for the same reason. I'd like to help. She's got over a hundred years head start on me and I think we could make a good team," offered Beth.

"Hoshi is a bad tempered, mean spirited, Bitch! There, I've said it and I won't say that again. You need to know what you'll be facing. I know you have the same goal and plenty in common. You're probably the only two people on the planet that I know who understand each other. She won't be welcoming and she can be mean. She likes to play mind games and she teases people with her intellect. She'll try to twist your words. Listen to me I'm going on and on. Beth, you'll need your wits about you," said Sakura concerned.

"Don't worry about me," said Beth twisting her right wrist upwards. "I'm a sly fox," said Beth smiling in a show of bravado. "I've an important question for you. Could Anwar read auras?"

"We'd talked about that and yes he could, he would have seen your pure Indigo color. He knew what an Indigo child was. It's probably a big factor in why he chose you, but he had to trust you too Beth," explained Sakura in a voice tinged with wisdom. Sakura broke hands and reached into her small black purse. She picked out a piece of yellow paper. On a post-it note was Hoshi's name and address. Below was a phone number with "Everard" next to it. Beth studied the note and glanced up at Sakura. "Everard is a friend of my husbands, he lives in Brussels. He owns a livery company," said Sakura recognizing the wrinkling of Beth's forehead. "A limousine company. He makes a good living off the bureaucrats. Brussels is the capital of the European Union. I'll let him know you're coming and he'll take care of everything for you. You are going to go aren't you?" pleaded Sakura.

"Yes, soon as I can," confirmed Beth. "Is Schelle near Brussels?" asked Beth.

"Close enough, Everard will drive you, you'll be spoiled. I've done that trip a few times. Schelle is about forty-five minutes North of Brussels by car. It's a trip on one highway the 'A12' I think," Sakura stated with a wave of her hand. "You could fly into Antwerp but we always stay in Brussels."

"I'll arrange through Mr. Wilks to fly to Brussels as soon as I can. Perhaps tomorrow if that's possible. I understand you're leaving tomorrow also?" inquired Beth?

"I need to fly to Yokohama and join my husband; we plan to stay a couple of weeks. I'll phone Everard and he can let Hoshi know that she'll be getting a visitor. She'll be curious. She doesn't have a phone or a computer so we use Everard to relay messages to her. It's quicker than the mail," said Sakura looking at the dark street outside. She took a quick scan of the empty restaurant and reached for Beth's hands again. "Beth, this was meant to be. Anwar selected you. As you get older in life you'll start to notice patterns, alignments or coincidences."

Before Beth could think, almost like a reflex she was saying, "There are no coincidences."

"I agree I wish you luck strong little fox. You've got my card it has my cell number should you need to contact me. Call me for anything, at any time, day or night," said Sakura knowing she must go. "I wish I could come with you. One last thing, then I really must go. Remember to call her Hoshi, if you call her Toshie she's got a wicked temper and for some reason it provokes her. Beth, please find that gate. Let's put Hoshi, Corom and everyone who has had to deal with her lately out of our misery. Can you do that for me?" asked Sakura passionately.

A few years ago Beth would have answered, "I will try." She now recognized the word try is a graceful way of saying no. "Yes, I will," said Beth confidently. The power surge in her head came through again; she heard "Yes" and smiled thinking of Subra.

"I can't thank you enough for doing this," said Sakura.

"My pleasure," said Beth thinking of Sanjeev and his posh watch. "Sakura, don't be so hard on Kaigara, she's trying to make it in a man's world. It's a different time now, you should be proud of her you know."

"I am," said Sakura smiling, "I have to go."

Sakura stood, flipped the strap of her purse over her shoulder and did something that shocked Beth. She leaned in and kissed Beth's cheek lightly. She did not pull her face away quickly but stayed close, gazed into Beth's brilliant green eyes and said, "Good luck my sly little fox."

With that she was gone confidently walking out of Azure and into the night. Beth tucked the yellow post-it note into her jeans pocket and moved towards the elevators. She sat with her back to the restaurant and was surprised to see it was now completely empty. She glanced at her watch, 11.50pm. Time literally had flown that night. She rode the empty elevator and looked at herself in the mirror. At the seventh floor she followed the signs for room 732. She reached into her rear jeans pocket and slid out her plastic room key. Gaining access to her room she slotted the key and watched the lights come on automatically. The room had been cleaned. The bed was turned down, items straightened, drapes closed and a little chocolate lay on the pillow with the breakfast menu. A pile of freshly laundered clothes was neatly folded on the bed.

"That was fast," thought Beth.

Beth walked over to the desk and unloaded her jeans. Lord Ganesha came out of the front right pocket, followed by a business card and a post-it note came out of the left. She looked at Lord Ganesha, "A good nights work, If I say so myself," said Beth feeling like she had made significant progress. She undressed quickly and threw her clothes on the armchair. She lifted the laundered clothes from the bed and gently placed them on the desk. She walked naked into the bathroom and looked at herself in the large mirror. Her thoughts turned to the smiling man in the restaurant. "Eat your heart out," she said mouthing the words into the mirror. Beth reached around the door and felt the robe hanging on a silver hook. She untied the belt and slipped into the robe. She pushed her feet into the hotel slippers and headed back to the bed.

"Well, my friend Subra, we're going to have a good chat tonight. I did well today," she said contentedly. Then she recalled the signals that Subra had sent her. "Thanks," she said softly. She wanted to sleep and talk this over with Subra but she was so excited, so energized. She felt like she had consumed seven cups of coffee. Schelle, IN DEN VOS, Toshie, Hoshi, Star, Everard, mean Bitch, holy water, Brussels, Belgium, the A12, Livery, all these words kept flooding into her head.

"Stop," she told herself. "Lie down in the dark and focus on your breathing." Beth felt the gentle rise and fall of her chest and tried to relax. Within ten minutes she was drifting off to sleep.

Chapter 13

Maid of the Mist

Beth knew she would need to concentrate to find Subra; he had been getting noticeably weaker. He was able to stay alive but he needed to expend a lot more energy to communicate. She needed his guidance and assurance at key times and Subra knew this. Beth had sensed his weakening but she did not want to admit it. It added pressure to an already stressful situation. Beth was finally being exposed to these wonderful exciting places. She wanted to experience it all. She wanted for the first time in her life to be a tourist. She knew that time spent enjoying this experience was precious time wasted. This guilt, anxiety and panic were overwhelming.

"There you are," thought Beth honing in on the faint but recognizable energy trace. Beth concentrated and amplified the signal. "Are you with me?" she thought.

"Yes but only just," was Subra's reply.

"Just is good enough."

"We've a lot to talk about but first let me say I'm proud of you little fox you did well today," said Subra in an earnest tone.

"I did, I made stunning progress today. I discovered Schelle, Belgium, IN DEN VOS, and Hoshi. I have to admit Hoshi sounds a bit daunting."

"If you can get me near the portal Beth, I'll feel it. I'll be able to feed off its energy. I should be able to signal to you if we're close."

"Great, what about Corom?" inquired Beth, "can you feel him too? Can you communicate with him?"

"Sounds like he's very weak but I should be able to feel his presence. I can't communicate with him directly, I would need you and Hoshi to be involved and I'm not sure that's a wise thing," cautioned Subra.

Beth's thoughts strayed to a future meeting with Hoshi. This would be a battle of wits with an experienced old woman. Would she willingly align her goals and join a joint search for the portal?"

"Never let the future disturb you. You will meet it, if you have to, with the same weapons of reason which today arm you against the present," said Subra in an encouraging way.

"I'm curious, when I find the portal how many Spirit Warriors can go through at one time?"

"Why do you ask?" said Subra in a puzzled voice.

Beth explained, "If both you and Corom can go through the portal it makes my pitch of cooperation more palatable for Hoshi. If only one of you can pass through then the other one and its guardian will be left looking for the new location of the portal."

"I see your point," Subra paused as if considering the options. "As long as Corom is close enough and has sufficient energy I can pull him through in one continuous energy stream. The key is one continuous energy stream. If I can locate him as I'm passing through I'll have one chance to pull him along with me."

"What does close enough mean? You said that time and distances don't mean much in your world. Does

Corom and Hoshi need to be standing next to us at the portal?" asked Beth concerned.

"No, close enough means that I can still feel his energy. Right now here in Toronto he's not close enough. I can't feel him. When we get to Belgium and we're closer, using your understanding of distance, I might be able to feel his weak signal."

"Is he much weaker than you? You keep referring to him as weak but you're not getting any stronger."

"I think I'll be stronger than Corom and I'll also feed off the portal energy," said Subra.

"What will this do to Hoshi?"

There was a pause as Subra tried to express the right words, "I'm afraid she's living off Corom right now. As a human, she should have died many lifetimes ago. I don't think she'll be able to survive Corom leaving her frail body."

"So her soul will find its own route to the spirit world?"

"Yes?" was the simple reply.

"You heard Sakura, I think she's ready to go. No one can say she hasn't had a good inning, as they say."

"Ah yes, I'm familiar with that expression, Beth uses a Cricket term! I never thought I'd see the two in harmony," teased Subra.

"Funny," thought Beth as sarcastically as she could. "It would devastate me if my actions killed someone but in Hoshi's case I think she wants to die."

Subra answered recognizing that Beth had switched to being serious. "Death is more universal than life, everyone dies but not everyone lives."

"I get it, you have to live life to its fullest, but Hoshi has outlived her will to live. Even she would probably say she has lived to the maximum." Beth struggled with her conscious knowing that if the plan worked Hoshi would become a victim of her actions.

"Those who welcome death have only tried it from the ears up. I agree with you Beth, if it wasn't for Corom Hoshi would be a long faded memory by now. If it weren't for Corom, Hoshi would also have led a more normal life. She's paid her price for longevity," explained Subra.

Beth became more concerned at the prospect of matching her wits with Hoshi. She showed bravado in front of Sakura but knew Subra could see right through that.

"Subra, what cargo was Corom carrying? What wisdom does Hoshi have?"

"I was told in my training that Corom was to retrieve a trapped spirit, a local spiritual leader who had great wisdom and the ability to connect with the dead. He died in a house fire in London. His soul or spirit was so far detached that he could not find a spirit guide to help him cross into the spiritual domain. He was trapped as a spirit in the physical world. His knowledge was so deep that the Universe collectively decided to send Corom to locate him and guide him back to the spiritual domain. Corom never connected with the estranged spirit. Corom never came back and fell to earth in Japan," explained Subra.

"What about the spirit?"

"After Corom failed it was decided that crossing over domains and attempting to return was too risky. I was selected out of necessity, and look what happened to me. I'm certain the spirit is still roaming, trapped on earth. Some spirits find a way to connect with a spirit guide and they will help them cross over. Some remain on earth as ghosts," said Subra.

"So I'd like to get this straight, as far as we know Corom didn't manage to collect his cargo of knowledge, Hoshi is wise because she's over 140 years old. Life experience is what I'm up against. I've got some of the brightest people's collective wisdom in my head. That makes me older than my physical age. That's something Hoshi will not be expecting. It'll be my secret weapon if you like," thought Beth contented.

"There are no secrets better kept than the secrets everyone guesses," said Subra hoping to make a point.

It was too deep for Beth and she'd moved on. "I'm still worried. What happens to me when you go through the portal? Will it kill me also?"

"Don't worry Beth, your energy is strong, you are young. You will survive this with a mild headache that will last a few minutes. You need not worry, I wouldn't do this if it harmed you in any way," explained Subra.

"Phew, that's a relief," thought Beth. "So I go back to normal right? I can eat and drink again?" asked Beth.

"Yes," said Subra simply. "You'll be normal but you'll have acquired a vast quantity of useless knowledge. As Bertrand Russell said, 'there is much pleasure to be gained from useless knowledge.'"

Beth was thinking hard and clearly concerned about her potential matchup. "When I meet Hoshi, she'll know that I'm an Indigo Child from my aura. Will she know that I have a Spirit Warrior within me?"

"I doubt it. I think Corom is so weak he'll not be able to sense me. Hoshi will know your aura is strong; she will try to find out why. She may piece together the puzzle. It'll be up to you to box clever and let her know when the time is right," said Subra being vague.

"When will that be?" inquired Beth.

"When the time is right," repeated Subra.

Beth was still feeling uncertain and unsure. "From what I've heard about Hoshi I'm going to need you to be a star."

Subra tried to select a quote to reassure Beth. He searched for one to show that he felt confident in her. "The main ingredient in stardom is the rest of the team."

"You're right, we're a good team," thought Beth feeling a little better.

"Beth, there's an old Japanese proverb I want to share with you. If he works for you, you work for him," said Subra, "Do you get it?"

"Yeah, we're a team and we're in this together. You don't know how much having you around helps me Subra," thought Beth.

"I do, but it's only temporary you'll be your own woman soon enough Beth. It's unfortunate that this happened to you it's a big responsibility. The lesson here is similar to the lesson Anwar provided. You took on the responsibility and you grew because of it. It's a well known fact that we grow more as individuals out of adversity than comfort," explained Subra. "You're still growing Beth."

"What was that word? That's it. Apport, I'd never heard of that word before. Reaching through space and time to transfer an object from one place to another. Hoshi did this with sealed jars of holy water. You once told me that you had your cargo and were about to head home. Can you remember that? You were hit by some kind of white energy beam. I wonder if it was Hoshi retrieving holy water?" asked Beth.

"You might be right. That makes sense. The only thing that could knock me out that way is a beam of pure energy. Nothing on Earth would produce that, it's not man made. It would have to be Hoshi and Corom. Now we know why; it was a call for holy water. They needed holy water to keep them alive. I got hit by their beam," said Subra finally understanding.

"I have another question while we seem to be on a roll," thought Beth excitedly. "When we get to the portal, will I see an image as a clue to the location of the next portal? This is the clue that you talked about?"

"Yes, we'll both see it," explained Subra.

Beth listened to the response and fell silent for a moment her thoughts still. "Will I need to describe the image for the next person seeking a portal?"

"No need to solve that one now Beth, do what's due. The task at hand is getting us both to Brussels then on to Schelle," said Subra trying to keep Beth focused.

"Do you need food? What should we do about the holy water? Should I get some?"

"No, while food is an important part of a balanced diet I don't feel I need any just yet. If I start to feel desperate I will let you know and we may have to resort to this but not yet," stated Subra confidently.

Beth and Subra continued to discuss the portal and Schelle. They talked about the IN DEN VOS vision that Hoshi experienced during her near death experience. After the discussion ran its course Subra called time saying he was getting tired and low on energy. Beth wanted to continue but agreed and woke herself. It was the early hours of the morning and Beth lay motionless. She was not asleep but the room was quiet, dark and calm. She rehearsed what she would say to Hoshi numerous times in her mind. She played out scenes in her head of how she might approach the conversation. 6am flashed on the alarm clock in bold green numbers. Beth swung her legs over the side of the bed and sat upright.

"I'm not going back to sleep, might as well get a jump on the day. I have to get to Schelle," said Beth in a determined way. She went to the hotel room safe and retrieved the letter with Mr. Wilk's contact details. She walked over to the phone and figured out the dialing instructions for the UK, explained on a plastic card clipped to the phone. Tapping the keys in sequence she could hear a ringing sound.

"Hello?" was the greeting it was a female.

"Hi. I was wondering if I could speak with Mr. Wilks, er David Wilks," asked Beth?

"What's it about?" she asked curtly.

"I'm Beth Martindale, I'd like to talk with him about the Generosity Account," said Beth, "I'm calling from Toronto."

"Oh I see, it's eleven in the morning here love, David's at work, you've called his home number," she explained in a more friendly tone.

"I'm so sorry," said Beth, "I'm new at this."

"No problem love, do you have his mobile?" she asked.

"I do, right here, I'll call that, thanks and sorry to bother you," offered Beth.

"That's not a problem, call back if you do need his mobile number or you can't get through," she said hanging up.

"She was really sweet," thought Beth. "Now let's do this right this time." Beth looked at the letter and tapped in the mobile phone number listed.

She could hear a ringing noise interrupted by a male voice, "Hello this is David."

"Hi David this is Beth Martindale calling from Toronto," said Beth with a nervous stutter.

"Hi Beth, just give me a second I'm just stepping out of a meeting so that I can talk with you, hold on a minute. There, I'm in a private room now. Good to finally connect with you how can I help you Beth?" asked David. His friendly tone settled Beth's nerves.

"I'm in my hotel in Toronto and it's six in the morning. I have to get to Brussels fast. I need to do a favor for Sakura Tanaka, can you help me?" asked Beth trying not to sound too desperate.

"Absolutely, Beth give me the phone number of your hotel and your room number and I'll have Tabitha from my office give you a call right back. She's got access to the travel system and will get you on your way using the fastest possible option," said David in a calm assured voice.

Beth told David her hotel details. When David disconnected Beth felt a mild form of panic. She wanted to get going and loose ends were testing her patience. She knew time was of the essence and that Subra did not have many grains of sand in the hourglass left. Beth jumped as the phone rang, "Hello?"

"This is the front desk we have an international call for you Miss Martindale," said a friendly male voice.

Beth heard a click; "Hello?" said a female English voice.

"Hello, this is Beth Martindale."

"Hello Miss Martindale, my name's Tabitha. I was asked to give you a call and help you with some travel arrangements, is this a good time to talk?" Tabitha inquired in a professional way.

"Yes, please, thanks for calling back so quickly Tabitha, please call me Beth," offered Beth.

"Thank you Beth let's get right down to business," said Tabitha.

The call was short as Tabitha recorded the details. She promised Beth that she would be flying out that day if it was possible. She instructed Beth to pack. Tabitha was a consummate professional. She promised Beth that she would not leave her office today until Beth's travel arrangements had been completed and were securely in her hands. She asked Beth if she had a preferred airline. Beth requested Jet Airways but insisted on a direct flight if possible. After the call Beth showered and dressed in freshly laundered clothes. She pulled on her trusty jeans and loaded her backpack with her belongings. It had been over an hour since the conversation with Tabitha. Tabitha sounded like she had stepped off the set of the popular English television soap East Enders. Having heard nothing but Indian and Canadian accents recently it was a shock to hear the stark contrast of a London accent. A knock at the door disconnected Beth from her thoughts.

Beth went to the door and without opening it asked, "Who is it?"

"Guest services Ma'am, I have an important printout of an email sent to your attention, travel arrangements I believe," said a male voice. Beth opened the door and was presented with an envelope containing a folded note. The young man started to walk away quickly and Beth thanked him before she closed the door. The phone rang almost immediately. Beth scooted over to the phone still holding the envelope.

"Hello?"

"International call for you Ma'am," said a male voice.

"Hello?" said Beth after the click.

"Hello Beth its Tabitha, have you got my email yet?" she inquired.

"It just arrived I haven't had a chance to open the envelope yet," explained Beth.

"That's fine, we have you all sorted. It'll be business class on Jet Airways direct to Brussels leaving this evening at 6.10pm. That's the fastest I could get you out of Toronto Beth. The full details are contained in the note including a contact mobile number for me. I've booked a great hotel for you it's centrally located and it's all prepaid by the Generosity Account."

"This woman has her act together," thought Beth.

"You're traveling on a UK passport so you can travel to Belgium no problem, no visa required. You told me about your ground transportation in Belgium. I've taken the liberty of contacting Everard at the number you supplied and he now knows your landing details.

He'll meet you at the airport and have a sign. I passed on the hotel information so he knows where you will be staying in Brussels. Your Toronto hotel will have a limousine on standby ready to take you to the airport. I've taken care of that on account also. I'd like you to contact the concierge to find out when you should leave for the airport. That should do it Beth you're on your way," finished Tabitha.

"Wow, you're good, thank you so much Tabitha," said Beth feeling relieved. "I don't know how I can thank you enough?" said Beth.

"You don't have to thank me Beth but I have to say I'm terribly jealous," said Tabitha playfully.

"Why are you jealous?" asked Beth.

"Come on Beth, Its Brussels, the home of the best chocolate in the world! You know what they say about Belgium chocolate?" laughed Tabitha.

"No, what do they say?" asked Beth giggling and playing along.

"Resistance is futile!" Both women laughed as Beth thanked Tabitha and ended the call.

Beth thought about her entire experience and was impressed with the Blue Phoenix Group. "These folks are good. I'm bringing Tabitha some chochies home," thought Beth. "She sounded like the type of girl you wanted on a girl's night out. I'm going to have to meet her when I get to London. Maybe have her show me the city?" thought Beth. Getting showered and packed did not take long. Beth contacted the concierge and asked him about the travel time to the airport.

"Your flight is at 6.10pm and you're not going to the US, customs is always longer to the US. From here I'd say you should give yourself about 45 minutes. You should get there at about an hour and fifteen before your flight. So if you left here at say 4pm that should be plenty of time to get there with no bags to check.

You have your seat confirmed, it's the new terminal and they're fast. I'll have the Limo ready for you out front at 4pm Miss," said the concierge.

It was only 8am and Beth had the entire day to kill. She felt guilty wasting the day this was Toronto! She could not leave until 4pm so what was she going to do? She looked at the young lady behind the tourist counter setting up for the day.

"Hello, I'm Beth," she said stretching out a hand.

"Good morning Beth, I'm Yvonne. Sorry I'm a little disorganized, I'm just getting settled. How can I help you?" said Yvonne shaking Beth's hand warmly.

"I need some advice," said Beth.

"That's why I'm here."

"I'm new to Toronto well new to Canada. I've only been here a day and I need to leave for the airport at 4pm today. I have between now and 4pm to fill my day. What do you recommend?" asked Beth looking at the pamphlets behind Yvonne.

"I have a couple of choices for you. You can see Toronto and the CN Tower or if you want something magical that you'll never forget I can get you face to face with Niagara Falls. The full force of the water splashing your face," Yvonne said in an excited voice. "There's one catch, the tour bus leaves in 10 minutes. I can get you on it but you have to tell me now. The day costs $80 Canadian and includes your transportation and boat ride. You'll be dropped back at the hotel at 3.15pm. This will give you time to shower and change if you need to. I can arrange a courtesy suite for you to do that upon your return."

A swell of energy surged through the base of Beth's neck and the words "Niagara Falls" popped into her mind. "Well, I know which option Subra is voting for," thought Beth. "I'll take it," said Beth. "I can do the CN Tower when I come back to Toronto."

"Great! Just fill out this form, name, room number, signature and we will bill it to your room." Yvonne picked up the phone and dialed. "Hi can I speak with Dave please?" she said hurriedly. "Hi Dave, I have a single guest here who would like to join the tour this morning can you can fit her in?" Yvonne paused to let Dave talk to her. She smiled and said nothing. Covering the mouthpiece she looked at Beth, "He's such a flirt." Yvonne turned her attention back to Dave uncovering the mouthpiece. "Have you had your Tim Horton's coffee this morning yet?" she asked. Beth could hear Dave talking but could not hear the words. "Good" said Yvonne. "You're in, the bus is not full, and Dave said he needs to swing down Front Street anyway. He wants you to cross the road and he will pick you up. Just look for a white bus it holds about sixteen passengers." She put the phone to her mouth again; "Prepaid by the hotel and she's wearing jeans and a white tee shirt, very pretty," Yvonne winked at Beth. "Go now, cross the street and have a great time. Come see me when you get back and I'll arrange the shower for you."

She instructed Beth with a sense of urgency. Beth picked up her backpack and headed for the hotel exit. She passed through the tall glass doors and nodded to the doorman. Taking a glance at the sparse traffic on Front Street she decided to jaywalk. She crossed the street and waited for the white bus outside a Lone Star Texas restaurant.

Beth had raced across the street but she had more time than she thought. The bus did not arrive until a couple of minutes later. It stopped at the curb and the door opened revealing the beaming face of a young man in the driver's seat. "Good morning, come on in for a fun filled day," he said in a perky tone.

Beth ascended the few steps onto the mini bus and quickly glanced at its occupants. There were about three couples of varying ages and a few singles spaced about the bus. Beth smiled at the staring faces as she found a spot containing two empty seats. The driver was wearing a headset with a small microphone wrapped around his face. Beth took her backpack and placed it in the aisle seat. She positioned herself near the window for a better view. The mini bus door closed and pulled away heading west along Front Street as the speaker system crackled into life.

"Good morning everyone we're going to have some fun today. My name's Dave and I am your driver on this magical mystery tour. Well, actually, it's not much of a mystery we're heading to the Falls. You guys are going to be seeing the falls from its most awesome vantage point, aboard the Maid of the Mist. I'll mention a few things to break the journey up along the way but we should be there under two hours, depending upon traffic. Let's start by looking to the left, you can see a great view of the Rogers Center, or as the locals call it, the Skydome."

Beth could see a rising walkway and a glimpse of a concrete structure with a crisp white dome topping the building. She recalled airplane video showing the roof opening for baseball games. She caught a glimpse of a large concrete balcony built into the structure. Over-sized gold colored statues spilled out from the building. Statues of fans all shapes and sizes exaggerated in a cartoon like manner were attached to the building as an art decoration.

"Next to the Skydome of course is the CN Tower," raved Dave.

Dave continued to pepper the bus with facts and trivia about the Tower, the Skydome, Toronto and its history as the mini bus weaved through traffic. At one point the mini bus started to climb an onramp onto an elevated highway. Dave informed the occupants that they were traveling along the Gardiner Expressway and they would be on here for a while. The Gardiner Expressway was a three-lane highway and although it seemed fairly busy it was moving quickly. Beth glanced out of the window and could see condominium buildings and glitzy billboards. It reminded her of that scene in Blade Runner. She laughed as she recalled sleeping through the end of that movie it was a bit slow. Suddenly Beth got a postcard view of the lake. She could see the harbor with docked sailboats. Most were white colored and she thought of the majestic sailboat docked in Tokyo Bay. Occasionally Dave would break the silence with a joke or an observation about a point of interest. It was clear that he enjoyed his job and Beth was warming to his fun personality.

"Folks we are now entering the QEW as the locals call it. This is the road that'll lead us to the falls it's called the Queen Elizabeth Way. I know we have a few Brits on the bus today so you can now go home and say that you've driven all over Queen Elizabeth," chuckled Dave.

A few polite laughs echoed around the mini bus at Dave's corny joke. Beth stared out of the window and drifted off. She was not sleeping but she was daydreaming and tuned Dave out. Overhead traffic signs flashed by and she read each one as if to mark her progress. Dave explained that this was a hotbed of historical action as the British defended the border from the invading Americans. Many British forts were erected on the Canadian side. The British and the local native Indians cooperated in these skirmishes against the Americans long ago. The names of the places were either native Indian like Toronto or remarkably British. Beth saw signs for Mississauga, an obvious Indian name and Oakville. She almost jumped out of her seat and craned her neck to see the next sign. Flashing by was a sign for Bronte Road.

"Bronte," said Beth softly. She immediately thought of the Bronte sisters, the parsonage museum and her home village of Haworth. "A little bit of home right here in Canada. There are no coincidences," Beth heard herself mumble.

The mini bus continued at a decent speed and Beth was starting to get a little bored. She decided to play the cloud game, to see if she could bust a hole in one. There was one small problem; it was a gorgeous day in Southern Ontario. Pure blue sky could be seen for miles, not a cloud in sight. The temperature was climbing up as the morning hours disappeared. The next sign that Beth noticed was a metal sign looking like sail boats with a Welcome to Burlington message.

"Burlington," said Beth remembering the Tai Chi group performing on Harbour Front. At the roads edge was a large billboard showing a beautiful woman stretching in a yoga pose. The caption read "Yoga with Dominique, voted Burlington's best Yoga teacher." Beth studied the billboard and thought, "I'd like to do that. I should get into Yoga when I get back home."

The traffic flowed easily around Lake Ontario and the mini bus was making steady progress. Moving through Burlington they passed over a bridge and Dave explained the stark scenery of Hamilton. Once a proud steel town it reminded Beth of Sheffield. Passing Hamilton the mini bus started to offer more scenic views. Dave talked about the wine-growing region of Niagara; he mentioned Ice Wine and talked about the famous wineries located here. Beth pictured herself enjoying her celebratory glass of Ice Wine and eating Belgium chocolates. Some of the place names reflected the wine-producing region such as Fruitland. Passing the township of Stoney Creek she saw specific names that reminded her of home such as Grimsby and Lincoln. Beth glanced at her thighs they felt warm from the sun streaming through the window turning her denim a lighter shade of blue. She thought about how much she had grown as a person these last few weeks. She felt stronger, resilient and more mentally prepared. She always lacked confidence and felt awkward, almost clumsy. She sat here today heading towards another experience and feeling excited about trying something new. It was more than that. She felt connected with the world as if she now had a purpose. Her life now meant something; people needed her to be on her game. She had responsibilities and she had not shirked them or laughed them off. She was delivering on her promises and handling tight pressure filled situations. She had shown a strong spirit and had kept her head. Beth smiled to herself as she realized she was not the same woman that left Yorkshire and she could never go back to being that person. She felt more confident in herself and her boundless possibilities.

"Is this what maturing feels like?" she thought.

It dawned on Beth that she also, for the first time, felt like a woman instead of a scared little girl. She could feel her power grow resulting from a sense of inner peace and her renewed confidence. Men always agree that the sexiest attribute of a woman is confidence. She recalled how she managed to push back with Kaigara and thought about the Beth of old. She would have been intimidated into silence. Beth sensed a large smile cross her face and she flashed her green eyes towards the window and soaked up the strong sun. When they reached St. Catherines Dave informed the passengers that they were starting to get close and would be entering Niagara soon. Beth could see signs to the USA and the Rainbow Bridge. The mini bus snaked an intricate path through Victoria Avenue and Eastwood Crescent before finally turning onto River Road. Dave was starting to get excited as he described the falls. He talked about their history with high wire walkers and people going over the falls in wooden barrels. He pointed to a huge plume of water spray that was visible high in the air causing a brilliant colored rainbow. Beth felt the excitement. You could not see the falls but you could hear a constant roaring noise from within the bus!

"Right people listen up," crackled Dave over his headset. "When I pull up to the curb I want everyone to get off the bus as quickly, but as safely, as you can. A young lady wearing blue will meet you. She'll be your guide and I think its Tammy working today. I'll have to pull away quickly and park elsewhere. You'll be whisked through the boarding process and avoid all the lineups. They'll kit you out in waterproof rain gear and help you onto the Maid of the Mist. My advice to you is go upstairs to the upper deck and stand at the front of the boat. That's the best vantage point to feel the full force of the falls. You'll get the best experience if you take the boat ride first then go and see the falls from above on the promenade. I'm sure that you'll have fun and remember, upstairs. Most people go to the front of the boat downstairs and it's too close to the water and too crowded," said Dave trying to be helpful.

As the mini bus drew closer the roar of the water became louder adding to the anticipation. The mini bus stopped at the foot of Clifton Hill close to the Rainbow Bridge. Everyone gathered their belongings and filed off the bus in an orderly manner. From the outside of the bus the roar of the falls sounded significantly louder and the air had a cooler misty feel. A young woman wearing shorts and a blue golf shirt beamed a smile at the group as the mini bus pulled away.

"Everyone, my name's Tammy I'm going to be your guide today. Your boat ride has been prepaid as part of the tour and I'm sure you're going to have a great time," she said doing a quick head count. "Follow me everyone please."

Beth walked with the group and entered the Maid of the Mist plaza. Tammy talked about the falls and the powerful diesel-engine boats that transport you from the Canadian docks past the foot of the American falls. The journey continues into the basin of the Canadian Horseshoe falls as the captain fights the powerful cur-rent and navigates a course clear of sunken rocks. It reminded her of a salmon swimming upstream. Tammy explained that there are two boats that depart in a cycle. Each boat can carry 600 passengers and are named the Maid of the Mist VI and VII. Each is 80 feet long and has two 350-horsepower engines. Tammy proceeded through this well rehearsed speech as if she had delivered it a thousand times. Her timing was impeccable for just as Tammy completed her speech the group was given recyclable blue plastic raincoats. Beth could feel the nervous energy in the group. The excitement grew when they were asked to enter a large brown stone tower, covered in mosaic vines. Inside were four high-speed elevators that took the group down to the docks at the river's edge. Beth could see the water streaming by and got her first glimpse of the Maid of the Mist VI.

Passengers were streaming off the boat as Beth looked at the sleek lines and pointed front of the boat. It had a second tier and a small shed like protrusion that she imagined the captain would occupy. She could see the location on the boat that Dave had indicated to be the ideal spot. Tammy waved the group forward. Beth could see more passengers filing in behind her group as the boat readied for another trip. The water roared in the distance and the plastic raincoat was starting to get hot in the sun. The group headed for the boat, Beth was swept along as if she were caught in the strong currents of the river. She headed upstairs and found a good spot at the front of the second deck. She hung onto the railing and watched hundreds of people pack in behind her. After what seemed an age the engines roared and the boat pulled away from the docks. The engines were noisy and the boat swung around and started to pass the American falls. They were larger and more impressive when you stared at them from the vantage point of the river. The water rushed over the edge and fell at great speed. Beth could not believe the pace of the water. Below were large dark stone boulders being battered by the force of the crashing water. A woman from the bus tapped Beth on her shoulder and pointed to the sky. Beth turned to see a beautiful rainbow arching through the spray and the sun.

"Beautiful," thought Beth her cheeks hurting from the fixed smile on her face.

Once past the American falls the boat started to pick up steam, the engines roared louder and the boat started to strain against the fast flowing current. The boat pressed on and the plume of spray hid the upcoming falls. It was difficult to see through the spray. The combined force of the wind and water hit the passengers full on. People huddled together and pulled their raincoat hoods over their heads for protection against the wet spray. The boat still powered forwards. Breaking through the wall of spray the sound of crashing water was deafening, exciting and heart pumping. Beth gritted her teeth but still had an enormous smile on her face.

"This is awesome, wow, what an experience," she thought.

The best was yet to come. The Captain took the boat right into the whirlpool letting the powerful engine strain against the current until the engines were flat out and yet the boat remained stationary. From this point Beth could see the falls in all of its thunderous glory. She stared upwards into a 172 feet high circular wall of fast moving water. It crashed onto rocks below generating the plume of spray high into the air. People on the boat were soaked and the noise was indescribable. The once mighty looking boat seemed tiny and underpowered when matched against the force of Niagara Falls. People laughed, huddled and gawped at the sheer power of the falls. Beth tried to imagine going over the top and crashing onto the rocks below in a wooden barrel!The boat finally gave up and let the current take it back down river giving the group another great view of the falls. A second rainbow glistened across the Horseshoe Falls and everyone pointed to the colored masterpiece. This was nature at its most powerful and it's most majestic. Only once, due to an ice flow clogging the river upstream has Niagara Falls stopped.

Old photographs document this dry winter scene. A "thundering silence" was how local residents described it. The water was flowing with great force as the boat fought its way back to the base of the falls to afford its passengers another stunning view. The Captain could only go so far due to the submerged rocks and the force of the current sweeping the boat backwards. After three valiant attempts the Maid of the Mist VI succumbed and let the current sweep the boat back downstream to the docks. It was exhilarating the whole experience shook Beth to the core. This was the only way to see the falls to appreciate its size and power. Her life now was about helping others and collecting new experiences. This was an experience she would never forget and was well worth the time and the effort spent getting here. The boat docked and Beth felt the strong sun drying her wet skin and raincoat. She took the plastic raincoat off and rolled it into a small ball. She threw it into a collection bin as she stepped off the boat. She also felt a swell of energy and her cheeks flushed.

"Incredible," popped into her mind.

"I agree Subra," thought Beth.

Subra had clearly enjoyed this experience and had fed on the raw energy. The ride lasted about 25 minutes but it seemed longer. Beth and the group were ushered back to the gift shop full of tacky items. Tammy wanted the group to see the falls from above to appreciate the sheer drop of the water. She escorted Beth and the group along the promenade to a fantastic vantage point where the water literally disappears. The river that feeds the falls was moving extremely fast she could see it pouring around Goat Island. Further upstream Beth could see the rusting hull of a grounded ship. Looking across the falls she could see people on the American side walking on a gantry. She looked down the river at the Rainbow Bridge cutting through a beautiful rainbow of many colors. The sun was strong and people were in a good mood.

"This was an awesome day," thought Beth.

Beth could see the little white boat with hundreds of tiny blue cladded passengers crammed onto the deck. The boat was powering towards the whirlpool. Beth could not believe she had just done this and could not take the smile off her face. A small blue and white helicopter hovered over the top of the Horseshoe Falls before taking off at great speed. The constant noise of the falls continued to bash Beth's ears. Tammy interrupted the bliss.

"Thanks guys the bus is here and you need to get on as quickly as you can. I do hope you enjoyed your visit, we enjoyed having you, come and see us again." She waved her arms and ushered the group onto the bus. Beth smiled at Dave the driver as she passed him and took the same seat.

"You can't tell me that wasn't amazing," shouted Dave into his mouthpiece with a high degree of excitement.

The group responded with a spontaneous round of applause. Beth was feeling energized her hair matted and a little wet. The mini bus pulled away into traffic and retraced its route back to Toronto. People settled into the comfy seats for the return journey. Beth started to recall billboards, houses and business signs that she recognized from her journey to the falls. The journey back was swift and the inside of the bus was calm and quiet. For some reason it seemed faster on the way home. Some passengers slept, some just stared out of the window trying to come down from the natural high. Beth thought about her day and how marvelous it was to collect that experience. She would never forget the sheer power of the water on the boat and against her face. Her thoughts turned to how far she had come in her life, no longer the clumsy shy girl who needed to focus. She smiled as she remembered Subra's reaction to the falls he enjoyed it too. She could not have imagined weeks ago in Haworth that she would have been staring into the might of Niagara Falls. Beth started to think about what she needed to do when she got back to the hotel. She would need to shower and change quickly. Her flight to Brussels would not be too bad. She would be spoiled by the yellow jackets. Beth had no real expectation of Belgium other than good chocolate and finding the portal.

What would she find in Schelle? What would Hoshi be like? How quickly could she find the portal? All of these questions danced through her mind. Beth could not sleep but the mini bus pressed on regardless. Dave was silently focused on the road as traffic increased closer to Toronto. Soon the traffic was heavy and moving fast. Illuminated billboards signaled a proximity to Toronto. The mini bus turned a corner and exposed the first city view with the CN Tower shining in the fading sun. Beth recognized this view as her first glimpse of Toronto when she came in from the airport. The mini bus soon dropped onto an off ramp that took them down to street level. Long shadows were cast by the tall condominiums and office towers. Dave spoke into the microphone.

"My first drop off is for the lady at the InterContinental, it'll be coming up here on the right."

"That's me," thought Beth glancing at her watch. It was 3.15pm, she had a short amount of time to shower and be ready for the airport pickup at 4pm. Beth felt the bus pull over to a stop and recognized the hotel entrance. She grabbed her backpack and headed to the front of the bus. "Thank you," she said smiling at Dave the driver.

"My pleasure," said Dave beaming back at Beth reminding her of Sanjeev.

Beth nodded to the doorman and entered the hotel. She made a direct line for the tourist desk and saw Yvonne on the phone. Yvonne caught Beth's eyes as she moved towards the desk.

She quickly completed her call, "How was it?" she asked.

"Awesome," replied Beth just about to hurry her along.

"Good, well I know you don't have much time but suite 202 is available. The towels are fresh just use this," said Yvonne offering Beth a plastic card key.

"Thank you so much," said Beth taking the key.

"You're welcome now go and drop the key back with me when you're done," said Yvonne.

Beth showered quickly. She washed her hair and pulled it into a ponytail. A quick change of clothes and she was on her way. It was 3.50pm when she entered the elevator to get to the ground floor.

"Feeling better?" inquired Yvonne.

"Much better, thanks," responded Beth returning the key. Beth felt energized, ready to tackle the next leg of her journey to Brussels and Hoshi.

Yvonne picked up the phone "Miss Martindale is ready," she said nodding to the phone and the recipient of her message. "You're all set, just see the doorman and have a great flight. Come and see us again."

"I have a strong feeling that I will" said Beth cheerfully, "again thank you for your help today you made the day a wonderful end to my Toronto visit."

"You're most welcome," beamed Yvonne.

"I do like these Canadians," thought Beth.

Beth strode confidently around the escalator cut away and out through the doors. As she exited the hotel the doorman greeted her and took her backpack. He placed it deep within the trunk of the limousine and closed it with a thud. Beth slid across the shiny black leather into the rear seat. A young Arabic looking man with a thin black mustache turned to greet Beth.

"Which airline please?" he said with a thick accent.

"Jet Airways to Brussels," replied Beth.

"Thanks, terminal one," was his response.

The doorman closed the passenger door with a smile and the limousine pulled away into traffic. The young man focused on his driving and did not talk with Beth during the drive to the airport. She said goodbye to Toronto knowing that she would be back. Beth knew she would explore the city, the Tower and see Sakura again, perhaps meet her husband. Familiar sights flashed by, the Skydome, the modern windmill, the plant based advertisements, the 427 and the lake views. It was not long before Beth was seeing airport signs. Soon she was entering the maze of roads that snaked their way into the various terminals. The limousine pulled up to a busy curb designed to disembark travelers so they could enter the airport terminal.

"This is you Miss, you're on account so you're fully paid up have a nice flight."

"Thanks," said Beth walking to the rear of the car.

The driver had managed to get there first and was handing Beth her backpack. He smiled awkwardly. Beth wheeled away in the direction of the terminal. Beth walked through the glass sliding doors to enter a large modern terminal. The terminal was brightly lit with an arched glass roof resembling an aircraft hangar. In front of her was a large panel with all the flights and their associated check in desks. Beth retrieved her itinerary.

"Flight 9W229 leaving at 18:10, where's that?" Beth squinted at the board before recognizing her flight at gate C. Beth looked down the check in hall; it was large, wide and organized in a semi circle. It was modern with high white tiled poles sporting black signs and contrasting bright yellow letters. She could see a yellow C in the distance and started towards it. Beth plotted a path between the passengers, families, luggage and a million other obstacles before she made it to aisle C. She turned into the wide aisle to see passengers in orderly lines waiting to get their boarding pass. Beth saw a familiar and welcome sight a well-groomed Indian woman in a smart long yellow jacket.

She beamed a smile and in a crisp Canadian accent asked Beth "Business class Miss?"

"Yes," replied Beth handing the woman her itinerary.

Beth was shown into an empty priority line and was checked in quickly and efficiently. With boarding pass in hand she made her way through security with relative ease. Once inside the secured area she started to notice the artwork strategically placed. Dancing figures suspended high above within a large skylight. The figures were made of glass and colored blue, yellow, red and green; it reminded Beth of the rainbows she saw in Niagara Falls. A week ago Beth would have been intimidated at the prospect of navigating her way through a large international airport. Today she felt confident and in control. Any doubt she might have had was now easily erased. She only had to think about the challenges the young girls faced in the Golden Tree to put her small challenges into perspective. Beth's timing was good. She waited about ten minutes before business class was called to board ahead of the remaining passengers. It was the usual immaculate routine with the yellow jackets; a warm welcome, Champagne, juice and water. Beth settled into her pod and watched movies until she felt tired.

The cabin was now dark and peaceful. There is something about a night flight where all is calm. The consistent low drone of engines and air circulation lull you to sleep. Beth felt her eye's getting tired and she snapped the entertainment screen back into its holder. She removed her earphones and pulled the warm blanket up to her neck. She reclined the seat to sleeping position.

"Time to chat with Subra," thought Beth.

Chapter 14

Hoshi - Truths, Falsehoods and the Pyrenees

Beth slipped quietly into sleep. The thick airline blanket provided needed warm and protection from the cool air conditioning.

"How are you my old friend?" asked Beth. Subra's energy came through louder and clearer than of late. "You enjoyed the Maid of the Mist, I could tell," thought Beth.

"I really enjoyed that experience. I managed to feed from the pure energy from the falls and the people. It was like having a large meal! A thing of beauty is a joy forever. It's faith in someone and enthusiasm for something that makes life worth living." Subra sounded charged.

"Subra, Schelle and IN DEN VOS; this lead seems a strong one to me. I'm good to go and chase this, right? I mean, there's no certainties but I know I don't have much time," thought Beth feeling concerned.

"Creativity requires the courage to let go of certainties. The portal will come to you when you're ready to receive it. Look how much you've grown already, how you feel about yourself and your outlook on life," explained Subra.

Beth paused and thought deeply, "No, that's not good enough. I need to be ready soon so I can find the portal before it's too late. I don't want to fail you due to my limitations."

"I seldom think of my limitations, and they never make me sad. Perhaps there is just a touch of yearning at times; but it is vague, like a breeze among flowers. Focus on what you want not on what you don't want," said Subra steering Beth in a different direction.

Beth switched topics in one fluid thought, "I'm looking forward to the challenge of meeting Hoshi but I've got this nagging feeling that she's barking up the wrong tree."

"One must be fond of people and trust them if one is not to make a mess of life. The only real mistake is the one from which we learn nothing. Beth you must trust your own instinct. Your mistakes might well be your own instead of someone else's," responded Subra. Beth knew the quotes Subra selected had deeper meaning and she often tried to find the deeper side to his responses.

"I need to learn from my mistakes and then they're not mistakes. Life's about learning, collecting experiences and helping others," she summarized.

"Wisdom is knowing what to do next; skill is knowing how to do it, and virtue is doing it. A woman uses her intelligence to find reasons to support her intuition," said Subra gently moving Beth to a better place.

"Got it. Use my intuition and back it up with facts and reason. I haven't formulated my strategy with Hoshi yet but when a woman tells the truth she is creating the possibility for more truth around her," thought Beth.

"Adrienne Rich, good quote. I believe you'll have to box clever and do subtle adjustments in your approach as the conversation unfolds," advised Subra.

"You're right, sometimes honesty doesn't work, it takes two and she seems the type who will be comfortable lying."

"Lying is done with words and also with silence," offered Subra.

"Another quote from Adrienne Rich. Yes, it'll be cat and mouse. You'll let me know if you feel the energy of the portal? I want to know I'm in the right place," thought Beth concerned at being on her own with Hoshi.

Subra tried to feed Beth some profound advice hoping she would pick it up quickly. "I will. Just remember that we learn what we have said from those who listen to our speaking."

Beth knew instantly where Subra was going with this. "She'll provide me with a clue that's why I have two ears and only one mouth. I'm confident but I'm realistic, this isn't going to be easy."

"All good is hard. All evil is easy. Dying, losing, cheating, and mediocrity are easy. Stay away from easy," teased Subra.

Beth laughed, "That's a good one; Scott Alexander I believe."

"I know you need to hear this but I think you're on the right track. Right now it's our only track so it's the right one. You have to be confident, you have to believe and prepare. Luck is where opportunity meets preparation and when we get the luck we'll be ready," explained Subra.

"When choosing between two evils; I always like to try the one I've never tried before," chuckled Beth. "Mae West sounded like a fun woman."

"She did! You're starting to get conscious access to the quotes; you now have this great resource at hand.

Use it when you meet with Hoshi remember though the good life is inspired by love and guided by knowledge," urged Subra.

Beth switched the topic of conversation radically and with no warning. "Why am I starting to feel attracted to men all of a sudden? Why is it that I'm noticing men looking at me? That's never happened to me before, never?"

"One simple word Beth, confidence," answered Subra. "If you think you can, you can. If you think you can't, you can't. You're right!"

"Confidence?" replayed Beth.

"Beth, you have a strong life force now. That's exciting for you but equally exciting to those who meet you and feel attracted to your energy. You have what we call the grand essentials of happiness," explained Subra.

"I haven't heard that term before, grand essentials of happiness?"

"The grand essentials of happiness are: something to do, something to love, and something to hope for. Right now you're learning to love yourself Beth. You have a job and a mission. Once you get comfortable with who you are you'll need a handsome man to complete your essentials of happiness. Don't get me wrong you don't need a man to exist, but your soul is telling you that you're ready to share your life and laughter with someone special. If you could only get this spirit out of your head!" laughed Subra.

Beth thought about the message carefully, "I see what you're saying. I'm ready; the time is right so I'm attracting this. You can't shake hands with a closed fist."

"Just as you're ready to find the right man, you need to prepare yourself to be as ready and open to receive signals to locate the portal. You have to be ready," said Subra in a serious tone.

"I understand it, I need to be truthful to myself," thought Beth.

"There are truths on this side of the Pyrenees, which are falsehoods on the other. To interpret truth you need to fully engage your intuition. Does this feel right? Beth you're heading into some heavy topics, be careful not to get into analysis paralysis, this can be simple. Trust yourself and don't resist. Things will come to you when you're ready. Just be prepared to see the signs," offered Subra.

"Yeah, you're right," thought Beth feeling much calmer.

"I have to go and you have to wake. Not only is another world possible, she is on her way. On a quiet day I can hear her breathing," Subra faded from consciousness.

"Arundhati Roy; that's a beautiful quote," thought Beth to herself.

She woke and glanced around the aircraft cabin to orient her self. The plane landed in Brussels in its usual smooth and timely manner that Beth had now grown accustomed using Jet Airways. The airport is located in Zaventem just outside of Brussels and has been voted the best airport in Europe; you could see why. It was clean, efficient and highly organized. The customs process was equally efficient with Beth explaining she was visiting Brussels on vacation. Beth left the customs officer and walked towards baggage claim. She passed the crowded carousels and entered the greeting area. It was 8.15am local time and the greeting area was only half full. Nothing looked full these days compared to the frenzied chaos of India. Centrally located a tall man stood holding a sign, "Martindale" written in bold black letters. Beth caught the man's eyes and nodded. His face immediately registered a smile as he navigated his route through the calm stationary crowd towards Beth.

"Good morning Beth, I hope you had a pleasant flight? Welcome to Brussels I'm Everard," he said in a friendly way. He spoke with clear English tinged with a slight accent. Everard reached for Beth's backpack and pointed in a direction for them to leave.

"Flight was great, nice to meet you Everard, Sakura and her husband have asked me to pass on their best regards," said Beth.

Everard was probably in his mid forties, he had a full head of dark hair carelessly swept back from his face. He wore matching pants and shirt, which looked like a dark blue uniform. He was a little overweight and had a beer belly.

Beth noticed his girth and thought, "Good Belgium beer."

He seemed very polite and was friendly enough as he chatted on route to the parked taxi. Everard's taxi was a shiny black Mercedes Benz. He opened the trunk for the backpack and then opened the door for Beth. As Beth climbed in she could imagine diplomats and politicians being driven around by Everard's company.

"Traffic is just filling in Beth but we should have you to your hotel by around 9am, sound good?" asked Everard.

"Sounds good."

The car pulled away and merged onto a highway. The traffic was light and the road was smooth. The pace of the traffic seemed slower than Toronto with not as many lanes. It was much quieter than India, no horn blowing! Beth watched the green trees and brick houses whiz by. The Benz was powerful, smooth and very quiet.

"First time to Belgium Beth?"

"Yes, I'm looking forward to it."

"Got any requests for chocolate from back home?" laughed Everard.

"No, but I'm going to take some home with me though," said Beth laughing.

"We're famous for beer, waffles, chocolate, a little peeing statue, diamonds, and our beautiful architecture. Go see the Grand Place. We're the capital of the European Union so we have many politicians. You're going to Schelle, which is a pretty little place. I wish I could say the same for Hoshi; she's an interesting old bird. Sorry, I shouldn't call her that, but she's fairly cranky, you'll see. The drive to Schelle isn't bad. I was thinking of letting you get settled in maybe take a nap or a shower. I will pick you up at the hotel for the drive to Schelle say 1pm? It takes about 40 to 45 minutes up the A12," said Everard glancing in his rear view mirror at Beth.

"Do I have a time booked to meet Hoshi?" asked Beth a bit surprised.

"Yes, Hoshi is keen to meet you. She wants to see you at 2pm. I've arranged for you and her to meet. It's going to be a gorgeous day and I know Schelle from my frequent visits. There's a restaurant that Hoshi hangs around, it's near a beautiful park. I can pull into the parking lot and let you two have a natter on the park bench near the restaurant. This seems to be her favorite spot in the whole village. I hope this is not too tiring for you but I was told that there was some urgency that you two meet," explained Everard.

Beth would have preferred an extra day, as this would have given her more time to prepare for Hoshi. The date and time had been set and she did not want to be the one to back down and appear weak. She needed to be ready and she would be ready.

"That's fine Everard. I'll be ready to meet Hoshi at 2pm. So I need to be ready for pickup in the hotel lobby at 1pm?" said Beth adjusting her watch to sync with the time displayed on the Benz dashboard.

"Great. I'll wait until you've finished your chat and drive you back into Brussels for the night. I'm available to take you to Schelle as often as you wish. Just make sure you arrange that with Hoshi before you leave. Hoshi doesn't have access to either email or phone so it's tough to arrange anything with her. She remembers everything for an old woman though. She's still mentally sharp," explained Everard occasionally taking his eyes off the road to meet Beth's in the rear view mirror. The Benz turned into busy city streets and then into the front of a crescent shaped building. "This is your hotel Beth, the Hotel Meridien. It's a decent hotel and you're central to all the action. The Manneken Pis is about a ten minute walk and the Grand Place is even less. There are fantastic places to eat within walking distance. You should go out tonight and explore. You have to see the Grand Place and it's worth seeing during the day and at night, totally different," said Everard with excitement and pride in his voice. "Anyway I'm keeping you; I'll see you at 1pm."

A doorman welcomed Beth as she retrieved her backpack and walked into the hotel. A stained glass revolving door opened up into a larger reception area. To the left the hall narrowed. In front of Beth was a large sitting area with a few people drinking coffee and reading newspapers. The sitting area had three large floor to ceiling windows flooding bright sunshine into the room. Flanked by cream-colored tall pillars the room was calm. The polished marble floor had a circular wheel design inlaid in tones of brown with a glass table at its center. A large brass chandelier with many lampshades hung above the table. To the right was a wooden reception area and check in desk. Two men and a woman in their early twenties staffed the desk.

One of the men raised his eyes to meet Beth "Bonjour."

"Good morning, Beth Martindale checking in," said Beth in a cheery tone.

"Certainly Miss Martindale," said the man in crisp English. "I have you on account Miss Martindale and we have a suite for you. Can I see your passport please and I'll go ahead and check you in?"

Beth handed over her passport and the young man typed information into the reservation system. He prepared the room key package slipping the plastic key into a holder made of card. "Is one key sufficient?"

"One's fine." Beth received her passport and the room key together with a small visitor's booklet.

"You're in room 722; the elevators are down the hall behind you and to the right. You'll need to insert the key to call the elevators. As a promotion we've included a small booklet with some really useful maps and tourist information for your sightseeing if you have time. Enjoy your stay with us."

"Thank you," said Beth smiling and turning to face the hall behind her.

She walked the hall, which came to an abrupt end as it swung away to the right. Turning the corner she saw the elevators on the left and what looked like a bar on the right. Beth pushed her card into the metal wall slot and pressed the button to call for the elevators. The elevator on the right arrived with a cheery dinging noise. Beth stepped out at the seventh floor and faced a mirror and a small desk with yellow flowers arranged in a vase. She glanced at the signs on the wall and turned left down another narrow hallway. She arrived at room number 722 and entered using the plastic access card. Beth activated the lights using the card slot in the wall although the room was flooded with natural sunlight. The room was spacious and neat. Wooden furniture accented the modern design. Beth walked to the window where she could see the busy street below. She looked out onto a church and in the distance could see an ornate spire high above the rooftops.

"Brussels," said Beth aloud. "Who in their right mind would have thought that I would visit Brussels? I thought I was going to India," said Beth shaking her head at the ridiculously sumptuous notion. Beth unloaded her backpack, showered and changed her clothes. She stocked the room safe with her valuables and later pushed her face into the streaming water jets of the showerhead.

She let some water enter her mouth and said to herself, "Just like the Maid of the Mist." As she said the words the water spilled out as the shower head continued to pelt her face with small jets of water. She recalled the spray from the falls. Beth did not feel like going out and exploring yet. There would be time later for that. She would stay in her room. She watched television jumping from channel to channel. She flipped through the tourist booklet and stored it in her backpack. She lay on the bed and relaxed. Beth stared into the mirror and practiced some well-rehearsed lines imagining how her conversation with Hoshi would go. She was nervous about this meeting and this was her way of preparing for the dialogue. She tried various approaches watching her performances in the mirror. 1pm could not come quickly enough for Beth. Finally it was time to head down to the lobby and meet up with Everard. The morning had dragged but Beth's strong intuition told her to stay within her room and rehearse, even though the exciting city of Brussels was within reach.

She glanced at her watch. To be honest she had looked at her watch almost every three minutes for the last fifteen minutes. It was time to head out and meet with Everard and Hoshi. Beth recognized Everard when she turned the corner and entered the hotel lobby area. He was pouring his charm over the young attractive receptionist who seemed to be enjoying the attention. Beth sized up the prospective couple and gave Everard a very slim chance of turning this into something meaningful. She gave him near impossible odds of turning this into something not meaningful. She smiled as she recognized that look of relief on the young woman's face when she saw Beth approaching.

"Are you ready?" was Everard's question.

"Yes, you?" responded Beth.

Everard nodded and headed for the stained glass revolving door that exits to the street. Beth followed and stepped into the bright light. The shiny black Benz was parked in the premium spot just to the right of the doorway and ready to drive off. Everard opened the passenger door for Beth as she positioned herself in the back seat. Beth was slightly annoyed at herself as she felt butterflies and knots forming in her stomach.

"Don't be nervous, you're strong and confident," she heard herself affirm.

Everard sensed this awkwardness. Before pulling away he stared into the rear view mirror to catch Beth's eyes. "It's going to go well Beth, nothing to get nervous about. She's a cranky old witch but you can handle her."

"Witch," thought Beth, "He used the word witch. How much did he know?"

"The drive's a simple one; it should only take about 40 or 45 minutes depending on the traffic. I'm going to take my time but it should be smooth sailing today. Beth, Sakura told me that this was going to be one of the most important meetings of your life. I don't mean to pry but when someone piles that amount of pressure on anyone you get uptight and nervous. My only advice to you is relax keep anything that you do simple. That's always worked for me in difficult situations," offered Everard.

"Thanks, that's good advice, I will," smiled Beth.

Everard slid the gearshift into drive and pulled away from the parking lot. After winding through a carefully planned street route he announced that they had made it to the roundabout that will get them onto the A12.

"We should be on here for about 25 kilometers," said Everard.

Beth was quiet running through key phrases in her head and trying to anticipate questions. "Keep it simple," Everard had said. That made more sense to Beth who was busy tying her nervous system into knots. The journey was smooth and uneventful; to break the thundering silence Everard turned the radio on. He selected a station that played light soothing instrumental music. It helped calm Beth. She glanced outside at the signs and did not recognize any. This was not Ontario with English sounding names. She saw names like Boomsesteenweg and Langlaarsteenweg. These were long and foreign sounding to Beth.

"Beth we're close now," said Everard turning the radio off. Steenwinkelstraat came into view. "This is Schelle Beth," announced Everard in a heavier accent.

The Benz glided down the road and smoothly pulled into a parking lot made of compressed stone chips. Beth could sense the tactile feed back of the car moving from a smooth asphalt road surface to the crunching sound of the dusty gravel. Everard pulled into a spot at the far end of the rectangular lot, which provided him some shade from the overhanging trees. Beth had been looking to the right. When she moved her head to the left a flat building came into view with a weathered wooden sign. Beth could just read the sign through the dust stirred up by the Benz.

In Den Vos Restaurant
Steenwinkelstraat, 49,
Schelle,
2627

Beth rubbed her eyes as if imaginary dust were blurring her view. "Do you feel anything Subra?" A surge of warmth flushed her cheeks and a message flooded her thoughts.

"Portal no, Corom yes."

Everard was looking into the rear view mirror directly at Beth. When Beth raised her eyes to the mirror Everard grinned. "If you're ready she's sitting on the bench like she normally does, right there," he said exaggerating his head movement to the left.

Looking to the left she could see a scene surrounded by trees and a small park. Opposite the restaurant a small isolated figure was sat motionless positioned at one end of a bench. Beth observed the petite frame clad in layers of clothes on a hot day. Her back was stooped as she faced the park. She had short black straight hair and wore a brown knitted sweater that was better suited for Fall. Beside her feet was a purse placed upon the ground. Hoshi looked smaller than Beth expected, she seemed less intimidating. Beth took a deep breath and reached for the handle on the Benz door. She heard a click and without really being present she found herself standing on the stone chips and clunking the Benz door closed. She could hear the stone crunching under her feet as she took steps towards the solitary figure. Beth knew that Hoshi could hear her approaching.

"Portal no, Corom yes," rattled her thoughts again.

Beth looked at Hoshi she could see a distinctive Indigo aura emanating from her tiny figure, it was strong and pure with no trace of any other color. "That's what I must look like?" thought Beth.

If Hoshi heard Beth approach she did not move to acknowledge her presence. She decided to remain facing the park. Beth rounded the arm of the bench and caught her first glimpse of Hoshi. She was indeed small framed and looking down at her feet. Her back was slightly arched and her hair was straight, neat and jet-black. It framed a face wrinkled with age. Her skin had an unusual color to it. It was a yellow color that darkened in the creases of her wrinkles. The yellow pallor was not a healthy glow it was the mustard yellow of dying skin. In stark contrast she had dark refined eyebrows and long dark eye lashes. Hoshi had a small puckered mouth and wore no lipstick. Hoshi rolled her eyes upwards to see who was casting a shadow over her favored sunspot. Her eyes were clear and bright, a deep chocolate brown with a fire burning behind them. This was the first indication to Beth that this woman was still sharp and engaged.

"Beth I presume," said Hoshi in an accent that sounded more Canadian than Japanese. She did not change her facial expression, which added to the impact of the greeting. It was almost dismissive.

"May I join you?" asked Beth respectfully.

"You've traveled a long way," said Hoshi moving her head to face Beth.

It was then Beth realized that moving was an effort for this woman. Our bodies were not designed to function for this long. Beth sat on the bench careful not to touch Hoshi. The silence was deafening but Beth just stared forward at the park.

"Do you know what an aura is Beth?" asked Hoshi.

This was not going where Beth had anticipated but she remembered the advice; keep it simple and go along with the conversation. "I know what an aura is and I know we both have Indigo auras," said Beth assuredly.

"Hmmm," said Hoshi. "What do you think that means?" asked Hoshi.

"It means everything and nothing," said Beth feeling pleased with her answer.

"Hmmm," said Hoshi starting to rock. "Sakura said I should meet with you. She's never said that before. She usually tries to hide me, not introduce me. Why does she want me to meet you?"

"Perhaps we are alike you and I."

"What makes you say that?" asked Hoshi.

"I believe we're more alike than you can imagine," said Beth strongly.

Hoshi stopped rocking and glared at Beth fixing her in those steely brown eyes. "How much do you know about me young lady?"

"Like I said we're a lot alike," said Beth vaguely.

"You know I'm an old woman, I like riddles but you're telling me nothing and yet you've traveled so far. I'm not sure that I'm seeing the worth of this conversation," said Hoshi bluntly.

"You might not see the worth but I wonder if Corom does?" asked Beth waiting to see the reaction. Beth certainly got a reaction from Hoshi. She glared intensely at Beth.

"Who told you about Corom? Bunch of delirious rants. Everyone hears voices at my age."

"Not everyone hears voices in your twenties and lives as long as you. Did you make him a promise?" asked Beth pointedly.

"You're not alone are you dear?" fired back Hoshi.

"That's right," said Beth pausing to see a reaction, "Everard drove me here today."

Hoshi smiled but she knew. "So you haven't answered me, why are you here?"

"You and I are looking for the same thing," said Beth keeping her options open.

"What would that be?"

"What's in Schelle Hoshi?" asked Beth using her name for the first time.

"I like living here it's quiet," bluffed Hoshi.

"IN DEN VOS" offered Beth. "The Toronto reference library helped you link IN DEN VOS to Schelle. Let's stop playing games. We need to cooperate," said Beth offering an olive branch. Hoshi studied the request but was not inclined to give in that easily.

"That place serves lousy coffee," snapped Hoshi.

Beth knew she was just blustering and she knew she was lying. Her voice altered slightly when she lied. Hoshi would be of little use at poker. "We can play with each other all day, you and I. I suggest we cooperate and join forces we'd be a stronger team," said Beth.

"What if I don't want to be a team, I'm happy on my own," said Hoshi resuming her rocking.

"You're not happy, I can tell. I know you don't want to hurt Corom he's your friend," that statement caused Hoshi to turn her head slightly and again glare at Beth. Beth swallowed hard and continued, "You have to get him home I understand that, more than you know," said Beth.

"Go on, say more," barked Hoshi.

Beth wondered if she should, she was giving her hand away. "Might as well go for it," thought Beth. "I know that we both need to find something then we can resume our normal lives."

"I'm old; I don't have a normal life. I'm ready to leave this world," said Hoshi softly.

"I know. You're getting tired of searching," offered Beth.

"What are you looking for dear?" asked Hoshi all coy.

"The same thing that you are," answered Beth cleverly.

Hoshi paused as if to say something dramatic that could turn the conversation. "Do you have a Corom?" Beth was rocked, what should she say? It was time to raise the stakes. She needed to hit back and get serious.

"Yes, Toshie, I have a Corom," said Beth using her real name and maintaining firm eye contact. It was time to be straight with each other.

It was not lost on Hoshi what Beth had just called her; she fixed her gaze squarely upon Beth. You could see the wheels turning in her head as she weighed her options. "My dear, I don't know what to make of you. You're a clever one but I'm still not convinced that you're genuine. You seem to know a lot about me but there's still plenty that no one knows."

"I want to help, you have to trust me. I want to help you find your gate," said Beth looking at her feet and avoiding the stare from Hoshi.

Hoshi continued to stare at Beth but she felt her world slowly getting revealed. Beth was a strong vibrant woman. Her skin was clear and her green eyes were full of fire. Her long hair glistened in the sunlight and she had a youthful strong body. Hoshi knew she could not compete with Beth's determination and zest for life. Her aura was glowing brilliantly and her energy source was strong. Hoshi was convinced that Beth had a Spirit Warrior within her. She recalled how she felt in her youth. She remembered how it felt coming to terms with sharing her mind. It had been so long that Hoshi could not remember being alone anymore. She did not want Corom to die; she had worked so hard to find the gate and try to release him.

"What do you know of the gate?" asked Hoshi in a more serious tone.

"I know that you've been searching for a long time."

"Beth, no more games, I'm serious," said Hoshi realizing that both women needed to be more open.

"Then do you want to talk with me honestly?"

"I'm convinced that you're not a reporter, you're not in this to sensationalize or get rich. For me to be totally open with you, you need to tell me why you're looking for the gate," Hoshi sighed.

"All right, dancing over time for some straight talk. I know all about you and why you're so guarded. I know more than you think because I'm in the same predicament. I need to find the gate so I can release my captive spirit. The spirits seek out an Indigo Child, a strong Indigo aura when they're in need of refuge. We both are afflicted with the same circumstance. If we sought medical help you know we'd be committed. Why do I mention that? You know that only too well. We can't eat, we can't drink, and we need to find this gate. I look at you and I see myself in the future," said Beth.

"Not a pretty sight my dear," chuckled Hoshi rocking her small frame.

"If we find this gate both Corom and Subra, my spirit, can pass through at the same time. The same time," repeated Beth to make sure Hoshi understood. This tweaked her interest.

"What have you found out about the gate's location so far?"

"This only happened to me a week or so ago. I've spent my time searching for the only lead I had, a Shell. It's led me to you, to Schelle and this IN DEN VOS restaurant. Sakura told me of you. She was reluctant and very guarded. She recognized that you and I are so alike," explained Beth.

"I'm losing this fight Beth. I was convinced that the IN DEN VOS in Schelle was the answer. I've covered every inch of that restaurant; I'm practically banned from entry now. I'm starting to think that I'm waving my sword at shadows," said Hoshi.

"Beth felt a sudden rush of blood to her cheeks as they warmed. "Corom yes, portal no."

"Thank you Subra," thought Beth. "What other leads do you have?" asked Beth.

"Dear, if I had any other leads I'd be chasing them. This is the best I've got and I was convinced, totally convinced, for the longest time. I'm not convinced now," said Hoshi dejected and staring off with a vacant expression.

"Sometimes when you look too hard you can't see what you want. It could be right in front of your face, in your blind spot," said Beth in an encouraging tone.

"Corom said to me once that he might be able to feel the energy from the gate, he's very weak, but he would still sense it," said Hoshi. "He feels its close but not here." Hoshi looked at Beth in an inquisitive way and Beth knew what she was asking with her eyes.

"Subra doesn't feel the gate at all."

Hoshi turned the corners of her mouth upwards in a smile of irony. "I've known for a while but I didn't want to accept that I was wasting my time. I'm out of options Beth. I hate to say this but I do need your help." Hoshi flashed her small brown eyes at Beth and for the first time she looked vulnerable.

Beth decided to make a move. She nudged forward closer to Hoshi and reached for her hand. She gently placed her hand on top of Hoshi's folded hands. In a calming voice Beth tried to reassure, "I'm here to help. I do understand what this is like. I've made a similar promise to Subra and I don't want to let him down either. I know you've been looking a lot longer than I have. Now there's two looking, someone to bounce ideas off."

Hoshi smiled without opening her mouth. "Thank you Beth. Seems like Sakura did the right thing. I want Corom to go home. I don't care what happens to me but I intend to keep my promise, I can't let him down."

"You've done more than expected but you still need some closure. I get it and I want to help. So this is as much as you have to offer? No insights left on the gate?" asked Beth gently.

"Nothing," was the dejected response from Hoshi. Beth felt her heart sink. The IN DEN VOS was situated right across the street. Should she go inside and try to find a gate?

"Should I look in the restaurant, perhaps I'll see something you didn't?" asked Beth.

"You can try, but I know you won't find it," said Hoshi.

The word "No" raced through her mind, a message from Subra.

Hoshi slumped over and looked despondent. She was not the fiery witch everyone had painted her to be. Beth felt sorry for Hoshi. She understood what she was living with. She was a frightened little girl living with a responsibility that until now she could not explain or share. Beth squeezed her hand.

"I know what it's like. You have someone you can talk with again."

"I haven't had that since my sister died. It's not fun watching people grow old and die Beth," said Hoshi shaking her hand. "People were not designed to live this long."

"Then we need to find this gate," said Beth in a determined voice. "I have energy Hoshi; I'll chase down our ideas. I want Corom and Subra to go home safely."

"Beth, what happens to me when Corom leaves?" asked Hoshi staring at her hands not wanting to hear the answer.

Beth thought for a moment, "I think we both know the answer, don't we?"

"I get a chance to go home too," said Hoshi gently.

"Yes, you get to go home and meet up with your sister again," offered Beth.

"That would be good," said Hoshi clearly tired of this existence.

The two women sat in silence holding hands and staring off into the green lushness of the park. The only sound was birds singing and the wind brushing up against the trees. They could not have been more different, raised in different times and in totally different cultures. Under normal conditions these two women would never have met, never have talked with each other. They were sitting together sharing the day because of an unexplainable bond that linked them across time. Beth tried to imagine what life was like for Hoshi as a young woman and how much effort it must have taken to adapt to today's world. The two women sat and talked about many things; life growing up as a young woman in Tokyo. How touching hands was an erotic gesture only reserved for serious suitors. She described the teahouses and how she missed her life. Time had changed the dynamics between men and women. They talked about the changes Hoshi has seen in her life and how hard it was to see her sister and friends get old and die. Hoshi spoke of her regret not being at her sister's funeral. Beth talked about her short life growing up in foster homes and child support centers. She talked with Hoshi about what it was to be a liberated woman still trapped in a man's world. How dating is complicated with date rape drugs, binge drinking, HIV, STD's and technology such as text and web cams. Hoshi listened and shook her head many times. The two women were clearly from different worlds and the gulf between them was immense.

"Beth, it's good to have a sister again," said Hoshi raising her face.

Beth's pink lips opened into a broad smile, "I know, people just don't understand what we're dealing with, and then you get labeled."

"You have to find that gate Beth, have to," said Hoshi.

From behind Beth could hear the familiar sound of crunching stone chips and glanced over her shoulder. She could see Everard who stopped in his tracks. He opened his arms wide and shrugged his shoulders as if to ask how things were going? Beth nodded at Everard who turned and walked back to the car.

"That means you have to go?" said Hoshi.

"For now, but I'd like to talk with you again, perhaps tomorrow?"

"About what?" said Hoshi?

"I need to talk with you some more, I might learn something that points me to the gate."

"I'm an old fool Beth, you're not going to learn much from me anymore," said Hoshi in a despondent way.

"Well, let's see, how about 1pm right here, can you manage that?"

"I'll be here Beth; I'll try to think of something that might help you."

"Help us," Beth corrected. Beth squeezed and released her hand. She looked deep into Hoshi's face, "We'll do this, have some faith." Beth stood and walked towards the car. "Have some faith. Yikes where did that come from?" thought Beth. Beth opened the car door and clicked the restraint in to place.

"Do I need to ask?" was Everard's question.

"It went well but I need to get more out of her tomorrow at 1pm same place," said Beth talking into the rear view mirror.

"Good, 1pm it is then. Back to the hotel now?"

"Yes," said Beth watching Hoshi still sitting on the bench.

The Benz pulled away and drove past Hoshi creating a swirling cloud of dust. Hoshi remained seated with her back to the departing car. Beth felt a deep connection and empathy for Hoshi, which surprised her. Until this meeting she had seen her as an enemy, a clever adversary. Now she had an affinity with her, she was like a sister, an older wiser sister. The ride back to Brussels was silent with Everard sensing that Beth needed to stew on what she had just heard. Beth replayed the conversation back in her mind and was starting to feel sorry for Hoshi. Hoshi knew she had backed the wrong choice with IN DEN VOS and Schelle. She had tried to make this combination work for so many years out of desperation. Beth had hoped Hoshi would have laid out an articulate series of discoveries that had led her to this location. Beth's visit had provided Hoshi the ability to look at her choices in the stark light of reality. It was clearly the wrong choice. Beth felt disappointed and needed some other clue to guide her to the next location for her search. She was more than willing to take on the responsibility of leading the charge. Her question now was which direction should she be charging in? She felt like a rudderless boat drifting. She had been given so many leads that neatly aligned to a date with Hoshi. These leads appeared to be so strong if they were all wrong now what? Her expectation was Hoshi would tell her something that provided that missing piece. Beth reran her entire conversation again in her head no missing piece. Perhaps it was not obvious, perhaps it was there but she needed to think differently? Beth felt two things from this back-seat mental activity; frustrated and a headache. Occasionally she would catch Everard looking at her in the rear view mirror but she would glance down quickly signaling her intention to remain with her thoughts.

Everard broke the silence by stating "Beth we're about ten minutes from the hotel."

"All right," said Beth simply.

The Benz smoothly traced a route through the traffic and the swelling streets back to the hotel. Upon arrival a simple goodbye and an exchange of details for the next day occurred. Beth felt deflated; she had built this up to be the conclusion to her journey, not a dead end. She had the same hopeless feeling that Hoshi had exhibited. Beth was in her room quickly. She did not stop or acknowledge any friendly greetings from hotel staff members. She pushed the door harder than she had intended and it slammed making a loud noise. She threw her backpack onto the bed and flopped down in the chair next to the desk.

"Damn it," she said in a low voice.

Beth sat and looked at her pitiful self in the mirror above the desk. "You messed up too," she mouthed the words to herself. She could see her face flushing and her cheeks felt hot. Her thoughts muddied and then became clear as Subra attempted to communicate.

"I can feel a strong energy source Beth." This snapped Beth back to attention and stopped her self-pity.

"You can?" thought Beth.

"There's energy. I'm not sure what it is, it's pure," Subra faded and Beth's cheeks cooled.

Beth suddenly recalled a conversation she had with Subra one evening. He explained how certain things on earth seem to emit a strong energy. Usually it is related to original works of art or sublime architecture. These specific things are items that took great feats of human endeavor. The energy put into their creation continues to emit long after. Fakes, reproductions and prints all take energy away. Subra had hoped he would be able to differentiate between the energy from fabulous art and architecture and the portal. Was this Subra's way of saying that he could not? Beth was starting to feel a little down. She had reached an unexpected dead end with Hoshi. She was sitting in one of the world's centers for chocolate and she could not eat. The food in Brussels with its mussels and waffles was outstanding and she could not eat. The choice of beer, really good beer, was overwhelming and she could not drink. The more she thought about it the more she became depressed. Beth slapped her thighs and stood in one swift movement.

"Right, stop feeling sorry for yourself and get out there and see some of Brussels. You can't eat or drink but you can soak up the atmosphere and see the sites."

Beth searched her backpack and found the tourist guide given to her by the hotel. As she browsed the attractions she was drawn to the Grand Place with its buildings and architecture. The brochure had a section on the Grand Place but she just looked at the pictures and ignored the text. On the bottom of the page it showed directions with a small map. The five-minute walk from the hotel clinched it for Beth. She grabbed the guide, tucked Lord Ganesha into her pocket and headed for the door. Once in the elevator Beth looked at the guide. The Grand Place was French; the Dutch phrase for this location was the Grote Markt. It was the central market square of Brussels and the most popular tourist attraction. The brochure talked about the Town Hall, the Bread House and the Guild Houses. She remembered flipping past these pictures in a magazine on the plane and paying little attention.

Chapter 15

The Grand Place, Brussels

A slight vibration announced the arrival of the elevator where the doors slid open smoothly. Beth walked to the exit and extended her hand to push the revolving door. She looked down at her wrist tattoo.

"Come on fox we're going out," she thought as she passed under the exterior grey metal awning. She noticed the evening air had cooled. She glanced at her watch 5.50pm. "Should I go back and get a coat?" thought Beth. "I'll be all right."

Beth made a right turn quickly locating her position on the guide map. She turned right again onto a downward sloping road. She walked briskly and the road opened into an intersection of three roads. Traffic was now restricted to pedestrians. A small crowd gathered outside a serving window, which held Beth's attention. To her right was a large brass statue of a seated man adorned with a bushy beard and mustache. Climbing onto his lap was a brass hound dog standing on its rear legs tugging at his sleeve. He held an open book in his free hand. Beth's attention was drawn to the small group of people huddled at the window opposite. She walked towards a tall two story building sporting flag-poles with three Belgium flags of black, yellow and red stripes. The building was located on a corner fronted with large glass windows, beige siding and a bright yellow trim. A sign read "Gaufre Du Bruxelles" next to a large replica waffle with a dollop of whipped cream in its center. Beth approached the building and could smell the sugary waffle aroma that was drawing the crowd in like bears to honey. She peered through the window at the waffles, and baked goods on display.

She did not feel hungry but she longed to sink her teeth into the waffle loaded with whipped cream, covered in strawberries and drizzled with dark chocolate. The open window served people waiting in line on the street. They left eating their food and looking contented. Inside she could see people sat at tables enjoying good food and conversation. On the sidewalk arranged symmetrically were wicker chairs and round tables. A small crowd sat outside eating and watching people walk by. Beth passed a man sitting on a blanket spread on the ground surrounded by two dogs, one large, one small, both sleeping. He had a baseball cap tossed on the floor looking for a handout. A small group of people was watching a man wearing a hat, mask and long raincoat. His costume had been painted to look like stone. He posed on a box painted in a similar manner. He remained still like a statue until he suddenly moved to the crowds delight. Beth loved the narrow cobbled streets it reminded her of Haworth but the signs looked different.

She saw a sign for the Grote Markt and turned left onto Rue de la Colline. She could hear laughter and loud echoes. As Beth entered the Grand Place its sheer beauty struck her. Her eyes could not take in all the nuances. She walked into the center of a large rectangular shaped opening. In the middle she saw an artist

with his paintings proudly on display. He had water-
colors showing different views of the Grand Place. He
signed them "Y. Ziaeian." Next to his stall a woman was
selling flowers. It was busy with people taking pictures
and movies of the surroundings. Tall buildings flanked
every side with narrow streets providing the entry and
exit points. When someone shouted or laughed you
could hear the sound reverberating back into the center forming a loud echo. You could hear the distinctive
sounds of shoes, boots and heels as they clacked their
way across the cobbles. The pink flowers for sale, still
in plant pots, provided a beautiful contrast to the stark
stone buildings. Beth's eyes were drawn to a building
top where she could see a gold statue of a man. He
was riding a horse perched high on the roof casting an
impressive profile against the sky.

"Where do you start with something like this?"
thought Beth overwhelmed. Beth's eyes were drawn to
the tallest building in the square the Town Hall. She
walked towards it in awe and wonderment.

"Sanjeev would have loved this," she thought.

The tower rose majestically into the sky and she
recognized the spire as the one she had seen from her
hotel room window. The building was a clean brown
sandy stone color with a slate grey roof. A Belgium
flag hung limp from a pole. It was a calm night with
no wind. The tower rose high and majestically into the
sky but something was not right. It took Beth a couple
of seconds to realize that the tower and the entrance
to the building were not centered. It was not symmetrical. The tower's position was skewed to the right.
The tower climbed for over five floors before it sharp-
ened into an ornately carved 96-meter tall octagonal
spire. Beth's eyes followed the spire skywards where
perched on the very top was a gold statue of the arch-
angel Michael, patron saint of Belgium. To the left of

the tower the building had ten windows and three levels. Between each window were carved statues of figures, gargoyles and animals. Eight windows lay to the right of the tower with an array of carved stone adornments. This was a stunning building; you could look at the detail for hours and still see new surprises. Beth walked closer to the entrance and looked at the carvings from a better vantage point. She saw hunched winged gargoyles with twisted faces protruding from the building.

Grey colored pigeons sat on their carved backs taking advantage of a safe resting place. She could see ornate figures of knights in armor brandishing shields and swords. Above a doorway Beth could see one knight standing on top of a winged serpent as he speared it with his sword. Next to him stood a figure sporting angel wings killing a horned serpent with a long sword. Figures of priests and cherubs also decorated the walls. The Town Hall was a feast for the eyes with too much to look at. It somehow worked. With all the detail it still looked masterful. Two smaller towers at each side of the building flanked the center tower. Facing the building the left hand tower had an old stone-faced clock clinging to its wall. There was so much to see Beth did not know what to do next. She could feel the energy of the buildings and the reaction of the people to their beauty. She spun around; behind her was the second largest building in the square. It looked darker, dirtier than the Town Hall but it was impressive in its own way. Beth was staring at the Kings House or the Bread House, as it was once known. Impressive gothic style columns and arches formed a perfectly symmetrical building. The centered spire was not as tall as the Town Hall but the building was impressive. Beth walked towards the building soaking in its design and beauty. Red banners hung on each pillar on the lower level announcing that it was now the city museum of Brussels. Another sign informed Beth that it was after hours and now closed. The Bread House stood on the site in the 13th century where bakers sold their bread. Stone buildings replaced wooden buildings with the current building built in 1536. The building has undergone many restorations but its gothic style was a feast for Beth's eyes. Beth scanned the different facades around the Grand Place. She saw red awnings, stone carvings, windows of all shapes and sizes, gold colored statues, gold accents and brightly colored plaques, too many to take in. Beth suddenly had an idea. She reached back into her rear jeans pocket and retrieved the guide.

"Let's do this right," she thought.

The guide started at one corner and worked its way around the square describing each building. Beth was centrally located and headed towards a corner weaving through the crowd and the people posing for photographs. She reached the corner and located the building at the start of the guide. She recognized the building in front of her as the one pictured in the guide. Her cheeks flushed and her neck became warm.

"What is it my friend?" she thought.

"The portal, I'm certain its here," said Subra.

"It's here?" asked Beth.

"Yes."

Beth did a strange thing. She turned and looked at the square expecting to see a neon signpost with an illuminated arrow. "Portal here!" it would read. Of course she saw nothing. She felt silly and excited.

"Find a Shell in this lot," she thought. "I'm going to use the guide, it's my best chance of not missing anything," she said aloud.

Opening the guide it started with a description of the Guild Houses. Beth stood in complete isolation

311

surrounded by people. She started to read the guide and its description of the Guild Houses. The guide explained that the Grand Place had more to offer than just the Town Hall and the Kings House. The beautifully restored and decorated Guild Houses were also spectacular. The name Guild Houses referred to a set of buildings surrounding the Grand Place; some were privately owned. After the bombardment of August 1695 the city requested that each Guild present their plans for restoration. In the middle ages houses had no numbering system so each house was adorned with a symbol, figurine or animal that represented the guild and identified the building. The guide indicated that it would start with the group of houses left of the Town Hall and would continue clockwise.

"There has to be a clue in here somewhere," thought Beth. "Keep your eyes peeled for a Shell." Beth stared at her guide. The first Guild House was a four level narrow building accented with gold. On the pinnacle of the elaborate shaped roof was a gold urn shaped sculpture. The house was called The Mountain of Thabor. Beth stared at the page. She had only seen this name once in her short life. She recalled rushing into the church hall to take shelter from the rain in Haworth. Her thoughts drifted to Dr. David Harrington the charismatic speaker who introduced her to the spiritual domain. He delivered his lecture in a room called The Mountain of Thabor.

"That's where this journey began," thought Beth. "That's the one and only time I've ever heard of The Mountain of Thabor, it's a strange name," thought Beth.

Subra was getting stronger from the abundant supply of energy and pushed a message through, "There are no coincidences."

Beth stared at the building looking for a Shell or a clue. She inspected the narrow facade. There was a sign located above the store housed on the ground floor. Written in white embossed letters across a small red and cyan striped awning was "Gautam Diamonds." Above the door was a plaque surrounded by a circle of gold colored decoration. In the center of a teal colored background lay a gold symbol that Beth did not recognize. She scoured the building carefully from top to bottom. Beth looked at the roof with its urn and two golden spheres. She looked at the highest window with its window boxes and green plants. The facade had gold accents and gold sprigs adorned with leaves. The gold accents topped the stone columns that supported the next level of the building. Beth studied the facade in detail but it held no clues. Tourists surrounded her but Beth felt alone in the Grand Place. She was so deeply focused she could not hear or see anyone around her. She unknowingly walked in front of a couple taking a photograph and continued to the next building. Glancing down at her guide she saw the words The Rose and stopped immediately.

"The Rose," said Beth quietly.

She thought of Anwar and his allotment full of roses. She remembered the rose he had given her on the bench. She remembered the white rose being the symbol for the county of Yorkshire. She recalled the birthmark on the forearm of Aklina being in the shape of a Rose. She remembered her search for Rose Akhter. It was not lost on Beth that the Guild Houses were starting to map out her journey.

"This is a coincidence," thought Beth, "this could not continue could it?"

Beth looked up from the guide with an eerie feeling sweeping down the back of her neck. She studied the building starting from the bottom. On the ground floor was a restaurant, in front were tables with red umbrellas where people sat and enjoyed a meal and drinks. Beth looked to the left where she could see a doorway surrounded by red colored wood. A bright red and cyan striped awning jutted out from the building. It had white letters stamped on the awning, "La Rose Blanche," the white rose. Above the wooden panels of the doorway was a ledge. Beth's eyes were drawn to a gold colored adornment nestled on the ledge. A large gold bowl with handles housed a golden stem. From the stem grew gold shoots to the left and right each decorated with gold leafs. The center stem grew tall capped off by a beautiful gold rose. To the right of the rose was a gold and cyan colored plaque with 1702 written in stylized gold numbers. This was starting to make sense to Beth. The buildings did mirror her journey.

She wanted to skip to the end but what if she missed a clue in one of the buildings. She examined The Rose building from bottom to top. Gold scroll accents separated each floor. Rectangular windows gave way to the top floor with three small windows. Scrolls were replaced with gold cloth swags. The roof had ornate symmetrical shaped scallops. Either side of the center urn was cyan and gold colored urns balanced precariously. Beth satisfied herself that she could not see a Shell and glanced downward back to her guide. Her hands were shaking and she steadied the booklet so she could read the name of the next Guild House. Beth was walking and reading. She stopped dead in her tracks as a wave of realization swept over her.

"This is meant to be. There are no coincidences," said Beth.

A man made a quick adjustment to his stride not expecting Beth to come to an abrupt stop. Beth was oblivious, wrapped up in the guide's message. The next Guild House was called The Golden Tree. The Golden Tree prompted images of stricken Indian women desperate to escape their lives in Sonagachi, the Golden Tree of Kolkata. Beth remembered the looks she saw on women's faces as she and Sanjeev passed by in that white taxi. So far the The Mountain of Thabor, The Rose, The Golden Tree had reproduced her journey in sequence.

Beth lifted her eyes and studied the building searching for clues. Two tall narrow windows flanked a wooden door with stained glass above. A row of small gold accents separated the first and second floors. The second and third floor had three rectangular shaped windows. Long stone-carved columns separated the windows. Wrapped around each column were golden accents of leaves and branches representing The Golden Tree. Small ornate stone carvings showing scenes of cherubs frolicking could be seen high on the facade. The columns ended in a splash of gold propping up a stone ledge with gold words. "MAISON DES BRASSEURS" could be seen under two stone lions. The lions reminded Beth of the marble lion in Anwar's allotment. Positioned between the lions was a stone plaque with small gold writing. The plaque was so high Beth could not make out the words. Above the lions the roof decorations were beautiful. Gold characters spelled ANNO to the left and 1698 to the right. Each plaque was flanked by curly tailed sea serpents. In the middle and surrounded by gold leaves and a row of gold swags was a colorful coat of arms topped off with a red and gold crown. This led to a plinth where a regal looking gold statue was perched. A man riding a majestic horse seemed to point inwards at the Grand Place. Beth glanced up and down again, sea serpents but no Shell.

Beth walked slowly towards the next building her stomach full of butterflies and her feet dragging as if in lead shoes. She stopped in front of the building daring not to look at the facade. She glanced at the text within the guide. The next Guild House was The Swan; Beth just smiled but felt faint from the excitement.

Before she could read she received a message from Subra. "We're close I can feel it, keep going," said Subra in a voice so strong Beth could feel it in her chest.

She read the guide. The Guild House The Swan is now a restaurant called "La Maison du Cygne" or House of Swan. Karl Marx and Friedrich Engels stayed here in 1847 during meetings of the German laborer's union. Trembling, Beth raised her eyes and immediately centered her gaze above a narrow stone door way. The door lay above four stone steps with a thin black wrought iron handrail. A wooden door topped with a glass panel welcomed guests. A small ledge above the door housed a vibrant splash of green foliage creating a framed border. In the center of this border against a royal blue background was a beautiful white swan. The wings were outstretched; it held its neck straight with its yellow beak facing forward. The swan looked as if it were to take flight from the building ledge at any moment. The beautiful white swan statue bordered by green foliage stood out from the stone and the gold. Either side of the swan was red and cyan awnings. People inside were enjoying exquisite food at a premier restaurant. Above the swan was a stone balcony supported by gold scrolls decorated with gold lion heads. Beth moved her eyes skywards and saw two stone cherubs holding a golden ring. In the center of the ring was a design that Beth could not recognize; it was a busy series of intertwined lines. To the left a striking red and gold plaque read AN.NO. To the right of the cherubs was another plaque in the same colors 16.98. Still higher was a triangular shaped stone roof with three stone statues of women. Each carried a small gold highlighted object. The swan reminded Beth of her time in Toronto and her visit to Kaigara, Sakura and Swan Property Investments. She remembered the Swan of the Pacific, the beautiful white-hulled schooner docked in Yokohama on the Tokyo Bay. The buildings continued to trace her journey in exact detail and Beth felt physically sick. She clasped her hand to her mouth and coughed loudly. The following Guild Houses were in sequence; The Mountain of Thabor, The Rose, The Golden Tree and The Swan had told of her journey.

Beth thought she had completed the Guild Houses in this row but the guide pointed out one more attraction. Joined to The Swan building was a thin building that had multiple floors but no ground floor. The building's first floor was a support structure of dark grey stone arches and columns. It looked a little out of place. A small crowd of people huddled under the arches and seemed to be interested by something within. Beth leaned against an ornate cast iron lamppost.

The guide informed Beth that the building was The Star and it was once occupied by Amman the Dukes representative in the city. The Star, Beth shook her head and felt the blood drain from her face. Toshie Osanami was the frightened young woman in Tokyo committed of fraud, having her mental sanity questioned. To escape persecution she followed her destiny to Belgium to find the gate. She had to change her name from Toshie to Hoshi.

"Hoshi, Japanese for Star" said Beth into the pages of the guide. Beth glanced upwards to inspect the building. The Star building was plain, supported by dark grey stone columns it was three levels tall. Above the arch was a plaque. An oval shaped cyan disk was visible surrounded by golden scrolls. It looked like a ring that you could put on a giants finger, plain and oval shaped. A few small accents of gold led to a modest triangular shaped stone roof. Sitting proudly on top of the stone triangle was a beautiful gold Star. It was angled to give a three dimensional feel.

"Hoshi, Star," thought Beth. "The Guild Houses continue to map my journey; this can't be a coincidence; The Mountain of Thabor, The Rose, The Golden Tree, The Swan and The Star."

She continued to read the guide. Under the stone grey arcade is a brass statue of a medieval Brussels hero. Legend has it that striking the forearm of the statue brings great luck. The statue is of Everard 't Serciaes.

"Everard, my driver," thought Beth. "That's it, strike the arm, that's the portal," thought Beth shaking with fear and excitement.

"Strike the arm," shouted Subra.

Beth walked under the columns and entered the arcade. A brass plaque was black from the grime and the oxidization. The plaque was three-dimensional with a figure reclining, his head to the left. The body and part of his face draped in a death shroud. His entire body was now a shiny yellow brass color. Many touches had rubbed the grime and dirt away. At his feet you could see the head of a loyal hound, yellow from the touches. Floating above the body was a cherub face surrounded by wings. The face was yellow but the wings remained black. Beth waited patiently and moved to the front of the line. Her heart in her mouth she was next. Most people were slapping Everard's arm with their fingers.

"Are you ready Subra, get ready to grab Corom?" she thought.

Subra was stronger than ever feeding off the pure energy. "I'm ready Beth, strike him."

Beth approached the brass wall sculpture and slapped his prominent right forearm with her fingers as she braced herself and closed her eyes. Nothing. Nothing happened.

She opened her eyes. In a panic she thought, "I must have missed his arm." Beth kept her eyes open and stared at a patch of Everard's forearm, yellow metal exposed from the touches. She saw her hand slap the exact spot. Nothing. Nothing happened. The people behind Beth nudged forward as if to indicate their impatience. Beth slapped the left forearm this time and incurred a comment in Flemish that she did not understand. Disappointed she beat a hasty retreat and screamed in her head.

"What happened? Nothing happened that's what. What were you playing at Subra? Why didn't you go through the gate?"

"That wasn't the gate Beth. Did you see a Shell? That wasn't the gate but don't give up it's near," said Subra loud and strong.

"Are you sure?" thought Beth.

"One hundred percent, I'm telling you Beth the gate, the portal, its here we just have to find it. I'm certain this is pure energy and it's coming from the gate," assured Subra.

"What do I do now?"

"The guide has tracked your journey through the Guild Houses why not follow the guide and keep going?" suggested Subra.

"You're right!"

Beth walked past a narrow street and under a Belgium flag attached to a flagpole protruding from the Town Hall. The flag fell limp in the calm night air. Above the flag was a round stone clock face. The face was black in color with gold Roman numeral markings and gold hands. The time on the clock read 7.25pm. Beth walked past the carvings of nobles, saints and allegorical figures. She marveled at the tall arches. She loved the gargoyles, some were beasts others squatting lions. Some had wings and beaks. Some had pigeons perching indignantly on their ornate backs. The birds enjoyed peering down on the crowds below. Beth stopped at the arch above the main entrance to the Town Hall. Two wooden doors studded with iron remained open.

"The gate," thought Beth walking towards the opening.

The open doors led into an area with a high vaulted ceiling. Beth could see another open door with a figure above the door carved into the stone. Through that was another open door that passed through the entire building.

"That's the gate," thought Beth. As she started to walk towards the entrance she felt hot.

"No, not through there, that's moving away from the energy," said Subra.

"So much for the gate theory," thought Beth.

Beth glanced up at the five figures on top of the door and examined each little cluster of carved stone figures forming a decorative arch. Not a Shell to be seen anywhere. Beth walked the length of the Town Hall until she came to the end of the building and another narrow street. She looked at her guide and skipped the section on the Town Hall.

Subra was screaming in Beth's head, "Yes, Yes, Yes."

"That's not useful," snapped Beth.

Looking at the guide she tried to orient her position and locate the next Guild House. By now the light was starting to fade. She started to read the guide again. The next Guild House was the House of Traders and on top of the house is the popular St. Nicholas or Santa Clause. Beth couldn't resist, she peered high on the roof and there perched on top was a gold figure of a man. Her eyes dropped back to the guide.

This Guild House was called The Fox from the trader's guild. Beth looked up to examine the building. She had seen Santa and she worked her way down examining the building. It had an ornate facade with a large window surrounded by stone arches, columns and gold accents. Faces stared out from the stone. A woman's face was prominent. She stared out from the building her face painted in brilliant gold. Surrounding her head was a star burst, an aura of solid gold (unlimited potential). Beth cast her eyes down the building, more windows separated by figures of women holding flowers and other objects. A gold accent created a border of leafs and scrolls between the floors. A large stone balcony with a stone railing jutted out from the building. The stone railing was held in place by stone spokes accented with gold. Between each tall window beautifully carved full sized stone women stood majestically. Five women draped in robes carrying objects painted in gold. They gazed down calmly on the crowds below. Under the balcony muscled men supported the weight on their shoulders, their faces showing the strain of the task.

A small unimpressive window above a narrow stone door housed a dirty figurine. It was painted gold but the pollution, dirt and grime had turned it to a dark yellow with large patches of grey grime. Beth rubbed her eyes and looked again. There was no mistake. Sat on a small ledge in front of an equally small rectangular window was a fox! Not any fox but the same design that Beth had tattooed on her right wrist. The fox was sitting facing Beth with its brush lying on the ground tucked between its legs. The fox had its front feet planted either side of its tail. Beth could not believe what she was seeing. Underneath the fox statue was a dark stained stone ledge that separated the window ledge from the door beneath. In the three inches of space that ran the distance of the ledge were badly stained gold letters. They were originally gold but the staining and pollution had turned them dark. Because they were attached to the stone they were raised and you could still see the message clearly.

IN DEN VOS

Beth closed her eyes and opened them to see if it was a trick of the light. IN DEN VOS was written below the sly fox statue.

"This has to be it," thought Beth.

The doorway below led into a small open room only large enough to house an instant banking machine. The brightly illuminated signs of the ground floor window proudly announced the name of the bank that offered the machines. The signs shone brightly in the fading light. The neon signs were Indigo colored with white lettering. The Indigo light shone down onto the cobbled slate flagstones outside. Battered from wear the stones were small and square shaped. Beth was shaking as she looked at the fox, the IN DEN VOS sign and her wrist. As she raised her eyes from her wrist she caught a glimpse of something sparkle on the dark slate floor.

The Indigo light from the banking machine sign had reflected by a highly polished brass stud inlaid into a stone cobble. Beth walked forward and examined what was embedded into the cobble. Her heart leapt from her body! It was a perfectly shaped yellow brass Shell contained within a slate square. It had no right to be there, no purpose. Beth felt a surge of energy swelling through her entire body. She instantly felt hot and dizzy. Her body seemed to take on a life of its own and she had the sensation that she was no longer in control.

"Step on the Shell," was the order rushing through her mind.

Without thinking Beth stepped on the well-worn brass Shell with both feet. Beth immediately felt a searing pain in her chest and neck. She could feel her knees buckle and began to fall. It seems strange now but in the time it took to fall to the ground Beth experienced so many things. She knew that Subra and his precious cargo had managed to surge out of her body and into the portal. She was convinced that she could feel him reach out and grab Corom.

"Thank you Beth," swirled around her head.

With Corom safe she could feel Toshie pass and leave her body for the spiritual domain. Beth felt happy and relieved. A cloud of Indigo fog surged into her mind but one clear image remained before the portal closed. The crystal clear image of an Angel was the clue to the location of the next portal. Beth did not know why but she had an overwhelming feeling that this image would be a part of her future. There was no doubt in her mind that she had felt this happen before she hit the ground. Beth blacked out from the electrical energy surge.

She woke almost immediately and felt embarrassed lying on the floor surrounded by strangers. She looked up at the young man standing over her extending his hand.

He smiled at Beth and in a thick Yorkshire accent said, "You all right? You took a fall over that Shell. Stupid place to put a brass ornament looks like it's worn because of all the people that's walked across it."

"Yeah I'm fine, bruised ego that's all," said Beth accepting his hand. Beth instantly felt a surge of energy rush through her arm. A small electrical charge crackled as their hands met. "Must be all this energy," thought Beth. She brushed herself off and looked at the handsome man before her. He was about five feet ten with hazel eyes, short brown hair, and fit body shape. He wore a plain white tee shirt and loose fitting jeans, black leather belt with black sneakers. He looked good. He smiled at Beth and showed an interest. A deep calming sense of relief swept across Beth so profoundly strong that she almost missed the next words.

"I'm Matt, I'm not used to being in the right place to pick up beautiful women," he said with a smirk.

"Oh and you think you've picked me up do you?" teased Beth.

"I mean lift up, lift up," he said in an embarrassed yet shy way.

"I'm teasing, Beth's my name," said Beth extending her hand for Matt to shake. Matt shook her hand firmly and Beth could see a strong ground aura of Indigo with spokes of Blue, Yellow and Orange. "A good combination for a man," thought Beth smiling at Matt.

"You sound as if you're from Yorkshire?" she asked.

"Yeah, I'm from a small village called Cullingworth, near..." Matt was interrupted.

"Haworth, where I live," she said flirting with her eyes and smoothing her hair into place. Beth felt her tummy growl she was extremely hungry. "Know any good places to eat around here Matt? I'm starving."

"Sure do, as my dad always used to say, eat breakfast like a? How does it go? Eat breakfast like a King?" he struggled to finish the quote.

"Eat breakfast like a King, lunch like a Prince and dinner like a Pauper, Adelle Davis 1904 to 1974," said Beth quickly. "Thing is I haven't eaten all day so I'm starving, I'll be eating like a King tonight," she laughed. "Thank you Subra, you took the cargo but you left me with a copy of all the quotes," thought Beth.

"So you're from Haworth, what a coincidence," said Matt, making conversation.

"There are no coincidences," said Beth looking deep into Matt's eyes.

"Shall we go I know a great little Italian down the way?" he said invitingly.

"Yes, I've got a few loose ends I'll need to clean up tomorrow, but for now let's eat," said Beth.

She smiled knowingly; she had kept her *two promises* to Anwar and Subra.

Beth reached out a hand and took Matt's. He was a little shocked but smiled his acceptance as the pair walked off together. Beth smiled and glanced up at the small statue of the sly fox as they passed by.

"I also need to go chocolate shopping," said Beth squeezing Matt's hand and laughing.